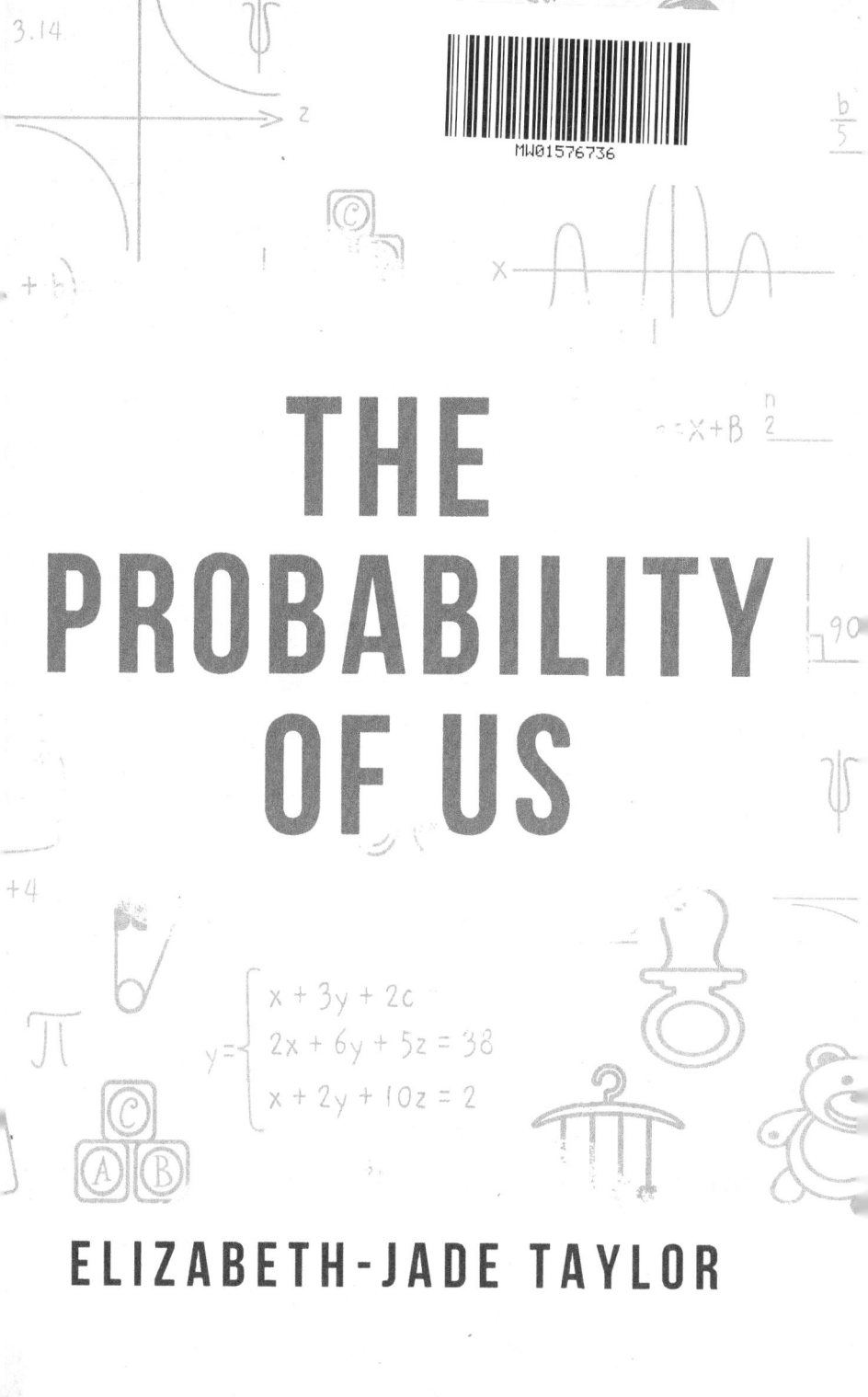

Copyright © 2025 by Elizabeth—Jade Taylor

All rights reserved. No part of this book may be used or reproduced in any form whatsoever without written permission except in the case of brief quotations in critical articles or reviews.

This book is a work of fiction. Names, characters, businesses, organizations, places, events and incidents either are the product of the author's imagination or are used fictitiously. Any resemblance to actual persons, living or dead, events, or locales is entirely coincidental.

Printed in the United States of America.

Edited by Melissa Dark Grove Press

Edited by Elena Page & Polished

Cover art and design by Alice Trijjet

Interior Formatting by Books and Moods

ISBN – Paperback : 979-8-9934423-0-3

First Edition : December 2025

*To all the women who have been told you can't
have both, you absolutely can
To my mother, for your encouragement
To my love, for being my witness*

CONTENT WARNINGS

Dear readers,

This page is to serve as a warning for the material that you will come across in this novel. While the story will have a happy ending, it's a contemporary romance that's deeply rooted in reality. Keep in mind that this book will contain the following ideas:

Absentee parents
Chronically ill child
Financial insecurity
Explicit language
Sexually explicit scenes (chapters 21, 22, 23, 29, 30, 32, 39)

Playlist

Let Alone The One You Love - Olivia Dean
Moral of the Story - Ashe
S****y Places, Pretty Faces-Ashe
Deserve Me - Kali Uchis & Summer Walker
Free Mind – Tems
Lady Lady – Olivia Dean
Take A Chance With Me - NIKI
IN THE MOMENT (feat. Tyler, The Creator) - Snoh Aalegra
who knew - Chloe x Halle
I Want You Around - Snoh Aalegra
Is it a Crime – Mariah the Scientist & Kali Uchis
12 to 12 – sombr
Lotus – Infinity Song
Pilot - Ravyn Lenae
The Healing - Zara Larson
Before You Go - Lewis Capaldi
Run – Joji
Bring It Back To Me – Martin Luke Brown
Jealous – Labrinth
Baby Steps – Olivia Dean
Getting Older-Billie Eilish
All That You Are- Sinead Harnett
Metamorphosis - Infinity Song
Great One-Jessie Reyez
I Didn't Mean to Fall in Love - Snoh Aalegra

"If we are bold, love strikes away the chains
of fear from our soul."

Maya Angelou

CHAPTER 1
Three Fines Means You're Not Fine

Jahlani

All things considered, Micah ending things with Jahlani on a random Tuesday afternoon over two bowls of mint chocolate chip ice cream is rather banal. Just another blip in her day. It's not a grandiose spectacle where she slaps him across the face, throws her melted green paste at him, and tells him to *go to hell*.

It's a far cry from that.

Instead, as they sit opposite each other in their usual spot—the black booth towards the front of the parlor—she considers two possibilities. The first is to confess the truth, which is that she despises mint chocolate ice cream. Really, anything combining those flavors together is an insult to her taste buds. The second thing plaguing her thoughts, as she swirls her spoon around the bowl, is how she allowed herself to end up here.

Here, across from a man who's been made to feel that the world revolves around him. She knows it's not his fault. Not really. If anything, it's his parents' doing. Always at his beck and call. Fixing his problems for him.

Jahlani's life is a stark contrast. If she wants even the bare minimum, she has to work twice as hard as the next person.

And sometimes that still isn't enough.

Some naïve part of her thought that was what made her and Micah compatible. That he would wake up one day and recognize that you have to work hard for the things you want in life, that things don't just get handed to you.

She believed they would evolve together.

But it's here on this arbitrary Tuesday afternoon, where the sky is that restless murky gray—the shade that makes you want to hide from the banshee-like wails of thunder and streaks of lightning—that Micah starts his breakup speech.

At a certain point in time between "we're not on the same page anymore" and "you're always working," she decides she's had enough and can't stomach this thing they call a flavor anymore. Letting the metal spoon clatter, she digs her nails into her palm, her knee bouncing under the table. And as he drones on, she isn't sure why, after all these years, she's felt the need to preserve his ego for something as simple as ice cream.

Jahlani averts her gaze to the large shop door as the bell overhead chimes. A woman weighed down by shopping bags stumbles in with two little girls, leaving a trail of muddy footprints as they make their way to the counter. Jahlani drops her head against the window, noticing the rivulets of water starting to build against the pane. She takes in the cramped brick buildings with rusted fire escapes, dog walkers, business professionals, and students as they share the darkening sidewalk of Lower Manhattan. She's suddenly envious of all of them.

They have intentions.

A destination.

Purpose.

And as her throat clogs, another devastating string of words falls past Micah's lips, waking her from her hazy state of insensibility.

"What?" she says, unwinding her arms. The green strings of her knit cardigan drag through the sticky mess on the table as she grips the edge of the seat. Suddenly, the booth is too small. There's not enough space for her to breathe.

Micah stares at her. "Did you hear anything I just said?"

She inhales deeply as she takes him in. "Uh, sorry. Repeat the last part?" She clears her throat, shifting against the leather.

She looks on, her heartbeat accelerating, as he pulls apart his napkin. His eyebrows furrow in concentration. He sighs, dropping the mangled scraps and presses the palms of his hands to his face.

"This is exactly what I'm talking about. It's like you're not even here. It's like I'm talking to a wall, Jahlani."

Her shoulders deflate, and she lowers her gaze.

"Oh," she says, feeling rather stupid, but what else *is* there to say? "I just have a lot on my mind," she says, rubbing her forehead. "Truthfully, I've been—"

"Jasmine thinks I need to be with a more present partner. Someone who listens to me," he says, interrupting her. "Someone who talks to me. And I agree with her."

At the mention of *her* name, Jahlani's head lifts.

"Jasmine?" she asks, hating how small her voice sounds. How afraid.

Because she knows Jasmine. They met at a fundraising event that his company held.

Last year.

Micah's eyes divert from hers, and it's all the confirmation she needs.

Jahlani runs her tongue over her teeth, nodding as she takes in his tense shoulders.

"So, let me get this right," she says. "You're ending things with me because *Jasmine* told you I'm not a 'present partner'?"

He sucks in air, scratching the back of his head. "Don't make this about her. She has nothing to do with it."

She rolls her eyes and folds her arms over her chest. "Spare me. She has everything to do with it."

He shifts forward, his mouth poised for rebuttal, but Jahlani raises her hand, letting out a derisive laugh.

"So, when did you have this riveting conversation with her about our relationship? Before or after you slept with her?"

Micah's shoulders fall from his ears, his eyes downcast like a scolded puppy. He lets out a heavy breath as he drags a hand through his hair.

"You weren't around, and I got tired of waiting," he says, his voice low. "Jasmine was there. She listened, and it was nice."

Jasmine was there. She listened.

The words ricochet through her head, and she waits and waits for something.

For anything.

For the words to strike through her heart, for her stomach to tumble into an abyss, for the flood of hysteria to overwhelm her senses, but it never manifests.

Instead, Jahlani lets his words settle over her like a weighted blanket. Heavy yet comforting because it's here, as she watches him, with his shiny curls, broad shoulders, and freshly trimmed beard, that the realization dawns on her: Micah and her were never going to work. And it's here that she realizes that, despite him unraveling their relationship in a few seconds, a small part of her is relieved it's over.

She's free.

Turning in the direction of the crowded streets, she watches as the rain escapes from the clouds. People run, using newspapers, tailored jackets, and purses to protect themselves.

Exhaling, she unwinds her arms, turning back to face him. "Okay."

And it must not have been the reaction he was expecting because his eyebrows raise. "Okay?"

"Okay," she says again, lifting her shoulders.

Micah pauses, clearly in shock, before scooting closer, jerking the round marble table between them with a tap of his index finger against it. "I just ended our two-year relationship and admitted to cheating on you, and all you have to say is *'okay'*?"

He puts air quotes around the word, and the whole thing is quite comical.

At least to her.

Lifting her chin up, she straightens her posture. "What do you want me to say?"

Scoffing, he pushes his ice cream to the side. "I don't believe this," he grits out. He rakes his left hand through his hair, but the strands fall back against his forehead. He braces his elbows on the table, gathers the shredded napkins, and crushes them further.

Poor napkins.

"See, *this* is your problem. I give and I give and you're like"—he pauses, eyes darting around the room—"you're like a machine."

At this, her eyebrow raises, as he continues.

"You don't know how to relax and take a break. You make everyone around you think they're not enough just because they don't want to *work* themselves to death."

Her eyes become smaller as she inches closer. "Not everyone has daddy and mommy's money to fall back on—"

"See? *This* is what I'm talking about. I haven't had to sweat for anything a day in my life, and you can't stand it, right?"

She falls back, pressing her fingers to her temple, looking at him. "You don't get it."

He exhales a strangled sound, and for a few seconds, neither of them speaks. He turns to face the window as it rattles, a thunderous clap echoing outside that startles several customers in the store. The whir of blenders and clang of spoons halt when the lights flicker overhead.

The conversations around her still momentarily, before continuing in hushed tones. She watches a few people leave, gathering their belongings. She realizes she should do the same.

Before it gets worse.

"Do you love me?" he asks, turning to look at her.

Her heart stops for a moment, and her skin prickles. She knows the right thing is to *say* it, but instead she scoffs.

"What?"

He moves forward, eyes bouncing over her face. "Do you love me?"

"I—" she pauses, searching his face, his gaze that seems to be pleading with her. "Of course I love you. Loved you," she says, correcting herself.

He shakes his head, running his tongue over his teeth. "Yeah, next time, try to say it without sounding like you're being held at gunpoint."

She clenches her fist, her skin tightening. "Oh, I'm *sorry*, was my affection not good enough for you? Did it not check all the boxes on your *'How to Love Micah'* list?"

His lip curls upward. "Screw you, Jahlani."

"No, screw you," she says in a harsh whisper. "*You* cheated on me. You left me."

"This is *why*," he says in a hushed tone. "This is why."

Her body trembles as she exhales. "Tell yourself whatever you need to sleep better at night, but you're not the victim here, and I don't have to prove anything to you."

She shakes her head, her heart pounding in her ears as he rubs his jaw, settling back.

"You know what?" he says. "You're intelligent, good at what you do, you've made it far for a woman, but this obsession you have with your career, your detachment … it's going to cause you to end up alone." He raises a finger, tapping it to his temple. "Wake up and realize that because you lost a good man. I'd hate for you to lose another."

Jahlani's lips part, her face flushing in bewilderment as she barks out a laugh.

"A good man?"

Drawing out a ragged breath, his shoulders slump. "I'm not trying to be mean. I'm just telling you the truth. If you worried less about that internship and spent more time on our *relationship* and me"—he waves his hand in the space between them—"we wouldn't be in this situation."

Cutting her eyes, Jahlani lets out a soft scoff, looking over his closed fists and drawn eyebrows.

So, this is who you really are.

Shifting closer, she sets a finger on the table.

"No. This *situation* wouldn't have happened if you weren't the type of man intimidated by a woman's intelligence. You're the problem. Not me."

Her inhale is long and drawn out, and she tries to control her chest rising and falling. She stares across the table as he wipes his hand down his mouth.

"Jahlani, I care about you, which is why I'm telling you this: you need to talk to someone. You need a therapist."

At this, her skin flushes. She looks around, suddenly remembering that they're in public. Lowering her head, she does everything to control her pitch from rising as more people walk in and out of the parlor, swallowing the acid in her throat.

"Fuck you, Micah," she says. "You don't get to cheat on me, blame me for this relationship falling apart, and give a half-assed attempt at psychoanalyzing me with some *bullshit* you probably read on WebMD. I don't need you or anyone else."

His jaw ticks. "Keep telling yourself that," he says before letting out a humorless laugh. "I can't do this anymore."

He stands up from the booth so that he towers over her. "I'm going to stay with a friend for a few days. We can talk about the living arrangements once we've both had some space."

She says nothing, her gaze fixed on the melted bowl of ice cream as he sighs, stepping past her and out the parlor door, the bell ringing above her. She sinks back into the booth, biting her nail, her mind spiraling. The saccharine scent of waffle cones being pressed drifts across the room as she inhales, then rises from her seat, throwing the remains of her food out.

As she steps out onto the damp pavement beneath the bleak New York skyline, the rain dampening her hair and clothes, she can't help feeling like it's crying for her.

With her.

At her.

Hastening to the subway, she forces herself through the crowded streets. She squeezes past cigarette smokers and bypasses several food stalls, shaking her head as numerous people try to hand her damp flyers. Her head remains tucked as she makes her way down the stairs to the platform, doing her best to avoid eye contact with other commuters because it feels like someone is running a fist the size of a gallbladder through her chest.

Jahlani steps onto the train, sinking into the first open seat she finds. The window is smudged with red lipstick that says 'love conquers all' and before she can process what she's doing, she wipes it away with her sleeve. Her shoulders slump, and she buries her face in her hands.

A feeble older woman sits next to her, reading the newspaper. Suddenly, it folds down and into the large, teal alligator purse propped in between them. Jahlani wipes the moisture from her cheeks with the back of her palm. She's not crying because she's hurt about anything that he said.

She's crying because—

"Honey, are you okay?"

What now?

Jahlani wipes her face with more urgency, mustering her best *my life is not on fire* smile she can as she turns to the woman.

"I'm fine, I'm fine. Everything's fine. Just got caught in a storm."

For the past two years of my life.

As she settles in for the rest of the ride, she convinces herself that this is for the best. She repeats the words in her mind as a quiet comfort, but they do nothing to soothe the trepidation that lingers as the train doors slide closed.

CHAPTER 2
Find Your Way Home

Jahlani

Jahlani is not a superstitious person by any means. To her, everything is a numbers game. It's logical. The Three Fates? Bullshit. Coincidences? That's just the human brain applying a perceived pattern to random events. A weak attempt to make something out of nothing.

And things happening in threes? One could say that's just paranoia, because from a mathematician's standpoint, a cluster of three is inevitable, given enough time.

But a believer would say that Micah ending things with her was the catalyst.

It's dark by the time she gets back to the apartment. She jumps in the shower, determined to wash Micah's words from her. After changing, she stands in the kitchen waiting for her chamomile tea to cool down. Taking out her phone, she sends a quick message to Imani, the only friend she held onto from high school.

Jahlani always had a tough time connecting with people. Her life differed from everyone she went to school with. She studied, kept her head down, and worked to keep herself busy. She didn't have the energy to explain that her mom probably wouldn't notice if she left and that her dad already had.

> **JAHLANI**
> Micah cheated. Don't call. I'm fine.

IMANI
Flights already booked. Does TSA still not allow weapons?

> **JAHLANI**
> Ha. I promise I'm fine.

IMANI
He didn't deserve you, Lani Banani.

Jahlani lets out a weak chuckle, setting her phone on the counter before dragging the stool from underneath the island.

What does that mean anyway? To deserve somebody?

The apartment is eerily quiet, only the low thrum of the A/C circulating and the dull pitter of the rain against the windows is heard. Summers in New York are her favorite. The breezes are kinder, and the people are softer. It's also the slow season for the company she's interning with. As she picks up her mug and takes a sip, the grassy undertones mix with the sweet, floral flavors, warming her throat.

Her laptop is still open from earlier that morning, and she clicks through the graduate student portal looking for her appointment link to register for her last semester.

But a red exclamation mark next to one email makes her catch her breath.

"No," she whispers, her voice echoing through the still apartment. She sets her cup down too fast, causing the liquid to spill onto her hand, but the sting is nothing compared to the burn in her chest as she reads the words *regret*, *unable*, and *financial support*.

The second email she sees sends her hands trembling. Standing from the chair, she paces the kitchen, twirling her necklace between her thumb and index finger. She moves back to the laptop, blinking, certain that she's read it wrong, but no. The words remain the same:

Due to under-enrollment, course number ISTX0200 will no longer be offered.

Jahlani lowers herself once more, her head spinning as she wonders how everything could get so screwed up so quickly.

No financial aid, and the last class she needs to graduate with her master's—gone.

For several minutes, she tries to just exist. To just *be*. She takes several deep breaths, trying to focus on steadying her heart.

When her phone blares, she doesn't bother looking at the contact and taps *Accept*.

"Hello," she says, her voice hoarse as she cradles it between her ear and shoulder. Static and heavy breathing greet her. "Hello?" she says again before pulling it down to look at the screen. Her eyebrows crease at the unknown number. She hears something and draws it back to her.

"Jahlani," the voice says, slurring. "Jahlani—"

Her eyes close as his voice carries through the phone.

"Why are you calling me, Micah? Whose number is this?" she asks, her voice constricting as she thinks of their last few moments together. Loud music and conversation spill through, and she rubs her chest, regretting picking up.

"Jahlani, please. Don't hang up. I just need a minute."

She glances at the time on her laptop, and she stands to look for a paper towel to clean the spilled tea. "Fifty-six seconds and counting."

He lets out a strained laugh. "Jesus, Jahlani. I didn't mean literally—"

"Fifty and counting."

"Okay, okay. I just called ... to tell you that I'm sorry about everything. Everything got so ... so—fuck," he says, laughing into the phone.

Jahlani breathes, clenching her fist before transitioning the phone to her other ear. "Are you drunk?"

He laughs again, as she rips a paper towel free, wiping the spill with more force than needed.

"I don't have time for this," she hisses, ending the call. She tosses her phone back onto the counter and lets it vibrate as she buries her head in her hands, unsure of what to do.

A weight of uncertainty settles upon her as she looks around. Except for a few things, nothing is hers. There's nothing to tether her to the space. Not anymore. She wonders if there ever was.

She moves slowly, each step drawing her closer to her past life. As she opens the door to the bedroom, it groans as it swings open, like it's in pain too. She steps over a pile of Micah's dirty laundry as she enters the cramped closet. When she sees the white box tucked in the corner, she pulls it out, settling on the floor next to it.

The scent of old paper and lingering coffee fills the air as she works on unpacking the contents—a framed photo of her at graduation with Imani, a random souvenir from her first client during internship, her high school transcript, and finally, a crumpled photograph of her and her mother right before she left for college. It's faded and spotty, and neither of them is smiling, but it makes her throat sting, like someone's clamping it shut.

She exhales, tracing her fingers over her mother's jet black locs, her rounded figure and firm jaw. Jahlani isn't sure how long she sits in the closet staring, but when her back pinches and her legs numb, she drags herself up.

And when she turns to leave the closet, she takes the box with her, having decided what to do.

$$x = \frac{-b + \sqrt{b^2 - 4ac}}{2a}$$

She's not surprised when Micah's stay becomes extended. A few days turn into two weeks, and by the time his second call comes, it's too late. She received the email a week earlier, letting her know of her acceptance into another graduate program.

In Florida.

The very place she had spent years trying to leave.

It didn't take long for her to pack up her things, leaving everything behind. It's become a tradition of hers.

With a grounding breath, Jahlani eases off the accelerator as she passes the sign welcoming her back into Florida.

She sighs, adjusting in her seat while reaching for the phone as his name flashes again. Normally, she hates driving long distances, but right now she welcomes it with open arms. It gives her a chance to *breathe*.

"What, Micah?" she says, sounding bored as she puts the phone on speaker.

"Jahlani," he says, breathing heavily. "I'm in the apartment. All your stuff is gone. Where are you?"

"Why do you care?" she says, making a left turn. "You broke up with me."

"Yes," he says with a hiss. "Because you refuse to change."

She drums her fingers on the steering wheel, pressing on the gas pedal. She savors the sight of the expansive highway stretching out before her, shimmering under the intense glare of the sun. Towering palm trees line the sides of the road, swaying in the warm breeze.

"No, Micah. Don't do that. Don't be that guy."

"What guy?"

"*That* guy," she says, hands tightening. "I didn't make you cheat, you made a choice."

He exhales, and she can hear him pacing. "Jahlani, just tell me where you are. I'm worried about you."

She lets out a choked laugh. "You're *worried* about me? Were you worried about me when you were screwing your coworker?"

"Jahlani," he says, his voice cracking. "Please. I miss you. It was a mistake. I'm sorry about cheating and for the things I said—I *miss* you. I love you. I want to talk about this."

Her skin flushes, and her foot presses on the accelerator even more. She watches as the speedometer moves up, wondering how far she's willing to push.

"You don't miss me, Micah," she says, her voice small. "And I'm already gone. I think I loved you because I needed someone to love. Not because I can't live without you, you know? There's a difference between loving someone because you need them and needing someone for love. I think you cared about me in your own way. I thought it was enough and that I could live that way, but I'm glad, Micah. I think no matter what my issues are, I deserve to be loved fully. So no, Micah. This is done. We're done."

Silence greets her on the other end as she takes in the widening stretch of the road, the lush fields, the rush of cars under the glazing warmth. A sense of calmness envelops her like a soothing wave washing over her skin.

She frowns, affronted by the sensation of tranquility that tames the anxiety brewing within. A juxtaposition to how she usually feels when thinking of her home because Florida is anything but *calm* for her.

Florida is years of neglect. It's months of conflict and confrontations. It's lost love, it's fending for yourself, it's getting out as fast as you can—and not looking back.

Run, run, run.

It is anything but calm.

"Jahlani," he says, his voice low. "Do you think we can—I don't know—be friends?"

She lets out a humorless laugh. *The audacity*, she thinks.

"Micah," she says in a soft voice, like she's talking to a small child, "you're going to delete my number because I deserve better. I hope that if you ever meet someone that you have a genuine connection with, you treat them better than you did me. I hope you make them feel tall. I hope you encourage them to go after what they want. I hope you love them unconditionally, because that's what we all deserve."

He lets out a pained sound, like a wounded animal. "Jahlani, just, at least tell me where you are. Tell me where you're going."

Her eyes shift to the navigation on her phone, and her shoulders fall from her ears as her grip loosens on the wheel.

"I'm going home."

CHAPTER 3
Flirting with Strangers

Roman

"You realize she's my daughter and not yours, right? I think I know her basic needs."

Roman adjusts the phone on his shoulder as he reaches for the package of diapers on the shelf. The muscles in his arm scream in protest as he extends, his body still not fully recovered from holding Lucy all last night. His mother huffs in his ear, and he can practically hear the eye roll.

"I know, but don't forget to grab the other stuff. We need—"

"The silver trays, paper plates, and the medicine from the pharmacy," he says, wincing as he picks up the basket again before exiting the aisle.

Soft music chimes through the speakers as he weaves through the bakery tables filled with pies, sugar cookies, and red, white, and blue cupcakes. He glosses over the beach towels and American flags as he narrowly avoids being run over by two little boys.

"You only said it to me about ten times before I left, Mom."

"I was going to say the fireworks, but yes, those too."

As he maneuvers around the store, he wonders how his mom is so meticulous and put together, and he's not. Of all the traits she could've passed to him, she didn't give him the one he needed the most.

"Okay, I'll get it. Bye—"

"Ro, wait. Your sister needs tampons."

Whispers crackle through the phone. "And pads, but not the ones with wings. She said the large ones, but not the thin ones." More hushed words, barely audible. "She said to make sure they're without the wings. And not the thin ones."

Roman rubs his forehead, trying to keep his annoyance in check. "Got it. Tampons. Pads. No wings. Large. Not thin." He repeats the list like it's a mantra.

He hears his sister, a muffled voice on the other end of the line. "What did he say?"

"He says that you're a leech and that you can go get up off your ass and get them yourself from up the road."

Such a shit stirrer.

There is an audible gasp, and the ruffling of the phone being transferred. "You little *shit*."

He stops walking, setting the basket on the floor. "Little? I'm older than you."

"Whatever. Don't forget that I watch your drooling monster for you. For *free*."

He rolls his eyes, leaning against a shelf that holds a selection of canned goods.

"Danica, she's lying. I didn't say that."

"Yeah, okay." She lowers her voice into a menacing tone, whispering, "Don't forget that I have something over you, fool. I could tell her right now."

He straightens his posture, gripping the phone tighter.

"You wouldn't."

"Try me, Pookie Bear."

Roman thinks about how this is the same girl who used to sit next to him at the dining room table on Sunday nights to watch him do homework. The same girl who cried to him when Angel Rankle turned her down before the Spring Fling Social her sophomore year. The same girl who begged him to live at home for college. The same girl who graduated in the top two percent of her class, got accepted to UM for political science on a full ride, and reads international relations documents for fun.

"Taylor called," he says, changing the subject. "Said he might pass through today."

She scoffs. "Oh, please. That won't work on me anymore. I'm a changed woman now. That was a trivial crush from high school. Puppy love," she says with a sniff.

Roman's lips twitch. "Really? I didn't realize you were such an evolved woman. What a shame. He was asking about you."

A pause. A breath. Some shuffling. "He was?"

Roman sighs, dragging it out, doing his best to sound sympathetic for his friend. "Yeah. Rachel left him last month. Something about them not being compatible."

An exhale. "Oh. I didn't know that."

He tries to muffle his laugh, clearing his throat. "Yeah. Well, he probably wants to be alone, anyway."

"I mean, I haven't seen him in a while. He could probably use the company."

Roman: one, Danica: zero

"Okay, I'll call hi–"

"Already texted him. Bye, loser." The dial tone reaches his ear, and he lifts the basket from the ground, smiling.

He makes his way toward the section with feminine products, grabbing what Danica needs before moving back to the groceries. He watches as a dad pushes his babies around, and a mother fights with her toddler, their cart filled to the brim with meats and wine coolers.

As he rounds the corner, he notices a woman struggling to grab a box from the top shelf, and his mouth moves before his cerebral cortex can process his entire view.

"What are you looking for?" he asks, his voice echoing throughout the shelves.

Her head turns toward his voice, and he finds himself thrown by the visceral reaction his body has to her. An oversized green cardigan sits on her shoulders, covering most of her frame, and he wonders how she isn't *sweating to death* in it. It's July. In Florida. He lingers for an extended amount of time on her face as he takes in her delicate nose. Eyes the color of bark. An upper lip that's slightly thinner than the bottom. High cheekbones. Masses of braided ebony curls. Warm brown skin.

Devastatingly attractive.

Oh hell.

He licks his lips, his senses going into overdrive, and he wills his voice to sound normal.

"I hate when they put all the good snacks at the top," he says, moving towards her with a sheepish smile. He can see that she comes up to his chin, and when she looks up, he notices her eyes are a lighter shade of brown. "This one?" he asks, extending an arm. Heat seeps through his arm as he tries to maintain his hold on the item for her. His fingers shake slightly as he waits for her confirmation.

"Uh, yeah," she says, and he pulls the box down, handing it to her.

He's almost certain she winces but can't be sure because she's leaning forward, and he's momentarily distracted by the shape of her hands, the amber necklace that rests on her collarbones, the scent of freshly picked apples that seems to dance around her.

"What?" he says, in a daze. "What's wrong?"

He steps closer as she inspects the package in her hands, her bottom lip protruding. He's staring, but she doesn't notice.

"Oh, it's fine," she says, waving him off as she gives a forced smile.

"Is that not what you wanted?" he asks, suddenly overcome with the urge to *get it right* for her.

She moves her head to the side, sending ripples of her perfume in his direction. He inhales, hopefully subtly, and exhales. She scratches her forehead, grimacing, then looks back at the floor.

"It's fine," she says slowly, but he's already taking it from her hand and placing it back. His hand shifts to the left, his fingertips brushing the edge of a different package.

"This one?"

"A little to the right ... yeah, that one."

He tugs the square packaging from the shelf, and his mouth twists into a grimace when he reads the words "plant-based" and "infused with coconut, chocolate, and almond" across the box.

"Huh," he says, leveling her with a look. "These look disgusting."

She lets out a soft laugh as he passes them to her, and he feels a sudden surge of energy. Like he's been asleep for a long time, and he's just now waking up.

"Thanks."

He frowns. "This is the part where you defend the honor of your *atrocious* choice of snack options, ultimately convincing me to buy them."

Her lips twitch. "But ... then I'd be lying."

"Ah," he says, nodding. "So, you admit that they are, in fact, terrible. I hope you're not in sales—you're not very good."

She shrugs, tilting her head to look up at him. "Joke's on you. I got Employee of the Month last week," she retorts, her mouth curving up at the corners.

He tsks. "It's rigged. Gonna have to call corporate."

She's full-on grinning now as he slides his hand into his pocket.

They lapse into silence, and it's deafening between them. Monumental. Roman is well aware that this is when he bids her goodbye, giving her a cliché '*happy fourth*,' but he can't find it in himself to make the first move. He should think of something to say, but everything that comes to mind sounds and feels certifiably insane.

You're beautiful.

Thank you for being too short to reach the top shelf.

Wanna get out of here?

He must be staring again because she clears her throat, stepping back. "Right, well. Thanks again." Turning away, she walks in the opposite direction. She's gone so fast, he wonders for a moment if he imagined the whole thing. Except, he couldn't have. There's a lingering fragrance, and as he turns his smile is still etched in place.

He can't remember the last time he felt so carefree. Flirting with strangers, if he can even call it that, doesn't happen for him anymore, and as he walks further down the aisle, it becomes more apparent why.

The pharmacy is located two aisles down, near the back of the store, and as he makes his way over, the rush, the *thrill*, of the encounter steadily simmers within him. His jaw sets tight as he comes to a stop at the end of the line. He takes in the rows of medication that rest on the shelves, organized behind the counter. A small table rests on the side, displaying signage about the dangers of skin cancer and the benefits of sunscreen. He grabs an extra bottle before moving to the window.

"Picking up?"

He nods, reaching for his wallet. "Yeah. Lucy Hayes."

The pharmacist hands him the package, and Roman cranes his

neck around the store, looking for signs of a green figure with dark braids.

With a deep exhale, he reads the description on the side, not watching his step, and collides with someone, causing his items and theirs to tumble out of both baskets.

"Shit. Sorry," he says, crouching to gather their items.

"Snack Guy," she says with a lilt.

At the sound of her voice, his head raises and he winces.

Snack Guy, he repeats silently to himself, and he struggles against the pull at the corners of his mouth.

He clucks his tongue. "Damn, you found out my name. I told my mom it was too common—she didn't believe me."

She slides her eyes back to the ground, shaking her head as she grabs her items, shoving them into her basket. "You following me around the store or something?"

CHAPTER 4
A One Percent Chance

Roman

"Yes, actually," Roman says, his face serious, but thinking of how serendipitous it is that she would be the one he crashes into.

Her hand wraps around the bag containing the medicine, and she holds it out to him.

"Thanks," he says, reaching for it. He tries, he really tries, to avoid making contact with her skin, with her fingers. But fate has other plans. So, as the package slips from her, his forefinger lightly grazes hers. His body is apparently determined to hold on to the sensation, knowing full well it will amount to nothing. This is nothing. Their gazes lock, and she sucks in a sharp breath before standing back to her full height.

Get a grip.

She clears her throat, jutting out her chin. "Someone sick?"

He looks down at the package, shoving it into the basket. "Something like that."

She gives a small smile, her features sympathetic. "Well, I hope they get better."

She's nice too.

She starts to move past, but he just can't help it. He enjoys inflicting pain on himself, you see.

So, rather than moving to a different cashier like a sane person, he finds himself in the line behind her. She types furiously into her cellphone as she gets rung out, her mouth pursed, her eyebrows drawn. He wants to know who's disturbing her and if he needs to have a word with them. He sees there's not much on the belt and watches as she absentmindedly shoves her card into the machine with more force than necessary before cracking her fingers as she reads whatever message comes through.

The cashier, a young kid with a smattering of freckles, clears his throat.

"Ma'am?"

She looks up from her phone, a tightness to her features.

"Your card declined."

He examines the machine and—

Yeah, those black letters are blocky and bold.

He shifts, watching as her eyebrows pinch even closer. She removes the card, wiping it against her stomach.

"Sorry, it's an old card," she says, clearing her throat. "Might have typed in the pin wrong." She inserts it again with shaky fingers. The anxiety rolls off her in waves, and he can't seem to tolerate the idea of her not feeling okay. Before he can really think about it, he's clearing his throat, pulling the piece of plastic from the card reader before it declines again.

"Baby," he says, slipping her card into her back pocket and pulling out his own. "I told you to order a new card last week."

Coaxing her to the side with a hand on her arm, he turns to the red-faced cashier.

"She's so busy with work, she must have forgotten. She's been making so many sales. She got Employee of the Month, you know," he says evenly as he removes the divider, pushing his items with hers.

"Just put everything together for me. This woman, I tell you, *incredibly* persuasive. Right?" He takes in her furrowed eyebrows and pursed lips before inserting his own card. "She's so modest." He steps back, gathering all the bags as the boy hands him the receipt. "Thanks, man. Happy Fourth of July," Roman says with a hand against her back.

He guides them out of the automatic doors, into the parking lot. The sounds of customers pushing their carts across the concrete, crying babies, and trunks slamming shut greet him. If possible, the temperature seems to have spiked at least ten degrees since he stepped inside. He walks with her, making sure they're in the shade of a few palm trees and the building's slated roof before turning to face her.

He holds out her bags, the oppressive humidity making his palm clammy against the plastic, sweat rolling down his side.

She stands, basking in the sun's rays, the light making her skin glow.

Jesus.

"Why did you do that?" She asks, blinking rapidly.

He shrugs, his hand slightly lowering. "I'm sure you would've done the same."

Her eyes flit to the cars in the lot before meeting his gaze again.

"No. I wouldn't have."

He blinks at her candid admission, not expecting it but pleasantly surprised anyway. His lips turn upward as she takes the bag from him. He rubs his jaw with his free hand and clears his throat.

"You know, most people would say thank you."

She looks up, her grip tightening on the bag.

"Thanks," she murmurs, moving to walk past him. "Sorry for the trouble."

But no, this can't be it, right? Surely, this ends differently.

"Are you from around here?" he asks, then cringes. He won't blame her if she pretends not to hear him and continues on her way, but her movements falter.

She turns on her heel, studying him for several moments, opening her mouth and then closing it.

He chuckles, running his knuckles under his chin.

"I'm not—I don't mean to … shit," he says, looking at his feet. He shuffles backward to leave. "Sorry. I'm not—I didn't do that so you would—"

"No," she says, interrupting him. He stops moving, examining her relaxed posture. "I mean, yes. I used to. I'm from New York," she says, blowing out a small breath.

Of fucking course.

"So," she says, looking back up at him with a small smile, "if you're a serial killer, I'm not the best prey." Her eyebrows pinch together then. "Or maybe I am. Nobody would look for me here, I suppose." She looks off to the side, appearing deep in thought.

The corners of his lips twitch as he lets out a shaky laugh. "Jesus, I'm not a serial killer," he says, chuckling louder as her words replay in his mind.

"That's what they all say," she mumbles. She fixes her gaze on him and steps further to the left.

He raises his eyebrows. "Are you … visiting family? Big Fourth of July celebration?"

And just like that, her face draws in, like a dark cloud swiftly appears in a clear sky. Her lips turn downward before pressing together. Her eyes fall to the ground, and her entire posture stiffens.

We were doing so well.

Roman rubs a hand across his mouth, taking a small step back when she says nothing.

"You don't have to—"

"It's complicated," she says, gripping the handle of her bag tighter. "I'm procrastinating. I haven't been home in a long time," she says, breathing out. "They don't even know I'm here. Not sure if they'd even be happy to see me. But I'm finishing my master's program around here—sorry, I'm rambling."

Her brown eyes are sharp and round, with an unwavering intensity that has his mind reeling.

"I really don't mind. You have a pretty fantastic voice."

And for some reason, he feels emboldened by her lack of retreat and takes a step closer.

"And I think they'd be happy to see you. For what it's worth," he says, towering over her as he rubs the nape of his neck. "Your family."

Her arms wrap around her silhouette. "You don't know me. What if I'm the problem? What if I'm the monster?" she asks, looking past him.

"You're not," he says, and then gestures towards her. "I mean, you don't look like one."

She twists her head, blinking up at him. "Really? And here I thought my fangs and claws were showing," she says, her eyes bouncing around his face.

He laughs as he inches forward to let a woman walk past with her cart.

"Well," he says in a low voice, "I think … I have a solution to our problem." He clears his throat, wiping his palm against the material of his shirt.

Now or never.

"I could take you out for a coffee, and you can tell me all about your origin story," he says slowly, gauging her reaction. "Fangs and all."

Her lips part as she stares at him, a slow smile on her face that makes his face heat.

Her eyebrow arches. "Presumptuous of you to assume I like coffee," she says, matching his pitch.

Roman reaches for his chest like he's been wounded, swaying to the side slightly.

"Don't … like … coffee?" He narrows his eyes. "You really are a monster …" he says, trailing off, eyebrows raised in question.

"Jahlani," she says, shaking her head.

"Jahlani," he repeats, savoring each syllable, testing it on his tongue and liking the way it sounds—loving the way it feels. "The evilest name I've heard since He Who Must Not Be Named."

She looks down at her feet, her smile faltering.

"I don't think your girlfriend—"

"Presumptuous of you to think I have a girlfriend." He jostles the bag of feminine products, flexing his fingers. "They're for my sister."

She says nothing, her expression wary. He takes another step forward, and his eyes flit to her pierced earlobes before moving back to the length of her nose.

"Come on," he says softly. "Don't say no. You have to admit that fate wants us together. Twice in one day? That's something."

At this, she laughs. And it's a glorious sound. One that he could get drunk on if she'd let him. One he'd make sure to hear at least seven days a week, 365 days a year. Her head tips back and her eyes close before they fall back to him, a lightness to them.

"That's not fate," she says, shuffling on the balls of her feet.

"It's not?" he asks, trying and failing not to sound winded.

"No," she says with a snort. "You're experiencing apophenia and confirmation bias. You're spotting a pattern that doesn't exist. You saw me once," she adds, stepping closer. "And you're choosing to focus on that, ignoring all the other times that we didn't cross paths. Us meeting? That's math. That's probability."

She waves her arm back towards the building, her stare unwavering.

"Let's assume here that the store is large enough that there's a reasonable chance of us crossing paths multiple times, but it's not so large that it's improbable we would never meet twice." She looks towards the store this time, before settling her gaze back on his. "Let's say it's 10,000 square feet. We were clearly not sticking to a single area of the store."

"Clearly," he murmurs, angling his body closer as she continues, her hands moving wildly.

"Our movements are random, and we've probably been in here for roughly the same amount of time. So, maybe we've only covered about one-tenth of the store in our time here. There's at least a point one, or a ten percent chance, of us meeting once." She licks her lips, eyebrows furrowed in thought.

"But we met twice," he says. "What are the odds of that?" She chews on her lip, looking away. "How do we get that number?" he asks, interest piqued, because *holy shit, she's a fucking math wizard.*

She exhales, looking back up. "You'd have to combine the probability of both independent events. Assuming that both numbers are the same, the product would be point zero one or one percent. But it doesn't mean anything. It's a rare event." She sounds less confident now, and it sends a sharp prickle through him.

His chuckle is low as he rubs two fingers against his temple. "Yeah, all you've managed to do is prove to me that your mind is just as beautiful as your face, and that I need to learn more about statistics if I have a fighting chance of keeping up with you in any kind of conversation." He shrugs, finally toe to toe with her. "Numbers don't lie, and I'd really like yours," he says, his pulse ticking to an abnormal rhythm, his tongue feeling rather heavy because the last time he asked a woman out, it didn't feel like this.

He isn't sure it ever has.

She blows out a gust of air, her eyes ricocheting over his features. "Did you hear anything I just said?"

"I did," he says, glancing at her mouth. "And I promise, I'm not a serial killer. I'm just a guy wanting to get to know a captivating woman."

"Why?" she asks, blinking rapidly.

He inhales deeply through his nose, sliding his hand into his front pocket. "You're funny, blunt, smart," he says, moving even closer.

Absolutely gorgeous.

"Unpredictable," he says instead, watching her skin flush.

She licks her lips, swallowing. "And that's a good thing?"

He shrugs. "It makes me curious."

"But, what if … I'm a serial killer?" she says quietly, her eyebrows furrowed.

God.

He laughs, dropping his head forward before taking in the serious expression on her face. "See what I mean?"

Her smile falls and the light in her eyes seems to dissipate as she moves further away from him. From whatever this is. From whatever it could be.

Her lips press into a thin line. "No, I don't, actually." His breath hitches as she seems to snap back into her default mode, her walls growing taller with each passing second.

"Jahlani."

She clutches her bag tighter. "I'm sorry about earlier, and …

thanks again for helping me, but I don't think this is a good idea for me. I'm just not in a good place right now," she says, wiping her hand against her thigh.

Roman's ribs grow tight as he gives a weak smile. "Yeah, okay," he says, while blinking. "Sorry, I don't know what—"

"No, it's fine—"

"—came over me, I have a lot—"

"—I'm just figuring out things—"

They both pull in shaky breaths before laughing. Roman swallows, stepping back.

"Maybe I'll see you around?" he asks, looking down as his phone vibrates. Danica's name and number flash across the screen along with a contact picture—a photo of her with Lucy. His daughter. The very reason he's in this store to begin with.

He declines the call, but when he looks back up, she's gone.

I'm just not in a good place right now.

And he knows she was right to pass up on his offer because, truth be told, neither is he.

CHAPTER 5
Everything All at Once

Jahlani

As Jahlani stands on the creaky wooden front porch, a strip of skin on her left arm starts to tighten and swell. Being away for so long, she had forgotten how mosquitoes love the taste of her blood.

She knows she can just open the screen door and knock. The crisp air conditioning would greet her, and she could take a chilling shower to cleanse herself of the Floridian humidity, of the strange sensation from her interaction with the guy at the store.

Her lips twitch at the memory, and she touches her mouth as soft laughter spills out, her chest flooding with *something* for the first time in weeks. A welcomed ache at the thought of what could have been because she didn't even get his name, and she's still thinking about him.

The sound of a passing car hitting a divot in the road startles her, and she blinks toward the house.

The chipped raspberry-tinted door, adorned in gold-plated numbers—*3141*—shines at her.

Go inside, she thinks, trying to compel herself forward.

And yet, she remains. Rigid. Unwilling to move even as a third mosquito burrows into her right ankle. Too long. It's been too long. What will she say? How will she *explain*?

Jahlani heaves out a sigh, turning back toward the metal that is her car, her month-old French curl braids swishing along with her. It looks out of place on the paved driveway. It doesn't belong there.

Wiping her palm against her arm, she glances toward the street, soaking it in. Something is off. Green and blue bins line the driveways of each residence. All the lawns are mowed, and the exteriors of the houses are smeared in fresh, modest coats of paint. Everything looks *cleaner* than she remembers. She's used to seeing overgrown weeds, barely-there fences, crumbling infrastructure.

Gentrification doing its work I see.

Glancing down at the keys in her hand, she wraps a tight fist around them. She'll come back tomorrow. And she'll have some kind of half-truth, some bullshit lie to vindicate her disappearing act.

Jahlani stares as two bushy-tailed squirrels scamper off around the corner. Lizards chase each other up into the palm trees. *Do you know what you're doing? Do you know where you're going?* she thinks, and then laughs at the *insanity* of it all because—*yes*, they have their shit together and, *clearly*, they know where they're going.

Slipping her phone from her back pocket, her finger hovers over the contact for Imani. When Jahlani checks the time, she realizes it's reaching half past four in California, so she'll still be at work.

She works to scroll past the number for her primary care physician, gynecologist, mechanic, and a few ex-colleagues before reaching the end. A painful reminder of her inability to form any *real*, lasting connections.

How pathetic.

Opening the app on her phone, she thumbs through her bank account before letting her head fall against the door.

It isn't supposed to be like this, she thinks to herself. She should be curled up in her own apartment, enjoying her summer break before her final semester of graduate school, not floundering around Florida with physical reminders of her failed relationships, zero dollars to her name, and the trauma of her childhood preventing her from stepping foot in the house she grew up in.

For the tenth time this week, she lets the hot tears build before soaking her face. Abrupt, choking sounds saturate the air as she trembles. She wipes with more pressure than needed, wanting nothing more for the stream to stop.

Pressing a hand to her quivering lips, she wills herself to calm down. To breathe. She attempts to gather her crumbling mind by playing out her next steps.

She'll stand for a few more minutes, making sure she's cried all there is to *cry* from her system. She'll check her eyes, cover the dark circles taking residence on her face, pinch her cheeks back to life. She'll smile once, twice, maybe three times until it's *doable*. Believable. A smile that hints at nothing being wrong, and that everything is *okay*. A genial stretch across the expanse of her face that proves that she made the right choice all those years ago when she distanced herself from her family.

Jahlani checks her appearance in her phone. Inky-brown, bloodshot ones glare back. The long drive—among other mental stresses—is catching up to her.

She needs a bed.

She needs a restart button.

The sun begins to set with vivid bursts of peach and hues of orange glowing across the skyline. This time, she pushes past the screen door and turns the key in the lock, the sound of the latch as loud as her heartbeat.

With an unsteady exhale, she steps over the threshold and is met with stillness. Her shoulders drop as she shuffles further into the house, closing the door softly. She just wants to get the reunion over with.

The house is shrouded in darkness. Faint glimmers of sunlight seep in through the two windows in the front room. The air carries a faint scent of freshly cut flowers, mingling with the subtle aroma of cedar found in polishing products. As Jahlani steps further into the space, the gentle hum of the air conditioning creates a soothing white noise. Slipping her shoes off, surprise runs through her feet as hardwood floors greet her toes rather than the ugly hunter green carpet she grew up with. Her fingers brush against the wall to flick the lights on, and for a moment, she wonders if she's broken into someone else's home.

A gray L-shaped linen couch has replaced the cracked leather one that used to take up much of the family room. An oak coffee table sits in the center, and a moderately-sized television covers the wall. As she steps further into the house, she becomes flustered. Everything is different. Upgraded. It looks pretty. Polished. There are no traces of the house she grew up in.

Trying to forget something, Mom?

Stepping through the hallway, she pushes open her bedroom door. A small gust of air flows past her lips as she looks.

Everything remains untouched, and she isn't sure how to interpret that.

The shelves housing her old high school textbooks remain frozen in time. Her hand skims her nightstand before moving to the vintage vanity she thrifted for her thirteenth birthday.

Caught in between the frame and mirror are several photos. Imani and her at prom *(she insisted on going despite Jahlani's protests)*, Imani and her on the hood of her first car, Imani and her in their cheerleading uniforms *(not a year she's proud of)*. Her chest squeezes as she comes across a beat-up photograph of her cousins, Trent and Teryn, from their tenth birthday party. She can't remember the last time she spoke to either of them, and she wonders for a moment if she's as bad as her mother.

Jahlani continues browsing through the room, viewing her old self. Everything looks fairly normal despite the scene outside the four walls.

And yet, something feels *off*. Wrong. *Something is missing*, she thinks, stepping back into the hallway. She walks further into the house and turns the corner. She sees the gleam of the machete before her, and bloodcurdling screams fill the hallway as Jahlani lifts her arms to protect her body, the knife clattering to the floor.

"Jahlani?" her mother asks, sounding breathless.

Jahlani clutches her chest as she leans against the wall to ground herself.

"Mom," she says, breathing heavily. "Jesus."

Her mother positions her hands on her hips and stares up at Jahlani, her lips tight.

"What did you expect? You can't just walk into a woman's house unannounced. *Especially* one that lives alone."

Jahlani's eyes widen as she takes in her mother's disheveled appearance. A sweat-soaked shirt clings to her shape as she wipes her chin with the back of her hand. She swoops to grab the knife alongside a basket of fruit by her feet.

"Well, I didn't expect a life-threatening weapon to be waved in my face. *God*. What do you even have that for?" Jahlani asks, her voice shaky.

"Mango tree," she replies, shrugging. "It's in the back of the house."

Silence engulfs and expands in the space around the two of them like a tight bubble. In a normal, functioning household, this is the part where the mother and daughter embrace. In a normal, *happy* story, the mother pulls the daughter close, breathes her in, and checks her over for any signs of hurt. Pain. *Heartbreak*. They ask questions. They're curious. They linger in the hallway, trying to cram years of life into a few hours. Everything all at once.

But this isn't a functioning, normal, happy household. So, they stare, and after a while, Jahlani unfurls her spine, looming over the woman who gave her life but not *purpose*.

Did she get shorter?

Jahlani reaches out to … to do what? Pet her? Shake hands with her? Hug her?

She lowers her hand, making a tight fist before pushing it behind her back.

"You look just like him," her mother says, clucking her tongue as she ambles toward the kitchen.

Him as in her dad. The other person who makes up fifty percent of her DNA. The piece snaps into place.

That's what's missing.

Her mom has scrubbed any remains of him from the house. His furniture. Collectibles. Pictures. Disintegrated. As if his entire existence had been a fever dream. Jahlani trails meekly behind her, breathing in her outdoor scent.

"It's been a while," her mother says, dropping the mangos onto the marble before rinsing them one by one.

Yes, four years is a long time, Mom. I missed you too, she thinks, and *no, I'm not doing okay* float through her head, ready on her tongue. Instead, she stays quiet, falling into sync with her mother. Jahlani pulls her sleeves up as she walks to the counter, washes her hands, and gets to work slicing the already rinsed mangos on the cutting board. For a while, the swift thud of the knives hitting the boards is the only sound that echoes throughout the kitchen. Jahlani notices that the layout is different here too. The golden teak wood cabinets have been replaced with a simple white base. Dressed around the island are four sleek leather barstools and instead of the electric stove, a glittering gas range sits on display in the middle.

Clearing her throat, Jahlani motions with her chin toward the stovetop.

"That's nice," she murmurs, glancing at her mother's face.

Her mother turns to look at the oven, before nodding slightly.

"A gift," she says, and that's the end of it. She doesn't seem too interested in having a conversation with her one and only child.

Jahlani waits and waits, slicing before lifting one to her mouth. The cool liquid of the mango springs against her tongue, leaving a tangy taste. Memories of humid summers, swarms of lovebugs, and lounging by the community pool with her cousins arise.

Then, as if on cue, her mother says, "Everyone will be glad to see you tomorrow. They haven't heard from you in years."

Jahlani exhales through her nose as she chews.

"Well, the phone works both ways," she mumbles, not looking her way. She resists the urge to knock the bowl of mangos over and scream at her mother, because she's *tired* and she hasn't bothered to ask if Jahlani's up to going.

It's a demand.

An expectation.

Her house, her rules.

When her mother doesn't say anything, Jahlani clears her throat, turning slightly to face her.

"Tomorrow?" She asks, trying to sound nonchalant. Trying not to let her irritation rise to the surface through any inflections in her tone, to let her mother down easy because she's not a child anymore. She should be allowed to say no and establish boundaries. She should be allowed to not want to be the subject of her family's judgment, ridicule, and outrageously invasive line of questioning. Her mother should understand that.

Right?

But her mother shrugs, slicing open another mango. "Teryn got accepted into some program for her master's." Her knife waves around in the air with 'some program.' *So did I*, she wants to yell. *Where's my party?*

Jahlani is quiet for several beats, chewing another slice, giving herself time to come up with a good enough excuse. She hums while nodding, wiping her hands against the front of her cotton leggings, heart drumming.

"I don't know. I'm really exhausted. And I still need to unpack," she starts slowly, returning to cutting. Careful with her choice of words. "I have a meeting at the school about my internship that I need to—"

Her mother's loud exhale stops her from saying more, and Jahlani sees from the corner of her eye that she's set her knife down.

Here we go.

Her dark eyes flutter around Jahlani's face before looking away, her expression stoic.

"Jahlani, they haven't seen you in years. You're going. Congratulate your cousin. They're your family. You owe it to them."

Jahlani's right eye twitches.

She *owes* it to them.

She doesn't owe them anything.

She just wants a moment to relax. To orient herself, but her mother continues, reminding her of why she left in the first place.

"You're lucky I even have room for you, showing up here out of the blue." Her voice rises slightly as she picks the knife up again, slicing expeditiously. "I was getting ready to rent it to one of your cousins when I got your little voicemail. So, *you* can go and be the one to tell them now that they'll have to find somewhere else to stay."

Jahlani squeezes her eyes shut, her shoulders curving inward as she takes a steadying breath. A part of her wants to pilfer the remaining mango and hide in her room for the rest of the night. The other part of her knows she has to *try* even though it's the last thing she wants to do. Even though she knows it'll be in vain.

Opening her eyes, she takes in her mother's thinning form. Her hollow cheeks. She doesn't look sickly, but she looks *older*. Jahlani unfurls her hands.

For what it's worth, I think they'll be happy to see you.

Her mind wanders momentarily to the man from the store again. His furrowed flat eyebrows, aquiline nose, and full pink lower lip. A selection of features she never thought she could be attracted to. His eyes, a striking combination of meadow green and sapphire blue. Those completely ruined her.

And he made her laugh.

Something that happens less frequently nowadays.

You were so wrong, she thinks. *This can't be what happiness looks like.*

For a moment, she allows herself to wonder. Her mind is a dangerous place, and she works hard to keep it quiet. It has a very treacherous habit of creating happy, safe realities, and in this one, he wrangles the ten-digit number from her, and she learns his name. In this version, she isn't emotionally unavailable.

Instead, this is the catalyst for their *something*.

He's charming and comes from a healthy, *stable* family. He knows how to love, and be in love, and be loved. He takes the time to show her how to do all those things. He's patient, and when she wants to stay late at work, he waits up for her. He's home cooking for her. He doesn't resent her for it. He's supportive and understanding because he's just that *good*. They would have nuclear, explosive sex, and she'd wonder where he had been her whole life because he was her *something* that became her *someone*.

She decides it's enough. His words encouraged her.

She reaches for another mango slice, restraining the sigh that is desperate to escape.

"What time does it start?"

CHAPTER 6
The Power of Presence

Roman

The stench of the sterile pediatric ward drifts through the air as Roman bounces his daughter in his lap, the scent clinging to him as if it's stuck to his skin. No matter how many times he steps into this place, the disinfectant, the antiseptic, the faint whiff of bleach, all of it hits his lungs like a slap, an unwelcome reminder of everything that's wrong in his world. He should be used to it by now. He's been coming here for months, after all. He should be numb to the chill, to the way the whitewashed walls seem to bleed into each other, creating a room devoid of color.

But every time he walks through the sliding glass doors, signs the paperwork, and nestles his daughter into his chest, it irritates his senses.

Now, he can't stand the smell of cleaning products or the sight of magazines.

Especially the travel guide ones.

He finds them to be insensitive and mocking since most people aren't afforded the luxuries of being able to go on vacation. This week's collection features a road trip to the Grand Canyon, a breathtaking photograph of the sun disappearing behind the cliffs, the winding river darkened, the minerals in various hues of red and salmon. A family of four poses with all teeth as they look into the camera.

Before Lucy's diagnosis, there was a time when he could have imagined himself out there with her. Now it further taunts him.

A reward for those who are deserving of it.

And he certainly isn't.

"Lucy Hayes?" A young woman in white scrubs covered in multicolored smiley faces waits for him by the corridor.

He stands quickly, still clutching Lucy as the nurse ushers them to the room, her cheerful face hiding a calm professionalism. The walls are a clash of rainbow colors and cartoonish sunflowers, a childish attempt to ease the tension of the place. Even as they float past them, he can't shake the gnawing panic rising in his chest as they get further down the hall.

The hospital, recently purchased by investors, is undergoing renovations. The new striking crescent blue of the pediatric ward helps to soothe his nerves as they finally make it into the room. It reminds him of the last time he took Lucy to the beach.

When the nurse shuts the door, he falls into their usual routine: he slips her out of her Winnie-the-Pooh onesie and into the gown the hospital provides. The whole time, she fondles her plushie, distracted. Happy. Oblivious. This is how it should be for her 24/7. She shouldn't be spending every waking minute in a hospital, strapped to machines. He sighs as he drops her against the pillow, kissing her cheek.

Moving to the other side of the space, he pulls out his laptop before lowering into the chair. The room is spacious, with a small TV mounted on one wall and a window that overlooks one of the courtyards on the other. Landscapers work on trimming the hedges as patients mill about.

Rolling his neck, Roman draws out his phone to read the schedule his advisor sent over once more, ensuring he's signing up for the right classes.

But when the landing page loads on the computer, the date he reads causes numbness to swarm his limbs.

"Shit," he whispers, refreshing the screen. He does this more times than he can count, the knots in his neck pulling tighter with each click, but it stays the same. "Fuck."

He missed his appointment slot for registration.

Sitting upright, he sifts through the available courses, and his stomach drops the further down he scrolls.

Suddenly, the door swings open and his mother walks in. He shuts the laptop, rubbing a hand over his jaw as he plasters a rehearsed smile on his face.

"I'm here, I'm here," she calls out, placing her bag on the side of the cot. Her overalls are covered in green and blue paint splatter, and her white and gray hair is piled in a messy bun. "How's she doing?" she asks.

She must have rushed over from the studio, Roman thinks, and the idea makes his heart sink.

He exhales harshly, folding his arms over his chest. "Doctor hasn't been in yet, but I don't know, Mom. She doesn't seem good. Look at her face."

His knee bounces as they both turn to her. Lucy's curls stack haphazardly on her head, her brown eyes wide, her cheeks rosy.

"Look at my gorgeous girl," his mom says as she smooths Lucy's hair, pressing soft kisses over her face, causing her to let out a garbled laugh. "My little girl. My brave girl."

His mom exhales, sinking down next to him, applying a hand to his thigh to still his bouncing knee. Pressing his hands together, he cracks his knuckles.

He juts his chin towards Lucy. "You see it, right?"

His mother's mouth twists. "It's probably nothing, honey. She's getting older, it's probably some extra weight she's put on."

He shakes his head, not feeling comforted by her words. "She's relapsed. Her whole body is swollen."

She squeezes his thigh. "Let's wait for Dr. Newark, okay?" She turns away from him, reaching into her bag. "There's no use in stressing over hypotheticals and potentialities. Did you eat?"

"No," he murmurs, taking the wrap from her hand. "Thanks."

He's two bites in when she asks the last thing he wants to answer.

"You got everything sorted for your last semester?" she asks, nudging his foot with hers. He busies himself with the sandwich, taking another bite. As he chews, he contemplates his answer.

"Yeah, everything's fine," he says, working on swallowing.

And it must not be convincing enough because when he does turn to look at her, she's pushed her glasses to the top of her head.

"Roman Alexander Hayes, don't you lie to me."

He shrugs in an attempt to play it cool. "I missed the deadline to register for classes. I have to go in person tomorrow to sort some things out. No biggie," he says, grinning.

She presses her hand to her temple, her eyes closing. "How?"

"I … misread the appointment date and time, but it's fine," he says, letting out a forced laugh.

She rubs the heel of her hands into her face, a heavy sigh escaping. "Christ, Roman. So what does that mean? Are you going to have to delay graduation again?"

A heaviness falls on his shoulders, and he bites back the burn in his throat as he sets the sandwich aside, no longer feeling hungry.

"No, Mom. They'll probably put me on a waitlist or something—no big deal," he says, waving his hand.

Wrong. It's a big fucking deal.

And it's as if she can hear his thoughts because she stands up and starts to pace. "It is a big deal, Ro. I need you to be a little more responsible, honey. For Lucy's sake," she says, disappointment coating her words.

"It was a slip-up, Mom. I'll handle it," he says, his voice coming out smaller this time.

They both turn when a knock sounds and the door swings open. A slender brunette in dinosaur scrubs walks through with a clipboard.

His shoulders tense when he realizes who it is. She keeps her head down as she reads over the clipboard.

"Hi, Gwendolyn. Roman."

He clears his throat, wiping imaginary dust from his pants as he stands. "Audrey."

Audrey looks up, gives a small, reserved *(completely fake)* smile before moving over to Lucy to check her vitals. His mom raises her eyebrows towards him.

He watches Audrey's lips turn down as she jots down notes on the chart. "Is something wrong?" he asks.

Her hazel eyes snap to his. "I'll let the doctor speak with you about it."

"Come on, Audrey," he says in a pleading manner, flashing a smile.

She waves a finger at him. "Ah ah, that won't work on me, Roman Hayes." She leans over the cot, tapping Lucy's nose. "Isn't that right, Lucy girl? Daddy's charm doesn't faze me anymore. Especially since he seems to have lost my number."

Roman's face flushes, and he scratches the back of his head, looking at the ground. Audrey straightens, walking away.

"Audrey, wait."

"Dr. Newark will be in soon," she calls without a backward glance.

The door slams shut behind her, rattling the hinges. He feels his mom staring, and he pivots to her.

"Not a word," he says, returning to his seat.

She holds her hands up. "Hey, I didn't say anything, Mr. Smooth Talker."

He groans, pinching the bridge of his nose. "I knew I shouldn't have gone out with her. I knew she'd be weird."

His mom shrugs. "Why didn't you call her? She seems nice. Educated. Pretty."

Roman sighs, shaking his head. "I just … didn't feel anything, and things just got hectic with Lucy, school, work," he says, rubbing the back of his neck.

His mom bristles at the mention of his job, turning away. It's another one of the many things he isn't doing right in her eyes. "I told you to quit that place. What does it have to do with engineering, anyway?"

"Nothing at all," he quips. "But I like it, and I like having a paycheck, and it's what pays for all of this." He gestures to the hospital room. At least, most of it.

She looks him up and down, arms crossed over her chest, before letting out a disapproving sound.

"Yeah, well. The quicker you graduate, the sooner you'll have a degree that will get you a real, secure job for you to take care of your daughter with."

His spine stiffens before he slips his mask back into place, tapping his mom's knee. "Don't worry, Mom, this is my last year."

The door swings open again, and Dr. Newark walks in, setting the clipboard on the edge of Lucy's cot. His dark hair—streaked with gray—has been gelled back, making him appear younger, and black frames perch on his nose.

Roman stands again, placing his hands in his pockets. "Dr. Newark. Tell me something good."

It's only when he steps further into the room that Roman notices the tight, uncomfortable smile resting on his face. Roman's shoulders fall, and the burning sensation in his throat returns. He looks down at his daughter, breathing evenly as she sleeps through the destruction of his world.

Dr. Newark shakes his head. "Roman, relapses happen. One minute, they're responding well to the corticosteroids, and the next, they're not. Right now, she's not. We have to give it time."

Roman grips the edge of the cot, his skin tingling at the cool metal. "How much time? It's been almost a year," he grits out.

Dr. Newark sighs, clasping his hands together.

"This condition that she has, nephrotic syndrome, it's *incredibly* rare. There are not a lot of cases found in the U.S., especially in children this young. We're lucky we caught it when we did. We're already two steps ahead. We knew that over the course of this new medication that there were possibilities for her to relapse, for the symptoms to return."

Roman looks down, feeling his eyes burn. "I just wish there was something I could do."

"You are, son," Dr. Newark says, nodding his head.

Roman wipes his face, feeling his mom wrap an arm around him, but that does little to comfort him. "What, watching her lie in a hospital bed every other week? Yeah, I'm dad of the year."

Dr. Newark chuckles. "Actually, yes."

Roman folds his arms across his chest, giving him a hard stare. Dr. Newark rubs a hand down his stubble, breathing out. He pushes his glasses to the top of his head.

"Most people don't realize how important it is for a child to feel loved. To be in a nurturing environment. Children have endorphins just like adults. Those positive emotions, her happiness, her *laughter*, those things stimulate the release of them. They help reduce her pain. They boost her immune system. They mitigate the trauma of all of this." He draws a circle in the air with his finger. "Don't think that you aren't helping her because you are. There's a lot of power in your presence, Roman."

Roman nods, wiping a hand down his face, some of the tension leaving his body.

Dr. Newark smiles, stepping towards the door. "Good. Chin up. We'll up her dosage on the steroids and see if that helps. I'll have the prescription put in, monitor her overnight, and then she should be good to go tomorrow."

Roman digs in his back pocket as it vibrates. "Sounds good."

VAUGHN

Marcus called out. Can you come in?

Tapping the screen, he moves to grab his bag before turning to his mom, who is engrossed in her sketchbook. "You good here?"

Deep blue eyes flicker to his. "You're leaving?"

"Someone called out," he says, shoving his laptop into the bag.

"Your daughter is *sick*, Roman. Let someone else handle it."

"Wow, I had no idea," he says dryly. "Thought we were in here for shits and giggles."

She purses her lips, resuming her sketch, the soft scratch of the pencil hitting the surface.

He runs a hand over his face, a new pressure building in his chest. "I'm sorry. I hear you, but I need the money. I'm no good just sitting here when I could be getting some extra cash to pay for her visits and medicine."

She waves him off, turning her nose up. "I'll keep you updated."

Shit.

His sigh is rough and slow. "I'm sorry. I promise it won't always be like this." He kisses her cheek lingering to breathe in her citrusy scent. "I love you." He shuffles to Lucy, chuckling as he wipes the drool that has seeped from the corner of her mouth. "I love you, my sweet girl," he whispers against her ear.

As he exits the room, he stumbles into the individual who managed to turn the room into an ice box several minutes ago. He murmurs a brief apology before moving past her.

"God, I'm going to regret this, but why didn't you call me, Roman?" Her voice is sharp.

Fuck him. She wants to do this now.

He pivots on his heel, scratching the nape of his neck. Audrey's arms are locked over her chest, and she rests her foot on the ledge of the cart that holds a monitor and several drawers of medical-grade supplies.

He sighs, dropping his hand. "Look, I meant to call. There's just a lot going on in my life, and I don't want to string you along with anything."

He doesn't need another person to disappoint.

She nods, looking up at him.

"Would it have killed you to say that to me the first night?" she asks, her voice coming out quieter. "I really thought that we hit it off, and then you just ghosted me like I meant nothing." Her eyes flit back to his, a glassy sheen to them.

You piece of shit, Roman.

He steps closer, looking down at her. "I'm sorry, Audrey. I think you're amazing. You're this badass pediatric nurse, and you're great with Lucy, but I'm just figuring stuff out right now."

"I understand," she says, the hum of the equipment and muted footsteps filling the silence between them.

He lets out a soft exhale, patting her on the shoulder. A pathetic attempt to console her from a distance.

"I really am sorry. I'll see you around?" he says, voice edged with finality.

"Sure," she says, her voice distant. "I'll see you."

The lights overhead flicker for a moment, as if the hospital itself is trying to remind him of his place. That people are dying here, people are in pain, and he's standing in a hallway making decisions that feel so insignificant against the backdrop of it all.

CHAPTER 7
I Am My Father's Daughter

Jahlani

Dear Ms. Jahlani Maria Jones,

This notification is to serve as a reminder that your bill of $197.79 is past due. Update your current payment method and pay your remaining balance as soon as possible to remain in good standing. Failure to do so may result in the loss of your ability to acquire future credit and/or loans.

For questions about your account, please reach out to customer service.

Hillman Financial

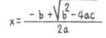

J ahlani's foot taps the dusty blue carpeted surface as she sits in the leather chair of the softly lit hallway of the Graduate Affairs building. She'd left earlier than she needed to, not wanting to deal with her mother's blatant disregard for her. Jahlani takes in the floor-to-ceiling windows as the afternoon light filters in with ease, crafting a checkered pattern against the walls. The campus is airy and large with sprawling bushes, and the chatter of students exploring.

She made the wrong turn twice on the way over, overwhelmed at the size of the campus, and having never been good with directions.

Now, as she sits and waits, the grip she has on her phone tightens with each breath. Her finger hovers over the contact for several ticks before she finally presses the call button. She finds it strange, the amount of unease that is ballooning in her stomach, rippling across her forehead, closing up her throat. It shouldn't be like this. She shouldn't feel like this, because it's only—

"Jahlani."

She releases a shaky breath, the rough polyester of her pants scraping against her sweaty palms as her knee bounces.

"Hey, Dad," she says, her voice sounding small.

Over the years, she's grown strategic in how she speaks with him. She's methodical. She breezes through the first part of her routine, mindful to keep her tone level with just enough interest to appear like she cares. Twenty minutes into him complaining about work, she brings up what warranted the phone call to begin with.

Rolling her shoulders, she clears her throat, a nervous utterance that echoes through the muted building.

"Hey, so I was wondering if you could, you know, maybe start paying back some of that credit card debt you owe me?"

The silence weighs heavily, stretching, expanding—a suffocating pressure—before her voice, thin and reedy, offers a fragile sound.

"You know what?" she says. "It's fine—"

"Sure."

Sure?

"Oh," she says, unsure of what to say next, not anticipating this response. "I really appreciate it," she adds, already hating how formal she sounds.

"How much?" he asks.

Ah, there's the other shoe, she thinks as she scratches her forehead, the smooth skin a familiar comfort.

"Well, uh, it's a lot–"

"Jahlani. Stop mumbling. I can't understand what you're saying," he clips.

A quiet exhale escapes her lips, a subtle release of tension. "It's twenty-five."

"Twenty-five hundred?"

She stifles her scoff, barely able to contain her irritation at his ignorance. The words escape her lips in a hushed tone. "Twenty-five thousand, Dad."

Silence bears down on the other end of the line. "You're kidding."

She sighs, her chest tightening painfully. "Well … you told me to use the credit cards to help me through school and that you would pay me back. And then you didn't, and the interest collected—"

"Right, but common sense would tell you to pay it back a little to avoid that, sweetheart. What happened to your big … fancy statesman job?"

She grits her teeth. "Statistician. I'm a statistician, Dad."

"Okay … well, what happened to that?"

She scratches the back of her head. "It was an internship. I didn't get paid much. It's more for the experience."

"Christ," he says, his voice gravelly. "Jesus, Jahlani."

She mutes the phone, pinching her nose as her eyes start to water. She knows she can just end the conversation here and now. She can placate him with her usual routine. But the notification from her bank flashes in her mind as she unmutes.

"Look, I'm not asking for all the money now, I just need enough to hold me over until the semester ends."

"Jahlani, baby. Hold on. I—" He blows out a breath. She hears shuffling and then a door closes on his end. He whispers now. "Look, I want to give you the money. I do."

"But?"

"Helen's pregnant."

She taps the mute button again, feeling the once-cold leather now warm from her body heat under her fingertips as she grips the armrest. Jahlani forces a smile onto her face, feeling the strain in her cheeks as she unmutes.

"That's great news, Dad." She tries to sound strong, but her voice does this strange warble. She clears her throat, exhaling through her mouth. "Congratulations. I'm happy for you. For you both."

"Yeah," he says, and she can hear the lightness in his voice as he drones on, oblivious to the damage he is doing. "It was totally unexpected. And we just purchased the house a few months ago, and—it's a girl! You'll be a big sister, and—"

And now you'll finally have a family that accepts you.

Jahlani recalls the night that he finally left. At that point, he rarely appeared in her bedroom. The last time he set foot in there was to build her four large white bookcases from IKEA that took up the length of the wall. His frame filling her doorway set alarm bells ringing, and when her eyes drifted to the metallic suitcase and duffel bag by his feet, she knew.

At that moment, she was torn. The angsty, hormonal teenage part of her was flustered.

But the rational, pragmatic, *sensible* part of her knew her parents arguments weren't traditional, and the way her aunts and grandmother would turn their nose up and speak to him whenever they would go over was debilitating, and so instead of throwing herself at him and crying in his arms like she wanted to, she slipped out of her bed, gave him a squeeze around his midsection that she swore wouldn't last more than ten seconds, and resumed her original position, typing away.

Her father's voice carries her back to the present. "And, anyway, Jahlani, you see how this isn't the best time for me financially. But I promise you once the baby is born and Helen's back at work, I'll send over the full amount. Okay, baby?"

No. Not okay.

"Dad—"

"Jahlani, I have to go. It's Helen. We'll talk soon, yeah?"

He ends the call, the dial tone seemingly mocking her as she drops the phone into her lap.

"Jackass," she says under her breath, rubbing her forehead. Tossing it into her bag, she slumps back against the chair.

A door opening at the end of the hallway causes her to stand up. She runs her hands down her shirt, smoothing out her blouse as a woman in heels walks toward her. Her hair is in a neat updo, and her eyes are a crescent blue that are hard to miss. She extends her hand to Jahlani, giving her a polished smile.

"Ms. Jones. I'm Dr. Evangeline Hunt," she says, taking her hand with a firm grip. "It's a pleasure to meet you. Please, follow me."

Jahlani slips her bag onto her shoulder, falling into step with her as they pass several offices and meeting rooms. She takes in the woman's floral scent, confident gait, and tailored pantsuit. When they get to the end of the hallway, they make two rights before finally reaching her office.

Dr. Hunt gestures for her to sit, and Jahlani clears her throat, sinking into the chair across from the desk. Her hands get clammy, the reality of not knowing why she is here to begin with making her stomach twist.

"You have a lovely ... office," Jahlani says, unable to come up with anything of substance. She's never been adept at small talk. She watches as Dr. Hunt moves around the large space with gentle but hurried movements.

"Can I get you something to drink? Tea? Coffee? Water?" Dr. Hunt asks.

Jahlani nods. "Water is fine, thank you."

She shifts in the chair as she watches Dr. Hunt pour them both glasses. She gives her a comforting smile when she presses it into Jahlani's fingertips. She's thankful for something to hold on to as she raises the glass to her mouth with shaky hands.

After sipping, Jahlani sets it onto the tiny coffee table next to her chair. Interlacing her fingers, she waits as Dr. Hunt settles across from her.

"I have to ask: why the transfer? You were close to completing your program in New York, right?"

Jahlani's palms grow clammy as unwanted memories of Micah flood through her mind like a broken dam. It had only been a few weeks, but Jahlani had already compartmentalized everything that had happened to her. What was the point in dwelling over things she couldn't change?

She crosses her legs, giving a tight-lipped smile to Dr. Hunt. She didn't feel like spilling her guts if she didn't need to. She'd give the abbreviated version instead.

Jahlani inhales through her nose, spinning the ring on her finger. "The university dropped the last course I needed to graduate."

Dr. Hunt nods, pressing some keys on her laptop.

Jahlani looks down at the ground as she says the next words, not fully believing them as they fall past her lips. "And I have family here." She shrugs, toying with the gold bracelet around her wrist. "I wanted to come back home," she says with as much enthusiasm as she can muster.

Dr. Hunt seems to buy it as she taps a finger to her lips. She unbuttons her jacket before shrugging it down her shoulders.

"Well, I'm thrilled to have you here. I know the program is in desperate need of more enrollment. Especially a woman of your aptitude," she says, sending a smile her way as she wrangles her hair out of its bun, dark waves trickling over her shoulders. She leans forward on her desk.

"So, Ms. Jones—"

"Please, just Jahlani is fine."

Dr. Hunt's lips turn upward. "Jahlani, I called this meeting because I have a proposition for you. Unfortunately, because you turned in your transfer paperwork so late, there aren't any more internships available that are similar to the work you were doing in New York."

And so it begins.

Really, it shouldn't matter what type of internship it is as long as she gets the credit to graduate. Except for her, it does.

For her, it means she has to work twice as hard now to prove that she's deserving of her job with whatever company she applies to when she graduates.

Because some will look at her gender and think that she isn't the right fit.

And others will look at her Blackness and say that she isn't capable.

And most will look at just those two, and nothing else will matter.

She won't even make it to the interview.

Jahlani nods, exhaling. "I see."

"I hope this doesn't deter you from the program in any way."

Jahlani lets out a mirthless laugh. "Honestly, Dr. Hunt, nothing has been going my way the past few weeks. My focus now is to finish my degree, however possible."

Dr. Hunt claps her hands together. "Good. I'm glad you say that, because I have an alternative for you." She leans forward, pressing her palms against the desk. "Our program allows you to collect your internship hours internally as well. Most students choose not to take that route because they're a shoo-in for a job with the companies that they intern with, which I'm sure you're familiar with, right? It's higher pay, better experience. All of this to say, you can still get your hours and complete your degree, but—"

Jahlani inches forward, her skin itching in anticipation.

"You would be teaching rather than applying it as you would in an external internship, with one of our professors here. You would be a graduate teaching assistant."

Oh.

Jahlani nods as she reaches for her water, finishing the entire glass. The room feels small, as if the walls are closing in on her.

"Oh, okay. Yeah, that sounds …" Jahlani trails off, trying to keep the disdain from her voice. After all, she's not in a position to be picky. Beggars can't be choosers. And right now, she's on her knees.

"That sounds good. Great," she says, giving a forced upturn of her mouth.

Dr. Hunt chews on her lip before she sighs, her shoulders deflating. "Look, I know it's not an ideal situation, but it has its perks. You would receive a biweekly stipend, and your tuition would be paid in full."

At this, the throbbing in her head seems to subside. Her spine straightens as she grips the cool glass between her fingertips. If it were plastic, she's sure she would have crushed it at this point.

"My tuition would be completely covered?"

Dr. Hunt gives a bright smile, showing straight teeth. "Yes, every single credit."

The email about her late loan payment burns a hole in her back pocket. The echo of her dad's refusal to give her what he said he would.

Her eyes move back to Dr. Hunt's.

"I'll do it."

Dr. Hunt smiles before typing something on her computer. "Great. Why don't you head over there now, introduce yourself, see what he needs, and I'll sort out all of the paperwork. You'll be with Professor John Jackson. I'm going to email you and him the details. He's located in the Mathematics Building on the west side of campus."

Jahlani nods, rising from the chair, and turns toward the door.

"Oh, Jahlani," Dr. Hunt calls out before Jahlani rounds the corner. She twists back to see her standing, arms braced on the table. "Thank you for taking on this role. I know it's not what you anticipated, but I appreciate your flexibility and willingness. Don't hesitate to reach out for anything."

Jahlani smiles, unsure of what to say before leaving the room.

She steps into the humid air, adjusting her braids behind her back as she maneuvers through the campus to Professor Jackson's office. Some people lounge around the quad with blankets, chatting with one another. The sun is generous today, offering a soothing warmth. The kind that makes her wish she were capable of taking a break to be able to enjoy it.

Taking a steadying breath, she climbs the concrete stairs into the building. The main entrance is carpeted in gray and offers windows that have a nook for students to sit on and work at. There are two hallways that sit on the sides of the elevator, paving a path to the lecture halls or the offices that house the professors. Jahlani walks to the directory, trailing a finger as she scans for his office.

Adjusting her bag, she turns the corner, making her way to room 205. The cream walls are covered in flyers offering tutoring services, upcoming university events, and programs offering financial assistance. As she gets closer, her stomach starts to tighten. Her mouth runs dry as she comes upon his open door.

From her angle, she can see a tall, dark-skinned man in a simple navy-blue shirt and black slacks. Silver glasses sit perched on his nose that slide down as he cranes his neck, shuffling papers around on his desk. Streaks of gray intertwine with the dark hair of his beard and coils on his head. His expression is stony as he mutters something to himself.

Clearing her throat, she raps on the door twice before stepping inside. He doesn't look up, and she wonders if she knocked hard enough. Flexing her fingers, she clears her throat again before speaking.

"Professor Jackson?" she asks, watching as he continues to move around the desk.

Maybe she's in the wrong room.

But the degrees that sit on his shelf say otherwise. He still doesn't look in her direction, and she feels her skin flush. Licking her lips, she leans her weight on the opposite leg.

"I'm Jahlani Jones. I'll be your graduate teaching assist—"

"No."

Her mouth snaps shut as the timbre of his voice transmits throughout the office. He still isn't looking at her. She blinks three times before finding her voice again.

"I'm sorry. I think there's been a misunderstanding. I'm completing my internship hours with you this semester?" She hates that it sounds like a question.

This time, he does glance her way. Dark, beady eyes drill into hers as they roam over her. The skin on his forehead is creased permanently, and several moles run down the side of his neck. Jahlani sees that his body is lean as he stands to his full height, removing his glasses to rub circles into his eyes. Clearing his throat, he places his glasses back onto his face before crossing his arms over his chest.

"You have the wrong professor. I don't require a GTA."

"Yes, but—"

His gaze slides back down to his desk, and he carries on moving around the room as if she's not there. Jahlani turns, leaving the room, heat creeping up her cheeks. She idles in the hallway, thinking back to her conversation with Dr. Hunt. She chews her bottom lip, thinking about how she needs this internship to complete her program. Without it, she's extending her stay, she's without any kind of income.

She's shit out of luck.

And she can't have that.

Exhaling a sharp, short breath, Jahlani rolls her shoulders before striding back in.

She walks until she's in front of his desk and this time he does stop. He stands tall again, his eyebrows pinching. She starts before he can, raising her chin up.

"I assure you that I've been assigned to you, there should be an email from Dr. Hunt."

At the mention of Dr. Hunt's name, his entire body stiffens. He shifts to his monitor, clicking and typing and reading as Jahlani just stands there. Unease and irritation prick her skin because *of course the professor would give her a hard time.*

Just when she thought things were looking up.

"Take a seat," he says under his breath.

Jahlani's shoulders slump, and she folds her body into one of the chairs opposite his desk. His office looks lived in. Shelves of books tower across both walls, and a brown coat rack stands in the corner where one single corduroy blazer hangs along with a leather messenger bag. She scans the rest of the room, landing on a painting featuring a Black man in a white long-sleeve shirt and dark wash jeans in front of a chalkboard. Four students, painted with elongated limbs and fluid motions, are raising their hands.

She sits up, watching him type on his computer, waiting. His focus never leaves the screen, and when he finds what he's looking for, his gaze flicks to hers and studies her for several seconds before opening his mouth.

"Your academic record is impressive," he says, not sounding impressed at all.

"Thank you?" she replies, but it sounds more like a question, so she clears her throat in an attempt to sound more confident. "Thank you."

He blinks, standing from his chair, and starts pacing back and forth behind the desk.

"In the Monty Hall problem, should you switch doors or keep yours?" He poses the question fast.

But of course, a test. Because her transcript somehow isn't enough.

Jahlani inhales deeply, not wanting to grant him the satisfaction of thinking that her transcripts and her ability don't correlate.

"You always switch. Two-thirds is better than one-third."

He runs a hand over his beard, moving from behind the desk to the other corner of the room.

"Are you more likely to roll one six from six dice, two sixes from twelve dice, or three sixes from eighteen dice?"

Her response is instant. "One six from six dice."

He mutters, and Jahlani takes this as a good sign. He moves swiftly back to his desk before lowering into the chair.

"What is the probability that the sun will rise tomorrow?" he asks, interlocking his fingers together on the table.

"99.99 percent, according to Laplace. Although, you're misapplying the Rule of Succession."

There's a slight twitch of his mouth that Jahlani doesn't miss as she exhales. "Look, Professor Jackson, I—"

"I have over 100 students enrolled this semester. With that being said, I'm not here to babysit you, Ms. Jones. You seem capable, but make no mistake, I will go above Dr. Hunt if I feel that you are unable to keep up. Understood?"

Jahlani swallows. "Yes."

His fingers dance against the mahogany as he looks across at her, his eyebrows less pinched than before. Jahlani's eyes bounce from him to the painting behind him, unsure of how to fill the silence.

"I like your painting," she says in a rush. "Who is it by?"

"Ernie Barnes," he says, his countenance remaining impassive. Jahlani blinks, hoping for him to divulge more, but when the silence expands, she sighs, shouldering her bag because she knows when she's not wanted.

"I'll be sure to email you once everything is solidified with Dr. Hunt."

Before he can say anything, Jahlani walks out, feeling more defeated than ever and wanting nothing more than for the semester to be over.

CHAPTER 8
Highly Inappropriate and Extremely Impolite

Roman

Roman knows it's his own actions that have put him in this predicament. He told himself he was going to do better. For his daughter. For his mom. But as he pushes through the glass doors, leaving his meeting with the advisor, he's starting to believe that being better is out of the question.

You need to be more responsible. Get a high paying job. Think of Lucy.

Moisture falls onto his hand as he stands on the staircase to the Undergraduate Affairs building. Looking up, a nimbus cloud greets him with a dark, vengeful smile. He curses himself for not checking the weather before leaving the house today. It's Florida after all. Did he pack a raincoat for Lucy? Abruptly pulling out his phone, he types a brief message to his sister.

ROMAN
Do you have her raincoat?

DANICA
Yes.

THE PROBABILITY OF US

> **ROMAN**
> Do you have an umbrella?

DANICA
Yes.

> **ROMAN**
> Do you have socks on her feet?

DANICA
Piss off Roman.

He grunts before hitting the call button on her contact. After one ring, her soft breathing greets him.

"I apologize for wanting to guarantee my daughter's safety and well-being amid this category-five hurricane," he says in a dry tone, looking at the sky.

His sister huffs out a laugh. "Okay, A: it's *hardly* raining. B: I'm not an idiot, and, in conclusion, it is *imperative* that you stop being a helicopter parent before I block your number and you never hear from me or your daughter again."

The call ends with a resounding click.

Roman pulls the phone from his ear, jaw slack as he stares at the darkened screen.

As he walks the length of campus to get to his next class, the humidity and rain cause pools of sweat to roll down his arms. The sun glares at him as he picks up his pace through the bustling campus. It seems to scold him for running late. His schedule doesn't leave much time for him to take a piss in a timely manner, apparently. He breezes across the quad and cuts through Freshman Orientation, letting out a breathless apology when he bumps into a young woman wearing a green sweater.

He does a double-take and his mind floats to the woman from a few weeks ago. Truly, he thinks it's for the best she said no. He doesn't have anything to offer. He's too busy trying to keep his life together.

What would have happened, really?

Maybe they would have hit it off. He'd let her steer the conversation, though, because he was fascinated with her. Her quick retorts and sharp mind. He had several questions that he needed answered and she'd maybe, hopefully, after a few minutes, be willing to answer them, but then she'd ask about his life, his story. And he'd be reminded by the fact that he's not someone who can go on dates with just anyone. He can't just bring strangers into his house, into his home. Because they'd get there, stumble through the door, and maybe even trip into a baby walker. He can't exhaust his energy on someone else when there's someone far more important that's needing his attention.

He can't have both.

Right?

So, even as he pushes through the double doors to the auditorium, he wills himself to think that everything happens for a reason. Despite being an engineering major, he believes in things like fate and destiny.

Starry-eyed. Quixotic. Impractical is what he is.

The lecture hall is spacious, dimly lit, and has the worst ventilation system in the university. Rows of worn-down oak desks line the auditorium, and two blackboards take up most of the front wall.

Hushed murmurs fill the space as Roman slips inside. He braces his hand on the creaking door so as not to draw attention to himself. Gliding up the carpeted stairs, he sinks into the first open seat he notices. Adjusting his bag on the side, he takes out his laptop.

He taps hastily, trying to pull up a blank document for note-taking. The room falls to whispers and murmurs before a different timbre greets his ears. It's a juxtaposition to the gritty tone that was echoing throughout the space only moments ago. This one is *gentle*. Soft. Confident, but not supercilious.

"My name is Jahlani Jones, and I will be the graduate teaching assistant this semester. I am looking forward to working with you all. I'm currently in the final semester of the master's program for Data Science and Statistics. I recently moved from New York City so I'm really, *really* struggling to adjust to the humidity here."

This earns a few chuckles throughout the room and causes Roman's gaze to drift upwards, his body humming in recognition because it's *his Jahlani.*

She stands in the middle of the room with the small mic curled tightly between her fingers. She walks across the space as she speaks, gesticulating with her hands. Her dark eyes rove about the room, and her initial nerves seem to ease as she continues. Sitting upright, he almost knocks the laptop off the desk.

His eyes follow her, soaking her in. Watching, lingering on areas that most would consider *highly* inappropriate and *extremely* impolite, but he just can't help it. He watches her from his corner of the room. Watching the way her angular flats turn outward when she steps, to the way her lips curve when she answers questions about her experience working with her internship company.

As he does his hardest to listen above the rattling, pulsing, thumping *thing* in his chest, he can't help but think she looks the same: unbearably beautiful and impossible to forget. Memories of *"What if I'm the problem?"* and *"I'm finishing up my master's program around here"* dredge up as he studies her. He sinks lower into the seat, wiping his hand down his mouth, trying to even out his breathing.

Her braids gather into a mass of curls that cascade dutifully down her shoulders, accentuating her high cheekbones and rounded ears.

The green cardigan drapes over her frame and he wonders how she isn't dead yet from overheating. Leaning forward with his elbows on his knees, he listens intently as she reviews her role and course materials. He seems to forget that it was less than an hour ago he was determined to remove the foot that Jackson had on his neck. And now?

Now, he's never been more thankful to a professor for failing him.

"Are there any other questions for me?" She asks warmly, innocently. Her eyes skate across the room, first to the leftmost side, then down the middle, where a hand has shot up.

"I'm sorry, but like what do you know about statistics?" The voice is nasally. Condescending.

Jahlani's smile falters, and her initial weariness seems to slip back onto her like a second skin.

"I can assure you that Ms. Jones is more than qualified," Professor Jackson says. "Besides, she isn't here for an interview, Mr. Torres, especially one conducted by someone who failed this class. Twice."

Jackson's voice is loud and razor-sharp as he stares at the boy sliding further into his seat.

Jahlani blows out a breath, answering a few more questions before finally reaching Roman's section. He inhales sharply, clutching the armrest, blood pulsing, mouth drying as her eyes catch his briefly and—

She continues her exploration without a second glance. He licks his lips and wills his heart to *stop thrashing so fucking loudly.*

She doesn't remember.

She doesn't remember him.

A flurry of emotion swarms his head. Disappointment, desperation, agony, wonder, and relief. Roman thinks it's for the best as he leans all the way back, combing his fingers through his hair.

But still. A small part of him wishes she had. *And then what?* They'd catch up? Go for drinks? He'd attempt to cook her something *outlandish* and end up burning it from nerves. She'd applaud his efforts with a gentle touch to his wrist. They'd order pizza instead. He'd figure out what her favorite toppings are—she seemed like an unconventional kind of person, and he was *completely* okay with that. He'd finally touch her. Kiss her. Maybe, quite possibly, have sex with her. Make up for lost time and missed opportunities. Quench this curiosity that had been brewing inside him for the past few weeks.

His body reacts before his mind does, and his fingers are in the air. Her eyes sweep over to him, trailing over his face, and—

There. That's what he wanted.

For her lips to part slightly and her eyes to widen momentarily before she remembers to school her features. For space and time to stand still as they converse with their eyes. For everything to fade into white noise as they try to make sense of this moment. Of each other.

For it to just be the two of them.

Roman lowers his hand, clearing his throat. "So, you'll be here the whole semester then?"

She nods, unblinking. "That's ... yes. The whole semester," she says through a stutter.

"And what about after?" He asks, his knee bouncing.

Her eyebrows gather as she clasps her hands together. "After?"

He nods, rubbing his fingers across his lips. "When it's over? What then?"

She takes a shaky breath. "Hopefully I'm a wildly famous statistician." She says it jokingly, a slight twitch in her lips, but her look says something else entirely.

He nods, sinking back into his seat, not completely satisfied with her answer, still watching when she breaks eye contact, still lingering when Jackson starts the lecture, still wondering how this could have happened.

It's not until the girl next to him starts shoving her notebook and pens away that he realizes the lecture has ended. He looks down at his laptop, and a blank document blinks back. He's left with a single thought as he watches Jahlani gesture toward something while she converses with Professor Jackson.

Fuck.

CHAPTER 9
You, Again

Jahlani

DISCUSSION BOARD POST INTRODUCTION MODULE

Directions: Please reply to this discussion board and one other peer by the end of the first week. Introduce yourself. This assignment will verify your status as a student for financial aid. Delay of disbursement may happen if you fail to complete this assignment by the end of the add/drop week.

STUDENT: ANTHONY L.

Hi, I'm Anthony. I'm taking this class again because I failed last semester. Is anyone able to tutor me?

STUDENT: ROMAN H.

Roman here. I'm looking forward to passing this semester with the help of Professor Jackson and Jahlani.

STUDENT: MALI T.

Hello everyone! I am Mali Thomas. I am a double major in political science and statistics. Don't ask me why I picked those two. Trust me, I have questioned my decision every day. May the odds be ever in your favor. XO

VIEW 134 OTHER REPLIES

$$x = \frac{-b + \sqrt{b^2 - 4ac}}{2a}$$

The lamp on his desk glows as Jahlani and Professor Jackson sit in silence, working to finish grading students' discussion board posts. He checks his watch before standing from his seat.

"I'm leaving," he says, moving to shrug his plaid blazer on. "Make sure those grades are in and that the door is locked before you leave."

"I'll take care of it—" she starts, but he's already gone before she can finish her sentence. "Have a good night, Jahlani. Oh, thanks. You too, Professor Jackson," she mutters bitterly.

Douchebag.

She yawns, her body screaming for a warm bath and pillow as she combs through the posts. Her finger hovers when she sees his name.

So, you'll be here the whole semester then?

"Roman Hayes," she says, reading his response, and can't help but think that *it suits him*. Her skin flushes when she reads her name on the screen, and she shakes her head. *You're his TA now. Nothing can happen,* she thinks as she stands and she can't help the sting in her chest. Her phone rings, Imani's name flashing across the screen, but she declines the call.

JAHLANI

> About to head home. I'll call you when I get in.

A wave of dizziness reaches her, and she catches herself on the edge of the desk. Blinking slowly, she clutches her head as it throbs. Reaching into her bag, she fishes for her bottle of ibuprofen, only to get pricked by a loose pushpin and come up short.

"Shit," she says, drawing her finger to her mouth.

Glancing at the clock, she tells herself she'll eat when she gets to the house. Her mom is guaranteed to have some kind of homemade dish in the fridge. Brown stew chicken, maybe some oxtail. Jahlani skirts around her mother as much as possible, unpacking, decluttering, and always waiting for the click of the front door before she leaves.

If she didn't know any better, she'd think she was living alone. It wasn't always like this with her mom. There was a time when they were together. Normal.

But the older Jahlani gets, the more out of reach it seems.

With the door locked, her steps falter as she makes her way through the desolate hallway, her head heavy and her body trembling. The day had been a whirlwind of lectures, assignments, and a string of impromptu group meetings. She hadn't had a moment to herself, let alone time to eat or drink. Her stomach twists in protest, but she forces herself to keep walking.

The sun has long since set, but the campus is still alive with movement, and the faint hum of fluorescent lights accompanies her footsteps. She reaches the exit, her hand grazing the handle, but as she takes a step forward, the room tilts. The world spins around her, dizzying her further. She manages to push the door open but barely has time to brace herself as her body sways dangerously, and her shoulder collides with the wall.

No, that's not right.

It isn't as solid as it should be. It's smoother. Warm. A deep, powdery scent lingers.

Jahlani blinks, trying to clear the fog in her brain. The wall shifts again, and she teeters, her knees unsteady beneath her. With great effort, she lifts her head, her heart pounding in confusion. A sturdy frame stands directly in front of her, a pair of robust arms outstretched, holding her upright.

Her gaze travels up, and her breath hitches in her throat.

Olive-hued eyes. Crimson cheeks. Fair skin.

Roman.

His features are so vivid, so striking against the shadowed light of the exit. His face angles slightly, brows furrowed, lips parted as if debating whether to speak. A few sable curls frame his forehead, and her hand, still resting against his chest, recoils as she untangles herself from him.

"Are you okay?" His voice is low, warm, and edged with a concern that makes her feel a strange mixture of deliriousness, comfort, embarrassment, and something else.

"I—yeah. I'm fine," Jahlani mutters, though her body still sways and her thoughts are hazy.

"Here," he says, stepping closer, one hand gently pressing to her back to steady her. "Let me help."

"I said I'm fine," she clips, trying to create space. But her voice sounds far away, and there's a low buzz in her ears. She stumbles again, and this time he keeps his hands firm on her arms as he guides her to a bench.

"Jahlani, you practically fell into my arms."

She tries to protest, but the words are caught in her throat, and she ends up leaning more heavily into him.

"Here," he says, his voice a steady anchor in her foggy mind as he pulls out a bottle. "Drink this."

She looks up at him, which is a *bad idea* because her head is clearing, and *God, he's unreasonably attractive,* she thinks. The movement makes her stomach clench again, and she feels the faintest tremor of nausea bubbling to the surface.

As she takes in the crease on his forehead, she folds her hands under her thighs. Her pulse is like a drum in her ears. She looks down at the drink in his hand, then back at him and she's suddenly hyperaware of how dry her mouth is. She squints harder, soaking him in. His torso seems longer than she recalls, his muscles more toned. And his scent.

She didn't remember him being so …

Overwhelmingly attractive.

Her lips thin at her train of thought. She shouldn't be thinking anything about him.

"You again," she murmurs, unblinking.

He sucks in a breath, sudden laughter escaping his lips. "Me, again."

CHAPTER 10
How to Start a Love Story

Roman

This woman is stubborn, Roman thinks to himself as he watches her look at the drink with cautious eyes. *It's charming. I'm charmed.*

"It's unopened," he says, waving the bottle of water in her face.

She continues to stare at it, like he just offered to spit in her mouth or something.

He sighs, rubbing his chin. "Look, I don't feel comfortable leaving until I know you're okay. So, the faster you drink, the quicker I'm gone."

Her eyes turn to slits. "I said I'm fine."

"Jahlani. You fell like a damsel in distress. Those are sure signs of someone who is *not* fine."

Pursing her lips, she reaches for it. Her fingertips brush his, and he prays she doesn't notice how sharply he inhales as he watches her drink the entire bottle.

"Happy?" she says, wiping the back of her hand against her mouth.

He offers a closed-lipped smile. "Very." He takes the empty bottle from her, throwing it in a nearby recycle bin. "How do you feel now?"

"Better," she mutters, staring down at her sneakers. Looking up through dark lashes, she gives a low "thank you." Roman folds his hands into his pockets, rocking on his heels as silence settles between them.

"What are—" he says just as she says, "Are you—"
Their eyes hold onto each other, and her lips part. He gestures for her to speak, a wide grin stretching over his mouth.

"Are you stalking me? Plotting your revenge murder because I didn't want to go out with you?"

He nods. "That's exactly what I'm doing. *'Florida Man Stalks and Kills Woman, Feeds Her to Undergraduate Students.'* It sounds pretty catchy, no?"

She locks her gaze onto his face. "I bet you think you're so funny."

"Hilarious, actually," he says, rubbing his jaw. "I'm surprised you didn't see the flyers around campus. My comedy show is this Friday. Be sure to check it out."

He bites back a laugh as she rolls her eyes, locking her arms across her chest.

He turns away, suppressing the urge to ask for her number. Again. He runs a hand through his hair before clearing his throat.

"Are you sure you're okay to walk?" He trails off, gesturing toward campus. "The clinic is right there. I can go get someone."

"No!" she blurts out, her voice sharp against the thinning campus. "I said I'm fine." Her gaze flickers down to her watch, the harsh glow of its face cutting through the deepening twilight.

"Look, thanks again for this," she says, standing up and shifting her weight to grip her bag. "I need to catch the bus."

She takes a step, her shoes tapping lightly on the pavement, already too eager to leave. To leave *him*.

And that spurs him into action.

He falls into step beside her, the sound of his stride almost too loud in the quiet of the evening.

Because he's eager too, apparently. Embarrassingly so.

"Let me give you a ride," he says, his tone insistent.

You're pushing it.

She must feel it too because she stops abruptly, the echo of her shoes fading into the night. He halts beside her, his gaze focused on her. Under the glow, he observes a slight flush to her cheeks, a lack of energy in her face. He pictures Lucy and, almost instinctively, the back of his palm presses to Jahlani's forehead. She's warm.

Stepping forward, he grabs her elbow to hold her steady.

"Are you sure you're okay? You don't look so good." He says, applying more pressure to her skin, before moving to her neck. His fingers raise as she swallows before she pushes his hand away.

"I'm fine," she rasps, touching her own skin. "I just need to get home and sleep."

He places them in his pockets as a precaution this time. He wonders how they must look to people passing by. Does he look as desperate as he feels?

"So, how about that ride?" He asks, his eyebrows raised.

Her pupils travel the length of the sharp scar across his forehead that Danica gave him, down the edge of his nose, to his throat, before going back up. He rubs his palms against his jeans.

"No." Her response is curt, the word almost swallowed by the hum of the campus.

"Why?" he says, stepping forward, voice low. "Are you afraid?"

"Afraid?"

He shrugs, dragging in an exaggerated breath. "That you'll fall for me."

And maybe he expects an eye roll. A middle finger, perhaps. Even for her to walk off. Instead, she lets out a weak puff of air, shaking her head toward the ground. "You have the wrong woman."

She resumes walking, her pace not as fast now. *Deliberately slower*, he thinks—he hopes—as he falls into step beside her. The lamposts overhead, casting brief shadows that stretch on the pavement.

"According to my ex, I'm not capable," she says in a low voice.

His smile drops, and his brows draw in. "What?"

She exhales deeply. "Apparently, I don't know how to relax. I'm incredibly uptight. Let's see, what else? I don't know how to have fun. I make everyone around me feel like shit because I like to work. Oh, I whine too much about being a Black woman in a male-dominated field, and if I ever do make it, it won't be because I'm not competent or actually good at what I do. It'll be because I'm a diversity hire." She lets out a weak chuckle. "So, I can assure you, wrong woman."

He stops walking, the crunch of rocks ceasing beneath his shoes, and to his surprise, she does too. He scratches his forehead, his mouth downturned.

"You don't actually believe any of that, right?"

She glances toward him before looking back down.

Shit.

"Jahlani," he says, his tone full of skepticism. "You can't—"

"Yeah, no," she says, touching the chain of her necklace. "I mean, maybe? I don't know. I shouldn't have said all that. I don't need a ride, okay?"

She turns back along the path, flanked by empty, looming buildings that feel as if they're watching. He quickens his step to match hers, closer than before because their shoulders brush. She cuts him a sidelong glance, her eyes sharp in the dim light.

He shrugs. " I can at least walk with you to the bus stop. It's dark out here."

She sighs, spinning to face him with a furrowed brow. "What?

No. I'm *fine*. The parking garage is in the opposite direction, and I don't need a bodyguard. A white knight. Whatever it is that you're trying to be here. I'm fi—"

"Fine, yes, I know," he says, interrupting while adjusting the velcro of his bag in a quiet, defeated gesture. The breeze rustles the trees, the sound too soft to mask the tension in the air. "Look, I have a young da—" He pauses. "Danica. My sister's name is Danica," he corrects himself, gripping the strap tighter. "And I would hate for someone to leave her alone at night on campus. I'm not trying to *be* anything."

"Okay, okay," she says, raising her hand. "Save your spiel for the debate team." Her words linger in the evening air, hanging like smoke between them, before she quickens her pace once more, her silhouette shrinking into the darkness ahead.

He shakes his head, smiling before doubling his strides to catch up with her.

"I'm sorry," he says after several beats of silence. When she doesn't say anything, he clears his throat, continuing, "About your ex. Those are some really … *shitty* things he said." His lip curls, thinking that if he were to ever cross paths with him, he wouldn't think twice about hurting him in the worst kind of way.

"Not your fault," she says, keeping her gaze ahead.

"And for that guy in class the first day," he says, rubbing his arm.

Her shoulders drop through a sigh. "Yeah, that's pretty normal."

"It's pretty fucked. I can't imagine what that's like."

At this, she does meet his eyes. "No. You can't."

He wets his lips, sending a small, hopefully sympathetic smile her way and her gaze falls to his mouth before she blinks, turning away.

"So, how was your Fourth of July?" he says, trying to defuse the tension.

"Fine."

"Just *fine*?"

"Yup."

"You're not going to ask about mine?"

"Nope."

"Ouch."

They round the corner where only one bus remains, but he knows they're too far to catch it. She must too because she slows her pace until she stops altogether.

"Was that your bus?" he asks.

She pivots to him, pointing an accusing finger. "This is your fault."

His eyebrow arches. "Mine?"

"Yes," she hisses. "If you hadn't—"

He takes a step closer. "Hadn't what? Caught you before you ate dirt and forced you to hydrate yourself?"

"I—" She blows out a breath, starting to walk down the row of benches. "What, no snippy comeback?" he asks, his laughter loud.

"Whatever," she calls over her shoulder. "Go write about it in your diary."

"Oh, I will," he says, and feigns writing into a notebook. "Dear Diary … today was a great day. I, the charming, sweet …" his eyes flit to hers and watch as she rolls her own, "devilishly handsome, Roman Hayes rendered the indomitable Jahlani Jones speechless."

Jahlani sighs, falling onto the rusted bench. "You forgot to add egotistical and arrogant to your description."

He laughs, folding his arms over his chest as he sinks down next to her. "True, but you didn't oppose the others, so that's a win in my book."

"What are you doing?" she asks through wide eyes.

He blinks. "Making sure you get on safely?"

He should leave. She clearly didn't want him around, but for some reason, he settles his bag in between his legs, patting his knees.

A breathless laugh escapes her. "Why?" she asks.

He turns to face her, the warmth of her knee brushing his, the cool wind whipping his hair. "Because it's dark out here and I'd hate to see your name on Channel Six News tomorrow morning."

She hums, turning away from him. "That's dramatic."

"It happens more often than you'd think," he says, his tone flat. "Trust me."

She crosses her legs together, removing her warmth, leaning forward. "Look, Roman. I'm fine. We've arrived safely. You've met your personal weekly quota for helping people in distress. Congratulations, you'll be able to sleep better at night knowing you're a good person—why are you looking at me like that?"

"You don't like getting help from people, do you?"

She shrugs. "I don't like burdening people with problems that I'm more than capable of handling myself."

Now it's his turn to scoff. "You're not burdening me. Now who's being dramatic?" He turns to lean against the overhang beam. "Besides, I need you."

"What?" She looks at him from the corner of her eye. Her shoulders are rigid, arms crossed in defiance, eyebrows drawn together.

"To pass Jackson's class this semester. I can't afford to fail again. Literally and figuratively. I have a lot of people counting on me."

His chest thrums thinking about when he received the initial email about his academic probation. He envisions the look on his mom's face if she'd found out.

She sighs, staring at him for several beats before turning away. "If you were struggling so much, why take him again? Why not get a tutor?"

He braces his arms on his knees, his muscles suddenly aching. *Asking the hard questions.*

"It's complicated. Circumstances prevented me from doing so at the time. It doesn't matter. I'm here now, and I'm serious about graduating."

She breathes for several moments, not saying anything, looking down at the ground. He uses the opportunity to take her in. Her hair is loose by her elbows, pushed behind an ear that has four studs. Another sweater, a different shade of green, shrouds her arms. Around the column of her neck rests the same amber necklace that she brushes subconsciously. He has questions, but he's been caught.

"You're staring."

"I am."

"It's creepy."

"You're nice to look at."

Roman knows he shouldn't have said it, but it's worth the reaction. Her eyes widen and her lips part before shutting. The wind picks up, forcing her fragrance to float between them. The tiniest hint of a smile appears on her face before it dissolves, and her scowl is back. She stands up, muttering while pacing. He exhales, leaning into the structure of the bus stop as he rubs his hand against his mouth.

"No," she says, moving back and forth, like a caged bird. "No."

He raises an eyebrow, unable to stop the smirk from building. "No?"

"No," she says, stopping in front of him. "It won't work, and it's not going to happen. If you want my help, *this* stops. I take my work very seriously. I have a lot at stake here too. So, forget that you ever asked for my number, because it's never going to happen, and stop doing all of this," she says as she waves a hand over his face and body, before sitting back down, leaving a noticeable amount of space between them.

He clears his throat, his lips curving. "All of this?" he asks, his tone playful.

She huffs, looking at him from the side. A few students walk past, speaking in hushed murmurs. Jahlani turns, lowering her voice to a whisper.

"Yes. All the flirty comments. And the looks. They stop now. I don't need anyone thinking that anything is going on between us, *especially* because it's against university policy," she says, her voice firm, as she looks toward the students.

He leans forward, resting his elbows on his thighs. "It sounds like you've given this a lot of thought, Jahlani."

"Roman," she says, her tone serious, causing the hairs on his arms to stand up because *fuck, his name sounds good on her lips.*

He snorts, leaning back. "Of course you're a rule follower. Were you in student government too? Hall monitor?"

She turns to him. "Roman. I have too much going on in my life right now. It sounds like you do too. I'm not about to have you jeopardize everything that I'm working toward. Put it to rest. It's not worth it."

He stares, not saying anything, breathing hard.

Shit. She's right.

There's too much at stake. Her eyes are wide and fragile, and he notices something else that he didn't anticipate—fear. It's subtle, layered in between her determination to get her point across, but it's enough to subdue him. His smile dissipates, like wax dripping from a candle.

"Okay," he says, his voice cracking. "I'll stop."

Her shoulders sag, and it shouldn't bother him so much, but it does.

"Thank you," she says quietly. "And for added measure, rules would be nice."

His lips twitch, and he sighs heavily. "Sure, Jahlani. Anything you want."

Anything at all.

"Rule number one: no staring in class," she says, glancing up as another bus starts to pull into the loop. Roman sits up, his mouth opening and closing.

"No *staring*?" he says, chuckling. "I have to look at you. Come on, that's unreasonable."

She looks to the ground. "Looking is fine, but you stare, Roman. A lot. You … linger. You … watch me. You look at me like you want something from me," she says, gently meeting his eyes. "Something that I can't give you."

Can't or won't?

Roman licks his lips, his cheeks flushing because *she noticed?* He leans forward, scratching the back of his neck. "You know, the fact that you saw that leads me to believe that you were staring too. You also lingered and watched," he whispers. "You want something from me, and the difference between the two of us is that I'm willing to give it. To give in."

They hold eye contact, and he leans forward, placing his hand on the bench next to hers, running his index finger along the plane of her wrist, the arch of her knuckles, and he revels in the sight of her shivers.

"You're already breaking the rules," she says, her voice cracking as she pulls away.

"You didn't say anything about touching," he murmurs. "But I'm going to take a wild guess and say that's out of the question too."

"That's my second rule."

The soft hum of the bus grows closer, a gentle rumble that pulls her from him. As it eases to a stop, there's a quiet hiss of air as the brakes engage, and the door slides open with a smooth, almost inaudible swoosh. She stands, but he grips her elbow, rendering her still.

"Would you have said yes?" His voice is low in the night air. "If we met again—if you weren't my GTA—would you have said yes, Jahlani? Did I ever have a chance?"

He isn't sure why he asks. Why he's so desperate to know because she's made it abundantly clear that nothing will happen.

But still.

He can't help but wonder if their timing had been better, their circumstances different.

Does she feel this too, or is it all in his head?

She turns to face him, and rich brown eyes bore into his. They flicker to his mouth, linger for a few seconds, drift over his countenance, deliberating. His pulse runs from him as she steps away.

"I already told you. I'm not the person you're looking for."

CHAPTER 11
Bayes' Theorem

Jahlani

"Alright, so today we're going to talk about conditional probability and Bayes' Theorem."

Jahlani pushes her braids behind her ears, walking around the room. "Everything was put online. You had a whole weekend to look over it and ask questions."

"Professor Jackson didn't upload anything," someone calls from the back.

Jahlani scratches her nose, moving to her laptop. "You sure?"

"There was nothing, Ms. Jones."

She rolls her eyes. "It's Jahlani. Just Jahlani," she repeats under her breath as she clicks through the course landing page.

After the first few days, Jackson saw an influx of students. He came up with the idea for them to split the class in half. Every week, a set portion would move to a different room with her while the others would stay back with him. She didn't expect to be teaching, *teaching*, but he has the type of authority that you don't question, and she likes the challenge. Some deep, dark part of her wants to prove herself to him.

"It's fine," she announces, facing them. "We'll just have to do double the work today."

Moving to the whiteboard, she writes the equation.

"Okay, let's look at the formula first. This is called posterior probability. All it means is this—" She continues speaking as she writes. "The probability of A happening given that B has already occurred. It's an equation allowing one to find the probability of a cause given its effect. Are you with me so far?"

She turns toward the students, seeing a scattered wave of nods.

"Amazing. Let's break this down further."

Moving to the opposite side of the board, she sketches a box with arrows.

"These arrows"—she points to them—"represent conditional relationships." She snaps the cover on the marker. "Okay, someone give me a pizza topping they hate."

"Pineapple!"

"Okay, whoever said that, you're not passing this semester."

A few chuckles wave throughout the room and she feels warm at the reaction. "So, here's an example of how this theorem works at the surface level. Let's say you're at a party. At this hypothetical party, you know that people who like pineapple on pizza are more likely to be from Florida—remember this is *hypothetical*," she adds when a series of gasps and gagging sounds are heard across the room. She waits for everyone to settle.

"Okay, let's change the example since we hate the pineapple one so much," she says, as scattered applause starts.

"Let's stick with pizza, but now it's a deep dish. At this party, we know that people who like it are more likely to be from Chicago. So, the fact that someone is from Chicago makes it more likely they'll like deep-dish style pizza."

She pauses, waiting for questions. When none come, she presses on. "Now, if we know that an individual likes deep dish, we have to ask ourselves, how does that change our belief that they're from Chicago? That is something that Bayes' Theorem will help us calculate."

Turning back to the board, Jahlani draws an arrow between the two factors, labeling them.

"So, P(A|B) is the probability that they are *from* Chicago, given that they like deep dish. And P(B|A) is the probability that someone from Chicago *likes* deep dish.

"So, maybe you start with some prior belief about deep dish preferences—say, sixty percent of people like it. But then, you learn someone's from Chicago. Bayes' Theorem lets you *update* your belief about whether they like deep dish."

She turns back and waits for students to write and type the information down. The door swings open, and she does a double-take. Her thoughts stutter for a moment because he's here in another long-sleeve that is doing a lot for his biceps, and doing everything for her body. She lingers as she watches him move up the stairs swiftly, settling into the third row, second seat in. The same every time.

She's suddenly irritated that she's memorized where he sits. *What a useless piece of information*, she thinks, and turns away from his frame, shaking the very detailed images of what she thinks his arms look like underneath from her mind.

She clears her throat. "Sorry, what was I saying?"
Looking back at the board, she drops the marker, wiping clammy hands on her sides.

"You were telling us the purpose of Bayes' Theorem," a voice rings out near the front.

Right. Bayes' Theorem.
She nods, picking up her water bottle and taking multiple sips. Setting it down, she moves back to the center, trying, and failing, not

to look his way every three seconds.

The rules. Stick to the rules.

"Okay," she says, stepping back. "Let's work through an example together. I want everyone to pair up. I'll give you a scenario, and we'll apply Bayes' Theorem to figure out how likely someone is to have a certain trait, based on new evidence."

She hands out printed scenarios, and student murmurs fill the air. Jahlani weaves around the room, helping here and there, but mostly letting the students work through the math themselves. From the corner of her eye, she watches Roman drum his fingers on his laptop. She hesitates before moving toward him.

Forest green eyes meet hers, and she tries to keep her face as neutral as possible.

"Hi," he says, sitting upright in his seat, flooding her with a slow smile.

She moves her braids back over her shoulders, and he tracks the movement, his nostrils flaring.

"Nice of you to show up," she says, trying to rein back her sharp tone.

He runs his pen across his lips, and she clears her throat, looking around the room as her body flushes.

"I know, I know," he says, shifting in his seat. "Catch me up?"

She scoffs, facing him. "Hate to break it to you, Roman, but that's not how this works. I have other students to help. Don't be lazy. Get here on time."

He runs a hand through his hair, rubbing the back of his neck.

"I had a situation," he says, his voice lower this time, eyes dimmer. "And, I thought you said you would help."

She crosses her arms over her chest. Leaning forward, she speaks in a low voice.

"I agreed to help someone who actually wants help, not someone who picks when to show up and half-asses things. If you want to pass this class and graduate, take it seriously."

His head rears back. "I am."

She straightens up, wrapping her braids into a high ponytail.

"No, you're not," she says, shaking her head and pursing her lips. "This is week two, and you've been late to almost every lecture. You completely bombed the last quiz. I can't help someone who doesn't want to be helped. That isn't putting in any effort."

He frowns, and she wonders if she came off too harsh. "Jahlani, I had a family situation."

She freezes, then lowers her gaze to the ground.

Always quick to assume the worst about people now.

"Shit," she breathes, shaking her head. "I'm sorry. Is everything alright? Did someone …" She trails off, not wanting to finish that thought, not wanting to be insensitive. Or at least even more so than she already has been.

His lips turn upward as he looks at her, and her pulse races. "Nobody died, if that's what you're thinking, and it's okay. It happens to the best of us. First impressions matter, and I haven't made the best one on you, I guess."

Her eyes soften as she chews her lip. He's so *pleasant*.

It pisses her off.

"Look," she says, releasing a slow exhale. "If you want help, office hours are every Tuesday and Thursday. I'm pretty much there the whole day. I also … linger around after class for a few hours, but don't broadcast that to anyone."

Jahlani walks away before he can say anything. Returning to the front, she turns her mic on again.

"Alright, let's go over the answers together."

For the next half hour, she works writing the different solutions onto the board, addressing misconceptions, keeping her tone airy and relaxed, encouraging students to share and discuss. The whole time, the nape of her neck prickles as he watches her. Only her. Every now and then, he checks his phone, smiles at something that makes her curious, writes things down in his notebook, but his gaze never leaves her form. *It's good*, she thinks. It means he's paying attention. That's all.

"Remember, Bayes' Theorem isn't just for parties and pizza; it's used in everything from artificial intelligence to risk management. Keep practicing, and you'll start to see it everywhere."

He watches for an unnerving amount of time as students begin to gather their belongings, and she knows she was too harsh on him earlier.

She just doesn't know *why*.

A tiny part of her thinks that he genuinely wants the help, and that other part of her, the part that's been burned too many times, thinks that he didn't mean what he said that day and he's just playing her like a fool.

"Before you leave for the day, a reminder about the Graduate Affairs Event for Data Science and Statistics next Friday. Jackson has promised extra credit for students who attend and stay for at least thirty minutes. We will be there the whole time to verify attendance." She meets viridescent eyes from across the room as she speaks the next few words. "I encourage you all to come out. Especially those of you who didn't do so well on our first quiz. It won't save your grades, but it will definitely help in the long run."

She checks the time on her watch.

"That's all I have for today. I'll be around for a few minutes for any lingering, life-altering questions that need to be answered. Otherwise,

I'll see you all again on Friday."

Jahlani waves goodbye to students while she collects her things. As the auditorium empties, she places her laptop, along with her charger, into her bag.

A familiar lavender scent hits her, and her hands start to tremble—her body reacting to his presence before her mind can gather coherent, safe thoughts.

"Was that jab meant for me?" His deep voice causes her hair to stand on end, and she refuses to look up as she continues to pack her notebooks next.

Grabbing a stack of papers, she lines them up, avoiding eye contact. "No idea what you're talking about. That was clearly an announcement for the entire room. You know, because the world doesn't revolve around you."

He scoffs. "You're mean today."

This time she does look up and—

He's closer than she realized, because she can see that he has a tiny mole under his eyebrow.

She stalls, trying to formulate a response that isn't purely driven by her overwhelming need to push him away, because he's not wrong.

She breathes out shakily. "I am."

His head rears back, and he smiles. "What?"

"I am really fucking mean to you today. I'm sorry. I just—"

"Don't like it when I'm late, half-ass things, and bomb quizzes after I've asked for your help?" he says, smiling wider, like this is a *good thing*.

She licks her lips, shaking her head. "Exactly. I don't like my time being wasted."

He holds up his hands. "I understand. I'm sorry, I'll try to do better."

"*Try?*" she says, a scoff slipping out. "You're unbelievable."

"Will. I *will* be better," he says, correcting himself.

She lets out a soft laugh, rubbing her fingers to her temple. "Yeah, I'll believe it when I see it, Hayes."

Shouldering her bag, she steps from behind the podium and moves toward the double doors. Roman is already in front of her, holding one side open.

"Thanks," she says under her breath, stepping into the university quad. A grassy lawn sits in the middle, flanked by two long paths that stretch to the main area of campus. The smell of the damp grass tangles with the aroma of roasted coffee beans emanating from the student café next to them. Students are spread out, swinging from hammocks, chasing dogs, noses buried in a textbook. She shields her face as the sun glares down on her, fishing her headphones from her bag. A sudden shadow blocks the light and she looks up.

"Can I help you?" she asks, not meaning it at all.

Go away, and take your stupid, laboratory-grown green eyes with you.

He slides both hands into his pockets as he looks down at her, smiling like he knows something she doesn't.

"I'll be there—for office hours and the event."

She blinks up at him. "You want a cookie or something?"

He laughs, throwing his head back. "No. No cookie, but you could be less mean. More friendly," he says, eyes raking over her as he steps closer.

She regards him warily. "I won't be *more* anything."

She walks around him, willing herself not to look back, even as the echo of his laugh calls to her.

$$x = \frac{-b + \sqrt{b^2 - 4ac}}{2a}$$

The following day, Jahlani sits in Professor Jackson's room for office hours when Roman walks in. His backpack hangs from one shoulder and he's wearing a black cotton long-sleeve with the arms pushed up. His expression is radiant as he sidles in. Like the dryer actually got all his creases out with "wrinkle control" turned on, and she finds herself on edge wanting to know what's got him so overjoyed.

She can't help the way her chest thunders against her ribs, and her knee starts to bounce.

She hates it.

She hates that she doesn't have control over it.

And more than anything, she hates that she didn't foresee it happening.

She looks at the time on the digital clock then to Roman as he pulls out his laptop and settles it over his lap.

"You're late," she murmurs, dragging her gaze back down to the computer and clicking through to find the lesson from yesterday. He lets out a soft laugh, shaking his head.

"Family emergency, and hello to you, too. I'm doing well, thanks for asking. How are you doing today?" he asks, giving her a blinding smile that makes her feel entirely *too much*.

Make it stop.

Clearing her throat, she rolls her shoulders back. She gives him a pointed look over the screen, her lips pressing together.

"I'm fine, let's get started."

He tilts his head backward, letting out a loud groan. When his eyes land on hers, they're firm.

"Come on, Jahlani. Give me more than that. It's not a crime to get to know each other, is it?"

"Yes. It is," she says, folding her arms across her chest. "And, there's only forty minutes left for office hours, we don't have time for that—"

Roman waves her off before standing up. "There's always time. Come on, it'll be quick."

And to Jahlani's absolute horror, he starts to drag the chair around the desk toward her. Her palms land on the surface, and her posture turns rigid as he sets it next to her.

"What are you doing?" she asks, leaning back as his lavender scent carries through the enclosed space.

"Moving closer."

She scrutinizes him and shifts her chair slightly to the left, which he apparently doesn't miss because his smile slips before it's back in place. "Why?"

He leans forward, resting his elbows on his knees. "I'm not contagious, Jahlani. It'll be easier for me to see the screen, and this way you won't have to talk to me with this giant monitor blocking you."

And before she can move further away, his fingers wrap around her armrest and drag the chair closer than it was before.

"Roman! This is too close," she hisses, dropping her hand back to the desk to prevent herself from moving any closer. "Someone could see and think—"

She stops herself, but it's too late. The damage is already done.

His eyes flash, and a slower, lazier smirk holds firm on his face.

"Think what, Jahlani? You're just a graduate teaching assistant helping one of your struggling undergraduate students. There's nothing suspicious about that, right?" he asks, his voice dropping low.

It's too much.

His stare, his smile, his carefree spirit.

Entirely too much.

"Come on," he whispers, shaking the chair with her in it. "Two questions, and then we work."

She purses her lips. "Two questions, and you move the chair back," she says, glancing toward the empty space in the center of the office.

He laughs, tipping his head back. "Deal. Why a statistician?"

"I'm good with numbers," she retorts, shrugging.

He sucks in air through his teeth, looking down. "That's unacceptable."

Jahlani scoffs, unscrewing the top of her water before taking a sip. "What?" she asks, raising her shoulders to her ears. "That's it. I like math. I enjoy it, and you didn't say there was a criterion for answering," she says, setting the bottle down and wiping the corner of her lips.

His eyes close partially, and he leans forward. "Jahlani—"

She holds up her hand, silencing him. "What's your other question, Hayes? We're wasting time."

He gives her another pointed look before rubbing his fingers across his jaw. He slouches back, seemingly deep in thought, and Jahlani fights the urge to laugh at how seriously he's taking this.

Is she really that interesting? Is she really worth getting to know?

Letting out a heavy exhale, she resumes clicking on her laptop. Her eyes flick to his momentarily before dropping back to her screen as she tugs on her ear.

"My favorite color is green," she murmurs, turning it around to show him the first half of the lesson. "So, we spoke about Bayes' Theorem—"

"Were they happy to see you?" he asks, shifting forward in his seat.

"What?" she asks, blinking slowly, taken aback by his question.

Roman scratches his wrist, staring at her intently. "Were they happy to see you? Your family."

She starts to shake her head. "I don't—I'm sorry. What?" she repeats, tilting her head.

He clears his throat, moving his laptop to the desk, and clasps his hands together. "The day we met, you said you didn't know if they would be happy to see you. I want to know if they were," he says, his expression somber.

Jahlani blinks, unsure of how to respond or react because *he remembers*, and better yet, he wants to know the outcome of her *silly little family reunion*.

"Why?" she asks, sounding breathless. *Why do you care?* she wants to ask. *Why do you remember?* she wants to scream. *Why are you made like this and why is it affecting me so much?*

Her mind drifts back to Teryn's graduation celebration—the sun burning bright, the music pulsing, and the chatter loud between her relatives. Even through the night, spirits were high and the conversation persisted. She went through most of it unscathed by their interrogations and statements. She spent most of the evening apologizing for not keeping in touch, promising to do better. Her mother barely said a word to her and ignored comments from relatives asking if she was happy to have Jahlani home. That hurt more than anything.

That, after all these years, her mother was still the same detached, nonchalant person she'd left behind.

Her cousins were different. Jahlani remembered Trent, the older twin by seven minutes, as the comedic relief. Laidback. He could hold a conversation with just about anyone, but the person she saw the other night was nothing like that. Trent was taller, muscled out, and dark all over. His expressions were deflated, and she spent all evening trying to figure out what was wrong. He was good. Deflecting, smiling, spinning the conversation back to her, but his eyes were wide and glistening. Unnatural.

And then there was the case of Teryn.

She straight-up ignored her the entire night. But Jahlani figured she deserved it for ignoring them all first.

"Some more than others," she says quietly. "It went exactly how I knew it would."

He nods slowly, drumming his fingers on his knees. "Hmm."

"What?" she asks, sitting up straighter. "What's that for?"

"Nothing. I just ... I think it's impossible to be around someone like you and not feel some form of joy," he says, his gaze unwavering. Jahlani feels her muscles relax as she searches for any signs of ridicule.

She swallows, looking down at her fingers. "How do you do that?" she asks, pulling at the skin surrounding her wrist.

"Do what?"

She looks up at his face. "See the good in everyone. Think that everyone is worthy of such high praise."

A gentle smile builds on his features. "I don't think that about everyone."

"No?"

He shakes his head, smiling down at his hands like he knows something that she doesn't.

"No, Jahlani," he says in a low voice. "I'm pretty sure I only think about you."

Her breath hitches when his words catch up to her. Her skin flushes as they maintain simmering eye contact. Her stomach flutters and she becomes hyperaware of her braids against her neck, her knee bouncing, his arms in his shirt, the part in his lips, his fingers tugging at his earlobe, the tick of the clock—

Clearing her throat, she breaks the connection first, gesturing to her laptop screen. Grabbing the tie on her wrist, she wraps her braids up before shrugging her cardigan from her arms. His eyes latch onto the movement, and goosebumps arise over her skin. She decides she's better with it on, and her gaze trails to the closed door. Standing, she takes a wide step around him to pull it completely open, cursing under her breath as she does.

"Let's start," she says, but her voice comes out shaky. High-pitched. As she walks back to the desk, she reaches for her water, turning away to finish the bottle. From her peripheral vision, she sees him adjust in his chair, dragging the laptop back to his lap.

"Why did you open the door?" he asks, tapping on his keyboard. Wiping a hand against the corners of her mouth, she settles back into the chair.

"Just a little warm in here," she says, avoiding his gaze. "Move your chair back. We've wasted enough time."

For the rest of the session, he doesn't steer the conversation away from the lecture, and she can't stop the wave of disappointment that consumes her when it's over.

CHAPTER 12
Bitter and Twisted

Jahlani

The Graduate Affairs Event for Data Science and Statistics is a large gathering for statisticians, computer scientists, data scientists, and anyone else interested in learning more about current research in the field. It also helps undergraduate students learn more about graduate school admission requirements and potential career opportunities.

In other words, it's one giant white, cisgender, male nerd fest.

Jahlani had come to terms with the fact that no matter where she went, there was a high probability that she would always be one of the few Black women in the horde.

The hulking downside to her industry is the constant requirement of having to prove that she deserves to be there as much as the next person.

That no, she isn't in the wrong class, and yes, she knows the difference between Binomial distribution and Poisson distribution. Yes, she graduated from her university summa cum laude with a faultless grade point average, but it was something she hadn't yet learned how to wear as a badge of honor.

The watchful gazes and upturned noses never quite screamed

'We're happy to have you here.' She attended several of them in New York during undergrad, and eventually learned what type of people to avoid to survive the night.

Jahlani brings a glass of water to her lips. So far, only ten students have shown up. Checking the time on her watch, she sees that the event ends soon.

I'll be there. At the event.

She cranes her neck around the room, looking for a familiar pair of forest green eyes and chestnut hair, but when she comes up short, she's suddenly reminded of when her parents had promised to show up for a presentation in high school.

It was her senior research project about the impact of stress on high-achieving students. She spent the whole year on the paper, practicing her speech in front of the mirror, with Imani, with her teacher.

Of course, neither of them showed.

And of course, they both had a shitty excuse. She knows that Roman isn't her parents, and truthfully, he doesn't owe her anything.

Given his track record for class, his words held no comforting syllable. The probability of him making an appearance was low to begin with. People don't just change overnight, and certainly not for some random person. Certainly not for her.

Even so, the bitterness that clouds her mind is hard to stop. It was the conviction in his voice that made her believe him. And his eyes.

And that's the problem.

The memory of them continues to afflict her thoughts for the rest of the evening. Even as she indulges in petty conversation. Even as she treks to the bus stop. Even as she unzips her dress and washes the makeup from her skin. Even as the silken comforter rests against her cheek. Even as she drifts off into a soundless sleep, the shine—their depth—still haunt her.

$$x = \frac{-b + \sqrt{b^2 - 4ac}}{2a}$$

The weekend passes by in a blur. And Jahlani is sure that she's over it. Over Roman not showing up.

She has a hundred other things weighing on her mind, so there's no reason for her to be checking the class roster to see if he's still active, and there's *definitely* no reason for the relief that washes over her when she sees that he is. And there is absolutely no reason for her chest to hammer as she watches the clock for their meeting to start during office hours on Tuesday.

Her phone vibrates on the desk, and she leans forward to pick it up. Her stomach pivots when she sees *his* contact name flash across the screen.

"Hello," she breathes out softly. *Wary.*

"Hey Jahlani," her dad says. "You busy?"

She checks the time again. Roman was officially late. Moving the phone to rest between her ear and shoulder, she checks her inbox for a message from him.

Nothing.

"Nope."

Her father clears his throat. "So, Helen and I were talking, and we think it's better to send the money when everything is done."

We?

She exhales slowly as a mounting pressure starts to build behind her eyes. She shifts to hold the phone, and it happens subconsciously. Suddenly, she finds herself transported to his Tudor-style home in New Hampshire. She's only ever caught glimpses over the years through static-filled video calls and low-quality photographs, but the open space layout is clear as day. Helen is in her early thirties. She's nice. And as Jahlani grips it tighter, she realizes she can't even hate the woman.

"Dad, I'm not asking you for the full amount right now." Her voice is tight and restrained.

He clears his throat. "I—okay. Okay. I can send you half soon, and then I'll have the rest for you another time."

"When?" she asks, her tone stern.

"Jahlani, it's hard right now, baby. Helen's IVF treatment was more expensive than we anticipated, and we started to renovate."

Jahlani's head tilts at this. "IVF treatment?" she asks, adjusting herself in the chair. "I thought you said it was unexpected?"

He blows out a gust of air, and the static sends an unwelcome chill across her skin. "Yeah, well. I mean that, with how long it's taken, you know."

Jahlani licks her lips, shaking her head slowly. "So, you had the money for IVF treatments for months, but you couldn't spare a single cent to pay back the loans you told me to take out?"

"Jahlani—"

She squeezes her eyes shut. "No," she says in a whisper. Then louder, "You can't keep doing this to me."

"End of next year, I promise."

This time, she laughs, but there's no humor behind it. "I need you to do better than that. You told me you would have this money once I graduated the first time. That was almost two years ago, Dad."

She releases a shaky breath, rubbing her temple. "Look, I understand that you have another family that you have to take care of, but this is your responsibility."

He kisses his teeth, his tone turning cold. "Why are you acting like this, huh? Did your mother put you up to this?"

She exhales. "Like what, Dad?"

"Greedy. Money hungry."

Jahlani blinks rapidly. "You're kidding, right?"

"You're like a child throwing a tantrum. You're twenty-six, Jahlani. Grow up and handle your own problems. You're not a kid anymore."

"But I'm yours," she says, her skin heating. "I'm still *your* responsibility. No matter how old I get, how far you move, how many kids you have with Helen, I will *always* be there. I'm not the one acting like a child here. You are, Dad. And that little gnawing feeling that you have inside right now, that's your guilt talking. Send me my money," she says, ending the call.

Leaning back, she takes several long, drawn-out breaths. Her eyes flit to the clock again before they scan the length of Professor Jackson's collection of books. Since Jahlani's position is funded through a grant, they didn't have the money to spare for her own office. Standing up, she notes that Roman is officially fifteen minutes late.

Of course he is.

Realizing that she has time to peruse Jackson's aged library, she skirts around the desk and up to a row of books lined in dust. As she skims the titles, she's surprised to see that none of them contain his name.

A particular text catches her eye, and she hooks her finger on the edge of the binding, pulling it out.

"What are we reading?"

She gasps, and the book tumbles from her hands and onto the floor. Roman bends down to pick it up, handing it to her. Her eyes take in his hunched figure, and for a moment, she forgets she's irritated that he's late, her body betraying her when their fingers brush as she takes it from him.

Shrugging her shoulders to ease her nerves, she returns it to the shelf, not making eye contact.

"Don't sneak up on people like that," she mumbles, moving toward the desk with a hand over her chest.

"Sorry." Her eyes snap up at the deep rumble of his voice. She takes in his flushed cheeks, wind-tousled hair. Effortless ability to look so ...

No.

She clears her throat and drops into her chair as he simultaneously sinks into the one opposite her. She rubs her hand against her temple, glancing at the clock.

"Forget to drink again?" he asks with a carefree smile, extending his bottle to her over the desk.

"No," she says, her tone more clipped than she intends. "I've just had a long day." She says, but his fingers are fast at work on his phone screen.

You're kidding.

Her eye twitches as she takes in his relaxed posture. He should be opening his laptop, apologizing for being late, thanking her for staying, for waiting. Her hand fists by her mouse as she resists the urge to throw a wad of paper at him.

Instead, she sighs. "Do you have everything?" she asks, typing. There's no reply from him so she looks over the screen. "Roman?" she calls out, eyebrows raised.

He looks up, clicking the phone shut. "Everything?"

In her head, she mocks him. In real life, she nods slowly as if she's talking to a five-year-old.

"For the exams?"

"Shit. Yeah, um—"

She leans back, running a hand over her mouth as he jerks his bag around. His phone vibrates again, and he checks the screen. "It's here somewhere."

Her eyes fly to the clock again, her body starting to grow heavy with fatigue.

His hand stops moving. "Shit."

She shakes her head, her lips flattening. "You don't have it, do you?" She crosses her arms across her chest, staring hard.

He slides a hand through his hair. "I must have left it on my desk. Fuck."

"Of course you don't." Jahlani scoffs, shaking her head as she closes the laptop, standing up abruptly. She grabs the stack of papers in front of her and starts shoving them into her bag.

"Jahlani, I'm so sorry."

Her hands work more quickly to pack, the sincerity in his voice making her stomach twist.

"Maybe we could just do this tomorrow, or we can run back to my place really quick? I'll cook? We can make a date out of it," he says. His tone is playful. Smooth. And on any other day, she would have brushed it off. She would have ignored him.

But tonight, she's pissed.

"Stop it," she says as she turns toward him, her skin on fire. She tries to keep her voice even as she speaks. "Just … stop."

The grin on his face falls, and he wets his lips. "Look, I really am sorry. A lot has been happening lately."

She scoffs, throwing her head back. "I don't know what's more insulting," she says, pointing. "You showing up late, wasting my time, or you thinking that you could *flirt* your way out of a sincere apology because I'm a *woman*."

His eyes widen and his lips part. "Jahlani, I'm really sorry. I had a thing."

She cocks her head, her voice wavering in pitch. "I wonder how this meeting would be going if I were a man. If I were *Jackson*." She points at the phone flashing on and off in his lap. "Would you still be playing on your phone? Would you have gotten here on time? Would you be prepared, Roman?"

Roman stands from his chair, mouth opening and closing. "I have the materials. I thought I grabbed them, but I guess I must've ..." He trails off, shaking his head. "Shit, I'm sorry. Truly." He shuts his eyes, breathing heavily. They snap back open. Wide and unwavering. "Look, I didn't mean to come on to you before. My intention wasn't to demean you like that. I swear." He blows out a breath. "I guess I just thought ... it's our thing."

Jahlani lets out a broken laugh, resuming her packing with more force and urgency.

"We don't have a *thing*."

From the corner of her eye, she sees him take a step forward. "Jahlani, really—"

She turns to him, unable to control herself. "And if you were going to show up late, the least you could have done was be prepared," she snaps before letting out a sardonic chuckle. "Silly me for thinking you would actually try."

Her chest heaves as his head jerks back. She shoves her laptop the rest of the way in, shouldering the bag before moving around the desk to the door.

"Wait, I can explain."

"And let you waste more of my time? Yeah, I don't think so." He steps in front of her. "No," she says. "I'm exhausted. I'm hungry, and I don't feel well, and I waited for you like an idiot," she mumbles to herself, pressing a trembling hand to her forehead. "I don't know why I waited for you."

His face twists. "Waited for me?" Realization flashes through his face. "The event. Shit. *Shit.*" She sidesteps him, reaching for the door, but turns.

"I'll have Professor Jackson assigned to you for the rest of the semester. There is clearly a conflict of interest here."

"Jahlani, you're upset, but if you would just let me explain. It was a family emergency."

Her laugh is dry as she steps closer. "That is always your excuse."

His nostrils flare. "It's not an excuse, it's the truth."

"And they happen. I get it, but last I checked, *common courtesy* means giving someone a heads up."

He exhales sharply, tugging on the back of his hair. "You're right, and I'm sorry, but my situation is a little more complicated than that."

His phone begins blaring, and this only incites her more.

She inhales deeply, tightening her hold on her bag. "Have a nice night, Roman."

He steps forward, grabbing her arm. "Wait, this isn't what it looks like. It's not what you think."

His fingers are warm against her flesh. Rough, and …

Pleasant.

She steps back, pulling away, feeling disarmed. "Roman. Please. Save it for someone with the tolerance, because you're not going to find it with me. I don't care. Not anymore."

At this, his expression hardens. "You sound just like him."

"Like him?"

"Like Jackson."

Jahlani sputters, her arms flailing. "What are you—what?"

He rubs his hands down his face. "He did the same *exact* thing to me last year. Judged me with only bits and pieces of information. Assumed things about me."

Jahlani presses a hand to her forehead. "What else am I supposed to think, Roman?" Her arms rise and fall at her sides. "Assumptions are sometimes all we have. They protect us."

He takes a step closer, his figure towering over her. "No. They cloud you. You're supposed to give me the benefit of the doubt," he says in a hushed tone.

"I did," she grits out, tightening her grip on her bag as she peers into his pinched expression.

He scoffs. "What? One time?"

"Well, fool me once."

She moves forward, reaching her boiling point, her mind racing through her confrontations with her dad. With Micah. Jackson. Him.

"You're *all* the same. You show up when you want to, do what you want to, go through life casually, never having to worry about anything, never considering other people. Everything is handed to you while others have to break their backs to even get half of what you have, to even be given a fighting chance."

His jaw clenches, and for a moment, she wonders if she's projecting.

"You have no idea what you're talking about," he says, his tone low as he steps forward.

His features become clearer. His left eyebrow has slightly more hair. His jawline is sharper than she realized.

It throws her off-kilter.

How obnoxiously handsome he is.

"Sure, I do, Roman." She steps closer, pointing a finger at his chest. "I've been dealing with people like *you* my whole life."

"People like me?" He repeats as he steps closer, causing her finger to brush his chest.

"Yes," she hisses. "Guys who like to cruise on by without a care in the world. You put in just enough effort because, let's face it, nobody's putting the heat on you—"

"What—"

"No matter what you do, you'll be great. You'll shoot, you'll score, and the crowd will go *wild*."

He shakes his head, rubbing his jaw. "There you go again, making all these crazy assumptions about me. What is your problem?"

She rises on her toes, leaning closer as his face lowers slightly.

"You're my problem, Roman. You keep playing me. You think everything is a joke, that we can just laugh away our problems. You asked for my help, and I'm here. I'm showing up and you're not."

She's close now, and he has to tilt his head to look down at her. Her nostrils flare, and the air shifts around her, sharpening in an instant. It's confusing what it does to her. So confusing that she draws in a ragged breath. There's a faint hint of what smells like clean laundry and lavender, and something else. It's the kind that wraps itself around you, settles deep in your bones, and makes your heartbeat just a little faster—like it belongs in a place where she's never been, but would happily lose herself in. It's intoxicating and grounding.

Heat travels up her stomach when his eyes flicker to her mouth. For a moment, she loses herself.

Because for some unhinged reason, she wonders what would happen if he closed the distance between them with his mouth. She wonders what it would feel like and if he'd be assertive yet gentle or fast and reckless. Jahlani doesn't say anything for several seconds, and something flickers in his gaze before he steps back. She instantly feels her body simmer down at his retreat.

She wonders if she's *losing her mind* because how can you go from wishing you'd never met a person to wanting that exact same one to pull you into their chest and press you firmly into a wall.

The look that he gives her is closed off. Far away. Not the usual expression she's used to seeing on Roman.

She knows she let her emotions get the better of her, and so she opens her mouth to apologize, but his next words make her freeze.

"Look, whatever guy has you all twisted up and bitter inside, take it up with him. I'm not the problem here."

He doesn't say it with an edge in his tone. There's no sneer or fever behind the words. He just sounds exhausted.

And for some reason, that disturbs her *more*. She could've handled it if he had said them in the heat of the moment, but his voice isn't loud, and his lungs don't tremble, and she knows that he *means* that. He must see that he's hit a nerve because he starts to reach out, but she steps backward with her hand raised.

"Jahlani," he says, his voice strained and desperate. "Do you remember when we first met? You asked me if someone was sick."

Taking a shuddering breath, she blinks rapidly, all of the energy seeping from her body.

No, she thinks to herself. *That can't be it. She can't have been that wrong.*

"Jahlani, it's—" His phone rings again, and his eyes drop. "Fuck. I have to take this. I'm sorry. I want to talk about this—*fuck*."

She nods, stepping back. "Take it," she says, throat hoarse, looking down.

Sick. Someone close to him is sick.

Her mind reels at the possibilities. His mom? Dad? The sister he mentioned on the way to the bus stop that night?

He grimaces, looking at her before pressing the phone to his ear. She licks her lips, her chest rising and falling as he stares intently at her while the other person speaks.

"Yeah, I'll be there soon," he says, his gaze burning into her as she shifts on her toes.

Why can't she leave?

He ends the call, blowing out a breath. "I have to go." He slips the phone into his back pocket.

She nods, twisting her mouth, a dull throb in her chest, as if someone just ran through it with the blunt end of a knife, not fully finishing the job.

Bitter and twisted reverberating through her skull, spreading through her body.

Her gaze must look far off, because he steps into her space again and her head snaps up. His eyes dance across her face as she tries to regulate her breathing.

"Jahlani, I have to go, but … I want to talk about this properly with you. I'm going to explain—"

"Just go, Roman."

He exhales deeply, throwing his head back before slipping his bag on his shoulder. He slides past her, brushing the tips of her fingers with his and she shuts her eyes at the tingling heat that spirals from it.

"You're wrong, Jahlani," he says quietly. "We have a thing."

CHAPTER 13
Off Limits

Jahlani

The funny thing is, Jahlani knows how inflexible Professor Jackson is and she still finds herself in his office the following morning. He outright refuses to transfer Roman to his group.

During the next lecture, she feels his presence more than ever. Her skin heats, and when he looks at her, they hold eye contact for a *strangling* amount of time. At the end of the lecture, as everyone files out, the hairs on her neck stand up.

She watches him making his way toward her, and her mouth dries. She remains rooted when several students suddenly crowd her with questions. She inhales, pulling her eyes from his.

From her periphery, she sees his jaw tick, and his hand tighten on the strap of his bag before he shakes his head, moving out of the auditorium. She lets out a slow exhale, turning her attention to the girl in front of her.

It's suffocating, really.

The hold that he has over her. His words. The guilt gnawing at her because she exploded on the wrong person. She exits the room, feeling more exhausted than usual, when her phone vibrates with a message from her cousin, Trent, inviting her out for drinks.

She gets ready to decline when *he* calls her name. Her eyes shut, and her shoulders tense when he moves in front of her. His eyes lack their usual lightness, dark shadows resting underneath his eyes, and his mouth is set in a firm line.

Jahlani scratches her forehead, letting out a deep exhale as she looks at the cracked pavement.

"Roman, I—"

"I have a daughter," he says, his voice hoarse. Jahlani's eyes meet his light green ones, her breath hitching.

Daughter. He has a daughter.

"What?" she asks, stepping back slightly to look at him.

"I have a daughter. Her name is Lucy. She's two. She's my everything—and she's sick," he says, his eyes darting away momentarily before meeting hers again.

He pauses, inhaling deeply, before shoving his hands into his pockets.

"I can't help her. At least, not in the way I want to, so I'm in school to get my degree to make a better life for her. So, sometimes I'm late because I'm up at night with her or have to work, and sometimes I'm on my phone because I'm checking to make sure she's okay. And sometimes I say *ridiculous* things around you because I'm attracted to you and you're *off limits*," he says, stepping closer. "You're off limits, and it makes me crazy."

She makes him crazy. His daughter is sick.

She was wrong about him.

He's not like them.

Jahlani shakes her head, her skin flushing hot, feeling her chest start to pinch with tension. "I don't understand. Why didn't you say something before?"

"I tried," he says, his voice even lower. "You assumed the worst and wouldn't let me get a word in." He exhales, rubbing his jaw. "I don't go around broadcasting my personal life. I don't tell people, because it's a hard conversation to have. I don't want her to be used as an excuse. I was wrong. I should have been on time. I should have been ready. My daughter being sick isn't enough to excuse my actions, and for that, I'm sorry. I have to own up to that, right?"

Wrong. So fucking wrong.

Jahlani's fists ball and she feels her stomach roll. "But this is—this is—I—"

Beyond anything she could have fathomed. Life-altering, game-changing information.

Because he's been genuine this whole time.

She assumed that he was another lazy, well-off student using his parents' money to get by.

Using *her* to get by.

She steps forward, the warmth of his fingertips brushing against hers, getting ready to say the most useful phrase known to mankind, but she hopes will help temporarily soothe the wound she had opened with him.

"Roman, I had no idea. I'm sor—"

"Is everything alright here?"

Jahlani takes several steps back, turning to face Professor Jackson before looking back at Roman with wide eyes. His entire body stiffens, but his eyes remain fixed on Jahlani's until Professor Jackson is next to her, briefcase clutched to his side, a stoic look over his features.

Roman's eyes slide slowly to Professor Jackson, and he gives him a tight-lipped nod.

"Just had a question for Jahlani, Professor."

Professor Jackson lets out something between a huff and a grunt, folding his arms across his chest.

"Next time, ask during the lecture and not *after* class is over when Ms. Jones is trying to get home, Mr. Hayes."

Jahlani's stomach plummets at his cold tone, and she opens her mouth to say something, but Roman beats her to it, his gaze sliding back to hers.

"Right. My apologies. It won't happen again. Have a good night, Jahlani."

Jahlani purses her lips, watching his figure retreat down the pathway until he becomes a blur. She turns to face Professor Jackson, opening her mouth, then closing it when he arches a brow. She looks in the direction that Roman just walked off in before looking down at her watch.

She might be able to catch up with him.

"I have to catch my shuttle. Have a good night, Professor Jackson."

She doesn't give him a chance to reply, a light jog in her steps as she moves toward the student parking lot. She isn't even sure what car to look for. She isn't sure about a lot of things most days, least of all Roman Hayes.

I have a daughter. She's sick.

Jahlani is panting by the time she makes it to the parking lot. Pressing a hand to her chest, she draws in ragged breaths.

"Shit."

Her phone vibrates in her hand again and she sees it's another text from Trent. She looks once more around the parking lot before walking toward the shuttle, deciding to take Trent up on his offer—Roman's truth ringing sharp in her ears.

$$x = \frac{-b + \sqrt{b^2 - 4ac}}{2a}$$

The bar Trent drags her to is an edgy, industrial space nestled in the heart of downtown. The interior is an eclectic blend of raw materials — exposed steel beams stretch across the high ceiling, and concrete floors are polished to a sleek, reflective finish. The walls are a mix of red-painted brick and matte gray panels, giving the space a modern yet gritty vibe. Large, black metal light fixtures with exposed bulbs dangle overhead, casting a warm, amber glow across the room. The bar itself is a striking centerpiece. Long, blackened steel with a glossy finish that contrasts with the matte gray countertop. Behind it, rows of neatly arranged bottles glow under soft, ambient lights, while bartenders move with practiced precision.

The sound of bottles being lifted, ice rattling as it's poured into glasses, and the quick, sharp snap of cocktail shakers as they're flipped and shaken with added flair, blend with the soft pulse of music and chatter.

It's a nice change of pace for her, and she finds her shoulders relaxing as they slip further inside. Trent guides her to a booth in the back before leaving to grab drinks.

"Jahlani."

She looks up at the sound of her name. "Teryn, hey."

Teryn's red locs cascade in loose curls down her back, the light blue fabric of her dress flowing effortlessly over her shoulders. She tosses her bag onto the table and slides into the booth across from Jahlani with a relaxed grace.

"Didn't think you'd be here," Teryn says, her voice casual but laced with curiosity. "I thought you hated bars."

"Yeah, well, Trent invited me," Jahlani replies, her eyes scanning the room for him. "I needed to get out of the house."

Teryn nods and starts to pick at the chipping nail polish on her fingertips. Low music filters through the speakers, but it's not enough to fill the growing silence between them. Looking around the space, she sees couples dancing, talking, and laughing.

Unburdening themselves.

Which is what she came here to do, not sit here in uncomfortable silence with her estranged cousin. So, *fuck this*, she thinks.

"Teryn—"

"Jahlani—"

They both meet each other's eyes and Teryn gestures for her to continue.

Jahlani sighs, straightening in the booth. "Look, I'm sorry about everything. I feel terrible about not reaching out."

Jahlani's mind floats to four years ago, when she finally left. She didn't tell anyone that she had no intention of returning. It would only take her two years, she told them.

Teryn tilts her head. "Did we do something to you all those years ago?"

Jahlani thinks about how she wishes she had the ability to go back in time. If she could, she knows that this is something she would do over in a heartbeat. She would learn to open her mouth and speak up. To communicate.

To let Teryn know that she was having a hard time with her parents and didn't know how to do anything *but* leave.

Jahlani shakes her head. "No, God no. It's complicated. It's mostly to do with my parents and everything that happened after my dad left." She extends her hand across the table, her fingers trembling slightly as she clutches Teryn's tattooed wrist. She looks into the dark tint of her eyes. "You did nothing wrong."

Teryn hesitates, then slowly folds her hand into Jahlani's, offering a small, watery smile. "Damn, I wanted to stay mad at you for longer."

A quiet laugh escapes Jahlani, but the moment lingers.

Teryn shakes her head softly. "I could have reached out too, you know? The phone works both ways, so I'm sorry. Wow, I've *never* cried in a bar before." She waves a hand over her face, blowing out her cheeks. Jahlani laughs, handing her a napkin.

Jahlani slides out from her side, then moves to wrap her arms around Teryn, a gentle vanilla scent emanating from her.

A deep voice laughs from the side. "You're hugging. I knew my trap would work."

Teryn rolls her eyes as they unwind from one another. Jahlani arches a brow at the three shot glasses in Trent's hand before reaching out to grab one.

"To family," Trent says.

"To family," Jahlani and Teryn echo as their glasses clink, and they tip their heads back to drink.

"Fuck, that's good," Trent says, laughing.

Jahlani nods. "I'll grab us another round. What's it called?"

"Green tea! But get it from the guy in the white shirt. He's the best one."

"That's not very specific when there's more than one, T."

"He's got the craziest eyes, like this super, intense green." He gestures with his hands, pointing to his face rather aggressively and it makes her laugh.

Jahlani shuffles through the crowd until she reaches the counter. She looks over the menu to occupy herself.

"What are you having?" a voice asks. And maybe it's the music or the thrum of the alcohol seeping through her system, but the familiarity of his voice doesn't register at first.

"Three green tea shots and—" Her finger glides down the menu in her hand. "I don't know, what can you recommend?"

She looks up, blinking rapidly as she absorbs *him* in front of her. Her eyes roam over his features, her lips parting, and the longer she stares, the more her head seems to empty.

Which seems to happen a lot these days whenever he's around.

"Roman."

CHAPTER 14
String of Thoughts

Jahlani

Roman looks different. *Better.* The white button-down does wonders for his chest and shoulders. The soft hue of the lighting makes his eyes appear even lighter. Trent's description echoes through her head, and she wants to kick herself for volunteering to come over here.

She feels less irritated than she would have expected at seeing him across the counter. She feels …

Curious.

I have a daughter. She's sick.

If he's surprised to see her, he doesn't show it, and that sets an acidic feeling in her stomach. Why does she care that he doesn't acknowledge her?

He slides a swift, rehearsed smile onto his face. "Sure, three green tea shots and a lemon drop martini coming right up."

She holds out her card with trembling fingers for him to take.

"On the house," he says, something sharp in his eyes.

"What? No. I can pay for my own drink," she starts, but he moves away before she can utter more protests. "Shit," she mutters under her breath, but she can't help the tug at the corner of her lips because what are the odds?

So, this is what you look like when you work.

She watches him from the other side of the counter. He's smiling, charming, oozing confidence as he works his way serving patrons. For a moment, she wonders if he lied to her earlier. He doesn't look like someone who is carrying so much weight. Her elbows rest on the counter, and she drops her chin in her hand as she stares, the warmth of the previous shots making her feel a little lighter.

Looser.

Exactly what she wants.

Her eyes slide over his physique as he works pouring drinks, the tension in his arms as he shakes the bottles, the way his head falls back when he laughs with the bartender to his left.

If I'm late, it's work.

I'm attracted to you.

You're off limits.

Her head falls to her chest when his eyes flash to hers, warmth flooding her stomach, before looking back up. He's still staring as he makes his way over to her. Setting the drink down, his eyes trail the length of black material covering her frame, the expanse of her collarbone, the curve of her shoulders, to the loose fabric at the top of her thighs. She brings the drink to her lips slowly, sipping the sugar from the rim, mixing it with the tartness of the liquid.

His eyes remain on hers. "How is it?"

Moving the glass, she turns her lip up.

Perfect.

"Disgusting," she says, lowering it back down to the counter.

And then, with her fingers, she makes a zero followed by a five. The sound that follows is loud and unforeseen. She watches as he sobers, shaking his head, and the room seems warmer because *she made him laugh.* His eyes are back on her, and his lips part, ready to say something, and surprisingly, she finds herself leaning closer to hear him when Trent slides next to her.

"Nice," he says, collecting the shots. Jahlani straightens herself, blinking as she grips her drink tighter. Trent nods toward her hand.

"What's that?"

"Lemon drop martini," she says, extending the glass to him. He leans forward, sipping from the straw while she holds it and something slimy glides through her stomach because she *knows* how this looks.

But anyone with an eye for detail would notice that their eyes are the exact same hue of brown, and that they share similar shapes in the arch of their nose and the curve of their mouths.

Leaning back, Trent nods in approval before making his way back to the table. Turning back, she sees that Roman has moved to the other end of the bar, and her shoulders drop.

Pressing her fingers to her forehead, she laughs to herself because *why should she care what he thinks?* Blowing out a breath, she walks away with her glass, not looking back.

As they work through their fifth shot, Teryn convinces them both to dance, dragging them to the center. She isn't sure how much time has passed as Trent disappears with a woman, and Teryn leaves to use the bathroom, leaving Jahlani alone. She moves to a more secluded corner of the room, finishing the rest of her drink which has her feeling fuzzy and warm, and *light*.

So light.

Shutting her eyes, she leans her head against the wall. She's warm everywhere, and her heart starts pounding. She shrugs her jacket off, dumping it on the floor. Soon, she feels a shift in the air. A tug in the back of her mind, and she opens her eyes, staring and saying nothing. Her body is warm and tingly from the drinks. *Only from the drinks* she tells herself.

Roman's eyes sweep over her, making her feel … making her feel *what*?

"Jahlani," he says, voice sliding out frustratingly deep and smooth. Too smooth.

"Hmm." She closes her eyes, trying to block him out. Trying and failing. Failing a lot more than usual.

"Are you, perhaps, stalking me?" he asks, his tone airy. Playful. Like they weren't arguing less than 48 hours ago. Like it didn't bother him as much as it did her. Like he's forgotten about it. She hears him shuffle closer and her stomach tenses, but she stays rooted to the spot.

"I didn't know you worked here," she says, monotone as she folds her arms across her chest. Her eyes fly open when his shirt brushes against her fingertips. Her cheeks flush under his gaze—no, *the lights*. It's definitely that—*yes, it has to be*. It's making the room hotter. "I'll be sure to add this to my list of places to never return to," she says. Willing the hum and warmth spreading throughout her body to *go away*.

He lets out a small gust of air, seeming *charmed* by her threat, which infuriates her because she definitely isn't trying to be with him.

"What? You think I'm joking?" She tries to sound fierce, but her speech is slow. Delayed. Her voice comes out more sluggish than she intends.

"No. I don't," he murmurs. "But I'm glad you're here," he says, stepping even closer. She's now pressed against his front, and she inhales sharply.

"I want to finish our conversation from earlier," he says, leaning over her, pressing a hand to the wall above her head, caging her in. "But you're drunk. So, it's going to have to wait."

And the liquor is definitely getting to her because she doesn't push him away. She licks her lips, tilting her head to meet his eyes.

"I'm not drunk," she says, her voice sounding weak. "I remember everything, and I wanted to tell you that I'm sorry."

He rubs the back of his neck, shrugging his shoulders lightly. "It's okay, Jahlani."

She scoffs, looking down at her feet, which are currently tucked between his shoes. "Don't do that."

"Do what?"

"Be nice to me," she says, looking off to the side. "I can't stand it, Roman." She turns back to face him, folding her arms over her chest, her fingers digging into her arms. "You did nothing wrong, and I had all these negative opinions of you. And I made you like them and you're *not*. You're ..." She trails off, clamping her lips shut when she looks back at his eyes that seem brighter. Hopeful.

"I'm?" he asks, his voice low as he draws in a breath, eyes raking over her features.

Charming in a way that's dangerous.

"A dad," she says, drawing out the word unintentionally, her body curving more into the wall. "You're responsible for a tiny human, and I've been making your life ... so much worse."

"Jahlani, you didn't know," he says, his voice softer this time.

She frowns down at the ground, not liking the way her throat clamps shut. "Maybe I am bitter and twisted."

Roman removes his hand from the wall, exhaling a ragged breath as he steps back, and Jahlani regrets saying anything because she's suddenly desperate for his warmth.

"I didn't mean that," he says, his voice heavy.

"Yeah, you did," she says, her eyes finding the ground again. "And it's okay, because I think it's true."

For several seconds, neither of them speaks. The distant sound of people laughing, the bass of the music, and the clattering of drinks being mixed, fill the tight space. Jahlani closes her eyes as her temple starts to pulse, and she draws her fingers to the sides, applying pressure as she winces.

He needs to go away. He's making everything worse. He's making her feel things that she has no business feeling.

Two fingers find their way to her jaw, and he turns her face back toward him. Her stomach flips and her eyes drop to his mouth.

"No, I didn't. I was frustrated at you and myself, but I don't think that about you," he murmurs, dropping his fingers from her face.

She shakes her head, her skin sparking where he touched.

"You're so gentle with me," she says, inhaling sharply. Her eyes bounce up to his. "And I'm so …"

"So?"

"Not with you."

His eyes wash over her before falling to her hand. His eyes narrow and he tilts his head. "What happened to your wrist?"

She blinks, folding her arms across her chest. "Some guy in here grabbed me when I was dancing earlier," she murmurs, her head starting to pound. "I just bruise easily. It's nothing."

A dark look crosses his features, and she watches the pulse in his neck tick as his jaw clenches. Her eyes close as the thrumming in her head increases and her stomach shakes.

"Who'd you come here with?"

She wants to slide down and take a nap. "Why do you care?"

"You're drunk. I need to make sure you get home safely."

She waves him off, swaying slightly. "I'm fine. I don't need your help."

"Stop being stubborn."

"I said I'm *fine*." She opens her eyes, pushes from the wall forcefully to prove her point that—*See? She's not drunk. Her mind is not a garbled string of thoughts, and she can walk in a straight line* but her heels are harder to walk in than she remembers, and she finds herself stumbling into his firm chest as his arms instinctively cage around her. Anchor her.

"Oh," she says stupidly, staring at his chest. "I guess I am a little drunk." She lets out a soft set of laughs before going limp in his arms, letting the weight of everything fall away against him. She can't seem to find the energy to pretend that she isn't happy that he came looking for her.

CHAPTER 15
Not a Cheesy Hallmark Film

Roman

It's been two whole minutes and Roman hasn't been able to move since Jahlani passed out in his arms. Two whole minutes of him staring at her parted lips and reddened cheeks. The shock of her laughter, he slowly realizes, is what did it. Laughing *at him*. But maybe her falling in his arms, her cheek pressed to his chest, her makeup *definitely* staining the white of his button-down, which he couldn't bring himself to care about, her delicate snores, and usually tense countenance all pacified, played a part too.

Shifting her body against him, he pulls a loose strand of hair away from her nose. She twitches, and he resists the urge to run his finger down its path. His eyes travel down to her parted lips as he watches her breathing even out. They're not their usual chestnut-brown color. They're lighter. Fuller.

Distracting.

His mouth dries as he takes in the crease of her lips, the way they seem to fluff out into this delicate pout *begging* to be kissed. His arms tense at the thought.

He certainly didn't expect to see her across the room tonight, and he definitely didn't anticipate encountering her drunk. Jahlani mumbles incoherently as he adjusts her in his arms.

God, what is she wearing?

It's everything and nothing at the same time. It's paper-thin. The leather jacket she had on earlier was covering the thin straps on her shoulders, but he had watched from a distance as she tossed it to the flo or. Now the delicate curves of her shoulders are exposed, as is her chest.

She's not wearing a bra. Her hardened nipples protrude against the barely-there barrier, leaving nothing to the imagination.

Was it against university policy to stare at your graduate teaching assistant's nipples? He averts his gaze, adjusting her to bend down and swipe the jacket from the floor. He manages with expert dexterity to wrap the jacket around her body without waking her. She shivers in response, curling further into him.

Shit.

Adjusting her, he guides them to the bench outside the hallway so that she's resting her head in the crook of his neck. Her soft breaths hit his skin and it's comical how much it's doing for him. His eyes travel down to her exposed wrist where he sees the bruise forming. He rubs a hand over the welt, testing the skin, and she winces, sighing against his neck.

Two days ago, she was tearing him apart. Now she's here again. Doing things to him without even trying.

"I don't ... need your ... help," she says, her voice laden with sleep.

Roman turns slightly to see that her eyes are still screwed shut. He chuckles. Her eyebrows are pinched, and her mouth is downturned. Even in her sleep, she's fig hting him.

He moves a stray braid from her face, grazing her cheek. "I know, Jones. You don't need anyone," he whispers into her hair. "You're so fucking smart, and beautiful. Stubborn as hell." He sighs, dropping his hand. "If you'd let me get a word in that day, I would have told you." He twists his neck to look down at her. "But something tells me, you're not ready to hear that yet."

Suddenly, her fists clench at her sides and she turns further into his neck, her damp forehead heavy against his collar.

"Roman."

His entire body stills as she tenses against him. Soft, harsh breaths fall from her throat. He blinks, unsure of what to do. He decides that he imagined the whole thing and that she didn't just say his name in her sleep.

He looks down, trying to catch her eye, because the only logical explanation is that she's awake, trying to get his attention and not the highly improbable explanation.

He licks his lips when he takes in her flushed cheeks and shut eyes. A more distinct sigh falls from her lips, and his head falls back against the wall. He feels her body further slump into his shoulder as he lets out a shaky exhale.

Well, fuck.

A woman with red locs that move with her rounds the corner, tapping away in a frenzy on her phone.

"Jahlani, I can't find Trent anywhere—oh, *God*."

She moves to Jahlani's side, crouching down so that she's eye level with her. She draws a hand to Jahlani's face, tapping her cheek as she attempts to lift her head from his shoulder.

"Jahlani, wake up. *Shit*. Where is Trent? I'm going to murder him when I find him." She talks fast and under her breath, not meeting his eyes as she lifts Jahlani from his shoulder. "Shit," she says through a winded sigh. "I need to find Trent."

She looks to the left and down the hallway which leads back out to the floor, and to the right before looking back to Jahlani. She lets out a groan, standing to her full height. Roman watches as her eyes dart around the building and back to a sleeping Jahlani.

Roman clears his throat, rubbing the back of his neck. "I can stay so that you can find him."

The woman looks down at him, her eyes thinning as she pulls Jahlani toward her. He throws his hands up.

"We know each other from school," he says, hoping that will soothe the weariness in her eyes, but he realizes he's mistaken when her lip pulls back. "I also work here," he says, but it comes out sounding more like a question, and he wants to shake himself. But her eyes soften, and the crease between her eyebrows unfolds as she lets out a soft "oh."

She shakes her head, her shoulders dropping. "Sorry."
"No need to apologize. I get it," he says as he rests his elbows on his knees. "Here, I'll even show you my driver's license."

Her eyes widen as she shakes her head. "You don't have to."

But he's already searching his pocket, and when his fingers grab the plastic card, he turns to show her. She leans forward, her eyes flashing between the photograph and his face before she moves back, nodding.

"Sorry," she says, blowing out a long breath. "I'm just—yeah. Sorry about her too," she says, motioning her head to Jahlani, who is still sleeping with soft breaths. "She's such a lightweight."

He doesn't mind in the slightest about that.

Roman turns to watch Jahlani, and he has the sudden urge to pull her back to him. He clears his throat again, shrugging as he adjusts himself on the bench.

"It's my job," he says, and he hopes that she doesn't see through his lie. He hopes it sounds convincing. He looks back up to face the woman and gestures in the direction of the floor. "Go. I'll be here."

She still doesn't look convinced, and Jahlani blinks her eyes open slowly, lifting her head from where it's resting against the woman. Roman grows rigid, preparing for the worst as she rubs at her eyes.

"Teryn," she murmurs, swaying. "I'm so tired. Let's just go home."

As Jahlani turns to face him, her blinks are slow and delayed as she traces his features with her eyes. The hair rises on the nape of his neck as he allows her to scrutinize him. He expects her to sneer at him, to say something about his proximity, but instead she does the last thing he expects.

She leans forward, until their noses almost touch, and lets out a deep sigh, her eyes bouncing and bright.

"You have the greenest eyes I've ever seen," she whispers, blinking slowly. "They're so beautiful."

Roman can't stop the smile that spreads across his face. "You're so drunk," he says with a laugh, shaking his head. "You need sleep."

His eyes dart to look up at Teryn, who looks at Jahlani with a raised eyebrow and tilted head. Teryn shakes her head, pointing to the floor, and mouths that she's going to find Trent. Roman gives her a discreet nod, turning his body to face Jahlani as she continues to speak.

"No, seriously," she says, her voice slurring as she waves her hand around. "They're beautiful. It's like … like they're not even real. It's so … infuriating, and I can't stop seeing them," she says, drawing an index finger to her head. "I can't stop thinking about what you told me that day. And your eyes—"

"Jahlani," he starts, but she continues speaking, her hands gesturing with each word.

"Your eyes looked so … angry," she says softly, slumping back against the wall before inching back down to rest her head on his shoulder. "I hated it. Don't look at me like that again, okay? I'm sorry about everything. I'm just … so sorry."

Roman shakes his head, rubbing his jaw. "You didn't know, Jahlani. It's okay."

He angles his head to meet her eyes, but he sees that they're closed and she's back to sleeping. He laughs softly, adjusting her into a more comfortable position against his shoulder.

Teryn rounds the corner sooner than he'd like with the same guy she shared her drink with earlier. He walks up to where they're sitting, gripping the underside of Jahlani's arms and lifting her from the bench.

He tilts his chin toward Roman, who is still sitting. "Thanks, man."

Roman gives a discreet nod, watching as they leave. His chest feels as though it's on fire because it should be him taking her home.

But he can't.

And it bothers him more than usual tonight.

It's well after midnight when he pulls into his driveway, the porchlight flickering in greeting.

"Dan, I'm here."

Roman drops his keys into the porcelain dish before bending down to quietly slip off his shoes. Rounding the corner, he takes in the dimly lit kitchen. A lone pizza box sits on the island. Danica sits crisscrossed on the three-seater couch placed in the center of the living room.

She scowls, at something on her screen, draping a blanket across her shoulders as she sits up.

"I'm gonna need you to get a babysitter—*what happened to your face?*"

Roman ignores her, moving to heat up the few slices of pizza left in the box, before rummaging in the fridge for ice.

"Roman."

"Dan, I'm fine. He was drunk. Chill out."

"Roman," she says, giving him a pointed look. "You're *way* too forgiving."

He inhales deeply, turning to grab a plate from the cabinet.

"How was she?" he asks, straightening the takeout menus before shoving them back in the nearest drawer.

Danica stretches her arms through a yawn. "Same ol', same ol', asking for some loser named Dad. Oh wait, that's you."

He gives a noncommittal 'hmm' through a mouthful of cold cheese as he simultaneously presses the bag of ice to his eye.

"I don't know why, though. You're kind of lame."

Brushing crumbs from his face and hands, he flicks her off before moving to sink into the seat next to her. Her laptop is open with a Word document.

"What are you working on?" he asks, nodding to the screen.

She sits upright, dragging the laptop between the two of them.

"I have to do a comparative analysis on two political thinkers on a specific topic, think liberty, equality, sovereignty, political obligation. So, of course, I've decided to focus on Simone de Beauvoir and Mary Wollstonecraft. Do you know who they are?"

He blinks. "Uh—"

Danica's lip curls upward, and she shakes her head. "You're an embarrassment to the family name. *Simone de Beauvoir*," she says rather sassily, "was an existentialist philosopher. Those are philosophers who feel that the nature of the human condition is a key philosophical problem. Her work focused on women's oppression. Women are seen as '*the other*.' Wollstonecraft, the mother of Mary Shelley—a.k.a the author of *Frankenstein*—predates Beauvoir. She focuses on empowering and uplifting women through education. Women are just as rational as men when given the opportunity to do so, and a woman's femininity is socially conditioned."

Roman blows out a breath, nodding. "Sounds interesting, Dan. Have you decided which topic to focus on?"

She purses her lips. "Not sure. Either a critique of patriarchy or gender norms."

His mind wanders to Jahlani's words from the other night. *You're all the same.* He wonders for a moment if she's right. The light tapping of Danica's computer keys slides through the air as he takes sips from his drink.

"Hey, can I ask you a question?"

"You just did."

"Is Mom … happy?"

Her fingers stop typing and a tentative smile appears on her face. "What?"

"Do you think Mom is happy?"

Danica snorts. "Fuck, I don't know. I mean, you gave her a grandbaby."

He shrugs, swirling the drink in his hands, continuing to press the ice to his face. "Yeah, but not the right way."

Her eyebrow arches. "The right way?"

He leans his head against the couch, blowing out a breath. "You know what I mean."

"No, I *really* don't. Please elaborate," she says, closing her laptop before turning to face him fully, chin in her hand, expectantly.

Roman suddenly feels embarrassed, but he knows his sister. If he lies, she'll see right through it. If he withholds, she'll pester him until he's six feet under. He shrugs, scratching the back of his head.

"You know, boy meets girl, they fall in love, she comes over for the holidays, Mom loves her, they marry, they have kids. Not my version."

She tilts her head, deliberating. "But your version is so much more … *fun*. Romantic, even. Think about it. Accidental-pregnancy trope becomes a single dad and an almost-college dropout working at a bar to support their kid. It has flair," she says, making jazz hands.

Roman sends her a blank stare. "I'm serious, Danica."

She shrugs. "What? So am I."

"You know what? Forget it." Setting his drink down, he starts to get up.

Her hand shoots out. "Aw, Ro. Come back. I'm sorry. I'm sorry." She pulls him back down on the couch next to her. She takes a deep breath, trying to poker her face. She motions her fingers, and he reluctantly hands her the ice pack for her to press against his face. He winces when she applies too much pressure. She grimaces, mouthing a *sorry*.

He exhales slowly, scratching under his chin. "I just feel like, if I had done things differently, Kareena would still be here, and Mom wouldn't have to keep giving so much of her life for us. I want her to be able to do what she wants and not worry about me and Lucy."

Danica shudders dramatically. "Don't say that she-devil's name."

Roman scoffs. "She's the mother of my child."

Her eyes snap to him. "No. She's not. She gave up that right when she left."

She exhales loudly, moving the ice over his eye before dropping it back to his lap.

Danica rubs her forehead. "Look, Ro. This is life. Not a cheesy Hallmark movie, you know? Shit happens. And Mom, she's fine. Stop worrying about her. She makes her own choices. Her happiness isn't on you." She waves her hand between the two of them. "It isn't on *us*. So, you know, don't put that kind of pressure on yourself."

She gives him a harder slap than necessary on his back before moving to pack her things.

"I will say, though," she starts, drawing the zipper up on her purse, "sometimes I agree with her about the bar when things like this happen." She gestures toward his face before moving to shoulder the bag.

He rolls his eyes, sitting up. "This is the first time this has ever happened."

Her eyes squint at him and she folds her arms over her chest. "Yeah. Why did it happen, Ro? Don't they have other people to handle drunk patrons?" she asks, raising a brow.

They do, but this one put his hands on Jahlani, and that he couldn't let slide, he thinks as he shrugs his shoulders, finishing his drink before standing. "Dan, it's nothing."

"It's not *nothing*, Roman," she says, raising her hands, before letting them fall to her sides. She blows out a breath, rubbing her forehead. "God, I just wish you would reconsider it, so that you're not somebody's punching bag," she says through gritted teeth.

Roman sets his glass down on the counter. He drops his hands onto Danica's shoulders before grabbing her left cheek and pinching it.

"Aw, Dan the Man, are you worried?"
She swats his hand away, the crease in her forehead deepening as she steps back.

"I'm serious."

He lets out a groan, looking to the ceiling. "God, you're starting to sound like Mom," he mutters before he looks at her. "I *like* what I do."

"But why a bar? Why there? There are plenty of other jobs. You're smart, and capable, and I just …" She shakes her head, her eyes wide.

"I don't understand."

"Why do you have to understand it?" he asks, his gaze hardening. "Why do you and Mom have to pick apart everything that I do?"

"Because, Roman."

"Because *what*?"

"Because," she says, her eyes jumping around the room, "you make really dumb decisions sometimes, and we just worry about you. We just want to *help*." Her words strike a nerve in his chest, knocking the wind out of him, but he refuses to let her know how much her words hurt him moving toward the fridge to grab a drink and setting it on the counter, his jaw tense. "No, you don't. You just agree with everything Mom says."

Danica follows, folding her arms across her chest. "No, I don't."

Roman exhales, running both hands down his face. "You know what?" he says, his voice hoarse. "I'm tired. I've had a long night, can we just … put a pin in this, please?"

Danica's arms fall to her sides, and he suddenly sees his little sister again. The one who used to look up to him. Not this new version that looks down on him.

"Sure," she says, grabbing her keys from the counter. "Love you, Ro."

"Love you too. Text me when you get to the house."

When he hears the latch of the door, he drums his fingers against the countertop before peeling his shirt from his body. Walking down the hallway, he gently opens Lucy's bedroom door, tiptoeing to undo a few buttons on her onesie. Most nights she sleeps soundly, but the new medication has made her more irritable. Planting a kiss on her forehead, he turns the sound machine on before moving across the hall to his room.

Still gripping the shirt, he starts to drop it into his hamper but notices a brown marking on the collar. He draws it closer, running his thumb over it before letting out a soft laugh.

Her makeup.

For a few seconds, he's tempted to leave it be, to tease her about it the next time he sees her, but as the plan formulates, Danica's words make a reappearance.

You make dumb decisions.

Messing with Jahlani is as dumb as it gets, he thinks as he drops the shirt on his growing pile. *She's responsible for your grades. She determines if you graduate or not.*

And then Jahlani's own words.

You think everything is a joke, that we can just laugh away our problems.

But as he wrestles with sleep, all he can think about is seeing her again and talking to her. Making her laugh.

And most importantly: fixing things with her.

CHAPTER 16
Ordinary

Jahlani

Jahlani isn't sure how she ended up back here in less than twenty-four hours. The bar looks just as classy in the daytime, the skyline a soft azure, clear and non-threatening, but Jahlani knows better than to trust it. The street is fairly quiet and the large windows of the bar are closed, protecting patrons from the oppressive humidity that September in Florida brings. Jahlani wipes her palms against her jeans, pushing her sunglasses to rest on her head as she steps up to the door.

Checking her reflection in the tint, she steps into the space, the atmosphere calming her senses. Low murmurs, dishware clinking and ice being poured filter through. She finds him too quickly, his tall frame bent backward as he laughs at something being said. Squeezing her fists closed and then spreading them, she walks slowly to the counter, rehearsing her speech in her head.

It's as if he senses her because his eyes meet hers before she's able to take another step. Her mouth seems to dry as every pair of eyes follow her as she walks.

She only focuses on one, as she reaches the velvet stool. Roman's dressed in black slacks and a white button-down, the sleeves rolled up to reveal smooth skin scattered with a few beauty marks. Several veins are peeking through. His hair is tousled in its usual manner, and his eyes shine bright.

He's stupidly *handsome*.

It sickens her.

Especially when he smiles down at her like they're old friends. Like they have a secret. Like he's *happy* to see her.

She clears her throat. "Hi."

"Hi."

She takes a steadying breath. "Can we talk—"

"Oh, hey! You're the girl that passed out on him last night."

Jahlani's eyes widen a fraction as she turns to the low-pitched voice. Her body flushes as she gives a tight nod to a girl with curly hair and round cheeks.

"That's me," she says, her lips forming a thin line.
"I'm Ashlynn. This is Vaughn," she gestures to a burly guy covered in tattoos with his arms crossed.

Jahlani clears her throat, interlacing her fingers. "Nice to meet you both. Roman, can I talk to you, please?" She adds, "In private."

Ashlynn and Vaughn exchange *the look*, the one that screams Roman has spilled every last interaction they've had with each other to the two of *them*. It makes her want to scream, cry, and throw up, because it can't have been a pretty picture.

Can you believe she's my GTA?
That's the raging bitch that flipped out on me.

As they round the corner, Jahlani is so wrapped up in her head she doesn't notice him stop, and she walks into his solid, well-defined back.

"Sorry."

"Are you okay?"

"Fine. I'm fine," she says, stepping back. Looking around, she sees that they're in the same hallway from last night. Roman stands against the opposite wall, his arms crossed over his chest, his expression unreadable.

She wipes her hands against her jeans again, feeling more nervous than before. "I don't want to keep you long. I just ... came to apologize for last night and to give you this."

She starts rifling through her bag. Straightening out the bills, she holds the money out in the space between them.

"Here."

He blinks down the two twenty-dollar bills in her hand, unmoving.

She clears her throat, shuffling on her feet. "It's not much, but I figured it's something to pay for dry cleaning since I probably got makeup on your clothes ... and for the drinks."

He continues to stare, unmoving. Jahlani sighs, dropping her arm when it begins to burn.

"Roman, I'm really trying here," she says toward her feet, unable to look him in the face. Two girls walk by giggling, disappearing into the restroom three feet away from them.

"I don't want your money," he says finally, once the door closes behind them.

She grits her teeth. "Take the money. I know it's not much, but it should cover most of it."

Pushing from the wall, he runs both hands through his hair as he towers over her. "You're infuriating, you know that?"

Her eyebrows draw together, heat spreading through her. "Well, take the money and I'll be out of your way."

He bends closer. "I don't want it."

"Fucking take it," she whispers through clenched teeth, slapping the paper against his chest. His hand immediately closes around her own. Warm and possessive. He traps her fingers, his jaw ticking as he looks down at her. Gently, he turns her palm over, removing the crushed bills, slipping them back into her bag.

"I don't want your money," he says again, his voice low.

His hand is still holding hers, and she knows that she should pull away, but she can't bring herself to *give a fuck*, because it feels nice. Really nice. She exhales, licking her lips, noticing his hand tightens in hers.

"What do you want?" she asks, the cotton of his shirt shifting under her fingertips.

Suddenly, the bathroom door swings open again, and the two girls walk back out. Jahlani pulls her hand back, creating a crater for them to walk through. One of the girls stops, facing Jahlani.

"You both are *so* cute together."

"We're not together," Jahlani says immediately, holding his gaze across the space. He looks away, his jaw ticking, and she's almost certain she saw a flash of disappointment cross his features.

We have a thing.

Except, no. They don't. They can't.

The girl frowns, seemingly confused, then moves to catch up with her friend.

Jahlani digs her nails into her palms, leaning her head back against the wall. "I didn't come here to fight with you. I just came to apologize. Take the money, or don't." She rubs her forehead. "Just please, don't say anything to Professor Jackson. I really need—"

"Why would I say anything to Professor Jackson?"

She narrows her eyes, as in, *you can't be serious*, pushing from the wall. "Oh, I don't know, Roman. Maybe because every time we've been in a room alone together lately, all my professionalism and decorum seem to fly out the fucking window. Maybe because I wrongly attacked the character of a student I'm supposed to be helping. Maybe because I got drunk at the bar that said undergrad works at, maybe because I *passed out* on said undergrad. You pick," she says, chest heaving. "The list is endless."

He works his tongue against his cheek as his hands rise, then fall back to his sides.

"I'm not ... a bad guy, Jahlani," he says slowly.

Her head rears back. "I know that."

"Do you?" he says, his tone incredulous. "Do you actually believe that?" He steps forward, closing the space between them, shaking his head.

"The fact that you think I would—" He blows out an exasperated breath. "Why are you so hellbent on making me into some villain?"

"I'm not," she says. *I don't mean to.* "I'm not," she says again, quite pathetically.

Roman sighs, looking toward the ceiling, his Adam's apple working through a swallow before looking at her.

"I'm not a bad guy," he repeats, his eyebrows pinched together.

"I know," she says, stepping back. "I should go. I shouldn't have come here."

"No," he says, grabbing her bag strap and tugging her forward.

"No?" she repeats, ignoring the tingles through her arm.

"You have yet to hear my side, and I just ... just don't leave. I meant what I said. Give me a chance to explain."

She scratches her eyebrow, looking toward the exit. "I ... don't think that's a good idea."

His jaw clenches. "*Why?*"

"Roman," she says, like a parent scolding their child. "Come on. Every time we're in a room together, it's ..." She trails off, shaking her head again and his eyebrows raise.

head again.

His eyebrows raise.

Confusing.

Unnerving.

She licks her lips, painfully aware of how his eyes track the motion. "Too much," she settles on.

His eyes shift over her, seemingly determined. "You asked me what I wanted. This is what I want." Checking his watch, he looks back at her. "I have to get back, but I'll be an hour max."

Spinning on his heel, he disappears behind a set of double doors. Tilting her head up, she lets out a groan before moving into the restroom. Setting her bag on the counter, she drags both hands down her face before turning the tap on. Letting the water run for a minute, she places her hands under it before pressing them to her face.

"Fuck," she says, slamming the tap off and staring at her reflection. She knew coming here was a bad decision. Now she feels compelled to stay when all she wants to do is go to the house and crawl into her bed for the rest of the weekend.

But as she pushes the door granting her access back to the lounge, she finds herself walking toward a booth in the back corner before sinking into the cushioned seat. She pulls a book and her reading glasses from her bag before settling in, her body fully aware that she's being watched.

She only makes it through one chapter when a drink lands on her table.

"Oh, I didn't—"

The girl, Ashlynn, sends her a sheepish smile. "He said you need to drink something," she says, before moving away.

Jahlani flips her book over, her gaze sliding to him across the way. He immediately meets her eyes and makes a subtle drinking motion and her lips part in disbelief when he resumes serving the woman in front of him. She deliberately pushes the glass to the opposite end, picking her book back up.

This time, she only makes it into two pages in before she closes it. Leaning back, she looks around the room before landing on him.

Chewing over her bottom lip, she checks the time before sliding her chin into her palms. Jahlani has never been into people-watching but she can't seem to draw her attention away from Roman as he moves around. She thinks that it will be different, after all, she was fairly tipsy last night, but the familiar tug enters her body as she looks at him.

He's still charming.

Still confident.

Still perfectly patient.

A juxtaposition to her. She isn't sure how much time has passed when she watches him disappear behind a set of double doors, returning several minutes later with a plate of fries and a burger. He sets it down in front of her before sliding into the opposite side, their knees brushing in the process.

"You waited," he says, smiling. "Thank you."

She nods, jutting her chin out. "I did. Are the fries my reward?"

She sits up straighter when her stomach involuntarily groans, trying to stifle the sound.

He laughs, pushing the plate closer to her. "The burger is for you. The fries are mine."

She hesitates, blinking at him as he pulls out ketchup, salt, and mayonnaise packets, squeezing them onto the side of the plate before popping one in his mouth. She watches as he chews and leans back against the booth.

"Thank you," she murmurs before clearing her throat. They eat in silence for several minutes, and the whole interaction is so fucking *ordinary*, it terrifies her.

Because it's nice.

It's something that she could get used to.

And that's dangerous.

Clearing her throat, she sits up, wiping her hands on the napkins he grabbed. "What did you want to talk about?"

He sips from his drink, wiping the back of his hand against his mouth.

"Where's the fire, Jones?"

She looks away because there's literally nowhere she has to be. There's no one checking for her. But the notion is too embarrassing and sad to air out, so she shrugs as nonchalantly as possible, not meeting his eyes.

"I just have some things I need to take care of. And I'm sure you need to get back to your daughter," she says, resting her elbows on the table. He wipes his hands with a napkin before sitting upright.

"My sister's with her. I have time. Plus, I don't like the idea of you thinking I'm playing with you. I meant what I said when I asked for your help, and I'm sorry I made you feel otherwise. That was never my intention."

Her shoulders slump, and she looks down at her finger, picking at a hangnail.

"I'm sorry too," she says, looking back at him across the table. She concentrates on the space between his eyebrows, unable and unwilling to meet his eyes as she speaks. "Earlier that day, actually, a few minutes before you came in, my dad … he called," she says in a small voice. "We don't have a great relationship … and yeah, I guess he upset me a lot more than I realized. And you were there," she says, letting out a short laugh. "It sounds so childish when I say it out loud.

'He upset me.' Jesus, I need to grow up."

She reaches for the glass of water, taking several sips, her face heating. Setting it down, she wipes the corner of her mouth, shifting in the booth. He's staring at her again and the hairs on her arms raise.

"It's not childish, Jahlani. Parents can be a lot. Have you spoken to him about it?"

Jahlani gives him a fixed stare. "Talking requires the recipient to listen. That's not a thing in Caribbean households. It's their way or the highway. I took the highway already and now I'm back, so I have to lie in the bed I've made."

Roman opens his mouth, but Jahlani shakes her head. "I don't want to talk about him anymore, okay?"

He raises his hands. "Okay, what do you want to talk about?"

Jahlani crosses her feet together under the table, causing their legs to touch even more, resting her chin in her hands.

"Tell me about your daughter. Tell me about your Lucy."

CHAPTER 17
Do It All Over

Roman

Roman has never been happier to have worked in this bar than today.

Because she stayed. She watched him from afar. She ate from his plate. She listened to him, and now she's asking about his daughter and she's not running away.

He likes that he's got her attention.

And he's going to do his best to keep her right where he can see her.

He smiles, scratching the back of his head. "Lucy, she's … that's my whole world. I love her to death."

Jahlani leans forward. "Do you have a picture of her?"

He scoffs, slipping his phone out and typing in his pin. He's ready to send the phone her way when she rises from her side of the booth and drops a few inches away from him, the entire length of her right side pressed to his left.

His body seems to stutter as she bends down to look at the phone. He clears his throat when her fingers brush against his on the screen as she zooms and pinches. Her eyes widen a fraction as she looks up at him, then thumbs through more photographs.

"She's beautiful, Roman," she says through a soft breath. "She looks just like you."

Heat swells in his chest, and he can't help leaning in, purposefully pressing closer to her. "You think I'm beautiful?"

She looks up, lips parting in shock; her eyebrows furrow, and she shakes her head, looking back at the phone.

"You're unbelievable," she mutters, swiping her thumb more. "Unbelievable."

He laughs, rubbing two fingers over his mouth. "I'm just asking for clarification purposes."

She didn't say no.

Clicking the phone shut, she tilts her head, sending a disapproving look his way as she slides it back to him. She turns to face him, resting her head in her hand again.

"You said she was sick," she says quietly, dipping her finger into the condensation from the glass on the table. "What's wrong with her?"

Roman blows out a breath, pinching the bridge of his nose. "Yeah. She has something called nephrotic syndrome."

"Nephrotic syndrome," she says, moving closer into his space. "What does that mean?"

He clears his throat, rubbing under his jaw. "Her kidneys leak protein, and it causes her body to swell. It makes her more at risk for infections, more tired." The words hang, heavy and clinical, as he thinks about when they first told him—how Kareena dissolved into tears at the word steroids, how Danica and his mother asked a million questions, how his knees wanted to give out under the weight of it. Jahlani must notice him disappearing before she nudges him.

"Her mom?" Jahlani asks, her voice quiet, probing.

Roman's eyes flicker, the edge of his jaw tightening. "We were co-parenting. She walked out when Lucy got sick. Said it was too much." His gaze shifts toward the window . "Last I heard, she moved out of the country."

"God."

Roman shrugs, offering a small, almost imperceptible smile, his eyes burning at the fact that his daughter has to grow up without a mother. "Her loss."

"How do you do it?" Jahlani asks after a long pause, her eyes flickering between Roman and the walls of the room. "Manage everything. School, work, raising her?"

Roman's smile falters, and he leans back in the chair, the creak of the plastic seat filling the quiet space. "My mom helps. A lot. My sister too. I don't think I would have survived this without them."

Jahlani nods, her lips pulling into a smile. "You're doing a pretty good job."

Roman looks up at her then, the faintest spark of surprise in his eyes. "Yeah?"

"Yeah," she affirms, bumping her shoulder into his. "You could just stop showing up to school, but you're making it work. You're doing your best. You should be proud."

He shakes his head. "But I don't manage everything. Not really. Why do you think I'm in Jackson's statistics course?" His voice is tired, but there's a hint of humor in it, as though he's learned to laugh at the absurdity of it all. The chaos. He clears his throat, his voice trailing off as he speaks the next words.

"Earlier, you asked me why I didn't say anything. When she got sick and Kareena—her mom—left, it messed up everything. We had a pretty solid schedule, but she always had this look in her eye, like she wanted out. I wasn't surprised when she left, but I wasn't prepared either. It was like someone pulled the rug right out from beneath me.

I couldn't keep up with school. The hospital bills piled up. I needed to work. To make money."

He exhales, catching her gaze. "The bar—it's easy money. Tips are great. The schedule was even better, but Lucy got worse. A couple of the professors were willing to cut me some slack, but Jackson"—he shakes his head, jaw ticking—"he told me that I shouldn't use her as an excuse. That I should've been more organized and to try again next semester."

Jahlani's lips part. "That's why you didn't say anything? You actually believe that? What he said?"

He rolls his neck. "His words were like fucking bullets, Jahlani. I felt like the shittiest person, the shittiest dad at that moment. I told myself that I would never do it again, but I …" He huffs, running a hand over his mouth. "I fucked up again."

The laugh that escapes is bitter. Hollow.

He swallows, shaking his head. "I misread the date to sign up for classes because she had relapsed before school started. Only Jackson's was left. I tried swapping because I know how he is, and I didn't want to risk failing again. My advisor told me to feel it out because a GTA was joining the course, but then …"

She drops her hand from her head and sits upright. Heat moves through his veins as he stares at her.

"Then?" she rasps, chest rising faster when his eyes drop to her lips. He turns slightly, lowering his head.

"But then … the woman I met at the grocery store with the big, beautiful brown eyes, sharp tongue, and sharper mind, that I hadn't been able to stop thinking about, turned out to be the mystery assistant."

Her scent is stronger than ever when he leans closer. The chestnut rays in her eyes sharpen.

His voice drops to a hushed whisper. "The truth is, Jahlani, I knew I couldn't handle having you as the GTA. I wanted to keep whatever image you had of me ... intact."

She lets out a strangled laugh. "That's presumptuous of you to assume you left any kind of mark," she says, a little quiet, a little breathless.

"See? How am I supposed to think about Bayes' theorem or multivariate analysis when all I can think about is changing your mind about taking a chance on me?"

For a moment, both of them still. No one speaks, and they watch each other's movements. He's sure he's going to break first, move in and brush his mouth against hers. Quickly, gently. Just a feel of her lips, but a bottle falls behind the counter, echoing throughout the bar, and they both lean back. Jahlani turns toward the sound, and he drops his head back, closing his eyes momentarily.

Fuck.

She turns back, but she shifts away, reaching for the glass of water. He watches, fist to his mouth to hide his smile, as she empties the glass. Setting it down, she toys with the rim, not meeting his gaze, seemingly in a trance.

He knocks his foot with hers.

"Hey, where'd you go?"

Her mouth twists, and she scratches her left eyebrow before meeting his eyes.

"I'm just ... so sorry. About everything. I wish I could do something to help," she says, staring outside. "I wish we could do it all over, you know?"

They fall into silence and he isn't sure how to respond, because truthfully, *no*, he wouldn't change a single thing that's happened between them so far.

He sticks out his hand, and she turns to face him, eyes slightly wide.

"I'm Roman Hayes," he says. "Nice to meet you."

Her smile builds slowly, and she slides her hand against his palm before grasping it tightly. It's smooth and warm and he doesn't want to let go.

"I'm Jahlani Jones. It's nice to meet you, Roman Hayes."

CHAPTER 18
Girl Fun

Jahlani

On Monday, something is off. Not in a bad way, but in a way that Jahlani notices the subtle difference in the air. A shift in the atmosphere— a lightness that glides through her chest, her toes, her fingers.

Except nothing has changed.

Jahlani still goes for her early morning run, her path illuminated by the streetlamps, taking the familiar curves around the neighborhood, sidestepping the cracks, waving to Mr. Thomas as he sits on his porch reading the morning newspaper.

She slows as she reaches the sidewalk by the house, wiping the sweat from her brow. The sun begins to grow comfortable in the sky, casting even rays of rose pink and soft orange. Chewing on her lip, she wonders if she's forgetting something. A birthday, an assignment, an important event, a deadline.

Nothing comes to mind as she changes for the day, not even as she gives her mother a light wave goodbye *(baby steps)* and makes her way to the shuttle stop. Thumbing through her phone, she sees a missed call from Imani.

"That's it," she says, murmuring softly to herself as she listens for the shrill sound of the bus brakes. She forgot to call Imani back.

Again.

Content that she's figured it out, she slips the phone back into her bag after sending her a quick text, stuffing her hands into the pockets of her jacket.

But when the bus turns the corner, and the doors hiss open, the feeling has returned.

It isn't until she's in the lecture hall hours later, as students filter in with hushed murmurs and laughter, that she notices she's checked the door every three minutes for brown tangles of hair, long arms, and that look that says nothing is wrong.

She realizes it's *him*.

She frowns, plugs in her laptop, busies herself with setup—then her stomach twists and her hands shake.

What the hell?

She glances at the door as more students pile in, and he's still nowhere to be found. She laughs to herself, wiping her hands against her pants.

Ridiculous.

She reaches for her water, taking several sips, waving when someone greets her before setting it back down. It's concerning the number of times her eyes glide over to the double doors, and it takes her almost tripping over the wiring around the monitor to snap out of it.

On Tuesday, she cancels office hours, using the time to update her resume. It isn't until Wednesday that she sees him again. She doesn't notice him at first—occupied with handing out the exam papers—until she gets to the row that he typically sits in and their eyes lock. Roman's chin rests against his fist and he gives her a two-finger wave, smiling small.

She licks her lips, her mouth suddenly drying before giving him a small wave back. She tilts her head and sends him a look that hopefully comes across as concerned.

Lucy he mouths to her, and she nods, handing papers to students until she gets closer to him. Their fingers graze as she hands the papers to him, and their eyes lock for an unnerving amount of time before she moves on to the next student, fighting the urge to indulge in his teasing.

Against the rules, she reminds herself, making a conscious effort the rest of the time not to look his way.

It gets worse as the days pass. When he's not there, she finds herself wondering what he's doing, if his daughter is okay. And when he is, she turns into a bumbling mess, her mouth feeling like it's been stuffed with cotton, her body flushing like the Floridian sun is targeting her. Like Apollo has it out for her.

Jahlani is frowning at the email she's reading on her laptop in Professor Jackson's office. She's so engrossed that she startles when a coconut, chocolate-covered almond bar is dropped next to her device. Her eyes lift to meet Roman's clear green ones as he drops into the chair opposite her, and her hands grow clammy.

She wonders if he's as affected, but when his phone rings and he answers with ease, she takes it that he isn't. His shoulders are relaxed, and he talks animatedly. There's no stammer, no hesitation.

He clearly isn't affected by her anymore, and she isn't sure why that sparks a fuse of irritation.

After all, she's the one who told him to stop. This is what she wanted, right?

They're cordial now.
She shouldn't read into the fact that he remembered the snack that she likes from when they first met. She leans back into the chair,

willing her hands to be steady, before unwrapping the bar and taking a bite. He smiles at her, nodding at whatever the other person is saying.

Disgusting he mouths to her, shaking his head, then imitates a gag.

Jahlani takes an obnoxious bite, closing her eyes and inhaling deeply before letting out a low exaggerated moan. But when she opens her eyes, he's staring at her mouth, a slight haze to them.

He isn't smiling anymore. She chews slowly, swallowing the bite with as much grace as possible as he continues to watch, his nostrils flaring.

"Delicious," she says, attempting to break the tension, but her voice cracks. Turning back to the computer to finish submitting her payment, she peeks over when Roman is suddenly upright.

"You can't watch her?" he asks, brows pulled together as he rises. Jahlani's eyes track his movement as he shoulders his bag. He rubs his forehead with his free hand.

"Shit. I have an exam today. *Shit.*"

Roman stops at the door, and Jahlani watches as he runs his fingers through his hair, tugging and twisting.

"Alright, I'll meet you down there. Bye."

Jahlani clicks the pen in her hand as she watches him rub his eyes, his shoulders taut as he presses his head against the door.

"Everything okay?" she asks, leaning forward to rest her elbows on the desk. From her peripheral she sees his jaw clench as he lets out a strained chuckle.

"Not really, no."

Jahlani nods, exhaling deeply. "What's wrong? Is it your daughter? Is she okay?"

Roman pushes from the door, turning to face her with tired eyes. His expression is grim and defeated. Like he just pushed a boulder up a mountain only to have it roll all the way back to the starting point. Like he's pulled a *Back to the Go* card.

"She's fine. I just forgot my sister's schedule changed, so there's no one to watch her, and I have to take this exam right now—*shit*."

"I can watch her," she says, her head tilting in the process, like she can't believe her own words. Roman's head tilts too, and his eyebrows raise to his hairline.

"You can watch her?" he repeats, his voice slow and just as confused, but his eyes flare with hope.

Oh God.

Jahlani shakes her head, looking down at a stray paperclip on the desk. She grips it, pulling it apart as she looks back up to meet his eyes.

"Yeah, I mean … it's the least I can do."

"Are you sure?"

"Yeah, it's not a big deal."

His eyebrows pinch together. "But—"

"Roman," she says, standing abruptly, blowing out a frustrated breath. "You have an exam you need to take, and I'll be in here for the next few hours." She walks around the desk until she's a few feet away from him. "Just bring her here. Stop being stubborn. That's my job," she says, laughing softly before grabbing his arm and pushing him toward the door. He stops in the doorway, looking down at her, her hands still pressed against his chest.

Two students walk by, chattering low, and she quickly removes her hands, stepping back as her body catches fire.

"Give me your phone," she murmurs, holding out her hand. He blinks down at her, but obliges, the cool metal a nice contrast to the heat caressing her. She types in her number before sending herself a message. "Go get her. I'll be right here."

She holds the phone back out to him, pulling her hair back over her shoulder. He grabs the phone, grabbing her wrist in the process, and before she can stop him, he's pulling her against his chest. His arms wrap around her waist and he buries his face in her neck.

"Roman," she says, but it sounds all muffled with her face pressed to his shirt. "People will see."

He pulls back, and she clears her throat, running her fingers through her braids. "You can't do that," she says, looking in the hallway for any lurking students, before turning back to him. "You could get us in trouble."

"Sorry," he says, walking backward. "Just—thank you. I owe you big time. My sister's downstairs. I'll be right back."

She shakes her hand, pressing a hand to her throat as she watches him jog down the hallway and around the corner.

What has she done?

$$x = \frac{-b + \sqrt{b^2 - 4ac}}{2a}$$

Lucy won't stop crying. When Jahlani offered to watch her, she thought she would sleep the whole time, but that lasted all of twenty minutes. Lucy's cheeks are rosy and her eyes are red-rimmed and watery as she sits in the car seat. Jahlani paces back and forth, waving her toy in front of her, worried that if she picks her up, she'll become even more hysterical.

But as Lucy watches her, she squirms in the seat, rotating and wriggling, her cries increasing in pitch.

"Shit," she says, looking around the room. When she sees the bottle of hand sanitizer, she unscrews the top, dumping copious amounts onto her hands, remembering Roman's words.

More at risks for infections.

Once she's satisfied, she crouches in front of Lucy, getting to work on her belt. When Lucy sees what she's doing, her wails turn to small sniffles.

"See? There we go, baby girl. All better already," Jahlani says, sitting back on her haunches to see what she does next. Lucy blinks at her with wide eyes before she pushes herself from the seat and stumbles toward her with outstretched arms.

"Up," Lucy says, opening and closing her fists. Jahlani shakes her head, because *of course Roman's child is okay with strangers.*

Jahlani gathers her in her arms, lifting her with added flair, causing Lucy to laugh. Lucy presses her hands to Jahlani's face.

"Name."

"*Jah-lah-knee,*" she says, making sure to enunciate each syllable while tapping her nose. Lucy's mouth twists, and she blinks hard as she works through the sounds.

"Lani," she says finally, and Jahlani shrugs, smiling.

"Close enough," she says, walking with Lucy on her hip back to the computer.

Lucy turns in her lap to look up at her. "Where's Daddy?"

Jahlani looks down at her face, and before she can stop herself, she's reaching for a tissue to clean her face. She wipes her tear-stained cheeks before moving to wipe her nose.

"He'll be back soon, baby, don't worry. We're going to have fun. Just us girls," she says, smoothing back her hair. "Okay?"

Lucy smiles, clapping her hands. "Fun!"

Jahlani chuckles as she pulls up an animated video for her to watch while she gets back to grading, wondering how anyone could ever walk away from a child like this. It doesn't take long for Lucy to become restless, and soon Jahlani finds herself chasing her around the office. She's so focused on catching her that she doesn't notice the door swing open. She collides with Roman, and he grips her arms, steadying her. She claps a hand over her mouth, laughing.

"Sorry," she says breathlessly. "I didn't see you there."

He looks down at her, his eyes soft. "I can see that. Having fun?"

But before she can respond, Lucy charges toward him, screaming. "Daddy!" She stumbles on the way over, and Roman and Jahlani both react.

"Be careful, baby."

"Careful, Lulu."

They both turn to look at each other, and a charged energy invites itself into the space. His hand still grips her arm, but it's turned to gentle caresses. Jahlani steps back so that he can pick up Lucy and stop her heart from flying out of her chest.

Make it stop. Please.

She watches Lucy drop her head to his neck and he presses a kiss to her forehead, rubbing circles on her back.

He's so good with her.

"Tired, baby?" he asks, dropping another kiss to her cheek. She nods, letting out a yawn. "Did you have fun with Jahlani?" he whispers, holding Jahlani's eyes from across the room. Jahlani sways on the spot, bracing her hand against the desk.

She likes when he looks at her like that.

And Jahlani's heart does fly out of her chest when Lucy nods, her eyes drifting shut. "Lani ... girl fun," she mutters.

Roman laughs when she starts to snore. "She's gonna be out for the rest of the night."

Jahlani nods, rubbing the back of her neck. "How was your exam?" she asks, starting to pack her things slowly, unsure of what happens next, but knowing she's not ready to leave this space with him.

He shrugs. "It was fine. I was a little distracted."

"Hmm. I'm sure you did well."

He sucks in air through his teeth, bending to pick up her car seat.

"Yeah. You heading out now? My car is in Lot E."

"The shuttle is on the other side. I'll be fine," she says, gesturing toward Lucy. "Get her home. You don't need to walk me."

He exhales, stepping forward. "You're not taking the shuttle, I'm giving you a ride, and I'm not taking no for an answer, Jones."

"Roman—" she starts to protest, but before she can finish her thought, he grabs her bag and walks out the door. "No—hey—"

"I'll be in the car," he calls over his shoulder, moving out the door. She stands in the office, tapping her foot, wondering if she really needs her bag. After remembering her keys to the house are in there, she follows after him, something unfurling within her chest.

CHAPTER 19
Mother Knows Best

Roman

"Seriously, thank you again. I owe you big time," Roman says, easing the car out of the campus lot. He adjusts the mirror, watching as Lucy's head rolls to the side, her lips puffed as she breathes out. He's trying to distract himself from the fact that Jahlani is in his car.

Finally.

"Roman, please. It was nothing." She leans back against the headrest, closing her eyes. "Besides, we had a great time. She's incredible." Jahlani opens one eye to look at him from the side. "She's smart. Makes me wonder where she gets it from."

Roman shakes his head, shifting in his seat as he rolls the car to a stop. "Funny."

She laughs softly, looking out the window at the darkened streets. The dashboard reads half past seven, and he wonders how he can drag out this ride. His eyes flit to the navigation on his phone.

The streetlights are blown out on some of the roads, making it difficult to see, and he catches her squinting. She leans forward until her nose is pressed against the glass.

"Roman, where are we?" she asks, turning back to look at him.

His hands tighten on the steering wheel, and he puts his foot back on the accelerator.

"Made a wrong turn," he mutters under his breath, not looking at her. "Sorry. We should be there in another … fifteen minutes?"

He watches from the corner of his eye as she chews on her lip, her forehead creasing.

He clears his throat. "Penny for your thoughts?" he asks, glancing over to read her.

She tugs on her bottom lip, smiling. "Nothing. Just thinking about how nice it was hanging out with your daughter today."

He hits a pothole, and they jerk forward. She turns to him with wide eyes, and he clears his throat again, his hands tightening.

"Shit, sorry. I didn't see it." He looks up in the rearview mirror to see if Lucy is still asleep and notices that Jahlani has turned to check on her too.

Fuck.

Jahlani shakes her head, and a strained chuckle escapes her. "Floridians really don't know how to drive."

"Guilty."

"Your poor daughter," she says, turning to look at her again. "How does she sleep so well?"

"Hey, I'm not that bad—I didn't see it."

"Sure," she says, not sounding convinced as she leans back in the chair. They drift into comfortable silence for a few minutes before Jahlani sits upright, turning to face him.

"Can I ask you something?"

He gives a subtle nod, unable to trust his body to do anything other than focus on the road.

"You're majoring in software engineering … but you work in a bar," she mutters, more to herself.

"Are you asking me or are you telling me?" he asks, pressing on the brakes as they come to a stoplight. His eyes glide to the navigation before moving to hers.

Eight minutes.

She shrugs, toying with the necklace on her throat. "When I saw you at the bar that night, you were different. You seemed to enjoy doing that. Why not get a degree in hospitality or business management?"

He nods, rubbing a hand across his jaw. "My mom is pretty traditional when it comes to success. In her eyes, it comes from the job title you have."

"And you disagree?"

He scoffs. "Of course I do." The light turns green, and he moves the car forward again, cutting his eyes to her. "To me, success comes from being happy. I should … feel something in what I do. It's not about the title or the money. It's about the people. It's about the little things."

"I'm confused. If you feel that way, then why software engineering?" she asks, completely turning her body to face him.

Roman's eyes flick to the rearview—to Lucy—then back to the navigation system. She must notice, because she lets out a soft "oh."

"What?" he asks, looking at her briefly. "What was that for?"

Seven minutes.

"Nothing. I was just thinking about how wrong I was about you," she murmurs, twisting the jewelry on her neck.

"Hmm. Not sure I follow. Care to elaborate, Jones?"

She huffs, rolling her eyes. "Nice try."

"Come on," he urges, his voice a low rumble. "It won't hurt my feelings."

The headlights from a car passing by cast a sharp light over her face and he sees the knot in her forehead as she deliberates. She huffs, her mouth twitching as she stares at her hands.

"Okay," she says, her voice soft. "I thought ... that you were just another privileged pretty boy—"

"You think I'm pretty?" he says, smiling broadly as he turns a corner, narrowly missing a stray cat.

"—but you're not," she continues, ignoring him. "You worship the ground that Lucy walks on. You take care of your sister. You're so loyal to your mom that you would jeopardize going after what you want just to keep her happy. You're a ... good guy, Roman. You're probably one of the best people I know."

His throat works through a swallow, unsure of what to say. He's so used to his mom's criticism of his choices, her words feel like a cure. A soothing balm that spreads throughout his body.

Five minutes.

"Roman?"

"Hmm."

"You missed the turn again."

He exhales, glancing her way. "I know."

From his peripheral vision, he sees her squint. "Why?"

Removing one hand from the wheel, he runs a hand down his jaw. "I'm trying to spend more time with this really infuriating woman I met over a month ago who claims she wants nothing to do with me, but says some really nice, really *thoughtful* things about me that make me think otherwise. Any advice you can give me? I'm dying over here."

He doesn't look over at her, knowing that he's said more than he should have, but not giving a shit.

Three minutes.

"I don't know," she murmurs, looking out the window. "You'd have to tell me more about her."

He inhales deeply, drumming his fingers along the steering wheel. "She's ... incredibly smart. Organized. Very Type A. Logical and driven. Honestly, the complete fucking opposite of me," he says, unable to stop. "She has this ... great laugh. It drives me crazy when I get to hear it, but she's also pretty closed off, so I don't hear it as often as I'd like. She doesn't like asking people for help or letting them know when she's struggling. She actually quite ... stubborn, but fuck if I don't like the thrill of changing her mind."

This time he does look her way as he gets caught by a red light, the glow casting beams within the car. She faces him fully, a pained expression crossing her face, before turning away as the car starts moving again.

"She sounds ... like a lot. Are you sure she's worth the hassle?" Her voice comes out quiet as she toys with her fingers in her lap.

One minute.

"Yeah, she's worth it," he says, drawing to a stop in front of a one-story house. He puts the car in park, before turning to face her. For a while, they both just stare, then he clears his throat. The cabin of his car has somehow increased in temperature despite the air conditioning being on.

"Roman," she says, her eyebrows pinched together in thought.

He leans forward, resting his elbow on the console. "Jahlani."

"What are you doing?" she asks in a whisper as she looks up at him. She licks her lips, and his eyes mark the motion, his patience running thin.

He knows the answer she wants but decides to tell her what she needs to hear.

"I'm trying very hard not to cross this line that we have here," he murmurs, tracing a finger through the air between them, "but the longer you stay in here with me, the harder it's becoming."

She shuts her eyes, her head shifting slightly as a sound of disdain climbs its way out of her throat. "I knew this was a bad idea."

His head falls to his shoulder as he watches her take several deep breaths. "But you came anyway."

Her eyes open, her lips parting. "You ... stole my bag," she murmurs. "I didn't have a choice."

He laughs, running a hand down his mouth. "You always have some kind of rebuttal."

She shrugs, turning to grip the door handle. "Thanks for the ride. Let me know if you need help again. I really didn't mind. I'll see you—"

Roman's hand shoots out before he can stop himself and he's pulling her closer toward him by her wrist. She lets out a sharp exhale, as she catches herself with a hand to his chest, a few inches from him. He wets his lips, his pulse punching against his skin as he draws himself further to her, their noses brushing.

"Jahlani."

"Don't," she says, her breath ghosting his mouth as she curls her hand into his shirt and he wonders if it's to restrain him or to restrain her. "Don't do it. You're a mess. I'm a mess. This won't work. The rules."

"*Fuck* the rules."

He sighs deeply, a low rumble in his chest, his jaw clenching as he grazes his nose across hers. A discreet exploration of what she's willing to give. The skin on the right side is slightly raised, a tiny ridge that tells a story. He makes a mental note to ask her about it next time. She lets out a shuddering breath, a tremor that flows through her body when his lips continue to trail along the bridge of her nose and begin a deliberately slow descent down the side of her cheek before he presses a soft kiss to it. It's gentle. Feather-light. A toe in the deep end of the pool to test the waters.

He sucks in air and pulls back, letting her wrist go. She blinks back at him, pupils skimming across his features.

"Thank you again," he says, his voice coming out thick. "For watching Lucy."

Her fingers trail across her cheek as she gives an absentminded nod. "Sure," she says, clearing her throat. "Goodnight, Roman."

He watches as she slips out of the car and walks toward the door. She spends an alarming amount of time with the key, and he rolls the window down.

"Everything okay?"

"Yeah," she calls back, but her breath is shaky. "Just an old lock." He sees it land on the floor and a string of curses fall from her lips. He unclips his seat belt and cranes his neck.

"You need me to—"

"Nope. I got it."

She pushes with her shoulder and the door swings open. As the porch lights flicker, he laughs as he pulls away from the curb.

At dinner on Sunday, Roman finishes at a record pace, and is almost ecstatic when Lucy spills hers all over herself, forcing him to change her.

But now they're getting ready to play a board game and he knows it's inevitable. Danica sets up everything in the living room while him and his mom stand side by side, cleaning the dishes together. He's a foot taller than her so it's easy for him to see the gray streaks poking out through her bun.

His eyes volley between scrubbing the porcelain dish with extra attention and gauging her mood. They had parmesan-crusted chicken with pasta, and he was determined to get the cheese off.

From the corner of his eye, he watches as she squints at a piece of food stuck to the plate, bearing down on the sponge to get it out.

"Hey, is your professor going to let you make up the exam?"

He blows out a breath, clearing his throat and focusing on a glass dish next.

"Oh, I was able to take it."

The scrubbing to his right ceases. She turns to face him, a breathless laugh escaping her.

"Okay," she says, drawing out the word, wiping the back of her hand against her forehead. She turns back to the dishes, grabbing a Tupperware container, creasing the plastic as she works the grease from it.

"I didn't know your sister was free."

"It wasn't Danica," he says as he grabs a paper towel to dry his hands with.

He scratches the back of his neck before adjusting the collar of his shirt. "It was a … friend."

She blinks, her arms raising in question. "A friend … what friend? Do I know them?"

He avoids her eyes as he grabs another dish, drying slowly. "No, Mom."

She drops the container, wiping suds on her jeans. She turns to face him, arms crossed over her chest. "Roman Alexander Hayes, have you lost your mind?"

"Mom," he says through a laugh in an attempt to diffuse the tension, "come on, it's not that big of a deal. I was in a bind. You couldn't watch her, and neither could Dan. My teaching assistant offered. It was only for two hours," he says before meeting her eyes.

All the blood drains from his face when he sees her pursed lips and narrowed eyes.

"Your teaching assistant, Roman?"

"She offered," he says, abashedly. "I needed to take the exam. What's the big deal. Everything worked out. I thought you'd be happy about this?"

"What's the big deal? My granddaughter was watched by a stranger. What if something had happened?"

"Jahlani isn't a *stranger*," he grumbles, shoulders sagging.

"Oh, so now she has a name."

Roman's jaw clenches as he works through several deep breaths.

She scoffs, hands rising to the air before they slap down to her sides. "I hope you know what you're doing."

At this, he freezes, his shoulders tense. He turns to face her. "What is *that* supposed to mean?"

She opens her mouth and closes it before pacing the enclosed space. She stops a few feet away from him. "I mean, the bar, college, the money, the bills. What are you doing?"

He snorts derisively. "Being a bad parent, apparently."

"Roman—"

"No, that's it, isn't it? I'm not doing enough for Lucy. I'm making all the wrong choices. I work a low-paying job, and I don't have my degree because I'm a fuck up, right, Mom? I'm a disappointment?"

She lets out a soap-opera level gasp and lowers herself into the dining room chair with a hand to her mouth.

He closes his eyes, guilt flooding through. Grabbing tissues from under the sink, he drags out the chair opposite her, lowering himself.

"I'm sorry. I didn't mean to yell," he says, placing the box beside her.

"You think I'm disappointed in you?" she whispers—maybe to herself, maybe to him—but he answers anyway.

"Yeah. Sometimes," he says, scratching the back of his head. He looks up to stare at her. "Are you?"

She meets his eyes as a fresh bout of tears fills. "Oh, Roman."

He didn't think it was possible, but he's fairly certain he hears his heart crack. "Not to parent you or anything, but this is the part where you say that you aren't," he says, trying to make light of the situation and failing miserably.

She drops her hand to the table, sniffling. "I don't want to lie to you, honey."

He rises from the table, bracing his hand on the back of the chair. "Am I that bad?" He asks, hating the way his voice fractures.

"Ro," she says, exasperatedly, wiping her cheeks. "You're so *young*, and I guess I just—I just get a little frustrated sometimes with the choices that you make, you know?" she says, wringing her hands. "And everything that happened with Kareena. I want you to have a good life, baby. I want you to be happy. I want Lucy to be healthy. I want a good life for you. For you both."

I want Lucy to be happy. A good life for you.

Her words slice through him. Is that not what he's doing? Is he giving his daughter a bad life?

He nods, unable to form words as he wills the sting in his throat to disappear. He rubs his forehead slowly as he tries to make sense of her words.

"When have I ever told you that I'm not happy?" he asks, blinking hard and fast. "What about my life is so awful?"

He watches as his mom scoffs, wiping under her nose. "How can you be with that job that hardly pays, Roman?"

He pinches the bridge of his nose, taking in a deep, centering breath. "Did it ever occur to you that maybe I like working there? That maybe a degree in engineering isn't what I want?"

"Oh, *Roman*. Ever since you were little, you wanted to do this."

He laughs, but it's short. There's no humor behind it as he gestures toward her.

"No. It's what *you* want. You have this warped idea of what success looks like, and I'm breaking my back trying to give you what you want, but I'm tired."

She stands from the chair and grabs his arms. "Baby, listen to me. As a parent, you make certain choices for your kids. Your life … it isn't just yours anymore. You have to think about Lucy."

"I am," he says, gritting his teeth. "That's *all* I do. Why isn't it good enough for you? What about me?" he says, pushing a finger into his chest.

Her lips part, and she shakes her head as she stares up at him. "What about you? You lost the ability to do whatever you wanted when Lucy happened. Your actions got you here. Take responsibility for them, that's all I'm saying," she says, pressing her face into his chest. "I love you, Roman. I love you so much. But these are the sacrifices you have to make as a parent—as a father."

He sighs, resting his chin on her head. Danica rounds the corner, eyes comically wide, and mouths a *what the fuck* at him.

He shakes his head, raising his eyebrows as if to say I *told you so* as he rubs a soothing hand down her back.

Clearing his throat, he gently plucks her from his chest, not meeting her eyes. "I'm gonna head out. Homework," he says, moving past her and Danica to pick up a passed-out Lucy from inside the collapsible playpen set up in the living room. He reaches a shaky hand for the door and twists. "I'll text you when we get in, okay?"

He shuts it, fishing for his keys in his front pocket. Unlocking the car, he starts to strap Lucy inside her car seat. He hears the front door open but doesn't look up.

"Dude, what the hell?" Danica asks, her tone scathing.

Clasping the final buckle, he triple tugs on them to make sure everything is secure before closing her door. He wipes a hand down his mouth before circling to the driver's side. He opens the door and pauses, turning to face Danica.

She stares at him with wide eyes, walking forward. The streetlight in front of the driveway illuminates her against the house. The cicadas hum and chirp in the distance, and he wipes at his brow as the humidity causes him to sweat.

"Do you agree with her? Do you think she's right?" he asks.

She shakes her head. "Of course not, Ro. She doesn't always know what's best. That is your kid in there," she says, pointing to Lucy. "Not hers. You're doing the best—" She sighs, shaking her head. "You're doing everything," she says in a small voice.

"I wish that were true, Dan," he says, sliding into the car and starting the engine.

"But, Ro. Come on ... was it wise to have your *teaching assistant* watch her? Is that even allowed? Do you like her? Is that why?" He inhales sharply, not saying anything, and her eyes widen slightly. "Oh fuck. You *do*."

"Dan, don't make a big deal out of it. She's not interested. Nothing is happening. She just helped me out."

Danica raises her palms. "Hey, man. You do you. Just be careful. You already have a lot on your plate."

He exhales, tightening his grip on the steering wheel. "I know, Dan. I need to get my kid home and start on my coursework."

She nods, stepping back. "Okay, just call if you need anything."

"Yeah," he says, peeling out from the driveway until she's a speck in the rearview.

He wonders if Danica is right. Despite everything that's happened, he's *starting to really like* her. She's headstrong, independent, and sharp in a defensive way that makes him want to know why.

And now she's met his kid.

But she's made it very clear that nothing can happen.

So, he'll have to settle for whatever this is instead.

CHAPTER 20
Invisible

Jahlani

Ms. J

Do we have 2 show work for the quiz if it's multiple choice???? Is it for a grade?

Harrison

Sent from my iPhone

$$x = \frac{-b + \sqrt{b^2 - 4ac}}{2a}$$

"I think you broke my wrist, Teryn."

Jahlani cradles her left arm to her chest, laying it on thick, as she uses her chopsticks to grab her California roll. They're sitting outside a restaurant two blocks away from the self-defense class that Teryn had invited her to. The air smells of ginger and soy sauce, and the dark wooden tables hold empty bottles of soju, sauce, and plates of sushi.

Teryn laughs, her eyes crinkling in the corners as she chews her own spicy tuna roll. "You're so dramatic."

The sounds of the plaza mix around them. The laughter as kids spill out from their afternoon karate class, the faint grumble of a truck's muffler as it drives past, and the occasional scraping of chairs and tables being pushed around the restaurant as people come and go. The chill of the wind helps cool down Jahlani's body as they sit outside. Teryn finishes her food, leaning back with a satisfied look. "Hey, can I ask you something?"

Jahlani nods, trying to maneuver another roll into the chopsticks.

"I know you said we didn't do anything when you left all those years ago for school, but you never really told me what happened," she says, her finger tracing the edge of her glass.

Jahlani sighs, shrugging, discarding the chopsticks, and settling for her fingers. As she chews, she contemplates how to respond.

Teryn shoves her straw into her glass, using it to make her ice rattle. "It's fine, Jahlani. You don't have to tell me—"

"When my dad left, my mom was different," she starts, wiping her fingers against her napkin. "I mean, you expect that. Your husband just left you and your kid. Things aren't supposed to stay the same. But he left, and it was like I was invisible." She wraps her arms around herself as the wind from outside bites her flesh, no longer providing relief. "She started dating, and at first, I was happy. She was moving on, but I think in the process, she left me without realizing it."

"Shit, I'm sorry," Teryn says, looking down.

Jahlani shakes her head. "Don't be. It was years ago. I'm a big girl now," she says through a strained chuckle. "I swore I wouldn't be like her, so I didn't date for a few years. And then I met Micah, and I don't know, I wasn't invisible anymore. And it just didn't seem worth it to come back, especially when I got into the program for my master's and he asked me to move in."

Teryn nods, toying with her lips. "What's the story there?"

Jahlani exhales, recalling their last conversation. "Apparently ... I'm emotionally unavailable."

Teryn kisses her teeth. "What a twat."

Jahlani snorts. "I'm sorry, 'twat'?"

Teryn shrugs, laughing. "What? I watch a lot of British television in my downtime."

Jahlani clears her throat and sips her water when her phone vibrates. Most of the notifications inform her that students have taken the quiz for this week, there's a Duolingo notification, and a message that makes her blood warm and stomach flutter. Her fingers are quick to tap the screen, and her face flushes.

> **ROMAN**
>
> Any chance I can take you up on that offer tonight?

Jahlani reads the message once. Twice. A third time, making sure that her eyes aren't *deceiving her*, because the past week, he's been distant. He barely looks at her during the lectures, and he hasn't shown up for any office hours. She chews on her fingernail, typing four different responses before finally hitting send.

> **JAHLANI**
>
> Sure.

Jahlani clicks the phone shut, setting it down on the table, feeling like a schoolgirl passing notes to her crush.

"What was that?" Teryn asks, raising a perfectly arched brow at her.

"What was what?"

Teryn points an accusing finger at her phone. "*That.*"

"Nothing. It was just a few messages from students."

Teryn folds her arms across her chest. "Girl, *puh-lease*. You can't fool me." She leans forward, folding her palms on the table. "It's a guy, isn't it?"

Jahlani withers under her gaze but forces out a snort. "No."

Her eyes widen, and she gasps. "It's the guy from the bar, isn't it?"

Jahlani shakes her head, trying to stave off the heat. "It's not like that … I'm just helping him out a little."

"Teryn," Jahlani says, giving her a droll stare. "Nothing is happening. Nothing *can* happen. It's against university policy, and I would very much like not to get kicked out."

Teryn shrugs, grinning. "Okay."

"What?" Jahlani snaps.

"Nothing. Just sounds like you've given this some thought."

"I—what? No … That's not true," she says weakly, not even sounding convincing to herself.

Teryn laughs again, wiping under her eyes. "Look, all I'm saying is … you clearly find him attractive, why not have some fun?"

"Fun?"

Teryn rolls her eyes. "Yeah. Fun. Ever heard of it? It's when you do something that you *want*. Crazy concept, right?"

Jahlani looks down at the table, sighing. "No. It's not part of the plan."

"Plan?"

Jahlani nods, twisting to sit on her hands. "Yes. I finish my internship hours, get my degree, get a decent-paying job, and pay back my debt."

Teryn raises an eyebrow. "And then …?

Jahlani shrugs. "Then maybe I'll start dating again."

Teryn kisses her teeth, giving her a *you can't be serious* look. "That's a shitty plan."

"Hey."

Teryn raises her hands. "I'm just saying, it sounds like you've been running past some pretty nice doors."

"Not all doors are meant to be opened."

"They're not all meant to stay shut either."

This one is, she thinks. *It has too.*

Jahlani drags the tablet closer to pay the bill, but Teryn beats her, tapping the screen with her card.

"Thanks," she murmurs, thinking about how she just finished paying for her credit card bill. "Look, all I'm saying is that plans increase the likelihood of success."

"Oh yeah?" Teryn says, smoothing out a few dollar bills and placing them under the saltshaker. "How's that plan working out for you so far?"

Jahlani's mind drifts to the past few days—her increasing desire to be *near* him. During the day, when the sun is the brightest, when her head is the clearest, she catches herself *wondering* about him. About how he's doing and if there's anything *else* she can do for him. Is what she's doing enough? She wonders how she can ease his burdens. When she catches herself wondering, she convinces herself it's out of guilt for the things she did and said. It has absolutely nothing to do with wanting to know more about him and his world.

Or with the way he looks at her when she's talking.

Or the way his lips felt against her cheek.

"It's working out fine."

$$x = \frac{-b + \sqrt{b^2 - 4ac}}{2a}$$

As Jahlani pulls into the paved driveway, she releases a shaky exhale. She takes in the bungalow, the front porch swing, and the patch of lilies on the manicured lawn. She was hoping for a bachelor pad. Something impractical for her to criticize him on. Something to smother the good guy image she had clearly missed. To change his flag back to red.

Agonizingly, the flag is getting greener by the second. Smoothing down her hair, she shakes out her hands as she makes her way to the door. She knocks, and it swings open almost immediately. She gives Roman a tight smile as she takes in his ruffled hair and bare feet. Her eyes stretch past him in an attempt to look down the hallway because her curiosity is growing by the second and he's not moving.

He stands in some sort of trance-like state, staring. He's in loose shorts and a white cotton T-shirt. His eyes sweep over her before moving back to her face. He exhales, blinking.

Her smile grows slightly, and she clears her throat. "Correct me if I'm wrong, but I think this is the part where you invite me in."

He stuffs a hand into his pocket, stepping back to open the door wider.

"Jesus, yeah. Sorry. Come in."

She brushes past him, wagging her index finger. "You'd be dead if I were a vampire, Hayes," she says over her shoulder as she takes a few cautious steps into his hallway. As she takes in the console table overflowing with unopened mail and the vintage mirror hanging on the wall, his palms move to her shoulders, easing her out of her jacket, his fingertips cool against the length of her arms.

What a gentleman.

Too quickly, they're gone, and she finds herself wanting to chase the sensation. To get it back.

Roman Hayes is husband material (*clearly*), and she wonders to herself why no one has snatched him up.

Her head suddenly revolts at the idea of him taking someone else's coat for them and pushes the thought from her mind.

"Oh yeah?" he asks, his voice a low murmur as he folds the jacket over his arm, staring at her pointedly.

"Yeah," she says, stepping forward to run her fingertips along his neck. She doesn't miss the way he leans forward slightly, or the way his pulse seems to ricochet.

"I wouldn't go for the carotid artery. You're too tall," she says, sighing. "I'd have to settle for the radial artery," she adds, tapping his wrist. He's staring at her finger, then meets her eyes with a quirked eyebrow.

"Thought about that a lot, have you?" he asks, tilting his head with a carefree smile that seems to think he's caught her.

You know nothing, Roman Hayes.

"Of killing you? Plenty of times," she says through a murmur before pressing her lips together to keep from smiling.

He smiles, shifting closer. "Plenty, huh?"

She squints up at him, exhaling through her nose before turning away and stepping back. She clears her throat, crossing her arms over her chest as she watches him place her jacket delicately on the hook and takes in her surroundings. It's all so … cozy. Where she expected black and white IKEA furniture, she finds natural oak, rounded bookshelves, and scenic paintings.

"Shit," she murmurs to herself, but he seems to hear.

"What?" he asks, sounding slightly panicked as he moves to stand adjacent to her.

She blows out a breath. "It's just not what I expected."

"Thanks … I think."

She nods, sliding her hands into her back pockets, looking around with raw curiosity. The entryway smells distinctly of citrus.

He cleaned for me, she thinks, and the thought makes her head swim and her chest gallop.

He turns to face her, scratching the back of his head.

"House tour?" he asks, moving farther into the kitchen. She

trails behind, brushing her hand against the mirror in the hallway as she walks.

"Sure. Is it okay if I wash my hands first?" She halts in front of the kitchen sink. "I read more about her syndrome after you told me that day."

"You ... read up on it?"

She shrugs as she turns on the tap to the hottest setting, pumping soap into her hands.

"Why the tone of surprise?" she asks over her shoulder to meet his eyes. He leans against the opposite counter, scratching his chin as he watches her move around.

"Just ... not the most riveting thing to read."

"It wasn't too bad. I learned a lot," she says with a shrug.

"You like reading?"

She tilts her head, contemplating his question. "I like learning. I like the act of gaining new knowledge. It doesn't matter the type. Reading, videos, hands-on. I'm a continuous learner." She rubs her hands together, then shuts the tap off, taking the paper towel from his hand.

She doesn't miss the way his eyes track over to the bruise darkening on her wrist.

"Jesus, are you okay?" He grabs her wrist, cradling it in his palm. He sweeps his thumb over the mark tenderly, sending shivers through her.

"Yeah, I'm fine."

He gives her a hard stare. "Jahlani."

"I'm fine," she whispers, pulling her hand back. "Promise. Teryn and I went to a self-defense class."

Clearing his throat, he steps back. "You should put some cream on that."

"Sure," she says, nodding. Waiting as his cheeks turn the shade of red she's grown to crave. To watch for.

Roman moves down the hallway and she trails behind him, soaking in the wall of framed photographs of him and Lucy.

She lets out a soft laugh as they turn into a carpeted bedroom. "Cute."

He shrugs, biting back a smile as she steps further into the room to inspect it.

The walls are painted in cerulean with hand-painted clouds and seagulls floating across the horizon. It's open and expansive, as if the sky and the sea itself stretched from one end to the other. A whitewashed crib with gentle distressing stood in the middle of the room over a sandy, circular rug. Lucy's chest rises and falls evenly as they tread throughout the room.

The quilt features sea creatures—seahorses, whales, and starfish—their pastel colors soft and inviting. Above the crib, a driftwood mobile sways, its seashells and starfish catching the light. In the corner, a tiny rocking chair, painted in a soft mint green, sits beside a small bookshelf.

On the right wall, a large painting of the beach at sunset fills the canvas. The gentle waves are captured intricately alongside the pink and orange streaks across the sky. On the far right of the painting is the back of a full-length man gripping the hand of a small child. A girl. Jahlani leans down, her fingers brushing the wall. She turns to find Roman leaning against the doorway.

"Is this—"

"Yeah."

She turns back to face the painting, continuing to run her fingers over the wall. "It's beautiful."

He clears his throat. "My mom did it."

Standing to her full height, she faces him with wide eyes. "Your mom did this?" she repeats, keeping her voice low.

He nods. "She did the whole thing."

She blinks. "She's incredible."

"Yeah," he says, looking around the room. "She was an art major in college. She owns a studio downtown. She holds classes during the week," he says, moving back out into the hallway.

"Does she freelance?" she asks, trailing behind.

Roman nods, rubbing the back of his neck. "Sometimes when business is slow," he says, shutting the door softly, before leaning on the handle. "When she's not watching Lucy."

She turns to face him and folds her arms over her chest. "So, what happened to you? Where's your talent?"

He laughs, pushing from the door so that he's in front of her.

"You saw the clouds in there," he says, hooking his thumb over his shoulder. "I did those."

She hides a smile behind her fist, clearing her throat to sound serious.

"Wow, that's something."

He draws near her. "Are you making fun of me?" he asks, tilting his head down at her.

She lets out a soft laugh, turning away to pad down the hallway.

"Who, me? I would never."

She thinks about him here late at night, staying up with a crying Lucy, as he guides her through the rest of the house, his hand resting every now and then against her shoulder, her elbow to tug her here, her back to guide her there. They return to the kitchen, and he pours her a glass of water, which she finishes immediately, her mouth apparently drier than she realized. He says something, but she doesn't hear.

Her eyes snap back to his. "I'm sorry—what?"

He leans forward, rocking on his heels. "I said you should come with us next time."

"Come with you …" She trails off, her eyebrows scrunching. "To the beach."

"Oh, I—"

"Or not."

She toys with the bracelet on her wrist, looking down. "Yeah, I'm just not a beach person."

"Not a beach person?" He repeats slowly, his head leaning to the side.

She shrugs, blowing out a breath. "I don't know how to swim."

Now his lips part and his eyes widen. "You live in *Florida*, and you don't know how to swim?"

"I just … never had time," she says, sipping from the second glass of water he pours for her. "What?" she asks as he studies her, eyes clouded in thought.

"I could teach you," he says. "I'm an excellent swimmer."

Her mind wanders to a shirtless Roman at the beach. The salt from the sea, the grain of the sand, the heat from the sun, her legs around his waist, her in his arms—

"No time," she whispers, and to her dismay, she sounds winded.

He tuts, finishing his own glass. "Make time, Jones."

CHAPTER 21
Distracting

Roman

Roman smells something sweet as he drops his keys on the console by the front door. In the hallway mirror, he sees that his cheeks are flushed. He loosens the tie around his neck, leaving it hanging as he works a few buttons undone walking further into the house.

The lights are off in the hallway.

"Jahlani?" he asks in a whisper.

When there's no response, he rounds the corner crossing the threshold to the living room, and the sight before him causes his heart to lodge in his throat. Lucy is wrapped in Jahlani's arms as they both breathe evenly, their eyes closed. The television still flashes with animated figures, causing different colors to extend over their features.

He wipes a hand down his mouth, staring at how peaceful they look unsure of what to do. He knows he should pick Lucy up, and put her in the crib, but the greedy part of him wants to take it in.

How right they look together.

Whole.

Roman tiptoes forward, clicking the remote to turn the television off and that wakes Jahlani. She blinks, before looking down at Lucy.

"Hey, what time is it?" she asks, her voice thick. She shifts against the couch, pulling Lucy closer to her.

He clears his throat, sinking next to her so that their knees brush. "A little after midnight," he murmurs.

"Hmm. Sorry for not putting her in the crib, she convinced me to watch the show and I couldn't say no to this face," she says softly, leaning her head back.

"Yeah," he chuckles. "She has that ability."

Jahlani nods, her eyes drifting shut again and he has to restrain himself from asking her to stay the night.

He stands abruptly, trying to put some distance and her eyes fly open again. "Here, let me put her to bed so you can get your stuff."

As he gathers Lucy against him, her head rolls against his neck and he can feel that she's hot. He inhales her powdery scent as he walks with her to her room. He places a soft kiss on her head as he lays her down in her crib, undoing a few buttons on her onesie before shutting the door softly.

He returns to find Jahlani leaning across the counter, engrossed in something on her phone.

This woman.

He stands for several moments in the archway studying her. Trying to process the shock of seeing her in *his fucking kitchen*. She's shed the oversized sweater from earlier and now stands in a white cotton T-shirt with a low V-neck. Her braids cascade down her spine while her black leggings hug the length of her toned calves.

Jahlani in his house might be his favorite version yet.

Her lips turn up at whatever she's watching, and the deep glow from the Edison bulbs above her seems to sharpen her. Put her in this golden spotlight that's hard to look away from.

Or is it him?

He strides forward until he's next to her because she's in his goddamn kitchen and isn't paying him any attention. He leans against the counter opposite from her.

Look at me. Pay attention.

"How was she?" He asks, his voice a deep rumble.

She finally turns to face him, her lips parting as her eyes wash over him. She shakes her head, looking back down at her phone.

"Yeah. I kind of love her. Sorry again for not putting her in the crib—she kept crying, and I sort of panicked."

He runs a hand through his hair. "It's okay. Do you want a drink?" he asks, moving to grab glasses from the cabinet.

"No, thanks," she says, still very much engrossed in whatever is on her phone. He pours himself one, bringing it to his mouth.

"How was work?" She asks.

He almost chokes on the dark liquid as he swallows, before setting the glass down.

Her back is to him, and he braces his hands on the counter to steady himself because it's all so domestic.

Her in his house. In his kitchen. Asking about his day.

She turns to look over her shoulder, one eyebrow raised. "Did you hear me?"

"Yeah," he says, wiping a hand down his shirt. "Sorry," he adds, scratching behind his ear. "I guess I'm just not used to anyone asking about my day."

And this seems to catch her attention, because her lips part ever so slightly, and she turns fully, mirroring his stance against the island.

"Oh. Well then, let me be the first to break the cycle," she says, a twitch on her lips. "How was your day?"

Roman swallows. "It was good … great. Nothing too crazy happened," he says, clearing his throat, hating how nervous he sounds, and he wonders if she knows how much power she has over him.

He closes the distance, sliding up to her, so that his left arm is brushing ever so slightly against her right.

"What are you watching?" he asks as he tilts his head in the direction of her phone.

"It's a pimple-popping video," she murmurs, turning back around to face it.

"A what?" he says, his mouth twisting as he peers at her phone.

She turns to face him, seemingly in a daze because she repeats it, more hesitantly. "A ... pimple-popping video?"

"What the hell is that?"

She clears her throat, seemingly embarrassed. "It's where a dermatologist pops people's pimples. They're actually really satisfying to watch," she says, almost shyly, turning back, and pressing the play button.

Stepping forward, he places a hand next to her arm on the countertop, partially bracing himself behind her. His chest flutters as his eyes bounce between the screen and the expanse of her cheek. The screen and the curve of her lip. The hair in her eyebrows, the arch of her neck.

For the next eight minutes, they stand side by side in his kitchen watching the video. She's quick to answer any questions he has, and he watches her intently. Anytime she shifts, whatever perfume she has on overwhelms him. It's sweet.

Distracting.

"See? It's interesting, right?" She turns to look up at him, smiling brightly.

He gives her a closed-mouth smile, stepping back to the opposite side.

Not like this.

"Hmm. Never show me those again, please."

Her smile falls and she clicks the phone off, flipping it over. He lets out a soft laugh. Folding her arms over her chest, she leans against the island. The clock reads that it's just past midnight. He knows he should send her off, thank her for watching Lucy, walk her out to her car, tell her goodnight, but—

She's in his kitchen, and he wants to keep her there.

"What am I smelling?" he asks, trying to distract himself.

She sniffs, turning her nose up. "Cinnamon rolls."

His stomach growls then, and she laughs slipping on his mitts. He watches, in a daze, as she pulls out the tray from the oven.

"They're done. I just put them back in there to keep them warm."

Snapping out of his stupor, he shakes his head. "Wait, why did you make cinnamon rolls?"

She shrugs, placing the mitts back in the drawer with the takeout menus.

She knows his kitchen.

"I used to make them with my cousin, Teryn, when we were kids, after my parents divorced. It's my comfort food. But, I'm not sure you deserve any," she says, nudging her head toward her phone. "Since you had so much to say about one of your favorite pastimes."

Reaching forward, he pulls one from the sheet, and bites into it.

"Holy shit."

Her eyebrows raise. "Good?"

"It's the best thing I've ever had in my life," he says, tipping his head back as he swallows before meeting her gaze.

She rolls her eyes, grabbing her own. He watches her chew through it. She tilts her head, seeming to analyze the baked goods as she swallows.

"It's okay," she says, chewing thoroughly. "It's missing something."

He grabs a second one. "What's in this?" he asks, his mouth tasting of sugar and dough and cinnamon. Of her creation.

Her eyes flash to him. "Not telling," she says with a teasing shake of her head.

"Come on, tell me." He pushes away from the counter. "You owe me," he adds with narrow eyes.

She gives a defiant shake, and he steps closer as she swallows the last piece of her bite, some icing lingering.

Roman swallows, gesturing to his lip. "You have some here."

Her hand flies to her face. "What? Is it gone?" She wipes frantically.

"Here." Roman's left hand slides behind her neck, tilting her head back while his right thumb brushes the corner of her mouth. He drags it down, brushing her bottom lip in the process. Her skin is smooth. Her lip, slightly damp. His finger lingers longer than necessary, and he hopes that she's okay with it, but also can't bring himself to care if she isn't. Their eyes lock and he wants nothing more than to take this a step further. He wants to know what else she would allow him to do. He wants to push himself against her, to make her feel what she's doing to him. He wants to know if this is just an itch or a full-blown rash. He wants—

"Got it?" she says, but it sounds raspy. Her hand lightly grips the one against the back of her neck.

"Got it."

He releases his hold on her, stepping back, his stomach clenching.

"Jahlani—"

"I should go," she says. "It's late." He watches her fly around his kitchen island. A blur of movements.

He blinks. "Yeah. Sure. Thanks again."

She slides her purse onto her shoulder, stepping toward the front hallway. He trails behind, flipping on the light switch as she presses her feet into her sneakers, not bothering to tie them.

She spins on her heels, patting her pockets, before she fishes her keys out. She blows out a breath, wrapping her hair into a low bun before flashing him a small smile.

"Goodnight, Roman."

Her shoes.

Crouching down to her left foot, he reaches out, pressing his fingers into her calf to steady her leg as he lifts it. She lets out a sound, but he ignores it, making sure to double-knot before moving to the other side. When he's finished, he taps her foot, dragging his fingertips over the muscle of her calf as he rises to his full height. In the process, they've inched closer—too close now.

She's looking up at him, blinking, her mouth slightly open, and he clears his throat when she breathes out slowly. Their eyes lock onto each other and he watches as several expressions play out across her features.

Confusion creases her brow, a trace of annoyance crossing her forehead, but her eyes say something else. They lower and fall to his mouth before moving back up. They search and stare and wait.

And his do the same as he leans in closer, searching and staring, and waiting.

It's there, the subtle shake of her head, and maybe she does it subconsciously, but it's enough to stop him. He rubs a hand over his mouth, stepping back.

"Goodnight, Jahlani."

She exhales slowly, reaching for the door handle and twisting.

"Goodnight," she says, her voice soft.

Back in the kitchen, he waits for the latch to click, for the tires to crunch across the driveway—then unzips his pants, the noise echoing in the desolate kitchen as he works over himself. He can't seem to stop his mind from reeling back.

He knows he shouldn't be doing this, but his hand tightens. He catches sight of her cardigan, draped over the back of the couch, and he squeezes his eyes shut, his head falling back as a soft groan escapes.

Thoughts of his arm brushing against her—her in his kitchen, *is it gone?* His palm on her neck, the tension in his stomach builds as he quickens his pace.

He thinks of his thumb on her lip, a breathless *got it.* His name from her mouth, the rise and fall of her chest, her body pressed against his, his erection pressed against his zipper, and he thinks *she fucking felt it she had to have* as he pulls and twists, his breath coming out harsh. The muscle of her calf. Him on his knees, her above him. Her hand on his wrist, her shifting ever so slightly against him, her eyes heady, and heavy.

He braces his free hand on the counter's edge as he lets go with a drawn-out groan.

His winded breaths echo through the space, and he sinks into a stool at the counter.

"Fuck."

CHAPTER 22
Friendly Friends

Jahlani

As Jahlani pulls onto the deserted highway, she tries to focus all her efforts on recalling pi—and none of it on him.

Because they have rules.

Because she's a professional.

But there is nothing professional about the way she's thinking about the ghost of his thumb against her bottom lip.

Calm down—nothing happened.

It's concerning how much influence he has on her body. She misses her exit and turns down the wrong street—twice.

As she bustles down the hallway and into the shower, she decides she imagined the whole thing.

But as she lies in bed, she dreams of tortured green eyes, smooth hands, and silky lips across her skin. Jahlani's lips part, and her stomach sinks as Roman's words make an appearance for the hundredth time tonight.

Got it.

And then his hand is slipping in between her thighs, parting them gently, his flesh hot on hers, his mouth moving against her skin as he rasps her name and she moans his—

She sits up suddenly—on the edge—and groans in frustration, wiping a hand down her face. She bites her lip, wanting so desperately to break her own rule. When the light on the clock alerts her to the fact that she's only rested for two hours, she folds herself back onto the bed. She fluffs the pillows, adjusts her silk wrap, flexes her hands. Feeling heat creep up her skin, she throws the covers aside before lying flat on her back.

After another few restless minutes, she resorts to a tried-and-true method: counting sheep. Twenty-two is all she manages before the need settles in again. The ache sweeps through her body, the *pressure* festering in her core.

Got it.

This time, the scenery changes. This time, they're in a hallway and he's letting his bag fall to the ground, peeling her cardigan from her shoulders before pressing his tongue against the column of her throat, her collarbone. He's pushing and pulling. Licking and sucking. Traveling across her skin, exploring areas that she didn't even know could make her *feel* anything before he turns so that his back is against the wall and she's threading her hands in his hair. Reciprocating. Moving in time with him.

Th en they're sliding down, her knees landing outside of his thighs as he explores her mouth, the curve of her ass as he draws her hips to press down against him.

Jahlani's eyes snap open, and she swings her legs over the bed. She takes several deep breaths before moving to the bathroom to grab some melatonin capsules.

As she closes the cabinet, she catches sight of her flushed skin and feverish eyes. She draws a hand to the corner of her mouth that he touched, dragging her finger in the same path, causing shivers to course through. Squeezing her eyes shut, she flips the tap on before throwing the pills back and drinking.

Moving back slowly, Jahlani falls back against her sheets. As sleep begins to take her under, she wonders distressingly if he's thinking about her the same way she's thinking about him.

And it's the lie that she feeds herself, that he isn't, which puts her mind to rest.

$$x = \frac{-b + \sqrt{b^2 - 4ac}}{2a}$$

"Hey, Professor Jackson, I'm having trouble figuring out—"

Jahlani comes to a halt, hand on the doorknob of his office. Because Evangeline is there. Striking, powerful, *could ruin your life with a few sentences* Dr. Evangeline Hunt is there—and she's *crying*.

In Jackson's arms.

"Jahlani," Dr. Hunt starts, trying and failing to untangle her limbs from a seemingly reluctant Jackson.

Jahlani's eyes widen as she takes a step back.

"I am … so sorry. I should've knocked."

Evangeline waves her off, giving a tight smile. "No, you're fine."

"Yes, you should have," says Professor Jackson, eyes remaining on Evangeline.

Feeling uncomfortable, because she had very clearly interrupted something, Jahlani starts to walk back out the door. Back into a world where she didn't wonder if Hunt and Jackson screwed each other on his desk.

"I'll come back later."

"Sounds like a great idea," says Professor Jackson at the same time that Evangeline says, "No, you stay, I'll go."

Jahlani blinks, unsure of what to do. She feels like a child with her hand caught in the cookie jar, and now her parents are fighting over how to punish her.

Jackson's eyes narrow as he steps toward her. His voice is low. Different. "Evangeline, we need to."

Jahlani turns away, a flush rising through at the intimacy of the moment.

Evangeline waves him away, stooping to grab her purse.

"We'll talk later, John." She turns to face Jahlani, giving her a pleasant smile. Her eyes are puffy and the bags that she's packing under her face look dark and sullen. She looks destroyed.

She squeezes Jahlani's arm as she passes by her. "Don't let him work you too hard," she whispers before slipping out the door.

For several beats, Jahlani and Jackson just stand in the room.

"I am really sorry. I didn't know she was in here."

He sends a thunderous look her way. "Don't you know how to knock?"

Jahlani's throat dries. "Yes. Sorry. The door was open. So, I just assumed—"

"Well, don't next time," he says, voice harsh as he rounds his desk.

Jahlani opens her mouth, then closes it, her face flaming.

"Right, sorry again. I'll catch you at a better time," she says, heading back out.

"Wait, Jahlani." He exhales, taking off his glasses, attempting to clean them before throwing them against the table. He rubs two fingers against the bridge of his nose. "Sorry. I don't mean to be so abrasive. What did you need?" he asks, stretching out his hand.

She steps back. "It's nothing. I'll figure it out."

He nods, busying himself with papers on the desk, and she turns out of the office. Walking out of the building, she shoves the papers into her bag, making a mental note to work out the problems later. She walks out to the parking lot, thankful that it's a Tuesday and she most likely won't see—

"Jahlani."

She finishes shoving her bag into the passenger side before turning to face him.

"Roman, hey."

He's parked three cars down and doesn't make any moves to close the distance between them. *Good*, she thinks. *Stay right where you are.* Clutching her keys, she starts toward the driver's side.

"Jackson?" he calls out.

She nods, sending him a tight, *take a hint* smile. "Yup," she says, "You here for a lecture?"

He nods, the October chill sending brown strands of hair across his face. "Unfortunately."

Jahlani thinks about how stiff their interaction is. They're good now. One might even go so far as to say they're friendly friends, despite the very vivid, very provocative sexual fantasies that have been growing in number.

Because it's becoming increasingly hard not to stare when he's heading out the door when the lecture is over, and it's difficult not to notice that he always has an extra water or snack when he makes it to office hours. She hates how much she's reading into everything, and she hates even more that she can't act casual.

Be *normal*.

Not think about the fact that she thinks about the way he smells as he's across from her. Not think about the fact that he does it for her.

She inhales. "Well, I'll—"

"Did you eat?" he asks, his voice light.

She looks down at her feet before meeting his concerned gaze.

"Yeah," she breathes. "I ate."

He nods, drumming his fingers against his car door, looking as though he's working himself up to say something that she knows she ultimately will turn down or say no to.

"Okay," she starts, dipping her head into her car. "I'll see you—"

"Are you busy?" he blurts out.

She stops, one leg halfway in, and blinks, straightening out. "Busy?"

He shrugs like this is entirely casual. Not a big deal. "Lucy's been asking for you, and I might need some help studying for this exam."

She shakes her head. "Roman, you know I can't."

He raises his hands up in defense. "Okay, okay, but Lucy really is asking for you." He slides his hands into his front pockets. "Think she might like you more than me."

Jahlani lets out a soft laugh. "Well," she says, sighing dramatically. "I do tend to have that effect on people."

He smiles, and even though he's at least six feet away from her, her body lights up as if he's right next to her. His thumb on her mouth, *got it*, his front pressed against her.

"I can't," she says, exhaling shakily. "I have plans."

His eyebrows draw in, and she realizes how that sounds. She feels the sudden urge to reassure him that *no, she's not going to get railed by some guy*, so she quickly amends her statement.

"With my mom," she says, feeling her chest flutter when the dark look passes from his face. She feels pleased and then wants to scold herself for doing so. "Rain check?"

His smile is small and doesn't quite meet his eyes. "Sure."

She sends him a small wave, slipping into her car and peeling out of the lot, trying—and failing—not to watch his figure disappear in the mirror.

$$x = \frac{-b + \sqrt{b^2 - 4ac}}{2a}$$

Jahlani hears the faint sound of laughter from the kitchen as she slips her shoes off and sets them on the rack. She sets the incense that's slid off the holder back into position, swiping the ashes into her palm to dump them out. Another bout of laughter is heard, and she swings around the corner into the kitchen to find her mother perched at the table with an older man. The house reeks of weed, and her eyes bounce between her mom's glazed eyes and the guy's beady gaze as she opens the trash can.

"Mom, I thought we were having dinner tonight."

"We are," her mom says a little too loudly. "But Dick will be joining us."

Dick stands. "Richard, but everyone calls me Dick."

His hand is dry and cracking as he extends it, but Jahlani shakes it, giving a tight smile.

"Yeah, she's real pretty, Yolanda," he says, moving to the fridge to grab a beer. "Just like you said. She takes after her mother." He gives her mom a wink.

Jahlani watches as her mom breaks out in a fit of hysterics, a new wave of realization washing over her as she takes them in because it's high school all over again.

"I only have enough food for the two of us," Jahlani bites out, pressing her hands to the counter.

Her mom waves a hand, kissing her teeth. "It's fine, just share it out for you and Dick."

Jahlani works her tongue into her cheek as she watches Dick move to sit opposite from her mom. Her eyes narrow as he lights his joint, smoke filling the air.

Her mom coughs, waving her hand in her face. "You know I don't like it when you do that," she says, in a small voice.

Jahlani purses her lips, shaking her head at how *docile* her mother sounds. How weak.

Her mother is not weak.

She watches with tense shoulders as Dick does it again, this time intentionally exhaling in her direction, a glint in his eyes.

"She said she doesn't like that, *Dick*," Jahlani says, sending him a pointed look, her skin flushing.

Her mom's wide eyes snap to hers and she sees something shimmer in them that she can't quite place.

"Jahlani, baby … it's okay—"
She shakes her head, suppressing the urge to scream back at her that *none of this is fucking okay*. Not the way she treats Jahlani, not the way she gets treated by men, and most of all, the way she treats herself.

Jahlani inhales deeply, clearing her throat. "You know what? It's fine," Jahlani says, moving back toward the door to slip her shoes on. "You two can have it. I have plans with a friend anyway."

$$x = \frac{-b + \sqrt{b^2 - 4ac}}{2a}$$

Jahlani is catastrophically terrible with directions, with reading maps, with finding landmarks. So, it's concerning how easily she gets to his place. It's useless, really. She'd be better off memorizing a route to the emergency room. Not the house of Roman Hayes.

Straight on the expressway for eight miles, left on Galen Way, past the dog park, and the first right on Leeland Street. She maneuvers the car into park, stepping out with the bag of food, smoothing down her hair. She doesn't get to knock because the door swings open, and he's there.

Hair dripping with remnants of soap, a faded tour shirt, and gray-washed shorts moving with him as he braces an arm against the doorway, blinking down at her.

She holds out the brown paper bag, feeling absurdly lame. Like a stray starved for attention.

Or maybe just for him.

"I brought doughnuts."

CHAPTER 23
Love on the Brain

Roman

When Roman sees her, the first thing that comes to mind is how much of a *terrible fucking idea* it was to invite her over again. It's far too intimate. It's too secluded, and worst of all, it's his house. Here, he used to be able to think. Here, he used to be able to breathe.

Here, he was safe.

It was pure.

Untouched.

There were no remnants of the sea green jacket. Of fruit-scented hair wash. No imprints of her laughter within the echoes of the wall, no woman-shaped impression in his sofa, no relics of her time within the confines of this house.

Here, he was free from the increasingly dangerous, eroticizing, loud, *unbefitting* thoughts of the woman who has bulldozed her way into his central and peripheral nervous system.

But now.

Now, it's ruined. He's ruined.

Because it's his house, and he knows it like the back of his hand. He knows the best places to sit for a good view of the television, the perfect temperature to set the thermostat at so it's not too hot for him and Lucy, the ideal time to start the washer and dryer so that it doesn't disturb his daughter. And now all he can think about is her.

In his kitchen. On the dining room table.

In his bedroom.

She leans against the doorway in a layer of fabric that *has* to be destroying the blood circulation in her body, but is doing *everything* to accentuate the roundness of her breasts, the muscles of her thighs, the curve of her arms, and—

"Roman. You gonna let me in or has the offer been rescinded?"

His eyes cut to her own, and he steps backward.

How could she possibly think that?

He shakes his head, letting out a strained chuckle.

"Shit, yeah. Come in."

Just thinking about how I could lock this door, spread your legs open, and work you up until morning against it. The bookshelf. The floor. Anywhere. Everywhere.

His fists clench at his sides as his stomach dips.

"Just thinking how nice you look," he finishes in a raspy, uneven tone.

He clears his throat again as a gentle smile seeps onto her face, like his pathetic attempt at a compliment actually *did* something for her, which is now doing something for him.

"Thanks," she says, sliding past him to slip off her shoes. He follows slowly behind her and moves to the fridge. "Do you want something to drink? Water, wine?"

"I'll take a glass of wine."

He looks up and sees that she's now positioned herself on top of the island. Quite comfortably, and he wonders *would she mind?* Would she really hate it if he drew her leggings down over her ass and thighs until they were a heap of fabric on his kitchen floor—if he worked his mouth over her body, slipped his fingers inside her, and watched her unravel with his name on her lips? Would it be so bad?

She murmurs something, snapping him back to the present conundrum: a very real, very titillating Jahlani on his kitchen island.

Slamming the cabinet shut, he pours her drink.

"Lucy's asleep?" she asks as he hands her the drink.

He hums in response, taking a sip from his own.

"Bummer," she says, pouting, and he wants to scream at her not to do that, but instead settles on reaching for a doughnut from the bag.

He extends one to her, and she takes it—the heat of her fingertips traveling his entire system. As she draws her fingers into her mouth, one by one, he's unable to look away.

He clears his throat. "What happened to your plans with your mom?"

Her eyes catch his. "Oh, so you don't want me here. It's fine. I'll take my doughnuts." She starts to slide from the counter, but his hand presses her hip back down and he stands in front of her to block her.

He rolls his eyes, taking another doughnut from the bag.

She sighs as she brushes her hands together before drinking from her wine glass. "Dick happened."

He arches a brow, and she sends him a pointed look. He raises his hands as if to say *you said it, not me.*

"That's his name. Richard, but *his friends call him Dick*," she says in a mocking tone. "My mom and I don't really get along." She sets her glass down. He shifts closer, reaching for another doughnut, and his arm brushes against her thigh, sending sparks through his chest.

"She developed this really bad habit when I was a kid, after my dad left, of just bringing home all these random guys. She would just shower them in affection and give them all this attention, and I was just kind of there. Forgotten. Like tonight," she says, laughing bitterly. "Tonight, she tried to make me serve him dinner like this is the 1950s and I'm his little housewife or something."

"I'm sorry," he says, his fingers drawing small circles against her leg.

She shrugs, tracing the rim of her glass. "I got used to it. I just worked harder in school, got as many scholarships as possible and left. I figured she wouldn't care if I did anyway."

"What about your dad? You never talk about him."

"My dad," she says slowly. "My dad has a new family with Helen. Helen is nice. They're having a baby. A girl. He's starting over. The perfect wife, the perfect daughter." She exhales, shaking her head, laughing silently. "Is it fucked up that I'm jealous of my unborn sister?"

She wipes at a lone tear, and his chest pinches. He wants to reach out and wrap her in his arms, but he doesn't. Instead, he continues to watch her, his eyes tracking her every movement.

"Ever since I moved back here, I've felt this weight on my chest. I'm doing everything wrong and saying everything wrong, and what happened with you just further solidified that my life is this bumbling mess."

Her shoulders are tense, and she doesn't meet his eyes as she slips off the counter and walks to the couch. She continues talking, and she sinks against the cushions.

He follows her, dropping into the space next to her, their bodies lined up together. She pulls a loose thread from one of the pillows as she continues speaking, her tone soft and murmured.

"Like, I'm twenty-six and I'm fucking drowning—*drowning* in debt because my dad is a useless piece of shit, and my mom won't even look at me, or hold a conversation with me and I shouldn't be here because this was not in my plan, like at all, but my stupid ex decided to cheat on me, and then my internship combusted, and it's just been one thing after another," she says, her glassy eyes meeting his.

Roman wants to find the right words to comfort her, to let her know that he's got her, and that he's here.

But most days he feels the exact same way.

And that scares him.

Because he has a little girl to take care of.

He has to be okay, no matter what.

"And then there's you," she says, scoffing, a tear spilling past. "You're always there. You're everywhere, and it's so irritating because in the grand scheme of things, my problems are so insignificant compared to yours, and that just makes me feel even shittier, and the cycle repeats. It's never fucking ending and I hate this," she says, her head dropping into her hands. Reaching forward, he tugs on her elbow, and she trembles against his chest.

"Jahlani, you're not a mess. You're just a person that got dealt some pretty shitty cards."

She pulls back, wiping under her eyes. "It's nothing. I'm being dramatic," she says, blowing out air between her lips.

He sighs. "Jahlani, nothing about what you just said was dramatic. Your parents neglected you. That's not nothing."

She nods, water filling her eyes. "Yeah, well when you put it that way, it sounds bad."

He pulls her back into his chest, shaking his head. "Baby, it is bad, and it affects you, and you're allowed to feel however you're feeling."

She exhales against him. "Do you think I need a therapist, maybe?"

His muscles tense slightly at the loaded question. "It might help to talk to someone about how you're feeling every once in a while, you know? Therapy isn't a bad thing."

"Yeah, I guess," she murmurs, burying her face closer. "I always wondered … why you smelled like this."

He clears his throat, his fingers grazing the length of her arm. Up and down. "Like what?"

She sits up, her hair framing her face. "I don't know how to explain it," she says, her lips twitching.

He leans closer, pushing her hair back before drawing her back to his chest. "Try," he whispers, skating his hand over her hair, her shoulder, her cheek. His fingers growing bolder over her body when she shivers.

"Roman," she says, her voice raspy. "If you keep doing that … I'll fall asleep."

His fingers stop their motion, and he settles back against the cushions, closing his eyes when his stomach clenches. She reaches up, grasping his hand and he looks down at her.

"Don't stop … it feels nice," she whispers, guiding his fingers over her scalp again. "So … yeah. Keep going. I'll fight it."

He swallows, picking up where he left off, and she curves further into his body. "You still didn't tell me what I smell like," he says, his voice rough.

She sighs, her own hand drawing down to her stomach. "Like lavender, and clean laundry, and … powder. Like a baby, which was confusing."

"Confusing how?"

"It was unexpected. Most guys smell like a night out, but you smelled like …"

He wets his lips, his blood turning hot under his skin. "Like?"

"Like a home," she says softly, pressing her face into his hand and inhaling. "You always do."

Fuck.

He isn't sure how long they sit there, but eventually she pulls back and mumbles something about needing to use the bathroom. When she steps back out, he's pulling out ingredients from the kitchen. Bracing his hands on the counter, he nods toward the water he poured for her.

"Drink this," he says, shoving a glass into her hands. Almost robotically, she brings it to her mouth. When she tries to bring it down, his hand is there, gently tipping the cup back up, his eyes on hers, urging her to empty it. When she finishes, she lowers it, letting out a shaky exhale.

"Thanks."

He reaches forward, prying it from her and setting it on the table. She wipes the back of her hand over her mouth.

"Better?" he asks.

"Better," she says in a low voice. She looks around at the food spread out. "What's all this?"

He slaps the table.

"Let's make cinnamon rolls."

She laughs. "Why? We just ate doughnuts."

He shrugs, scratching under his chin. "You said it calms you down. We don't have to actually eat them."

She smiles, walking until she stands next to him in the kitchen, her body brushing against his. "I'm in charge of whisking."

For the next twenty minutes, they stand side by side in his kitchen, laughing, talking, and forgetting.

Jahlani questions him about high school, and he obediently offers up the information, telling her about anything and everything she wants to know. Occasionally, his hand will skate down her back, her elbow, her fingers. He pushes each time. Seeing what he can get away with it, which is apparently a lot.

Because every now and then, she'll press her shoulder to his, she'll touch him as she laughs, she'll move a little closer. She'll break a rule and invite him into her space.

After they slide the tray into the oven and set the timer, Jahlani settles back on the kitchen island, her glass in hand, her braids in a loose bun.

His chest thunders against his ribcage because she looks comfortable.

She looks comfortable in *his home.*

And it's everything and nothing and he needs it to be *something.*

"Can I tell you a secret?" Jahlani says from her position on the island. Her feet swing from the edge. She's onto her second glass of wine as they wait for the timer to go off. He stands adjacent to her, his own glass in his hand.

"Mhm."

Her eyes widen, and she lets out a giddy laugh. "Okay, but you can't tell anyone."

He snorts, setting his glass down. "Okay."

She laughs again, biting her lip. She fans her face before exhaling slowly. "Okay, you know Dr. Hunt?"

He crosses his arms across his chest, his mind firing through all the faculty from the school. "Vaguely."

Jahlani makes an annoyed grunt. "Come on, she has blue eyes, brown hair ..." She trails off when he continues to stare. "Okay, well. I caught her and Jackson hugging in his office earlier today!" she says, seeming so impressed with herself for *gossiping* that he can't help the slow grin spreading on his face. She sighs, reaching for her drink. "It sounded juicier in my head."

Roman laughs, sending his head back. "Yeah, I can see that." He spins, inspecting the food in the oven before grabbing two porcelain plates from the cabinets and setting them down. With his back turned, he asks, "You think something's going on?"

He turns back around as she frowns, looking into her glass. "I don't know. I guess it wouldn't be allowed if they were," she says, meeting his eyes.

He inhales, wondering for a moment if they're talking about the same thing, but she swiftly changes the subject.

"Your turn now. Tell me a secret. Tell me something deep and dark and tragic," she says in a mockingly deep voice.

He laughs, folding his arms across his chest. "What do you want to know?"

She shrugs. "I don't know. You seem to know everything about me. I'm always spilling my guts to you, so it's only fair." She pats his shoulder, "Tell me something, and make it good."

He sighs, shaking his head.

"Come on," she croons. "Tell me all your secrets," she says in a horrible, witch-like voice.

He laughs, dropping his glass in the sink. He wipes his hands on the back of his shorts, turning to face her.

"Okay," he says, drumming his fingers on the countertop. "I don't like celebrating my birthday anymore."

She tilts her head. "Okay. Tell me more."

He exhales. "Um, well, I don't feel like I'm worth celebrating."

His words hang in the air between them, and the timer goes off. He rotates, turning it off and grabbing the oven mitts.

Jahlani is next to him, peering down as he tries to maneuver the tray out without burning either of them. "What do you mean you don't feel like you're worth celebrating?"

Setting the tray down, he slams the oven door shut with his hip.

He shrugs, removing the lid from the icing. He slathers it onto the first bun before handing the spoon to her.

He sighs, watching as she moves onto the third one.

"I'm a failure, Jahlani. I can't take care of my kid. She's always sick and I can't do shit. I'm always just there. Watching. I failed school. I already know that my mom is disappointed in me. She actually admitted it the other night ... So, yeah. There's nothing about me that's worth celebrating."

She hums, glazing the final bun before dropping the spoon into the sink.

"Well, it was dark. And a bunch of bullshit," she says, turning to face him.

His head rears back. "What?"

"Most of those things you just described are completely beyond your control. Did you make your daughter sick? Can you force your mom to be proud? Can you go back in time and make sure you pass your classes?" she asks, leaning forward slightly.

He shakes his head.

"Right, so. Maybe focus on the things that you can control, and you'll find all the things that make you worth celebrating."

"Like?"

She narrows her eyes. "Oh please, you're not slick. I'm not gonna say a whole bunch of nice things about you. Your ego is big enough."

He lets out an exaggerated exhale. "Can't blame a guy for trying."

She bumps his shoulder, looking away. "Like, I'm not going to tell you that you're ... annoyingly determined, and have ... incredible patience, or that your daughter is lucky to have a dad like you in their life, because that would just be ..." She licks her lips, looking up at him.

He angles his head down, closer to her. "That would be?"

She blinks at him, and he doesn't miss the way her eyes fall to his mouth, before stepping back.

Rubbing her hands together, she steps toward the tray. "Think it's cooled down enough," she says, looking up at him. Ripping off a piece, she chews, letting out a small moan of approval.

Fucking hell.

"It's good. Try it," she says through another bite.

She holds out the other piece between them. Stepping closer, he tilts his head down, grabbing her wrist that holds the piece. Her lips part when his mouth meets her fingers, and he feels her hand grow limp as he deliberately licks the icing from her fingers.

"You're right," he says. "It's delicious."

She shakes her head with wide eyes. "Roman, what—"

He pulls her forward until she's flush against him, her wrist still caged in his hand, her other hand warm on his abdomen.

"What are you doing here, Jahlani?" He asks, whispering.

"You invited me," she says through heavy breaths. "Should I go?"

He presses her closer, wrapping his free arm around her waist. "No, that's not why," he whispers. "That's not why."

She shifts against him, and he shuts his eyes as the sensation causes the pressure against his shorts to increase.

She's barely touched you, get a fucking grip.

"I came because I needed to get out of my house. You know, neglectful parent and all," she says through a strained chuckle.

He lowers his face, turning them so that she's pressed against the kitchen island. "No, that's not why, Jahlani."

Letting her wrist go, he wraps his hand around her waist as he curves her into his body. His heart knocks against his chest as he drops his nose into the curve of her neck, followed by his mouth.

"Roman," she says, but it comes out all raspy and weak and *not like* the Jahlani he knows.

Oh fuck.

He pulls back to see that her eyes are closed, her cheeks flushed.

Suddenly, her eyes open and bore into his, and he tries to control his breathing. "Tell me why you're here, Jahlani, because I'm trying not to cross the line even though … I'm fairly confident you already have. So, maybe just lie to me. Tell me it's in my head."

Her eyes bounce around his face. "I came because I …" She licks her lips. "I—" She looks down at his mouth before meeting his eyes. "I wanted to, Roman. It's not in your head."

He swallows, not moving, wanting to give her a chance to push him away because she's been drinking, but her hand is suddenly against the front of his shirt, and she's twisting it, forcing him to stay.

"Is that what you wanted to hear?" she asks, tilting her head. "That I wanted to be here. With you. That I like being around you, Roman, and I shouldn't," she says, moving so that she's inches away. "I shouldn't be here, doing this. And yet it's all I've been able to think about because I crossed the line way before you did."

And then she's fully pressing their mouths together, dictating the duration of the movement, the angle of his head, the amount of pressure, and it's not enough at all.

Not at all.

His palms press flat against the small of her back, traveling up until one hand covers her neck and she sighs into his mouth. She pulls her head back, and his eyes open as he gazes down at her. Her skin is flushed, and her eyes are low.

For several seconds, they watch each other. His fingers ghost over her mouth before traveling to her jaw. He inhales deeply, leaning back in, but not completely closing the space. Wanting to be sure.

But he's the one sighing when she presses her mouth to his again with more intensity than before. This time it's harder, like she's angry.

Like she's desperate.

He slides his tongue across the bottom of her lip before pulling gently. The next meeting of their mouths is open and deep, and he tries to savor the motion of their tongues infusing, its languid pace punctuated by the warm, intoxicating taste of grape and cinnamon and a whisper of vanilla on her lips.

He *really* tries, because he doesn't know how long he'll have her like this. All loose lips and pliant and *her* against his form.

Nothing like the Jahlani that he's grown accustomed to.

No, this Jahlani is risky. A rule-breaker. Willing to fall into the abyss with him.

They move together in earnest, and all the blood seems to rush to his groin in an instant when she pulls his bottom lip between her teeth. He groans and she pulls back a fraction, her words a whisper against his mouth. "Did I hurt you?"

"No, you didn't," he says against her lips. Sliding his hands under her thighs, he forces her onto the counter. Gripping her knees, he drags them apart until he's standing in between them. He guides both of her arms around his neck and sinks her fingers in, gripping the strands in earnest as he guides her mouth back to his.

His hands move up to clutch her neck as he works his tongue over her top lip. They both groan as their tongues meet, and her legs lift to wrap around his hips.

She pulls away and they both breathe against each other until he's moving her braids, tilting her neck, and sucking. Her moan is soft. Quiet even.

He wants her louder. Screaming. But then it occurs to him as she draws her hand to her mouth to stifle a slightly louder moan that she's trying to be respectful. She's trying not to wake his daughter.

She's being considerate.

He pulls her mouth back down to his and gives her a punishing kiss for being so *goddamn good*. For being *off limits*.

Jahlani's hand starts to lower. Slow. Discreet. It brushes over the front of his drawstring. Pulling back, he lowers his head watching as she tugs the knot loose. The snap of the waistband reverberates through the room. He watches intensely as her fingers start to inch down. He inhales sharply, catching her wrist.

"Being around you," she says breathlessly. "It's not good for me. I lose sight of my goal, my dream. You make me want to give it all up. You make me want to find a way to fit you into my plans, and I can't have that. There's only this."

His lips brush over the side of her neck. "Jahlani—"

"Do that again," she says. "It feels fantastic."

Like a puppet under her control, he moves his mouth over the bridge of her neck again, and again, until she's bending into him.

"That feels amazing. Why does that feel so good?"

And he isn't sure how long they stand there together. Her in his arms, her legs around his waist, his tongue on her neck, but every second it turns more frenzied, more rushed, less controlled. It's like they're trying to make up for all the times they missed out, and it still isn't enough.

He hears the static from the monitor before she does, and he pulls back to meet her eyes, but it's too late.

Because Lucy's cries sound through the kitchen, and she drops her eyes to the screen, touching her mouth. He watches her blink, her expression morphing into one of guilt as she looks away.

"Jahlani—"

"Go. Take care of her," she says, still not meeting his eyes.

He steps back as she adjusts her shirt, feeling torn.

"I'll be right back, just—don't move, please. I want to talk." He walks backwards, watching her shoulders hunch over as she nods her head, not seeming to fully register his request. He dashes into the bathroom that's in the hallway, sees his tousled hair, bruised lips, manic eyes, and thinks about how fucked he is because it was so much better than he imagined it being. But in all his imagined scenarios, he never made it to this part—the aftermath.

He knows she's a rule follower, he knows she's sitting on his island overthinking everything that just happened, if he could just soothe Lucy quickly.

He hears the soft click of the door closing and walks back out to the kitchen, a sniffling Lucy in his arms.

"Fuck," he whispers, moving to the entryway to turn the porch light on. He doesn't bother chasing after her. She needs space to think. He understands, really. He rubs Lucy's head, bouncing her before moving her back to her room and placing her in the crib.

They crossed the line. This time together, he thinks as he moves to the kitchen to place the cinnamon rolls in a container. He snaps the lid shut, shoving the container so hard it slides down the counter and falls off the edge.

"Damn it," he mutters, tugging his hand through his hair.

Wiping a hand down his face, he reaches for his phone to text her, but stops himself, throwing it onto the counter.

Sighing, he bends, picking up the larger pieces of glass before sweeping the remainder with the broom. As he drops into the stool, he decides that he'll give her two days.

After that, all bets are off.

Because if there was one positive thing that came from tonight, it was that he knows she wanted this just as much as he did.

CHAPTER 24
The Sober Theory

Jahlani

Ms. Jahlani,

Please give me an extension on the quiz that was due two weeks ago. My girlfriend of three years left me and I'm really going through it right now. Your understanding in this matter is highly appreciated.

Thanks,
Justin

$$x = \frac{-b + \sqrt{b^2 - 4ac}}{2a}$$

"Let's talk about principal component analysis, or PCA. Yes, it will be in the midterm in less than two weeks, so look alive people. So, what happens when you have, say, too much data, and it starts to look like a giant, unmanageable mess?"

Jahlani gestures at the projected slide, where a scatter plot filled with overlapping points appears.

"This looks catastrophic. But we can't just ignore it because it's big. That is where PCA comes in—by reducing the dimensions. You're basically summarizing a big chunk of data into a smaller set of important 'components' while keeping the most critical information.

Does that make sense so far?"

She turns back to face an almost empty room. Those who are there look like zombies. They offer the barest nods of understanding. She checks her watch, hoping to cut the lecture short. She can barely manage the migraine she's nursing right now.

A broad-shouldered guy in a small pair of frames raises his hand. "You won't lose data by doing that?"

Jahlani nods, reaching for her flask of ginger tea. "Yes, you're technically losing some information, but PCA is designed to keep the most critical parts. It works by finding the directions of maximum variance in your data, which, mathematically, we call 'eigenvectors.' These are the axes that matter most."

Turning, she writes the word *eigenvectors* on the board and underlines it.

"The great thing is that PCA gives us new axes that help us see patterns in our data we might have missed before. It's all about simplification without losing the essence of the story."

She pauses and looks around the room, more zombie-like stares. Sighing, she sets her cup down.

"Tell you what, I will end the lecture early."

A burst of cheers echoes throughout the room.

"*If* we get through these last two exercises with full participation. Meaning, I need all of you to tap your shoulder buddies and get them awake. You don't spend all this money on tuition to *sleep*."

She watches as several students tap the desks of others, and drowsy eyes lift and blink. A familiar pair never meets hers, and she's thankful, she thinks. She's been trying—and failing miserably—to not think about her actions from two nights ago.

Clearing her throat, she sets her drink back down.

"Welcome back to the land of the living. Here's what's happening:

I'm going to give you a dataset. Your task is to calculate the first two principal components."

Jahlani's eyes flick to her watch after thirty minutes, and she moves back to the front of the room.

"All right, I think you've got the basics down. Next week, we're going to talk about factor analysis, which is similar but focuses on underlying relationships between variables, rather than just reducing dimensionality. Please make sure you complete the practice module, as it will give you feedback on how to address any issues you encounter."

As students trickle out, Jahlani heads back to Jackson's office.

Two hours later, all she manages is a page of cat drawings. Jackson had already passed through letting her know she can head out early if she wants to, but she decides to stay, not wanting to go home. She still hadn't spoken to her mom and has had other things occupying her head lately.

She needs to focus on her essay. She needs to focus on getting her degree. She tears the fresh sheet of doodles from the notebook, crumpling it before throwing it across the room.

"Jeez, what'd I do this time?" Roman's toned arm reaches down to grab the crumpled paper, unraveling it.

Jahlani stands from the chair in record speed as her chest starts to pound.

"Roman," she says, running a trembling hand over her head. "What are you still doing here?"

He turns the crumpled paper toward her, giving her an arched eyebrow. "Didn't know you could draw. It's not bad."

She moves around the desk, snatching the paper from him, his familiar lavender scent overwhelming her before she moves back to the security of the grand desk.

"It's nothing. Something I do when I can't focus." She doesn't meet his eyes as she starts straightening papers. Checking the time on her laptop, she sees it's well after six.

From her peripheral vision, she sees his arms cross his chest and for some ungodly reason, her body seems to have a visceral reaction to the sight. She recalls those arms gripping her waist, pulling her in—

"You avoiding me, Jones?"

Her hands stop moving.

Absolutely.

"No, Roman. I'm not avoiding you."

"Well, you haven't looked at me once in the"–he looks down at his watch–"fifty-six seconds that I've been here," he says, closing the door.

She scoffs. "I'm busy, and in case you forgot, we had class today and Wednesday." She stands straight, crossing her arms over her chest. Her eyes flit to his for a moment and her body burns thinking of the way those same eyes looked at her in his kitchen. "Happy?"

A small smile grows on his face. "Ecstatic."

She moves again, placing her laptop in her bag.

"Okay, well. It's late, so I'm going."

"Can we talk?" he asks, tone low. He paces toward her, gripping the back of the chair across from her.

She shakes her head, her pulse quickening as she shoves her beat-up charger into the bag next.

"About?"

"The other night."

She stops moving, shutting her eyes. Her mind wanders back to his breath on her neck, his fingers on her thighs.

She opens her eyes. "I have no idea what you're talking about."

Now it's his turn to shake his head. "You're stubborn as hell."

He scoffs as he removes his bag from his shoulders, resting it in the leather wingback chair.

"Thanks, I get it from my mom." She resumes her task of packing her things. "I still have to submit this paper to Jackson."

"Jahlani." His voice sounds closer, but she doesn't look up, focusing her efforts on her bag and willing her body to stop flashing hot.

"And I need to input grades for the project—"

"Jahlani."

"And I need to finish all of this by tonight—"

"Jahlani, stop." He grips her wrist, halting her movements. He's made it past her security. Breached the place she thought she was safe. He towers over her, smile gone. Bending closer, he utters his words in a harsh tone. "You don't get to kiss me, run off, and then pretend that nothing happened."

Her eyes widen. "Will you lower your voice?"
He drops her hand, stepping back a fraction to fold his arms over his chest.

"Oh. So, you do remember?"

She exhales. "I—it's not—there's nothing to talk about. It shouldn't have happened Roman, okay? It was a lapse of judgment. I was drunk."
His eyes narrow as a soft scoff filters past his lips. "You're kidding."

She lifts a hand up in exasperation. "Roman, take a look around you! Do you see where we are? It shouldn't have happened," she grits out. "It shouldn't have. I shouldn't have done that, and we shouldn't be talking about it, *especially* here," she says, her voice serious. Unwavering. His expression is unreadable when she finally has the courage to look up. He nods his head as he stuffs his hands into his pockets.

"So, the only reason you touched me is because you were drunk?" She nods even though her stomach revolts and it feels as though someone is shoving a rock down her throat.

"Pretty much."

He rubs the back of his neck, stepping forward. "Have you been here all day?"

She nods, shouldering her bag. "Yes, and I really need to—what are you doing?"

Now a toe's length away, his eyes scan her face with an intensity that she wishes didn't affect her. She wishes to go back to before he could extract this type of reaction from her. It's too much and nothing at all.

His eyes flicker to her lips and his hand, warm and assured, slides to the side of her waist, pulling her closeles. "Testing a theory. At least, let me … just once."

"Roman, people could see."

"Just once." He breathes against her mouth, sealing the space between them.

And truthfully, Jahlani knows she can put up more of a fight, but as he walks them backward into the bookshelf and slides his tongue against hers, her flight and her fight mode seem to malfunction. He slides her bag from her shoulder and the sound of her things spilling out does nothing to cease their movements. He slots his thigh in between her legs, and she lets out a low moan when he shifts against her.

He pulls back, pressing a firm kiss to her neck. "I'm sorry you felt the need to run. You were probably so frustrated." A firm kiss to her lips. "I would have taken care of you. Let me try now," he says, guiding her hips to rock on his thigh.

She shudders, allowing him to do it once, twice, and then her sense of hearing seems to heighten and she's confident she heard footsteps just outside the door, and so she pushes him back.

"Roman. No, we can't. We can't."

He blinks, breathing heavily seeming to come out of a daze. "You feel this too, right?"

She shakes her head, adjusting her jacket when it slips down. "Nothing can happen. Nothing *else* can happen."

"*Jahlani.*"

"We *can't*," she says, her voice strained.

"Why?"

"Because … I'm your GTA."

"And?"

"*And?* And someone could find out."

"How would anyone?"

"When you look at me," she snaps, finally meeting his eyes.

He wipes a hand down the corner of his mouth. "When I look at you?"

"Yes," she hisses. "When you look at me it's different. It's not—I don't know how to explain it." A humorless laugh escapes her. "You look at me like—"

"Like I think about you. Like I want you," he supplies, sounding defeated.

Her stomach twists and she blinks. "Yes."

He drops his hands to his sides. "Like I can't think properly when you're around, and even when you're not, I'm pretty miserable on the days that I can't see you. The slightest shade of green makes me think of you and all I want to do when I see you is touch you. Hold you. Fuck you."

She blinks rapidly. "That's not … you can't say that."

His eyebrows raise. "What? Say that I want to fuck you? Well, I do. I can't help that. I can't help the way I look at you. I can't help thinking about you. About wanting to be around you."

A scoff slips out, and she's suddenly angry at his carelessness.

"Roman, you're talking about risking your diploma. For what—a quick fuck?"

He steps forward and his eyes narrow. "Is that what you think this is?"

"I don't know what this is," she snaps, pressing a hand to her forehead.

"Is that what you want?" he asks, quietly. She exhales, meeting his gaze.

No, what she wants is to be free of this constant need to see him.

"I don't know what I want," she says, her voice small. "But I do know that this won't end well."

"You don't know that."

She shuts her eyes, lowering her head. "Roman, I'm attracted to you. I am, but I need you to think about the bigger picture, because I am. I can't afford to change my plan anymore. I need this to go well so I can fix my life, and you need your degree to take care of Lucy."

They lapse into silence, the sounds of students transitioning to other lectures filtering through. She opens her eyes, stepping back.

"Shit," he says, dragging a hand through his hair, taking several steps back. His eyes meet hers. Firm. Intense. Lingering.

And she finds herself leaning forward as he walks up to her, wrapping his hand over her jaw as he presses another firm kiss to her lips.

"Damn it. Damn you," he says in between the collision of their mouths. "Fucking hell."

"I'm sorry," she says, when he allows her to catch her breath. "I'm sorry," she repeats once he unwinds himself from her, stepping back.

"Don't," he says, shaking his head. He runs a hand through his hair. *"Jesus.* I have to go."

Her heart squeezes in her chest as she watches him pick up the contents of her bag and set it on the desk before moving to slide his bag on his shoulder.

"Roman" she calls out, stopping his movements. "We're okay, right?"

"Yeah, we're good."

But even she knows he's lying as he walks through the door.

CHAPTER 25
How It Should Be

Jahlani

Jahlani used to love the holidays. When she was younger and both her parents were around, it was the things she looked forward to the most as a kid. Growing up in a somewhat religious Caribbean household meant that Halloween was a no-go for her. She spent most of them sneaking around with her cousins for candy. But Thanksgiving and Christmas were *everything*. At Christmas, they'd decorate the tree together, she'd make a list, and then she'd take turns going shopping with each parent, a true *non-believer*, but she wasn't upset. Always too logical to believe in things like the Easter Bunny. The Tooth Fairy. Bloody Mary. It was the act of spending time with her parents that she liked.

Thanksgiving is her favorite.

Was her favorite until the divorce. Every year until high school, they would alternate holidays, until she left for college and then she just stopped showing up for either one. Not that they noticed or cared.

Which is why she can't stop the twitch that grips her left eye as she reads the confirmation email her dad had forwarded to her last night. A round trip to visit him for the weekend. She immediately dials his number, chewing on her lip as she waits for him to pick up.

"Jahlani."

"Dad, hey."

She exhales, deciding on her next words carefully. "The plane ticket?"

"Yeah."

She blinks slowly. "Why?"

His sigh is deep and heavy and so *him*. "Well, Helen figured …"

Ah. Helen.

Jahlani doesn't hate Helen. Truthfully, she's a wonderful person—an elementary school teacher who volunteers at a homeless shelter on weekends, walks when she can to cut carbon emissions, and takes care of everyone. She takes care of him. She reminds my dad to take his medication. She makes sure he takes care of her.

And that's the problem.

"Jahlani? Did you hear me?"

She blinks, shaking her head. "Sorry, bad connection," she mumbles.

"Okay, well. Let her know what you want."

Her head rears back. "Dad, I'm not coming."

Silence greets her on the other end for a moment before he clears his throat, the noise loud in her ear.

"Does that date not work for you?"

"No, I just …" She sighs, running the tips of her fingers across her necklace. *Don't think you actually want me there.*

Jahlani pulls the phone away from her ear as her throat tightens. She takes a shaky inhale before blowing out the air and drawing the phone back to her ear.

"Dad, I'm confused. You're *confusing* me. The last time we spoke, you called me greedy and a whole bunch of really *hurtful* things. Why would I want to spend Thanksgiving with you?" she says, letting out a bitter chuckle.

"Because I'm your father and we haven't seen each other in years."

Jahlani can't help the sound that slips out. "So, that's supposed to excuse everything that you said to me? Because we share some DNA? And what about all the other years? You didn't seem too concerned about buying me a plane ticket then."

His sigh is ragged. "Look, baby. I'm just stressed out. I didn't mean to take it out on you, okay?"

Bullshit.

And as she sits on the bench, she's struck with a sharp realization.

She looks up at the sky, her throat tightening. "Dad, *no*. It's not *okay*. It's not," she says, letting out a shuddering breath. "Would you want another man to treat me the way you do?"

His laugh is deep through the phone. "What, with love, Jahlani?"

"This isn't love, Dad," she whispers over the line, wiping under her eyes, thinking of Roman with Lucy. "This can't be. You don't know anything about me. Whenever you call I feel like shit. I don't think it's supposed to feel like this."

He clicks his tongue. "Jahlani, don't be silly, of course I love you."

Jahlani nods, trying to fight the tears that form in the corners of her eyes as she grips the phone tighter.

"No," she says, her voice coming out sharper than she intends. "This is toxic. One minute you love me, the next I'm greedy for wanting the money that *you* promised me. You don't call me for weeks, *months* sometimes, and when you do, it's to tell me you're having another baby."

"Jahlani, what? That is not true."

"Yes, it *is*. And I'm just ... exhausted," she says, swiping under her nose. "I'm exhausted. So, please don't try to manipulate me into wanting to spend the holidays with you," she says, her voice shaky. "I need to focus on me, and I can't do that when you're making me feel guilty for wanting my basic psychological needs met by the person who gave me life."

"Jahlani, can you just–"

She ends the call and drops the phone onto the swing, burying her face in her hands as she tries to stave off her tears. She's not sure how much time passes when Roman's car pulls into the driveway. She sits up straighter, checking her face in her cellphone, before sending him a small wave.

He starts to walk toward her, and she moves to gather her things, slipping her bag onto her shoulder. She makes it a point not to linger when he's here. She shows up on time, she leaves on time. She's punctual.

Professional.

How she should have been from the beginning, and Roman hasn't been giving any pushback, and she's thankful and really irritated about it for some outrageous reason.

She clears her throat, starting to stand when his hand shoots out to her shoulder, pressing her gently back into the seat. His eyebrows are knitted together and there's a *look* on his face.

"What's wrong, Jahlani?"

"Nothing," she says fast. Too fast.

He sighs, removing his hand before dropping into the space beside her. He rubs his fingers over his eyes, his shoulders taut under his dress shirt. The past few weeks seem to have taken a toll on him. It's the middle of the semester, which is always the hardest. She sees the list of tasks on his laptop right before he leaves for work every day. His hair seems more unruly than ever, his pants wrinkled, as she takes him in. The mid-term was today, and she's excited to tell him that he passed despite their awkward dance over the past two weeks.

"Are you okay?" she asks. He turns to her and doesn't say anything for a while. She turns away when it becomes too much. "You passed your mid-term by the way."

She sees him lean closer from her periphery. "You were crying, Jahlani. What's wrong?"

"Nothing," she says, sharper this time.

He rolls his neck, wetting his lips. "Look, I know things are weird between us—"

Not weird. How it should be. Corrected.

"—but you can still talk to me. It doesn't have to be awkward. We don't have to tiptoe around this. Around each other."

She lets out a soft laugh before sighing and rolling her eyes. "Ah. Good, because my feet were *really* starting to hurt."

He bumps her shoulder with his, shaking his head. "Tell me."

She blows out air between her lips. "It's nothing. Well, it's not nothing. It's my dad. He bought me a plane ticket to go see him for Thanksgiving."

Roman sits up to look at her. "And that upset you?"

She purses her lips, tilting her head. "I'm not upset about the ticket itself. It's more about what it represents."

"Which is?"

She shrugs, looking down at her feet. "His new life. His new family. He doesn't *actually* want me there," she says, shaking her head. "It was Helen's idea to invite me." She looks back at his clear, very bright, very *seeing*, moss-colored eyes.

He frowns. "And that's what's upsetting you?"

She turns her entire body to face him, nodding. "I just wish he'd thought of me for once. I get it, I'm not a kid anymore, but it hurts being an afterthought or not even being a thought at all to the one person that evolution had determined is supposed to care about me the most," she says, quietly. "It's kind of heartbreaking."

Roman doesn't say anything for a while, but he looks at her as if he's unlocked some secret window into her soul.

And a part of her likes to think that he has.

His jaw works, and he opens his mouth as if he's about to say something but then he stops himself. Instead, he drapes his arm around her, pulling her so that her cheek is pressed to his chest.

"Your dad is an idiot," he says, his voice raspy and quiet. "And I'm sorry he ever made you feel like this."

"Yeah," she says through a watery chuckle. "But that seems to be the pattern with the men in my life."

And at this confession, he's pushing her up to look at him, his eyes hard as he wraps his hand around her jaw, his thumb swiping across her cheek. "Not with me, Jahlani. Never with me."

She nods, her lips trembling as he draws her back into his chest. The monitor crackles to life and she swipes sweaty palms against her jeans as she stands up. He does the same, so that they're face to face.

"I should head out," she says, unable to meet his eyes.

"Yeah, thanks again."

She sends him a small wave, turning to walk to her car when he calls her name. His arms grip the railing of the front porch. The wind whips against his hair, flushing his cheeks.

"I won't be in class this week."

She smiles, trying to hide the fact that her stomach dropped at the prospect of not seeing him after tonight.

She nods. "Okay."

His eyes narrow slightly as he nods, before releasing the railing to step back. "Have a good Thanksgiving, Jahlani."

"You too, Roman."

$$x = \frac{-b + \sqrt{b^2 - 4ac}}{2a}$$

Jahlani spends her days prepping next to her mom. She crushes, slices, and mixes dutifully before helping her separate items into Ziploc bags to marinate in the fridge.

She watches her grate cheese over the baked macaroni while she works on dicing onions. Thinking about her conversation with her dad, she clears her throat.

"Dad asked me to visit him for Thanksgiving," she says, cautiously, watching her mom from the corner of her eye. She sees her shoulders tense, but she continues working on the cheese.

"Oh, yeah?"

"I told him no," she says, looking up at her. "He's never asked me before. I don't understand why he did it now."

Her mom meets her eyes. "You can go if you want, Jahlani. It won't bother me," she says, wiping her hands off and moving to grab the cheese sauce. "I'm used to going alone to your grandmother's."

Her chest pinches at her words and she sets her knife down. She sighs, walking closer to her mom.

"Mom, why did you and Dad separate?"

Her mom's eyes flash with something before she slips her mask back on. She lets out a chuckle that sounds forced, moving away from her.

"Why are you asking me about that, Jahlani?"

She chases after her as she opens an overhead cabinet, rifling through it.

"Mom," she says, closing the door, forcing her to look at her. "I'm not a kid anymore. Tell me," she says, in a gentle tone, *hoping, praying, wishing* to get through to her.

"I don't walk to talk about this," her mom says brusquely and all the anticipation fizzles in Jahlani's chest as she brushes past her. After a moment, Jahlani moves back to her cutting board, chopping in silence.

THE PROBABILITY OF US

She wonders if she's cursed to never fix things with her parents.

$$x = \frac{-b + \sqrt{b^2 - 4ac}}{2a}$$

At work the next day, Jahlani feels more lethargic than usual during class and office hours and decides that it's her cycle that's making her feel this way.

Only a few students show up, so she decides to cut the lecture short, choosing to upload everything online, telling everyone to enjoy their break as they exit.

And it isn't until later that night when her phone vibrates with a message, that she feels that familiar smite of energy that she's been missing the past few days.

> **ROMAN**
> You're welcome to join us if you want.

> **ROMAN**
> No pressure.

And it isn't until the next morning that she realizes just how badly she needs it.

CHAPTER 26
Fight Girls Over Boys

Jahlani

J ahlani isn't sure what to expect as she pulls into the tree-lined cobblestone driveway within the cul-de-sac (*of course*). She didn't anticipate going and yet she finds herself at his doorstep. Well, his mother's doorstep. The dashboard reads half past six as she puts the car in park before stepping out to admire the house.

Its brick walls, with accents of cream-colored trim, glow slightly from the golden light of late afternoon. A wreath of dried leaves and red berries is hung proudly on the front door, a seasonal touch that blends with the muted autumn colors of the trees lining the street. In the yard, a few pumpkins sit on the front steps. It's nice. Really nice. Everything she imagined it would be, and the thought upsets her more than it should. She should leave. Turn back before anyone notices her.

"You must be Jahlani. Come in, come in. It's *freezing* out there." A woman who she can only assume is his mother stands at the door, flapping her arm, a polka-dot apron wrapped around her. Despite their eyes being different colors, she sees traces of him in her. She ushers her into the entryway and Jahlani does her very best not to gawk at the mid-century modern finishes and listen as she talks, insisting that Jahlani *"drop the formalities"* and call her *"Gwen."* She takes the tray of food Jahlani had pilfered from her family and red wine she'd found on a shelf that seemed appetizing and tells her to join *everyone* in the living room.

Jahlani's stomach flips at this, because *who is everyone?* She's not good in intimate settings with people she doesn't know. She doesn't even know *why she fucking came.* Panic starts to bubble inside her and she stands awkwardly in the hallway, deliberating on faking a stomach bug when Lucy swings around the corner.

She lets out a loud shriek when her eyes land on her. Jahlani falls to her knees to catch her, smiling.

"Hi, baby girl. I missed you," she says, pressing her cheek against hers.

"Lulu, stop," his voice calls and her heart thunders against her sternum.

Her eyes meet his over the top of Lucy's head, and as gracefully as she can while holding her, she rises to her feet, not missing the way her knees pop.

"Jahlani," he says, slowly walking to them until they are toe to toe. Jahlani sways Lucy in her arms as she toys with the necklace at the column of her throat.

"Hi," Jahlani says, feeling awkward.

He smiles down at her, sliding his hands into his pockets. "I'm glad you came. I didn't think you would."

She nods. "Yeah. I'm not really sure how I ended up here."

He grins. "I think I have an idea."

"Yeah?"

"Yeah. It's me. You missed me." He clicks his tongue, shaking his head. "I knew you were obsessed with me, Jones."

She inhales, her body tingling with *want, need, mine.* "What if I did? Miss you?"

The grin stretching across his face fades slowly. "Hypothetically speaking," she says, whispering in the quiet hallway. "What would you say? What would you do?" she says, shifting her grip on Lucy, the familiar warmth of her wrapping her in a happy bubble.

He steps forward, rubbing a hand over his jaw. "I'd say ..." He blows a gust of air through his lips. "I wouldn't know what to say, actually. Fuck," he says, shaking his head, scratching under his chin.

She lets out a soft laugh. "Ha. Now who has nothing to say."

His eyes lower to hers with an intense gaze. *Want, need, mine.* "Yeah. You tend to have that effect on me."

She sucks in a breath, stepping back in an act of self-preservation.

He nudges his head toward the living room.

"Let me introduce you to everyone."

$$x = \frac{-b + \sqrt{b^2 - 4ac}}{2a}$$

Within two hours, Jahlani learns more about the Hayes family than she knows about her own. She learns that Danica is a political science major with a minor in women's studies and is fully committed to embarrassing Roman every waking second. Taylor is a friend from high school who graduated with a biology degree and is now in his second year of medical school. Gwendolyn flits in every now and then, offering bits of the food, refills, or memorabilia from Roman's childhood for her to look at. She disappears when another knock sounds at the door.

Danica rolls her eyes. "I swear, this woman invited the whole damn neighborhood."

Taylor bumps his shoulder into her. "Hey, be nice."

"Do *not* tell me what to do."

"I'm not—"

Jahlani sips from her glass of wine, eyes bouncing between the two of them when Roman sidles up next to her.

"What?" he says.

She shrugs. "Nothing."

He squints at her. "I know that look."

She nods in the direction of Danica and Taylor, who have now taken their lovers' spat to the backyard.

"Is something going on between them?"

"Dan and Taylor? Nah."

"Roman," she says, staring pointedly.

He sighs, rubbing the back of his neck. "Danica might have had a thing for him back in high school, but …"

"But?"

Roman winces. "I might have gotten drunk one night and told him."

Jahlani gasps. "No."

"Yeah," he says, bowing his head.

She covers her mouth with her hand. "How could you?"

He looks down regretfully. "It wasn't my finest moment."

"So, what happened next?" she says, drinking from her glass again, turning to face him.

He blows out a breath, laughing. "Danica beat the hell out of me." He lifts the hair falling across his brow. "That's how I got this."

He points to the scar running across his forehead. Jahlani tsks in mock pity, running her fingertips across the strip of skin.

"Poor Roman."

His eyes catch hers and she freezes momentarily before removing her hand, her body flushing. *Want, need, mine.*

"Sorry, I don't know why I did that," she says into her glass, suddenly very interested in an intricate bird painting on the mantle.

"It's fine."

He clears his throat. "So, Taylor pretty much shut her down. She didn't talk to me for about three months."

Jahlani laughs. "Three months?"

"Oh yeah. It was bad. Mom even thought about putting us in family therapy," he says, scratching under his chin. "Eventually, she woke up one day and asked what I wanted for breakfast, like nothing had happened. She's over him now, but I think she's secretly been plotting some form of revenge."

Jahlani steps forward, pointing to them outside. "Roman, I hate to be the one to tell you this, but she's very much *not* over him, and she's *definitely* plotting her revenge."

He turns to watch them, his brows furrowed.

"I'm going to get a refill," she says and starts to move toward the kitchen when three new bodies fill the hallway. One is Gwendolyn with an uncomfortable smile on her face, the other is an older gentleman, holding a bottle of red wine and wearing an even bigger smile, and the third makes Jahlani's stomach flip because she has a look in her eyes as she stares at Roman. One that Jahlani's grown to recognize within him.

Yearning for something you can't have.

"Audrey," Roman says as she waves the food in her hand cautiously.

"I made pie."

$$x = \frac{-b + \sqrt{b^2 - 4ac}}{2a}$$

Much to Jahlani's dismay, the pie is *really fucking good*. She deliberately avoids eye contact with Roman as they seat themselves around the table. She isn't sure why she's so upset. They're not a thing. She has no right to feel anything yet she does.

Want. Need. Mine.

Suddenly his breath is tickling her ear. "You okay?" he asks in a hushed tone.

"Yeah. Fine," she says, giving him a closed-mouth smile, not meeting his eyes. "Danica, can I get the butter, please?"

From the corner of her eye, she can see his hand drag down his mouth as he watches her before turning to adjust Lucy in her seat. For a while, they all pass around plates of food and chatter aimlessly. Jahlani constantly turns down food, claiming that she already ate, and the conversation volleys around with Lucy being the main star of the show. Audrey somehow managed to weasel her way next to Lucy and has now taken the role of helping Roman feed and soothe her.

Jahlani's knee bounces under the table when Roman reaches forward to give her a napkin and their hands touch. She takes large gulps from her glass.

"Jahlani, what do you do for work?" Audrey asks.

All eyes float to her and she shouldn't feel intimidated, especially considering she stands in front of twenty times that amount at school, but still.

It's his family, she thinks, feeling compelled to make a good impression.

"I teach."

A chorus of oohs and ahhs spread throughout the room and she feels her face warm at the attention. Audrey tilts her head.

"Where do you teach?"

"At the college. I'm a graduate teaching assistant—temporarily," she feels the need to add. Audrey's grin spreads like the Cheshire Cat and Jahlani can't help but feel like she's fallen into her trap.

"Temporarily?" she parrots, making a point to wipe the mashed potato from Lucy's chin.

Jahlani clears her throat. "Well, the plan is to become a statistician.

I'm doing it for my internship hours."

"Wow," Audrey says, blinking. "I remember during my internship how busy I was. It was *such* a crazy time. I barely saw my family. Do you get to see yours often?"

Jahlani blinks, tilting her head slightly as she nods.

"I mean, I live with my mom, but my dad lives in another state with his wife," she says, sipping from her wine, her face burning. Audrey turns back, her smile faltering slightly before she slips it back on.

"Oh. I'm sorry to hear that," she says, turning back to tickle Lucy, who suddenly spits up her food.

Huh.

"And that, folks," Danica starts as Roman moves to start wiping her up, "is one of many reasons I sure as hell won't be pushing anything out anytime soon—so you have nothing to worry about with me, Mom," she says, tapping her hand. "I'll be well on my way to the Supreme Court." This earns a collective chuckle from everyone, and Jahlani can't help the slimy feeling in her stomach when she looks up to see Roman looking at Audrey. It's not long before they all start to clear the table and spread out into their respective locations as Gwendolyn waves away everyone's help.

Jahlani turns from the kitchen, mumbling about needing to use the restroom. Once inside, she locks the door before pressing her forehead against the cool wood. Lowering herself onto the edge of the bathtub, she bites at the skin on her thumb. Dropping her hand, she then laughs to herself at the sheer *stupidity* of the entire situation.

She didn't fight girls over boys.

And she sure as hell wasn't about to start now.

Especially considering that nothing *could* happen. Not again.

Turning the tap on, she lets it run over her hand before she presses them to her cheeks, cooling the warmth that had spread through from the wine.

Opening the door, she almost collides with Audrey.

"Oh, sorry—"

"It's okay."

"Did I—"

"—totally, my fault. I was standing too close," she says breathlessly.

Jahlani nods, wiping her hands against her shirt as they lapse into silence. She starts to move to the side, but Audrey steps in her path.

"Hey, I'm sorry about earlier. I didn't mean to come off like that. Well, I *did*, but it wasn't right, and I'm sorry."

Jahlani exhales slowly. "I *really* wish I knew what you were referring to," she says in mock seriousness.

Audrey's lips lift slightly before dropping. "The holidays are a difficult time for me. I don't know what I was thinking back there," she says, shaking her head. She meets her eyes before looking away. "My mom passed away a few years ago, and I guess … I just assumed you had this perfect family … and yeah," she says, exhaling shakily. "It's stupid."

Jahlani shakes her head, the muscles in her neck loosening. Thankful that for once, she didn't assume the worst.

"Not stupid, and I'm sorry about your mom, Audrey," she says. "Were you close?"

Audrey inhales, tilting her head in thought. "She was a complicated woman, but she was my mom, you know?"

Jahlani nods, thinking about her mom and her own complicated feelings toward her. She thinks about how she should *try harder*. Be better.

Audrey sighs, adjusting her bag on her shoulder. "Anyway, I'm heading out. Happy Thanksgiving, Jahlani."

"You too, Audrey."

She watches Audrey slip on her shoes silently and speaks before she can process what she's saying.

"Audrey," Jahlani says, crossing her arms over her stomach. Audrey's eyes flit to hers as she starts on the other shoe. Jahlani scratches her forehead. "If you … if you ever want to talk about your mom, I don't mind listening. I know a thing or two about complicated mothers," she says, shrugging. "I mean, I'm sure you have other—"

"That would be nice," she says, smiling as she stands to her full height. "I … thanks, Jahlani. I appreciate it."

"Sure," she says, giving her a small wave as she walks out the front door.

Slipping back out into the living room, she finds Danica setting up a game of Catan. She looks up when she sees her, smiling brightly.

"Hey, what color do you want? Typically, I'm blue, but you're a guest, so you can have first pick."

"I'm not staying," she says gently. "It's getting pretty late and my car isn't too reliable these days."

Her face falls. "Oh. Dang it. I wanted to impress you with my road-building skills."

Jahlani lets out an airy laugh. "Maybe next time," she adds, unsure of why she would promise such a thing.

Danica smiles, pulling her into a quick hug. "Sure, it was nice meeting you."

Slightly taken aback by the gesture, she slides her bag onto her shoulder in a daze, waving goodbye to Taylor who helps Danica set up the pieces. She moves into the kitchen, and is forced to wait two minutes while Gwendolyn packs her *a little bit of everything*. She's pulled into another hug before she walks out of the house into the darkened street. Dropping the food into the back seat, she slams the door shut before moving to the driver's side. She looks up, feeling his presence before he can say anything.

For a moment, they just stare at one another, and she's tempted to get in the car and run him over. But she's also tempted to tell him to run up to her and take care of her against the car.

She points back at the house when he starts down the driveway toward her. "I figured you were busy with Lucy—I didn't want to interrupt—"

He stops a few feet in front of her, his eyes dark. "Jahlani?"

"Yes?"

"Give me the keys."

"What are you doing?" she murmurs when he invades her space, the front of his navy sweater brushing against her fingertips.

"You've been drinking. You can't drive yourself home."

"Oh. Okay."

She doesn't say anything else when his palm wraps around hers to pry the keys out. With a hand on her back, he guides her to the passenger side where he opens the door. She turns back to face him.

"But Lucy—"

"In, Jahlani."

"Yeah. Okay." She drops into the seat, and when he shuts the door, she buckles herself in. He slides in on the other side, and if she wasn't so warm, she'd laugh at how cramped he looks against her steering wheel. She leans her head against the cool glass.

"You know how to get there?" she murmurs through a yawn.

"Yeah. Close your eyes, Jahlani. I know where we're going."

CHAPTER 27
Waiting

Jahlani

When Jahlani comes to, the dashboard reads that it's five past nine. She blinks, sitting up in the car, looking out the window.

"This isn't my house," she says in a croaky voice while squinting through the windshield. "This is …" She trails off, turning to face an impassive-looking Roman. "What are we doing here?"

"We're going to talk," he says, opening his door and moving to her side. She leans away when he opens it.

"You kidnapped me," she says breathlessly. "Why?"

He leans down, meeting her eyes. "Because we're going to talk."

Cupping his hand around her elbow, he tugs her forward until she's out of the car. The palm trees loom like shadows and the crickets are loud in his driveway. It's a familiar scene and she's annoyed by how much comfort that brings her. He shuts the door with his free hand, not letting her go as he gently steers them into the house. She watches through parted lips as he bends down to undo her laces, slipping off her shoes before placing them neatly next to his own. Her stomach burns and he leaves her there in the dimmed hallway to walk toward the kitchen. She stands, blinking, warring with herself before she pads in softly after him. She stops at the edge of the island, his heated gaze stalling her.

"What are we here to talk about, Roman?"

With one hand braced on the edge of the kitchen sink, the other holding a clear glass of *something*, he looks like a man on the brink. His hair sticks up in every direction; his eyes a storm. Pushing off, he rounds the island, sinking into the stool farthest from her. Setting the glass down, his eyes don't leave hers. Neither says anything; a low chime signals the dryer is done.

Jahlani breaks first. "I think your laundry's done," she whispers.

"Come here," he says softly, with a tilt of his head. She hesitates, only briefly, before she moves forward, until she's an arm's length from him. He exhales, leaning forward to grip the bottom of her shirt, pulling her the rest of the way. She braces her hands on his shoulders, taking a soft inhale when his palms move to her thighs. Her eyes close as he drags them slowly up and down the length of her jeans. Her eyes snap open.

"Roman?"

"What happened back there?"

"What?" she asks, looking down at him.

"Why did you try to leave without saying goodbye?"

"I told you. You were busy with Lucy and—"

"Bullshit," he whispers, pausing his movements.

She clenches her fist, eyebrows furrowing. "No," she murmurs, "Not bullshit."

He removes his hands from her, leaning back in the chair his expression softening.

"Tell me what happened."

Dropping her hands from his shoulders, she takes his glass from the table and finishes it.

"Do you want more kids?" she asks, finally.

He doesn't miss a beat. "I don't know. Maybe."

"I grew up an only child, you know. It was lonely," she says, rotating the cup in her hand.

She steps closer into him, and he lays his hand on her waist, rubbing slowly as she continues, not really knowing where she's going with this, but knowing that she needs to say it.

"Audrey seems nice—pretty, smart, good with kids. She'd make a good mom." She watches his face for something, anything.

He shrugs. "Sure. I guess. Never thought about it."

"What happened between you two?"

His sigh is sharp as he pushes her back slightly, standing from the chair.

"You're angry at me," Jahlani says, watching him pace, her stomach doing a violent flip.

"No."

"Is it because I'm asking about her? About Audrey?"

His laugh is humorless. "No."

She stands, walking up to him. "Then what? Do you want me to go?"

He stops pacing then, running both hands through his hair before looking at her.

"No, Jahlani. That is the *last* thing that I want from you."

She presses the heel of her palms to her eyes. "What then, Roman? What do you want from me? Why did you bring me here?"

"What do you want from *me*, Jahlani?"

"I—" Her hands fall to her sides, and she takes in his dark expression. "I don't know."

Need. Want. Mine.

He walks forward, grabbing her arms.

"You're sweet to my mom, my sister, my *kid*, but then you push me away. I'm confused. Help me out here."

She looks up at him with wide eyes. "I'm sorry," she says weakly.

He sighs, intertwining their fingers, drawing her in to follow behind him. They move in silence down the hallway to his bedroom. He pauses at the door, turning to face her.

"This conversation isn't over. We're going in here, we're changing, we're brushing our teeth, and then we're going to sleep and talk in the morning—because I can't spend another night apart from you. We've both had a lot to drink, and I don't think you're ready to hear what I have to say tonight. Okay?"

She blinks. "Okay."

He exhales, turning back around to push the door open. For the next several minutes, they do exactly as he said. He drops clothes into a neat pile on the bed for her before moving out to give her privacy. When she's changed, she meets him in the bathroom and waits patiently as he unwraps the toothbrush for her. Their eyes meet at least twelve times (*not that she's counting*) in the mirror as they complete the most mundane human tasks that have somehow become some of the most intimate in the past fifteen minutes together.

When they slip under the covers, he asks her if she wants the lights on or off, and as they disappear into the darkness, she isn't sure who reaches for who first, but her legs become twisted with his and her arms get trapped against his chest.

His heart thrashes loudly and the sound of their breathing becomes its own symphony.

Just as she's about to drift off, his voice rumbles against her ear.

"There's nothing going on between me and her," he says. "Not since you, and even before then."

"Okay."

"There's just you, Jahlani. I only see you."

She shifts against him, body warming, her leg tightening against his, the familiar urge seeping through.

"Roman." She breathes heavily into his chest. "What are we doing?"

"Going to sleep."

"Right."

He tightens his arms around her when she shifts again to get more comfortable. "We both drank tonight," he murmurs.

"I'm not drunk," she grumbles into his chest, her body starting to relax.

"I know. I'm just waiting for you to catch up."

CHAPTER 28
Safe Zone

Jahlani

As the amber sun strikes through the windows, Jahlani curses herself for not remembering to shut them last night before Roman dragged her against his chest. With a groan, she burrows herself further into his pillow, inhaling the subtle aroma.

"You're grouchy in the morning. Why am I not surprised?" he asks, his voice heavy.

She turns to face him, her eyes squinting in an attempt to block the light. He shakes his head, getting up to draw the curtains in. Her head slumps down and she mumbles out a "thank you?" turning her face back into his pillow.

She feels the mattress dip as she flips onto her back, stretching out like a cat. The shirt he gave her raises, revealing the plane of her stomach, along with a few scars. His fingers begin to run across the exposed flesh before tapping on one of the circular scars and she inhales sharply.

"Chicken pox," she says, her voice a broken whisper. She clears her throat, lifting to watch as he presses his mouth against it, his fingers flexing against her lower stomach. Her head falls back as a shiver runs through her. He does this a few more times, her body heating further with each pass of his lips.

When she can't take it anymore, she rolls to her side, and stares at eyes the color of the sea.

I think I'm drowning, but I don't want to be saved.

"Good morning," she mumbles, her voice raspy.

"Morning," he says, his eyes creasing around the corners.

"What time is it?" she asks around a yawn.

"A little after seven."

"Hmm." She fights to keep her eyes open. "Lucy?"

He drops on his back next to her, rubbing his hands down his face. "Mom likes to keep her after a big holiday, spend time with her, and usually I'm working."

"That's nice," she says through another yawn and he laughs beside her. "I had a dream about this," she murmurs after a while. "About what it would be like to wake up next to you."

He turns to look at her. "And?"

"And ... it's different," she says, her eyes flitting to his.

He sucks in a breath. "Not sure if I like where this is going."

Of course, he sleeps without a shirt on, she thinks as her eyes roam his chest with naked curiosity, and then her hand follows, feeling the soft rhythm of his chest rising and falling as she traces patterns along his skin.

"It's different in a good way," she says. "Your hair kind of splits in every direction." She places a hand through the silk-soft mess and his eyes close, his breathing turning heavy. "And your skin looks smoother, like you're at peace." Her fingers brush over his lips lightly. "And your lips are fuller."

"Stop," he says as his eyes snap open. He grabs ahold of her wrist to keep her hand in place.

"Why?" she breathes out, leaning forward slightly. "You started it."

He shakes his head. "We need to talk, and if you keep touching me like that, I'll kiss you. And if I kiss you ..." He presses a deliberate kiss to her fingers, heat sparking low in her belly. "I won't hold back this time." Her eyes drop to his mouth, and she licks her lips, leaning forward to finally close the space between them. To do something.

But then her body betrays her in other ways by letting out the loudest growl humanly possible. The hand Roman is holding tenses immediately, and she closes her eyes, the licks of embarrassment engulfing her fast.

He starts, "Are you—"

"Nope."

"—perhaps—"

"I'm fine."

"—hungry?" he finishes, shaking with laughter next to her. She sighs, pulling her wrist from his to drape it across her face.

"I'll go make something."

She huffs, shaking her head. "Just leave me here to starve. I'm already dying from embarrassment." She then grabs the lip of the cover, throwing it over her head.

He squeezes her calf through the sheet as he walks to the door. "Rest some more. I'll wake you when it's ready," he says, still laughing.

$$x = \frac{-b + \sqrt{b^2 - 4ac}}{2a}$$

Jahlani pads through the hallway, having showered and brushed her teeth before slipping back into the clothes Roman had given her last night. She smells like him, and she likes it a little too much.

As she steps into the kitchen, the distinct buttery scent of pancakes and smoky bacon makes her mouth water. He's on the phone with his back turned as she walks out.

"I can't today, man. Sorry."

He turns to her when he hears the stool scrape against the tile, and he seems to forget that he's on the phone when the person on the other line yells at him.

"Yeah, I have to go," he says as he drops the call, throwing it down. Jahlani lets out a small chuckle.

"Who was that?"

"Nobody important," he says, looking her up and down. She looks past him at the food, licking her lips. She scrunches her nose.

"That's a lot of food—are you expecting more people?"

This seems to snap him back to reality. He turns back to the food, dropping the plates on the island in front of her. He scratches the back of his neck.

"I might have gotten carried away."

Both her eyebrows shoot up as she drowns her pancake in syrup, then creates another dipping pool.

"Hmm."

"In my defense, I usually cook for myself plus a baby."

Jahlani cuts a piece of the pancake before shoving it into her mouth. She can't help the moan that follows, and her eyes snap open to praise him when something dawns on her.

"You don't cook for people?" she asks

He shakes his head.

"Like ever?" she asks, reaching for the orange juice he poured for her.

He shrugs. "No one comes over."

She sets the drink down and wipes her mouth with the back of her hand. "What do you mean 'no one comes over'?"

He pops a piece of bacon into his mouth, chewing. "I mean, no one comes over. I always go to them. Danica comes over every now and then, and mom and Taylor, but that's about it," he says, brushing off his hands.

Jahlani works through a swallow, licking her lips. "No guy friends?"

Roman shrugs. "We text every now and then, but I got busy when Lucy came around."

Jahlani nods. "And no other friends?"

Roman snorts. "You mean women, Jahlani?"

She nods, bracing herself for the number, but he shakes his head. "No. No women."

Jahlani narrows her eyes. "Except me."

He nods, his expression solemn. "Except you."

Suddenly, her mouth is dry, and she reaches for water. Setting the glass down, she meets his eyes again.

"So, I'm the first and only woman you've ever brought back here?"

Roman folds a hand over his mouth, nodding.

"Huh," Jahlani says, nodding, sliding from the stool.

"What, you don't believe me?" he says, his eyes following her as she scrapes the remaining food from her plate before setting it in the sink.

"I believe you. I'm just ... trying to figure out what to do with this information."

His eyes lower to her mouth. "Hopefully something good," he says in a low voice, brushing against her as he drops his plate in the sink. She steps back, exhaling.

"You said we needed to talk. Let's talk."

He sighs. "Okay, but let's do it over a game."

$$x = \frac{-b + \sqrt{b^2 - 4ac}}{2a}$$

They've transitioned to the dining room table adjacent to the kitchen island, and Roman cuts the deck in his hands.

"I don't play many card games," Jahlani says while watching his hands work to shuffle the stack.

"No?"

She shakes her head, frowning. "My family isn't the board game kind." *They aren't really the family kind either.*

"This game is easy. It's six rounds. The goal is to have the least number of points at the end of all the rounds. You can look at two cards to start. Remember the number. You can also discard at least two black cards and three color cards of the same number. Got it?"

Jahlani nods, listening with rapt attention and he leans back, rubbing his fingers over his mouth.

"What?" she asks.

"You're competitive—it's cute."

Jahlani flushes at the compliment. "I'm not competitive. I'm just determined to get things right the first time. There's a difference."

He shakes his head, starting the game. Three minutes in, Jahlani loses the first round. Roman's eyes glint like he's riding a rush.

"New rule: loser of each round does what the winner decides."

Jahlani's lips part. "You can't do that," she murmurs, shifting in her seat.

He shrugs, looking over her body. "My house, my rules."

She sighs, sliding her cards to the discard pile. "What do you want?"

"Tell me what happened last night," he says, not looking at her as he reshuffles for the next round.

She blinks over at him, suddenly deciding she has nothing to lose and everything to gain. "I'm attracted to you, and I shouldn't be, and I—" she clears her throat, trying to steady her breathing—

"missed you in class. And thought that I—" His gaze meets hers, and her palms grow clammy. "And I thought I would get to spend time with you in a safe zone so as not to feel tempted," she says in a rush, startling herself with her honesty.

He grins. "Safe zone?"

She waves her hand around the room. "This isn't a safe zone. There's no one around to stop us."

"But my mom's house was full of people," he murmurs to himself.

She nods, folding her hands under her thighs while he deals.

They start the second round, and Jahlani feels more confident. So confident that she calls the round.

But Roman has a better poker face than she thought. Her face falls when she realizes she's lost again. She practically throws the cards in his face as he laughs.

"What truth do you want now?"

He shakes his head, leaning forward. "No truth this time. I want you to do something," he says, eyes flashing.

Jahlani throws her head back before grinning at him. "I'm not prank calling any—"

"Take your pants off."

CHAPTER 29
An Itch

Jahlani

Jahlani's mouth dries, and a weak laugh tumbles out. "What?"

Roman leans back, shuffling the cards again before dividing them.

"Take your pants off," he repeats, sending her a look that makes her body tighten. "And spread your legs for me," he adds in a low murmur.

Jahlani wets her lips, her body thrumming in anticipation.

She hesitates before she rises to her feet, her gaze locked on his as she hooks her hands into the shorts he gave her and slides them down her thighs. Folding it neatly, she sets it on the other end of the kitchen table before gliding back into the chair. The shirt he gave her is oversized, but it's not big enough to hide her completely when she opens her legs, anchoring both feet behind the chair legs. She shudders as the cold air meets her center.

"Good enough?" she asks, slightly winded, even though he hasn't done anything.

Hooded eyes drag to hers. "Fucking perfect."

She starts the round with shaky hands, distracted when his eyes dip to the lace covering her, the dampness spreading, but with more determination than ever to win.

"I win," she says, smiling triumphantly.

Roman leans back, spreading his palms out. "Your wish is my command," he states, and the filthiest thoughts run rampant, but she pushes them to the side, resolved to see this 'talk' through.

"What happened between you and Audrey?"

"She wasn't you," he says immediately with a shrug.

"That's not an answer," she whispers, shaking her head.

He scratches behind his ear, bracing his elbows on his knees as he stares at her, contemplating his response.

"She didn't excite me. She didn't make my blood boil or my mind race. She didn't challenge me. She didn't make me want to do better or be better. She didn't make me want to drop everything at any given moment to be with her. She didn't make me crave her scent or her smile or her touch. She didn't make me want to carve out space for her. She didn't make me feel weak and strong at the same time. She didn't make me curious. She wasn't you."

He leans back in his chair, spreading his legs. "Better?" he asks, her voice thinner now.

She nods, her heart starting to beat at an unhealthily fast pace. "Better," she croaks.

Roman wins round four and determines that he wants her to take her hair down, which she finds odd, but does anyway, letting her braids tumble down her shoulders in waves. When she asks if that's all he wants, he hesitates.

"That's all," he finally gets out, his voice sounding husky.

Jahlani wins round five, determining that it's only fair he loses a piece of clothing since she had to. Reaching behind him, he drags the shirt over his back, folding it neatly and depositing it on top of the shorts she'd removed earlier. Jahlani wonders if she should feel embarrassed at how much wetter she gets but decides to embrace it instead. After all, he wants her like this.

"Last round?" she asks, voice hoarse. He nods, flipping over his cards. This one seems to go on forever. Jahlani's body tingles as the air conditioning hums on, fanning over her bare legs. She rolls her neck, jittering her foot against the floor.

Reaching forward, she swaps a card she knows has a low number. He doesn't make a sound as she smiles, feeling proud. When it's her turn again, she flips the card over, her mouth falling open.

"What? How?" she sputters, tapping the card. "This should be a negative four."

He shrugs, reaching to flip over his last card. Her eyes narrow.

"You shuffled the cards," she says, tone disbelieving. "That's not fair," she finishes, brows knitting. "That's cheating."

He raises his palms up. "Hey, I never said you couldn't."

"Whatever cheater," she sneers, earning a chuckle from him. "I lost." Her eyes drop to his mouth before jumping back to his eyes. "What do you want?"

His jaw clenches, and she inhales sharply when he pushes his chair back.

"On the table."

"On the table," she repeats slowly, wondering at all of the possibilities that *here* could mean. The possibilities the demand entailed. She rises from her seat, stepping the two feet toward him until she's between the edge of the table and his knees. Exhaling, she presses her palms flat against the wood, testing its weight, before sliding on top. The temperature seems to climb several degrees when she unfurls her legs again.

"Here? Like this, Roman?"

He rubs a hand over his mouth, his fist clenching and unclenching before he reaches to cup the back of her calf, his fingers sparking an inferno.

"Just like that," he says, his voice rough. He leans forward, his other hand joining to massage both of her calves, and her head tips back slightly, her eyes slipping shut.

"What else, Roman?" she asks, fighting the urge to slide off the table and onto his lap, the pressure becoming almost unbearable between her legs.

He stands then, and her head falls forward to meet his stare that's full of desire and promises and *heat*. His palms slide to the back of her knees and pull her forward. Her pelvis meets his in one fluid motion that has her lips parting. His head bends until his mouth is an inch from her neck.

"Tell me what you're thinking," he murmurs, his mouth brushing the column of her throat. Her hands curl against the table, but she keeps them in place as her body shudders at the contact.

"I'm thinking … that I should have been meaner."

"Why?" he rumbles, traveling his lips to the arch of her shoulder.

"Because nothing good will come of this."

He chuckles against her neck, pressing an open-mouthed kiss there that makes her shiver. "I can think of plenty of good things that will come of this. Tell me what else you're thinking," he says, wrapping both hands in her hair to expose more of her neck.

She bites her lip, determined to answer him. "I'm thinking—" She pauses, shuddering when his mouth starts to suck against her throat. "I'm thinking that I'm still not the person you're looking for, but I'm not sure that I care anymore," she says breathlessly, before moving to push him back to look him in the eyes. "I'm thinking that I'm tired of thinking and I'm tired of talking."

He nods, his hands moving to cage her jaw, both thumbs brushing against her lips.

"Me too," he murmurs, pulling her face to his. "Me too."

Their mouths meet, and if possible, it's even better this time around. There's no restraint when he opens against her and strokes his tongue with her, when she moans at the contact, when he pushes further into her.

Want. Need. Mine.

One hand leaves the surface to drag through his hair, pulling him close, urging him on, holding him steady. She uses the leverage to guide him back to her throat, which he does so dutifully, licking and sucking. He kisses her collarbone, drawing her in closer, lifting her knee against him.

Pressing her other palm against the table, she shifts against him, earning a low groan from him as she gasps. She does this several times, until his head drops into her chest and they're rocking against each other, her lace impossibly wet. Pulling his head back, she kisses him softly before stilling her movements to meet his eyes.

"Roman, I'm not ... good at this." She exhales shakily, licking her lips. "I just—"

Leaning forward, he kisses her once. And then again, working their tongues together, before pulling back to drop into the chair. Jahlani takes deep breaths, observing him. His hair is messy, his chest is red from where she had her hands on him, and his pants have a wet spot on the front, either from her or from himself.

Want. Need. Mine.

"Spread your legs," he murmurs. This time, she doesn't hesitate when she widens them. She drops both palms for balance and watches his chest rise and fall as he wets his lips.

"Touch yourself," he demands, his hand running across his jaw, eyes dark.

Lifting one hand from the table, she flattens it against her stomach before sliding it under the lace. She exhales shakily as she slowly starts to rub, her head falling back, a breathless moan escaping.

"I could watch you do this for hours, Jahlani. Days," he says, letting out a rough laugh. "Hell, I could watch you solve statistical equations for hours and be perfectly content." She inhales sharply, her nipples hardening when she bears down on her fingers.

"I don't believe that for a second," she says, before letting out a low whine. "Not a second."

He leans forward, eyes glazed as he watches her grind against her hand. Her stomach clenches and she stops her rhythm when he stands, towering over her.

Want. Need. Mine.

"I'm a patient man, Jahlani. I don't care how long it takes. I don't care how long anything takes when it comes to you and I mean it."

"Roman," she says, swallowing. "I need more."

"I know," he says as his index finger slides against the curve of her abdomen, back and forth, never shifting to where she wants it to. "One of these days, I'm going to watch you touch yourself until you come for me. But not today."

She tries to even her breathing, but then both his hands are pushing the white cotton of her shirt up and over her breast. Warm hands roam across her chest and circle ever so gently, dampening her further. One hand leaves and hooks into the lace, tugging them down slightly.

"Good?" His voice sounds strained.

Yes, yes, yes.

She nods, biting her lip as his fingers hover over her core. She wants him to touch her. No, she *needs* him to touch her there. She arches her back, pressing into him.

"Is that what you want, Jahlani?" He drags his finger against the fabric, pinching softly, and she chases the pressure.

"Tell me what you want, and I'll do it. Anything," he says.

"Just … touch me."

"Where?" He murmurs, drawing his hands up her shirt to cup her breasts. "Here?"

She gasps when he starts to rub her nipples. "Here, Jahlani?" He asks, continuing to touch her. He massages and strokes and watches as she unravels beneath him.

"I … had a dream about this," she confesses. "About you."

His fingers glide down back to her center, grazing with more pressure, and he pulls back, his lip curving upward.

"Hmm. Tell me what happens."

"I don't remember." She groans, pressing her cheek into his chest, when he slips his hand underneath.

He chuckles. "Liar."

"In my dream, you talk less."

He tsks. "Ridiculous. Even like this, you still find a way to insult me. You're incredible."

Suddenly, his knuckle slips against her and she gasps. The back of his hand cups her head, lowering her until she's flat against the table as his fingers continue to slide through. His lips meet her neck again and deliver delicate, flowery, thoughtful kisses. He continues rubbing in slow, dizzying motions that have her pushing her face into the table to stifle the sounds escaping her throat.

How? How does he know?

"You're a liar, Jahlani. You said you weren't good at this," he says as his mouth closes around her nipple and sucks. "But look at you."

She grips his hair, gasping, drifting off because she can't help it. It feels good. Really good. Which is also bad. Really bad.

"I'm not even doing anything ... it's all you," she says through a moan when his teeth graze her chest.

"Not true," he breathes. "You're doing so well," he whispers. "All the sounds ... and the way you're taking my fingers. So good. So perfect."

And then he's finally circling her there, and her back's arching into him as she chases the pressure.

Her moans grow more uncontrollable when he alternates between sliding his fingers into her and drawing circles, and then his mouth is on her. Licking her bottom lip, he invades her as he inhales her sounds. His fingers start to move faster, and one hand travels to press her stomach down. She separates from him as she clenches, her eyes screwing shut at the fluttering sensation.

"*Roman—oh my God.*"

She slips her hand into his curls, as he sucks on her neck. Her eyes screwing shut as he slows his fingers to teasing grazes. His tongue mimics the same pace, and she can't take it any longer. Her breath stutters, her fingers claw at his hair as her chest pinches. She drags his mouth back to hers as warmth floods through her, and the tension in her body snaps. An intense moan draws from her mouth, and she bites on his bottom lip as her body jolts, twisting through the sharp pulses. Roman continues his motions until she pushes his hand away.

"Roman," she says, after her heartbeat comes back to a state of normalcy.

"Hmm."

"What if it only feels this good because we shouldn't have it?"

She licks her lips, meeting his eyes. "What if it only feels this way because it's forbidden? What if it's just an itch that needs scratching?"

He sighs, brushing a thumb over her swollen lips. "It's okay. You'll figure it out eventually."

She's about to ask him what he means by that, but he's hooking his thumbs into his pants and pulling them down. He drags the remaining fabric from his body, leaving him naked and hard in front of her. Sitting up, she grips his neck, while the other hand reaches out to stroke him. He groans, shifting against her once, and then again before he drops his face into her neck, trembling, and cursing.

She lifts upward, letting his erection bump into her clit, and they both groan into each other, repeating the motion until he pulls back abruptly. She blinks up, feeling dazed and desperate.

"Condom," he breathes out.

"Oh," she says, exhaling. "I have an implant, and I haven't—it's been a while."

He nods. "Yeah. Me too."

"Okay," she says, smiling before reaching up to kiss him, slow and sure. She breathes as he widens her legs and starts to push in. Roman takes his time, pausing to fuse their mouths.

"Shit. I had a dream about this too," he says through a groan and a chuckle. "I had a dream about fucking you on my kitchen table."

She bites her lip, her stomach fisting at his words. He starts to rock against her gently and she shuts her eyes.

"Okay?" He breathes against her neck.

So, so okay. So fucking okay.

"Yeah." She breathes against his chest. Suddenly, his fingers are digging into her hip bone as he presses all the way in, and her eyes fly open to look at him.

His jaw ticks as he pulls back all the way before pushing in again. He's watching their bodies meet through hooded eyes. He moves his fingers to brush over her clit, and she moans.

"*Fuck*," he says, brushing over her again. "Fuck, Jahlani."

And then he's kissing her, and it's greedy and hot, and he's laying her back against the table again, less in control this time, pushing the cards so that they scatter to the floor. Her arms move to push the clothes off and stay above her when he starts to move faster.

"I thought about you," he says through grunts. "I thought about you just like this. Legs spread for me on my kitchen table."

His fingers move back to rubbing her and she arches against him. A familiar heat starting in the base of her feet.

"Fucking look at you," he groans, moving harder, pressing her further into the table.

"*Oh God.* I'm going to—"

He keeps a steady pace as he pushes into her. Her moans become choked. Breathless.

And when he pulls her leg out more, changing the angle, twisting his fingers through more of her curls and wetness, praising her more while dropping kisses to her stomach, her neck, her chest, she feels an insatiable fire spread below that she begins to chase as she lifts her hips against his. Her toes splay then curl when he pushes her hand from her nipple and he sucks, rocking into her.

"*Roman.*"

Her lips part and she moans as her body breaks in liquefying pulses. She's aware that she's chanting out his name but can't seem to stop or care as she twists her face into the cool wood of the table as her hips jump and her back arches. Too soon, he's pulling away from her and it takes more energy than she thought it would to sit up on her elbows. He's breathing heavily, staring down at her with *so much* it makes her dizzy.

He's tugging her forward and she happily complies as he pulls her from the table. He drops into the chair from earlier, tapping his thigh. Breathing heavily, she tests the weight with one leg before he's grabbing the other and pulls her forward to sink down on him.

She doesn't move, trying to wait for her body to adjust to him again. "Was this part of your dream?" she whispers against his mouth.

Both his hands start to help her shift. "This and so much more," he says, groaning.

She throws her head forward, pressing their chests together as he moves her faster and harder. She whimpers, her body vibrating as she builds up again. "*Roman*," she says, eyes wide in shock.

Jahlani's stomach caves in as she grinds harder against him. Her chest burns, short gasps bursting out as he helps her move over him. Most people don't know this about her, but Jahlani is an avid reader of romance novels. She always thought it was *so fucking ridiculous* when the main couple finally got around to having sex and he would command her to come, and she'd instantly do so. She figured there was no way the human body worked that way. You can't just finish because someone tells you to.

But as the words slip past Roman's lips, all demanding, and rough, and *needy* she can't seem to help the way her body bends into his as she lets go or the desperate moans that echo through the kitchen, or the way her body tingles and pulses and swells as he continues moving in her.

"*Fuck.*"

His arms band around her back as his head falls into her chest as he pulses inside her. He drags his face against it, his mouth unhurried as his teeth bear down on her flesh through his orgasm. She moans when he reaches her nipple and bites down on the flesh softly.

"Shit," he groans, panting heavily. "*Shit.*"

Pulling back, he looks into her eyes before moving to kiss her. They kiss and kiss and kiss, and she's getting too worked up again. Too soon. Too fast. She knows she should stop, but his pressure is steady, his mouth deliberate, and she wants to hold on to this feeling for as long as possible.

Roman chases her lips, standing to set her against the table, sliding a hand under her ass to guide her against him, and she lets him. She doesn't know how much time passes. Maybe a few seconds, maybe minutes, but she can feel herself tightening again. The combination of them together makes her *stupid with want*. Her mouth glides with his as he cups her cheek, fusing them as if his life depends on it. She pulls back when she feels it happening *again*. His eyes bore into hers.

Dopey and medicated.

"Again," he says against her lips. "Again."

This one is low and pulsing and draining ,and she convulses against him softly, crying out. There's a low ringing in her ears as she comes to, and he falls against her chest, pressing soft kisses against her.

"Tell me what you're thinking," he says.

"I'm thinking that was the best scratch of my life," she says through pants.

He laughs into her chest, pulling her up and toward the bathroom. He doesn't stop touching her. Not as he grabs towels. Not as he starts the shower. Not as he bathes her, then himself. Not as he's getting dressed. Not even as she's getting changed herself.

"Now what?" she whispers lazily once he's pressed her into the cocoon of his chest.

"Now, we sleep. I need you fully rested for what we're doing later."

"Which is?" she says through a yawn.

But she drifts off before she hears his response.

CHAPTER 30
Imprint

"You're doing so well."

"Roman."

"Just like that. Keep going."

Suddenly, she's spinning to face him, her legs dropping as she points an accusing finger at him.

"Roman, I told you I didn't want to do this," she hisses, narrowing her eyes at him.

"Lani, you're doing so well. Come on. Don't stop now."

They were currently in the shallow end of a family-owned local pool. After waking from a much-needed nap, he decided the rest of their day would be best spent with him teaching her how to swim. After much protest on her part—and several persuasive tactics on his—he finally managed to convince her.

They were on their second round of him trying to get her to kick her feet for an extended amount of time. She lets out a string of expletives, dropping her legs. She crosses her arms over her chest, scowling up at him.

He laughs, grabbing her arms to steer her around him.

"Okay, how about we try floating."

Unwrapping her arms, he guides her body so that she's in front of him.

"Lean back," he says. She sighs, giving him a pointed stare. "Lean back, baby. It's fine. I've got you."

This seems to work because she exhales, leaning back into his arms and a ripple of satisfaction trickles through his system. Sliding his arms under her thighs, he lifts her legs, guiding her body into place.

"Lani, relax. Tip your head, arch your back—perfect. Spread your arms a little more. Yeah, that's it," he says, keeping one hand steady under her back. "Just like that."

The water flows across her body, down her breast, over her exposed stomach, between her thighs and he has never been more jealous of an inanimate object. He's also incredibly glad the pool is dead today.

He stares down at her, smiling. "See, you're doing it."

"Barely," she says sourly. "You're holding onto me. It's cheating."

"Helping," he says, spinning her gently through the water. After several minutes of him guiding her, she starts to relax and they fall into silence, the slight ripple of the water the only sound.

"Roman," she says, closing her eyes as she floats with him.

"Hmm."

"I've been thinking about going to therapy," she says, exhaling. "The campus offers some services. Some extra sessions for free since I'm on payroll, and I don't know. I might do it."

"I think that's a great idea."

Her eyes open slowly as he continues to turn her.

"Okay," she says. "You can let go now."

"You sure? I'm perfectly content holding on."

Forever, if that's okay with you.

She nods her head slightly, and he gently slides his hand from under her and she immediately starts to sink. He grabs her immediately, and she stands on both feet, sputtering. He laughs, wiping the water from her face.

"Don't laugh at me," she says with a scowl.

"I'm not," he says, trying to keep his mouth straight. "I'm not."

"I can see your lip curling," she says, pointing at him.

He turns his back to her, diving under the water and swimming a lap before coming back to stand in front of her. He wipes his hand down his face and pushes his hair back.

"Ready to try again?"

After several seconds of silence, she asks, "Why are you doing this?".

"What?" he says, chuckling.

"Why are you wasting your time like this?" she asks, folding her arms across her chest.

His eyes narrow at her question. He isn't sure if she's talking about swimming or about her.

"Nothing with you is a waste of time," he says evenly, his hand cupping her ankle.

She purses her lips, looking down at her feet underwater. She looks back up at him, unblinking.

"I'll never be good at this," she murmurs.

And if this were a few months ago, her statement would have felt like a hot poker to the chest, but he's figured it out. He's figured her out. He sighs, wanting to tread carefully, but also wanting to push back—to push against her, into her.

"You'll be great at this."

"You should find a more willing student."

Now the hot poker *is* in his chest and his eyebrows do furrow and he's standing to his full height in the water pushing her until she's sandwiched between his chest and the wall of the pool. Her hands rest on his biceps when he bends his head.

It was meant to be a reassuring gesture. A quick brush to let her know that he isn't going anywhere and that he doesn't want anyone else, and that she's so *fucking stubborn* but when their lips meet, he doesn't realize how tetchy he feels about her comments, and it quickly dissolves into an invasive one. Her nails dig into his arm, and she lets out a soft whimper when he deepens the kiss. His tongue sweeps against her and he drags his hands down her face, controlling the depth and speed and pressure, because he can.

Because he needs to.

Because he can't control anything else.

Pulling back, he rests his forehead against hers, his thumb tracing her mouth.

"I don't want anyone else, Jahlani. It makes me angry when you say things like that, so … don't, okay?" he says, breath uneven against her.

Cupping his jaw with her hand, she drags him back to her, kissing him with just as much aggression and he pulls back again, grabbing her jaw to stop her from chasing him.

"Did you hear what I said?" He asks.

She looks down, nodding. "I heard you, Roman."

He looks down at her, taking in her wet eyelashes, bruised lips, and bright eyes.

"God, you drive me crazy," he says before gathering her against his chest to kiss her with more languid precision.

"Roman Alexander Hayes! I thought that was you!" a voice calls from the side. Jahlani immediately pushes him away and glides to the side.

Alexander she mouths, hiding a smile behind her fist. He shrugs, turning back around to face the full government name-calling individual.

"Elliot," he says, reaching his hand out to clap his. "It's great to see you, man."

Elliot squats at the edge of the pool, smiling. Roman notices Jahlani sliding away and catches her wrist, pulling her back.

"Eli, this is Jahlani. Jahlani, meet Eli."

Jahlani sticks her hand out, and they shake. Elliot smiles at her before turning back to him.

"So, what's going on with you, man? I haven't seen you since Lucy was born."

Roman scratches his hair, feeling sheepish. "Yeah, man. I'm sorry. Things just got crazy."

Elliot holds up his hands. "Hey, I get it." Then with a frown, he amends, "Well, actually, I don't get it because I don't have a kid, but I get the sentiment."

Elliot turns to Jahlani, his mouth curved upward. "How do you know, Roman?"

She parts her lips. "I—"

"We're together," he says, not missing the way her eyes snap to him. "We're together," he repeats, liking the way it sounds.

Elliot smiles, shaking his head. "I figured, with the way you were practically swallowing her."

Roman flicks water at him, and Jahlani turns her head into his shoulder.

Elliot laughs, clearing his throat. "What brings you by?"

Roman sends a thumb Jahlani's way. "Teaching her to swim."

Elliot nods. "Ah. Well, Jahlani, you're in good hands—Roman wiped the floor at all the competitions."

Her eyebrows bend. "Competitions?"

"He didn't tell you? He used to swim competitively—that's how we met."

She looks up at him, shaking her head. "No, he didn't."

"It's nothing," he says, his cheeks burning.

Elliot narrows his eyes. "It's not nothing. You went to col—"

"Hey, how's Rosie?" he interrupts, shooting him a *don't fucking go there* look.

He nods slowly in understanding. "She's … good. Well, I'll let you both get back to it." He stands, slipping his sunglasses back on. "Hey, you should swing by next weekend. She would love to see you. We're playing board games." He turns to Jahlani, grinning. "You too, if you're not sick of him by then."

Jahlani laughs, shaking her head as he waves goodbye.

"Who's Rosie?" she asks when he disappears through the double doors.

He lowers his shoulders into the water to hide his trembling. "His grandmother. She raised him by herself after his parents died."

She frowns. "That's so sad."

He sighs, nodding. Suddenly, she's wrapping her arms around his shoulders and her legs around his waist.

"We should go next weekend."

The smile that spreads on his face is uncontrollable. "Yeah?"

"Yeah," she says, kissing him softly. "Invite Danica too. She wanted to show me her road-building skills last time in Catan."

He laughs, throwing his head back.

"Okay, sure. Whatever you want, Jahlani," he murmurs against her lips.

$$x = \frac{-b + \sqrt{b^2 - 4ac}}{2a}$$

They swim until their fingers prune up and Jahlani's stomach rumbles. It's quickly becoming one of his favorite sounds—right after her laugh.

It means he gets to take care of her in a different way.

In a domestic way.

In a way that shows he's good for something.

They sit in his car in a near-empty parking lot, working their way through fries, milkshakes, and burgers. She offers him a bite of her sandwich, and he leans forward, taking what he assumes is more than what she was offering when she pulls the food back, cursing at him. As they wipe their fingers and faces, she looks at him pointedly.

"Why didn't you tell me you used to swim competitively?"

He shrugs, chewing and swallowing his food. "It was a long time ago."

She scoffs. "Not that long ago, Roman. You were swimming at the collegiate level," she drops her phone in between the console, scrolling through a series of articles. All about him.

"What happened?"

"I became a single dad?"

She shakes her head. "Try again."

He expels a breath of air. "What do you want me to say?"

"Try the truth."

He wipes his mouth with a napkin before tossing it in the plastic bag between them.

"I didn't enjoy it anymore."

"Why?"

"It was something that my mom put me in as a kid and I was just naturally good at it. Coaches pushed my mom into making me do swim meets and competitions and sure it was fun at first, and then I got to high school, and I couldn't do what everyone else was doing. I had to keep my grades up and monitor my diet and focus on training and I just felt like I missed out on having an authentic teenage experience."

"Why didn't you say no? Why didn't you quit?"

He shakes his head. "I didn't want to disappoint my mom. She worked so hard with me and Dan. No help from anyone, I couldn't do that to her."

She twists her lips. "What happened when you got to college?"

He sighs, leaning back into the seat. "That's where I messed up. I had a lot more freedom than I was used to. The guys on the team were cool. More relaxed. Party people. It was fun and I got ahead of myself and you know the rest," he says, meeting her eyes.

"Lucy," she finishes softly.

"Lucy."

"Do you regret it?" she asks, tilting her head. He shakes his head.

"No. I will never admit this to anyone else but I'm glad Kareena got pregnant. It gave me a quicker way out because I knew eventually, I wouldn't be able to keep up."

Her eyebrows move together. "Keep up?"

He shrugs. "I knew I'd drop the ball eventually."

She scoffs. "How could you have possibly known that?"

"It's what I do."

She shakes her head, looking down at her hands. "That's called a self-fulfilling prophecy and a rather negative one."

"Yeah, I guess so," he says, looking at her from the corner of his eye. "What are you thinking?"

She sighs, leaning forward to grab his hand. "I'm thinking that you put *way* too much pressure on yourself and that you need to learn to take a step back and take it all in every once in a while."

He nods, humming as he watches her dance her fingertips across his palm.

"So software engineering became your backup," she murmurs, tracing his lines. He wets his lips, the tips of her fingers brushing over areas he didn't realize were so sensitive until just now.

"I thought it would sound good to my mom. Software engineer as a son has a nice ring to it," he says, chuckling weakly.

Jahlani tuts, dragging her index finger down the middle of his palm to the edge of his hand before starting over again. He's embarrassed at how he starts to press against the seam of his shorts, but *fuck she has to know what she's doing, right?*

"What would you have done then?" she asks.

"I can't tell you," he says, pressing two fingers to his lips, watching her.

Her eyes flick to his and she applies less pressure. "Well, now you have to tell me, otherwise I'm going to think the most outlandish things."

He shakes his head, lips parting when lifts his hand up to her mouth.

"A magician?"

"No."

"Sex therapist?"

"Nope."

"Dental hygienist?"

"You're so close."

"Come on, just tell me," she says, pressing a soft kiss to the inside of his wrist and it's impossible to hide his hard on at this point.

"Truthfully, I'd love to get my business license. I'd love to own something someday. Probably the bar."

"That sounds perfect," she murmurs, brushing her lips against his thumb.

"Yeah?" He breathes out, all the blood seeming to rush from his head.

"You'd be so good at it, Roman. You're very charismatic and

determined. You fit there," she says, pressing a bolder kiss to his palm. "You should look into it."

"Can't," he drags out, closing his eyes. His cheeks flush from her praise and her lips.

"Why?"

"Lucy. No time," he says, choppily trying to calm himself down. His eyes fly open when he starts to feel the flat of her tongue over his index finger.

"Jahlani," he says, dragging her mouth to his. "You should really stop before I'm forced to take drastic measures."

"Like?" she whispers, teasing.

"Like, screwing you in my car."

"Oh," she says, eyes flicking down. "I've never done that before. I don't know if …" She trails off, meeting his eyes again. "I want to try."

Fuck.

Leaning forward, he catches her mouth, pushing the plastic bag from her lap with the food in a frenzy. She tastes of the milkshake and the salt of the fries. Grabbing her waist, he helps her maneuver over the console and hover his lap. Her hair is still wet from their time in the pool, but he reaches up to take it out of its bun, letting her braids shroud them.

"You always do that," she murmurs against his mouth, shifting closer but not fully resting her weight on him. "You always take my hair down."

"I like it"—he threads his hands into her scalp—"when it's down. You always have it up at work and it drives me crazy because I want to do this." He tugs against the roots gently to expose her neck. "And this," he says, massaging her head gently while he drops soft kisses to her neck.

She sighs, finally dropping herself onto him and he groans. Her hands fist against his chest as she holds herself steady.

"Okay?" he asks against her neck.

She nods slightly. "Yeah, I just don't want to hurt you."

He lets out a broken chuckle. *Please fucking hurt me*, he wants to say but decides not to. Instead, moving both hands to drag her cover-up to her waist, and press her against him. Looking down at him, her teeth pull over her lip as he guides her over him.

"You're not hurting me, Jahlani."

He presses an open-mouthed kiss to her lips before leaning back to drag her over him again.

"Roman," she says through a breathless moan.

Her hands fist his shirt tighter, her mouth dropping back to his as he moves her faster over him. His hands move to untie her bikini top, and he drags the green fabric from her chest and throws it to the side.

She pulls back from his mouth when his hands slide under her cover-up, over her stomach, and ghost over both her taut brown nipples. Her hips stop moving and she lets out a strangled gasp.

"Keep going, Jahlani."

Her dark eyes meet his as she moves above him again, lips parting, another shuddering moan escaping as his hands roam her chest. Her hips start to bear down harder, and he groans at the teasing sensation.

"This is everything I didn't know I needed, Jahlani, you know that?" he says, while tugging on her chest.

"Roman," she breathes, hips melting against him.

"I love when you call my name like that," he says, pinching her nipples.

"Roman," she rasps, her chest heaving. "I'm—"

Her hands tangle with his own against her chest, not pushing, not encouraging him to touch her a certain way, not to pull them, they just rest on top delicately as she breathes out a series of expletives. She snaps her hips against him a few more times before she's moaning excessively in the cabin of his car, her fingers curling to apply a slight pressure against the veins in his hands.

And a sudden thought strikes him as he watches her come undone, their hands pressed together, his length desperate to be inside her.

How much longer do we get to do this?

She falls forward, breathing heavily and he moves her hair to the side, pressing a soft kiss to her ear.

"At Thanksgiving dinner, you said you were staying temporarily. What does that mean?" he says, against the shell of her ear. He kisses against the piercings that glint on her ear, and she shudders.

"What?"

"Thanksgiving. What did you mean?" he says, his hand tightening on her hips.

She sits up, blinking slowly. "You really want to talk about this now?"

He leans back to look in her eyes. "I just want to know what it means," he says, cupping her jaw. Her eyes bounce all over his face.

"You know what it means, Roman," she whispers.

And suddenly that clock becomes more vivid in his head. He licks his lips, tightening his hold on her face.

"Do you want this, Jahlani?"

This. Us. You. Me. Together.

The silence is deafening in the car. She turns her head. "I don't know."

And really, he's not surprised by her response. It's inherently Jahlani. And he would have believed her if he didn't know her so well. And he does know her well. And it makes him want to laugh and cry and jump for joy but also scream at The Fates for making him fall in love with someone who is so determined to not *feel too much*.

But he knows she's not ready to hear that and he's already treading on dangerous waters with this conversation, so he shoves it down.

"Well then," he says, drawing her face back to him to kiss her cheek, "you have time to figure it out because I already have my answer. In the meantime, I'm going to keep looking at you. I'm going to kiss you when I feel like it, and hold you when I see you, and fuck you every time I have the chance because yes, you're worth the risk, and no, nothing about it will be quick."

"And what if I say no?"

He shakes his head, adjusting her on his lap. "You won't."

"How do you figure that?"

"Because you want this as much as I do—maybe more," he says, swiping his thumb along her mouth.

"It's risky," she murmurs, sliding her hands under his shirt. "We'd need some better rules of engagement."

"Meaning?"

She inhales, thinking deeply as she runs her hands over his shoulders. "No eye contact at all during lectures. Don't raise your hand during class. And no office hours anymore."

He lets out a soft laugh. "So, you're basically going to ignore my entire existence."

She sighs, toying with a piece of thread on his shirt. "You and I both know that's not possible."

And it's her admission that does it for him because he finds himself nodding, sliding his hands against her thighs.

"Yeah. Okay. I have one condition," he says, leaning forward to kiss her.

"Mhm," she says against his mouth.

"We don't talk about you leaving," he requests, dragging her cover-up over her head this time.

"Deal," she says through a shiver, leaning down to catch his lips. "Roman," she says after several minutes of haze-inducing kissing. She pulls back, meeting his gaze. "Don't try to stop me from leaving."

How much longer do we get to do this?

The question dries in his throat, his heart thundering in his chest.

He doesn't say anything as he gathers her in his arms, pushing his shorts down, and then her bikini as he helps ease her down. Their foreheads meet as they breathe against each other.

She nods before letting him kiss her freely. Deeply. Slowly. Halting her when she tries to move against him. Pressing into her when she takes him in a little more. Sighing when she pulls at the hair on the back of his neck.

"Jahlani. Can I tell you something that will probably scare you shitless? You had me the minute you walked into class that day. I tried not to be curious about it. About you. I thought it would go away. I would barely see you. Plus, I had Lucy to worry about. How are you doing?"

She mumbles in response. He kisses her cheek. "Good. You're doing so good."

"Roman." She sighs quietly, kissing his jaw as she rolls against him.

"I made up all these crazy ass scenarios in my head. That you hated kids, that you didn't like guys with green eyes, that you were into something boring like bird watching. Which I actually think I'd be completely okay with if it was with you." A strained, breathless laugh leaves her lips.

"And then I saw you that day, about to pass out. You didn't even know, but I had a really shitty, rough day. Like—incredibly shitty. I was exhausted, but then I saw you. Do you remember?"

"I remember."

"Right, so. Shitty day, desperate to go home, and then I see you. And you look even worse than I feel. And I'm wondering to myself, 'Why isn't anyone taking care of her?' And then I stepped to you and the question became, 'Why won't she let anyone take care of her?' And Jahlani, I really, really was so tired. But I couldn't leave you. I didn't want to leave you. I was just too damn curious about this woman. Scared yet?"

She swallows. "Like I'm watching a slasher ... except I'm the main character who trips and falls." He laughs into her neck before groaning when she starts to move faster.

"There's nothing to be afraid of. I think I figured it out. Figured you out. And I realized it didn't matter if you didn't like guys with green eyes, or that you hated kids. All that mattered was that you were okay. That someone was taking care of you, and at first it didn't matter if that someone else was me or another man, but Jahlani," he says, pulling back to look at her. "I really want it to be me."

And then to his satisfaction, she's contracting against him. Her head falls back, and he catches her wrist, caging them against his chest as her groans surround them. With one hand still trapping her wrists, he moves the other over her clit slowly.

She looks at him through hazy eyes, moaning his name as she grinds against his hand, coating his fingers, and that's what does it for him.

The look of pure elation on her face.

"Jahlani," he says, shuddering violently as he pulses inside her. His hips still as he breathes deeply against her collarbone. His fingers continue to brush against her, and the plane of her stomach, and her breaths turn heavier, louder, longer.

Her thighs grow tenser, and she's arching into him, and then she's gasping as she drives herself against him. He captures her mouth, kissing her, trying to imprint himself on every version of her.

How much longer do we get to do this?

Because he wants forever.

CHAPTER 31
Family-friendly

Jahlani

Jahlani feels as though she's cheating on her family as she pulls into the cobblestone driveway for the second time. She should be trying to mend things with them—to be better, to try. But things here with them are easier. Calmer. Happier. Here, she doesn't have to think so much about what she's doing. This time, the door is covered in Christmas decorations. Somehow, she finds herself in the kitchen with Gwen—which she doesn't mind. It's refreshing. She talks about everything. Her latest project, a crazy buyer, how she got into art, and then Roman.

"I just worry about him," Gwen says, scooping out pasta into a bowl.

"Worry?"

"That boy just always seems to have his head in the clouds. He's been like that since he was a kid, and I hate that he's still working at that bar," she says, sipping from her wine. "It's a shame."

Jahlani is quiet for several moments, mixing the salad.

"Roman is brilliant, Gwen," she says, slowly. "He has this way with the customers. He's so expressive and controlled. He's very personable and works so hard. It's not easy what he does, but he's good, and he likes it. He's happy. Shouldn't that count for something?"

Gwen sighs heavily. "Happy doesn't pay the bills, baby." She pats her arm as if to say, *you're so cute, so young, so naïve.* "It doesn't cover the cost of her health."

Jahlani lets out a long sigh, scratching her temple because she understands now.

Why Roman is the way he is.

"Gwen, you should be proud of him. You should cheer him on. Support him. What you think matters to him."

She sets her glass down, her head tilting. "Did he say something to you?"

Jahlani shakes her head. "No, I just … I see how hard he works and how good he is with Lucy. He's trying. He has a lot on his plate, and I just think you might be being too hard on him," she says, her voice quiet. "Sorry if that's overstepping. I'm gonna … set this on the table." Jahlani squeezes past her, not waiting for her reaction.

The rest of the night is spent playing an intense game of Catan over milk and cookies. Roman is patient, taking his time to explain the rules, brushing his fingers over her thighs, resting his arm on the back of her chair, and reminding her to drink. It's well past eleven when they get back to his, and he's tucked Lucy in.

He shuffles out to the living room, lifting her legs to drop them in his lap as she hits the play button on a show. He peels both her socks off before moving to massage them. She drops the remote across her chest, leaning further into the couch.

"What's going on?"

"They're trying to figure out how to kill their sister's husband."

He snorts. "That's sick."

Jahlani shrugs. "He deserves it. You'll see."

Twenty minutes later, Roman is nodding at the screen. "I see." She laughs, looking at him.

"What's that look?" he asks after a beat.

Jahlani sighs, looking toward the ceiling. "Nothing. I'm just happy."

He turns to her. "Yeah?"

"Yeah."

"Good. I like it when you're happy."

She sighs, turning back to watch the show. "Me too."

And as they watch the main characters argue on whether to cut the brakes of the husband's car, his fingers rubbing soothing circles, Jahlani thinks about how maybe it is possible for things to come in threes.

Lucy.

Roman.

Her growing relationships with everyone.

Despite everything she's been through with her parents, Micah, her financial dilemmas, and school, she feels something she didn't foresee happening anytime soon.

She feels hope.

$$x = \frac{-b + \sqrt{b^2 - 4ac}}{2a}$$

"Okay," Jahlani says, clapping her hands together in the front of the lecture hall the next day. "We have two more topics and then we're done."

A few students whoop from the back. Jahlani laughs, feeling light and airy and *good*. Her eyes gloss over Roman, who sends her a wink. She averts her attention back to the screen, pulling up the next PowerPoint.

For the past week, she's been blissed out. She's glowing. Thriving. Healthier. Apparently, great sex and even better conversation does that to a person. There's a loud energy that seems to thrum around her when she's sharing the same space as him and they meet each other's eyes. The first day back in class was ... disastrous. She bumbled her way through the lecture, making mistakes to the point that several students had to ask if she was feeling okay.

All because of him.

Later that night, they laid out even more ground rules that resulted in her being pressed into the kitchen island. She moves around the room as students take notes. The loud chime of her phone receiving a text message sends a thrill through her.

RO
Come over.

Her body burns and she can't stop her lips from turning upward.

JAHLANI
Don't text me. I'm working.

RO
Okay.

RO
I'll stop if you agree to come over tonight.

RO
I have perfected the craft of cinnamon rolls.

She snorts at this, getting ready to type a reply when a student calls her.

"Uh, Miss ... your messages are showing up on the screen."

Jahlani looks up and she reaches forward to rip the HDMI cord from her MacBook. She lowers her head, cheeks flaming, before looking at her phone.

"Would you look at the time—I'm late for an appointment."

"We still have forty-five minutes—"

"Class is over," she says in a rush, typing on her phone as students filter out, not looking up.

JAHLANI
We'll talk later.

$$x = \frac{-b + \sqrt{b^2 - 4ac}}{2a}$$

"New rule," Jahlani says in the entryway, slipping off her shoes. "You can't text me anymore."

She stops when she rounds the corner, unable to fight the curve of her mouth when Lucy stumbles to her. She lifts her up, placing her on her hip as she walks toward Roman.

"What's all this?" she breathes out, stepping toward the dining room table that's laid out with food. He shrugs, rubbing the back of his neck.

"My way of apologizing. I tried to get all your favorites. I even"—he lifts the box to reveal pineapple pizza—"got this monstrosity."

She scoffs. "This isn't going to work."

He sighs, dragging a hand down his face. "I know."

"That could've been way worse."

"I know."

"That could've been expulsion."

"Yeah."

"And was really, reckless—"

"Yup."

"Of me," she says, setting Lucy down on the ground. "I shouldn't have used my laptop, or I should've turned off my notifications. I'll do it tonight," she says, stepping into his arms. "This is crazy, Roman," she says against his chest.

"We'll be more careful," he says, his body rumbling against her. "Two more weeks until the semester's over."

She pulls back, her stomach dropping. "Already?"
"Yeah. And then you're all mine," he says, smiling.
As long as this isn't an itch.

CHAPTER 32
Opportunity

Jahlani

Dear Ms. Jahlani Jones,

Our team would like to thank you for applying for a position with SION Consulting. At this time, we would like to formally extend an invitation for you to interview with us. Please reply to this email within the next forty-eight hours with a date and time that works for you.

If you are no longer are interested in this position, please disregard this email.

Thank you,
Angela Keighton
Director of Human Resources
SION Consulting

$$x = \frac{-b + \sqrt{b^2 - 4ac}}{2a}$$

Jahlani stares at the email in her inbox two weeks later, blinking. She isn't sure *why*, but she isn't jumping for joy. She should be touching the ceiling right now. Her head should be through the goddamn roof.

After all, this email is a position for her dream job.

The job that she's been clawing, punching, and kicking at for the past few years. A once-in-a-lifetime opportunity. A chance for her to free herself. To be happy.

But she isn't jumping for joy.

She's frowning instead. She remembers applying for the job at the start of the semester, she remembers seeing the qualifications and meeting them all. She remembers asking around for recommendations—Jackson included—but she doesn't remember the position being in California.

Over two thousand miles from here.

Across the country.

And she isn't sure why that information is so vital until her eyes meet his across the room. A few days ago, as she held Lucy while he shoved his shoes on in a rush, he bent forward to kiss Lucy's head, and then did hers too, and it was so intimate and sweet and *so much more* than she had ever expected.

And that was a problem.

Because now he's what's wrong with her. He's the reason why she isn't jumping for joy. He's the reason why she's questioning all her choices, why she keeps breaking her own rules, and keeps wanting to break them.

The reason the lump in her throat forms and her hands start to tremble. The reason she bumps into Jackson, mumbling something incoherent about needing to step out. The reason she flies down the hallway, turning corner after corner until she's back in his office.

Safe. Alone. Away. Her skin flushes as her heart hammers. She unbuttons her cardigan, shedding it as she paces back and forth in the empty room.

The door swings open, and Roman walks through.

Her eyes widen as her pulse increases. "What are you doing? You can't be in here."

Stepping all the way in, the door snaps shut as he leans against it. "I wanted to make sure you're okay."

She laughs, but it's strained. Mocking. "I'm fine."

"You don't look fine."

"Roman," she whispers as she continues pacing back and forth, "I said I'm fine. You shouldn't be here. Someone could see."

"See what? We're not doing anything." His phone vibrates, but he ignores it.

She steps toward him. "You can't be in here," she says, gritting her teeth. "Leave. Go back to the lecture. Please."

He steps forward, eyebrows pinched together. "Did something happen with your parents? Did someone do something to you?"

Yes, I realized that I haven't been able to wash you from me yet. I realized that I fell for you. I realized that no matter what, I'm going to sabotage this somehow.

"No. Nothing happened," she says, lip curled. His phone buzzes again.

"Then, what's wrong?"

"Nothing! I just—are you going to get that?" she snaps.

He arches a brow, turning the phone off before placing it on the desk.

"No, I'm not going to get it. We're talking."

She covers her face with her hands, inhaling and exhaling to lessen the shaking.

Without realizing, she finds herself on the edge of Jackson's desk. Roman steps further into the room, and it's not long before warm hands engulf her own, prying her fingers from her face. He's too close, and her mind wanders.

She fastens her chin toward her chest as his finger curls under it. "Jahlani, look at me."

She licks her lips, her stomach twisting at his light touch.

"You shouldn't be in here," she says to the ground in a quiet voice.

"I know."

He steps forward, trailing his fingers from under her chin to her cheek. Back and forth, and back again. She shivers, turning her face into his hand, closing her eyes when his arm slides around her waist, curving her body into his. His thumb finds its way to her bottom lip, and he swipes against it slowly.

"Jahlani," he says, voice gravelly. "Fuck, I—"

Her body hums and seems to fold into him. Into his touch. It seems to scream *here, this is it, this is what you were missing. Him.*

Her eyes open as she peers up at him, their heavy breathing mixing together, his green eyes pouring into her own ebony-infused ones. She's so warm and desperate and he's barely touched her. His head tilts closer and their mouths are a fraction away.

"Anyone could come in," she says against his mouth. "Jackson could come in."

But her body's a mess for him.

So, when he breathes against her mouth telling her that he missed her she closes the distance, sending her fingers through his hair. His hand moves to grip the back of her neck, pressing their mouths together, holding her steady as they kiss slowly.

"Can't do it," he says into her mouth as his tongue meets hers. "I don't know if I've told you this, but your rules are bullshit."

Her hands slide under his sweater as she roams his hard chest and stomach. A rush of cold air meets her as he steps back, dragging the shirt up his body. Both arms wind against her back, lifting her to deposit her further on the desk. Her legs fall open as he steps in between them, his hand gliding up her thigh, disappearing under her skirt.

His fingers trace slow, soothing circles over the lace, and she moans into his mouth, gripping his arm as she tries to get more.

"*Roman.*"

He pulls the damp material to the side, grazing her bare clit with his fingers. Her eyes screw shut as her mouth falls open in a soft whimper. As his fingers graze over her, his tongue meets the side of her neck with fast, bruising motions. She bites her lip as her body grows warmer and she starts to tilt and circle against his fingers.

"Should we stop, Lani?" His lips graze against the column of her throat as he continues to massage her, never changing his pace. "I shouldn't be in here, right?"

He pulls back, gripping her hair, twisting her head to whisper into her ear. "I shouldn't be touching you like this in Jackson's office. I should stop, right?"

She shakes her head, exhaling slowly.

His fingers slide into her, and an abrupt moan falls out of her. He stays there for several moments, grazing, tapping, collecting, before he slides them and rubs over her. Her stomach clenches and she lets her legs fall open further as he continues the slow motions of his fingers. Her head falls against his chest as her body starts to throb, the familiar ball of tension starting to grow.

It doesn't take as long as she expects as she presses her fingertips into his arms, her body unwinding in satisfying layers. As her body travels to some state of normalcy, he continues rubbing. Tilting her head up, he presses their mouths together in a frenzied, almost clumsy rush. Sliding her hand down to his, she removes it before sifting both hands back through his hair.

He pulls back and away, and she almost cries out because she's not ready for it to be over. Not yet. Maybe not ever. But as she leans against the edge, she sees him turn the lock on the door. She watches through hazy eyes as he steps back in front of her, snapping open the buttons of her blouse. When he works the last one open, he drags it down her arms, kissing down the same path.

She watches through drunk eyes as Roman leans forward, caressing her knee. The multicolored stack of papers on the desk is almost enough to throw her off track and the insanity of it all rushes toward her, but then he's pushing himself closer, and her eyes flutter shut as she grows hotter, wetter.

"I wanted this that night," he says, kissing her again. "When we argued. I've thought about it every night since. I've thought about this since the first day I saw you in class. You still don't think it's fate? That we're here like this together?"

"Roman," she says through a sigh. "Just shut up and kiss me."

And she pulls his mouth to hers, forgetting everything that led her to this room in the first place.

"Guess what?" he asks, pulling back as his fingertips become firmer as he moves to her thigh, massaging.

"What?" she murmurs, eyes stuck on the movement of his hands on her flesh.

"After today …" He trails off. She watches as he grips her foot, pressing a kiss to it, before moving to her ankle, calf, inner knee, thigh. He repeats the same action to her other foot and leg before standing up to slide her panties all the way down. He kisses her intensely before making his way down her body and licking her. "After today," he breathes against her, meeting her eyes, "you aren't forbidden anymore."

Her mouth falls open and her eyes close as he works his lips and teeth and tongue over her. She grips his jaw with one hand and uses the other to anchor herself to the table to angle her hips, to push them against his face and then she's coming apart, and she bites her hand to stifle her scream.

He moves back up her body, leaving a trail of kisses against her knee, the top of her thighs, her chest, before making it to her lips where the kiss is slow and lazy.

Explorative.

When he pulls back, she slumps back against the desk, covering her face with her arm, exhaustion tugging at her. She opens her eyes and looks around at the mess they made before laughing hysterically.

"What's so funny?"

"I think we broke Jackson's pencil holder." This sentence alone brings a new wave of hysteria to her as he pulls her up. He kisses her, silencing her.

"What now?" she asks, staring at the mess around them.

"Now, we go back to class."

She lets out a breathless chuckle. "I don't know how I'm supposed to go in there and pretend like we didn't just do this."

He winks at her as she slides her clothes back on. She sees the glint of his phone, and powers it back on, shaking her head as she sets it down to put her shirt back on. She bites her lip, feeling giddy until she sees his phone flash from her peripheral.

It happens fast and all at once. The notifications that stain his phone are a combination of Gwendolyn, Danica, and then Audrey. That one sends her hand trembling.

"Roman," she says, her voice sounding hollow and distant. He doesn't hear her as he bends down to straighten the materials from Professor Jackson's desk. She licks her lips, taking a short step toward him.

"Roman," she says, louder this time, and this time he hears. His eyes meet hers and she watches as his smile instantly dissolves. His eyes travel to the phone in her hand and his forehead creases.

"What's wrong?" he asks, taking several steps forward. Jahlani holds out his phone, and he removes it from her grasp, inspecting the messages. His thumb sweeps across the screen with increasing ferocity, his face contorting, his shoulders dropping.

Jahlani steps forward with her arm outstretched, but Roman takes an abrupt, almost flinching, step back before turning to face her, his eyes not quite meeting hers.

"I have to go," he mutters, looking around the room with wide eyes. "I have to go."

Jahlani nods, running a hand over her head. "Go."

"My bag—my stuff," he stutters, patting his pockets. He digs his hand into his front pocket, retrieving his keys. "My laptop—"

Jahlani shakes her head, a sharp pressure building in the back of her throat as she watches Roman.

"Roman, *go*. I'll bring it to you later. Go, quickly."

She watches him nod absentmindedly, shuffling backward before connecting his eyes with hers, and she sees it: the guilt, the dread, the consequences, all flashing behind his eyes. Her stomach churns and she shakes her head when he hesitates at the door.

Go she mouths softly, watching as his knuckles turn white on the handle. With a final desperate look, Roman pulls the door open and leaves.

When Jahlani hears the latch of the door close, she leans her weight against the desk, taking deep breaths. Pressing a hand to her chest, she closes her eyes as she tries to time out her breaths evenly. When she feels her pulse slow, she's left with a single, lingering thought:

She should've stopped him sooner.

CHAPTER 33
Vitals

Roman

The creak of the door opening startles Roman from his attempt at sleeping. Wiping down his face, he clears his throat, sitting upright. The leather chair cracks in protest as he shuffles. Goosebumps arise on his arms when the A/C unit that hangs on the wall kicks in. Looking toward the cot, he sees that Lucy is still sleeping.

His exhale is long and low as he stands, rolling his neck and stretching his hands overhead.

"Knock, knock," Audrey says, walking in with a teal clipboard decorated with smiley faces. "Just wanted to check her vitals," she says in a hushed tone.

She's wearing navy scrubs with anchors and multicolored fish. He blinks, trying to get his bearings as he stretches. After a few minutes noting the monitor, Audrey sets the clipboard down and turns to him, a hand on her hip.

"You okay?" she asks, a tilt to her head. Her hair hangs loose by her shoulders and sways with her as she inspects him.

Fucking terrible, he thinks as he runs a hand through his hair, blowing out a breath. "I'm good."

She stares for a few seconds, her eyes narrowing slightly.

"Okay," she says, sending a sheepish smile before returning to write more notes on the clipboard. They lapse into silence, Roman frowning at his phone because Jahlani Jones—*the love of his fucking life*—said she'd be here an hour ago, and she's late.

She's never late.

Audrey turns to face him again, cradling the clipboard against her hip. "Hey, are you sure you're okay?"

He sighs, clicking his phone closed, before sliding it into his pocket. "I'm fine. How's she doing?"

Audrey nods, running a finger down the notes she wrote on the clipboard.

"She's good, Roman. Her temperature is going down, which is great," she says, looking back up. "But I'm only asking about you because your shirt is inside out."

Roman takes a moment to inspect his outfit then and realizes that *shit, she's right.*

He shakes his head, letting out a weak laugh. "I need coffee."

He gets up, moving to pour himself a cup, except he completely misses the Styrofoam, spilling dark liquid across his hand and the counter.

"Shit," he mumbles, his reaction slow as he watches it trickle down the sides. Within a few seconds, Audrey is next to him, pressing paper towels onto the counter. They work in silence, the soft hum of the monitors filling the room. He walks them to the trash can and returns to find the cup has already been filled for him.

"Thanks," he murmurs, reaching for it still feeling dazed after he takes several sips. Audrey leans against the counter, her arms crossed over her chest. She nudges his shoulder with hers and smiles.

"She'll be okay, Roman. Promise."

He nods, watching the rise and fall of Lucy's chest as he drinks. He hears a sharp inhale from Audrey and turns to face her. She rubs the back of her neck before meeting his eyes, a slight tint to her cheeks.

"Hey, I just wanted to say I'm sorry about Thanksgiving. I was out of line. I shouldn't have acted that way, and I'm completely mortified by my behavior. My mom—" She wipes the counter again. "She died two years ago. From a brain aneurysm."

Roman lowers the cup to the countertop, his eyes widening.

"Shit, Audrey. I'm so sorry. That must be ... I can't imagine," he finishes rather lamely.

She doesn't talk for several moments, wiping at her face. "Yeah, so, anyway, she was all the family I had and ... I guess I was just looking for someone to care about me again. The same way you care for Lucy, you know? And I'm not telling you this as an excuse, but I think my actions were misplaced when I saw you with Jahlani."

Roman nods, scratching the back of his neck. "I'm sorry too. I just—"

"It's okay. She's intense. Intelligent. Pretty. I get it."

He sighs, pressing his fingers to his eyes. "Yeah, but I messed up. We were together when the calls were coming through. I think she blames herself for what happened. Me not being there in time for Lucy."

Audrey nods, folding her arms over her chest. "Well, don't jump to conclusions just yet. I'm sure everything's fine."

You don't know her like I do.

"Yeah, thanks, Audrey."

"Sure," she says, moving to the door. "Try to get some sleep, Roman."

Audrey pulls it open then and Jahlani appears on the other side, her eyes bouncing between the two of them before settling on Audrey.

Roman's pulse intensifies, his body tingling as he watches her stand in the doorway, his backpack on her shoulder.

"Hey, Audrey," she says in a low voice, her eyes moving back to Roman's, sending him a weak smile.

"Jahlani, hey," she says, turning to look back at Roman, before meeting her gaze again. "I was just on my way out."

Jahlani's eyebrows crease. "Is she okay? Is she doing better?"

Audrey waves her free hand in the air. "Oh, yeah. She's good. She's a fighter, that one," she says, smiling, but Jahlani's eyebrows remain pinched, clearly not reassured. Audrey reaches out, squeezing her shoulder. "She'll be okay, Jahlani. She's in good hands here."

Jahlani smiles then, nodding before moving her eyes over to Roman again. Audrey drops her hand from her arm, stepping to the side.

"I'll get out of the way. It was nice seeing you again, Jahlani."

Jahlani toys with the gold chain around her neck, nodding.

"Yeah. You too, Audrey," she murmurs, giving her a polite smile that Audrey returns.

Roman watches Jahlani and Audrey shuffle around each other before Jahlani steps fully into the room and closes the door. She exhales, drops his bag on the floor, and moves to Lucy with quiet, tentative steps.

"She's okay?" she whispers, hovering her finger across her cheek, never fully touching her. Roman nods, moving to the opposite side, watching her.

"She'll get discharged tomorrow as long as her temperature keeps going down."

Jahlani shakes her head, standing upright and his heart squeezes because she's here. Maybe he's wrong about what he saw.

"That's good," she says, letting out a breath. "That's great. I'm glad."

She smiles, but it doesn't seem to reach her eyes. He blows out a breath, moving back to the chair lowering himself into it. He clears his throat.

She moves around the bed then, walking toward him slowly. Cautiously, like a baby deer.

He extends his hand to her and after a second of hesitation she takes it, lowering into his lap. He can't seem to help himself when he pulls her closer to bury his nose into her neck. He inhales deeply.

"You smell heavenly."

Like home.

He feels her throat work through a swallow, and he kisses her softly before pulling back to look at her.

"You're quiet," he says, shaking his leg to get her attention. "Talk to me."

When she doesn't speak, he drops a kiss to her forehead.

"Jahlani—"

"I'm going to California," she says in a rush.

Roman's heart drops into his stomach as she continues to speak, not meeting his eyes.

"It's for an interview and I know the timing is bad with Lucy, but it's for my dream position, and I can't—" she stammers, letting out a shaky exhale. "I'm sorry."

"It's okay—she's fine," he says, drawing her closer to his chest. "I'm happy for you. I'm sure you'll do great, baby. How long are you going for?"

"Just for the weekend," she whispers. "It'll be good for us to get some space, so that you can focus on Lucy, you know?"

Roman shakes his head, pulling back to look at her.

"When is it going to get through to you that space is the last thing that I want from you?"

Her eyes trail to his lips, linger for far too long which he's *completely okay with*, before meeting his eyes.

"Do you need a ride?" he asks, his tone gentle.

"A ride?" she murmurs, unable to tear her gaze from his mouth. He can't help the lurid images that flash through his head—them in his bed, him shirtless and bare, her knees anchored on both sides of him as she straddles him, his fist in her hair as she presses herself down, him moaning her name.

He exhales before meeting her gaze. Her lips curve upward, and she gives him a knowing look.

"To the airport."

She sighs, running a shaky hand over her braids. "No. It's too much trouble."

"Nothing's too much trouble when it comes to you, Jahlani."

"Don't say things like that," she whispers.

"Like what?"

"Just ... you know. Like that."

His eyes shift to her lips once more. Shaking his head, she slides off his lap, removing her warmth. He watches her slide her bag onto her shoulder and kiss Lucy on the forehead.

When they reach the door, he stills as she looks up, meeting his gaze. Her face is etched with something he can't quite place—anguish, frustration, a rawness that takes him by surprise. He runs a hand through his hair, gripping the handle of the door with white-knuckled intensity.

"Just call me. Please. Can you do that? Can you just—" His voice cracks. For a moment, everything freezes. There's only her, standing there, looking at him like he holds the answers to something she hasn't figured out.

His breath catches, his chest tightening in a way he didn't think was possible because she looks desperate, vulnerable—completely at odds with the woman who usually imprisons her feelings.

"I'll call you," she whispers, her voice sounding small. "Promise."

Roman's gaze softens, and he drops one final kiss to her lips.

But he's seen that look before. It's the same one Kareena wore before she left.

CHAPTER 34
Limits

Jahlani

It's close to sunset in Los Angeles and Jahlani squints to see her best friend against the dusty skyline. The airport is overrun with people, and she cranes her neck to see Imani, her phone pressed to her ear. Ducking and weaving in between people, she makes it to the end of the curb where she finally catches sight of her red highlights and glinting piercings. As she steps toward her and Imani catches her eye, it's like she's been struck. Everything she's bottled for months surges up, and she stumbles into Imani's outstretched arms.

Imani holds her close, resting her head on top as Jahlani's shoulders shake.

"Come on, Lani Banani. Let's get you fed."

$$x = \frac{-b + \sqrt{b^2 - 4ac}}{2a}$$

The refrigerator's low hum fills the one-bedroom as Jahlani tries to string a coherent thought together. The sun begins to sink across the wood flooring, casting a soft tangerine sheen. Outside, the streets are quiet as people turn in. Laughter flares in the hallway, then a door snaps shut.

"Imani, I feel … funny."

"Yeah, three edibles will do that, babe."

They had spent the past three hours catching up about nothing and everything. Jahlani's head rests in her lap as they sit on the couch. Imani passes her fingers through her braids, combing out the knots that have formed over the past week.

"How do you feel about the interview tomorrow? You think you'll get it?"

Jahlani blows out a breath. "I think so. We had a virtual meeting already, so I think my prospects are high. Plus, it's woman-owned." Imani hums, her fingers continuing to glide through her hair.

"Imani, you'd make such a good mom," Jahlani says softly after a few minutes of silence. Imani's fingers stop their motion in her hair, but she grabs her fingers, forcing her to continue. She does so dutifully. "You're the fiercest person I know," Jahlani murmurs. "You don't take shit from anyone. You're strong and poised. You take such good care of me." Jahlani twists in her arms to look at her. "Hey, remember that time in eleventh grade when Robert Lind said—"

"Said you were pretty for a Black girl," she finishes in a deadpan tone.

"Yes!" Jahlani throws her hands up, shaking her head at the fond memory, before inching back down and readjusting herself on her lap. She begins toying with a loose thread on her cardigan.

"I've never seen you angry, Imani. You punched him. You got suspended for it."

"Yeah, well, he deserved it," she grumbles, but Jahlani can hear the smile in her voice.

"You got suspended for me," Jahlani says, her voice quieter now. "I didn't understand it at the time. The way you explained it, the backhandedness of his comment. You were so mad. You grabbed my arm, and you said, 'Jahlani, don't ever say thank you to anyone who compliments you while tearing down your race in the process. You're beautiful regardless of complexion. He's a piece of shit.'" She sighs, teasing the loose thread, unraveling it farther.

Jahlani drops her hands with a sigh.

"What if I'm a bad parent?" she asks in a low voice. "What if I'm like her—like my mom?"

Imani sits up straighter, her hands gently guiding Jahlani to sit as well until they're facing each other.

"Jahlani, what are you talking about? You're *nothing* like them."

Jahlani's eyes cut down to the quilt draped over the linen. "I think about what Micah said a lot. I think he was right a little, Imani. My parents ... they messed me up badly and I don't feel okay."

Jahlani looks to the ceiling before she stares into Imani's eyes with watery ones. Imani's warm hands wrap around Jahlani and ease her down until they're lying side by side. She presses a delicate kiss to her head.

"Damn you for keeping this shit from me," Imani whispers against her hair, rubbing soothing circles across her arm. "I hate seeing you like this. And to answer your question, you would make an *exceptional* mom. I know that because you care enough not to make the same mistakes that our parents did growing up."

Jahlani nods, letting her words settle around her.

"She's really sick, Imani," Jahlani says after some time has passed. "What am I supposed to do? I care about them both so much, but I'm not what they need. They deserve better. He deserves someone who can give him one hundred percent, and I'm not there. I don't think it's fair to her for me to want more from him. You know? I don't want him to turn into my parents. I don't want him to neglect her for me."

Imani sighs. "I think ... Roman should decide what he needs

and what's best for both him and his daughter and you need to allow yourself to experience just being in the moment. Allow yourself to enjoy whatever this is between you and him without worrying."

Jahlani swallows. "He's so ... whole and put together, and I'm not. Who wants that?"

"He does, clearly," she murmurs, sitting upright.

Jahlani shakes her head. "I'd ruin him, Imani."

"Or maybe you wouldn't."

"He'll get tired of me—"

"Or maybe he never gets tired of you."

"He'll want me to love him in a way I'm not capable of—"

"Or," she says, grabbing Jahlani's hands, "Maybe you already love him the best way you know how and that's enough for him. Don't you think you should let him decide his limits?"

Jahlani shakes her head. "I already know his limits, and I know how this ends."

$$x = \frac{-b + \sqrt{b^2 - 4ac}}{2a}$$

Two days later, it's well after midnight when she gets back to Florida. She ignores Roman's sleep-well message, choosing instead to curl into a ball, crying herself to sleep. The next day, she convinces him that she's come down with something and insists on not wanting to pass it on to Lucy.

Jahlani can hear her mom banging around the kitchen and against her better judgment, leaves to investigate. She shuffles down the hallway into the kitchen. Multiple pots sit on the stove, while carrots, lentils, and half-chopped celery take up the countertop. Blinking, she walks in, lowering herself to the dining room chair.

"What's all this?" Jahlani croaks.

Her mom moves back to the largest pot, lifting the lid to stir what's inside.

"It's soup. Dick's not feeling well, so I'm making him some. Gonna head over to him in a minute."

Jahlani's fingers twitch watching her mom. She waits, and waits, and waits, but the offer never comes. She doesn't ask if Jahlani wants any. She doesn't try to force-feed her. She doesn't even look at her.

"Mom." Her voice reverberates in the small kitchen. Her mother's sunken eyes meet hers. "I have to talk to you. Can you sit for a second?"

She looks over at Jahlani, moving to the pantry. "Can it wait? Dick likes his food hot. Won't touch the microwave—radiation and all that," she says, rummaging through the shelves.

"No, it can't," she says through a shaky exhale.

Her mom returns with various-sized Tupperware, setting them on the countertop before looking at her with a sigh.

"What is it, Jahlani?"

Jahlani starts cracking her fingers before spinning the necklace at her collarbone. "I'm leaving," she says, her eyes flitting to hers before looking down at the fruit-printed tablecloth. "I took a job in California. It's a good job," she says, setting her hands on the table, looking at her. "It's my dream job."

Her mom blinks, seemingly unfazed and then returns to sorting the Tupperware. "Well, that's good. I can rent out that room, then. Dick has a friend—"

"Mom," Jahlani says, her knee bouncing. "Are you being serious right now?"

She continues to sort the Tupperware. All the tops on one end and their respective bases on the other. "What? Dick thinks it'll be a good source of income."

"*Mom*," she says, pushing from the table with shaky hands. "Please. *Please*. I'm begging you right now." Jahlani covers her mouth, working through the lump in her throat. She wipes under her eye with her thumb. "Do you even know the statistical probability of me being successful? How incredibly low it is, considering neither of my parents went to college. Not to mention they had the world's *shittiest* marriage. I mean, the odds were *really* stacked against me. But I did that. I graduated twice without *you*—" she jabs a finger in her mother's direction— "without *Dad*. Without any of you. And despite this, despite this astronomical accomplishment that I've achieved that you have yet to acknowledge, you decide to concern yourself with some random asshole? Why don't you care about me? You bring all these men in here, and you cook for them, you clean for them, you provide for them, and you neglect me," she says, pushing a finger into her chest. "Your daughter, your child."

Her mother blinks, her lips thinning. "You're twenty-six, Jahlani. You're not a child anymore. You're a big *grown* woman now," she says, waving her hand in her direction. "You got grown and you left, and you realized too late that the world isn't kind to people like us," she says haughtily, pointing a finger at her. "So don't blame me, child."

Jahlani shakes her head. "You acted like you didn't want me around after Dad left," she says, wiping her nose. "I was a kid. And you just ... left me."

"*Left you?* No, baby, your father left you. I provided for you."

"You're not listening to me," she whispers, sinking back into the chair.

"I'm listening. You just don't like what I have to say. You had a roof over your head, food on your plate, and clothes on your back. I'm sorry I was such a bad mother. I'm sorry that I didn't want to be alone after he left."

Jahlani scoffs, rubbing her forehead. "I didn't say you're a bad mother. And you weren't alone."

Her hand slams down on the counter, startling Jahlani. "I *was* alone, Jahlani. My husband left me, and I knew it was only a matter of time before you did too, because that's what kids do. They get *older*. They want their own lives. So, excuse me for not wanting to die in this house alone." Her mom folds her hands over her chest, breathing heavily. "I can't go back in time and change the past, baby."

Jahlani shakes her head. "I don't want that. I just want a healthier relationship with you. I want you to listen to me when I talk. I want us to be better." Jahlani licks her lips, wringing her hands. "We could talk to a therapist—"

Her mom kisses her teeth, moving about the kitchen again. "I'm not going to a therapist," she says, voice hard. "Therapists a re f or people with issues," she hisses, spinning to face her. "And I don't have any, so you better tread carefully, Jahlani."

Jahlani wipes under her eyes, before exhaling through her nose. "I'm not saying that."

"Well then, what are you saying? Do you need a therapist?"

Jahlani's mouth falls open as she takes in her mom. Her lip curls and her eyes burn, and Jahlani knows, she *knows* that she isn't going to change her mind. She sighs, standing from the table.

"Yeah, I do," she says, starting to move back to her room. "I'm going to try it, Mom. And I hope that when I'm better—when I'm healed—that we can work on this. On us. Because despite what you think, I still need you. I still need my mom."

CHAPTER 35
If You Say So

Jahlani

That day, Jahlani does leave the house, finding herself on Teryn's doorstep where she then curls into a ball on *her* mattress with Teryn and Derrick, her cat, in tow this time. By the third day, Roman sends her a text of him and Lucy at the pool. Later that night, he sends her an Uber Eats delivery of all her favorite snacks, which sets her off again.

On day four, she knows she can't hide anymore. She cleanses her face as best as possible, trying to scrub any remnants of her tear marathon, and drives as slowly as possible to his house. Quite possibly, making the wrong turn on purpose.

With a shuddering breath, she gets out of the car. Within her being two feet of the door, it swings open, and he smiles down at her. Setting down her things, she walks into his arms, breathing him in.

"How are you feeling?" he asks, pressing a hand to her head, rubbing circles on her back.

"Good. Better," she says, burying her face further into his chest. He pulls her face back, planting several quick kisses against her lips before dragging her inside. "Lucy?"

"She's asleep right now," he says in a low voice. He busies himself while she takes in the house. "There's some leftovers that I can heat up if you want," he calls out with his head buried in the fridge. "It's fried rice—your favorite."

Jahlani's stomach clenches. "I'm not staying," she says, tightening her grip on the basket. He turns, looking down at her shoes, only then seeming to notice she didn't slip them off like she normally does. She doesn't miss the flash of disappointment but decides to ignore it.

"I just wanted to drop this off for Lucy," she says, setting the basket on the island. He moves toward it, unwrapping it carefully. She clears her throat. "It's nothing crazy—just some books and toys." She trails off when he reaches the photograph of the three of them. He goes quiet for an abnormal amount of time and nausea rises; she lowers herself onto the stool beside him.

He turns to face her, and she sees it then, in his *eyes* and before she can stop herself, her hand covers his mouth as she shakes her head. "No. Don't say it."

He pries her hand from him, his brows pinched. "What?"

"Don't say it," she repeats, more desperately.

"Say what?"

She sends him a look. "You know what."

"What? That I love you?" Each syllable is a shot to her system, destroying the intimacy, leaving her bruised and torn.

Because she didn't deserve them. She feels him reaching toward her, and she opens her eyes pulling back. "I told you not to."

He reaches for her again, but this time she slides from the stool. She paces, rubbing her knuckles against her mouth.

"I got a job offer. I'm taking it."

"What?" He breathes out, reaching toward her. "That's incredible—"

"It's the one in California," she says, through trembling lips, her mouth drying as soon as the words fall out.

He blinks and then blinks again, rearing back. "California?"

She nods, her chest squeezing. "I—"

And then she watches all the puzzle pieces fall into place. He lets out a laugh, full of derision and she feels herself shrink. She nods, wiping away a tear before rushing to explain. "You had so much going on with Lucy and I didn't want to distract you."

"Little late for that, Jahlani."

She shakes her head. "I'm sorry."

"When are you leaving?"

She swallows, her skin crawling as the words fall past her lips. "I have to … figure some things out. Tie up some loose ends, but as soon as possible."

He runs two hands through his hair. "Jesus Christ, Jahlani. Am I one of your loose ends?" He asks, looking toward her. "Don't answer that."

"Okay," she says, lowering her gaze to the floor.

"So, what is this? Are you done?" He asks, his voice hoarse.

She nods, fighting a fresh wave of tears. "We have to be."

He shakes his head, crossing his arms. "We don't have to be."

"Roman," she says, wiping her face in exasperation. "You—"

"Jahlani—"

She points a finger at him, stepping closer. "No. *No.* You said you wouldn't do this," she says, hissing. "You said so."

"But that was *before*," he says, rubbing his chest, like he's in pain.

"Before what?"

"Before the idea of you leaving became real," he finishes, his voice cracking.

Jahlani exhales, bracing her hands on her head. "Roman, please don't make this harder."

"Did you at least try to find something closer?" he asks, arms outstretched.

Her hands fall to her sides. "It doesn't matter. It doesn't change anything."

"It changes everything," he says, raising his voice. "I *love* you, Jahlani."

"Roman, *stop*—"

"No. I'm fucking crazy about you—"

"*Roman*—"

"And you're tearing us apart, and I cannot figure it out for the life of me. We could be so happy together," he whispers, closing the space between them to grab her face. Her hands press to his chest to stop him.

"No."

"*Why?*"

"Because I don't want this."

His eyes narrow and he draws her face closer. "You don't want this?"

She nods. "You asked me that day in the car, and I didn't know before, but now I do," she says, trying to sound confident. "I don't want this."

He exhales heavily, his breath grazing her lips.

"You know, I've learned a lot about you the past few months and one of the biggest things is that you're a terrible liar," he whispers slowly. "You love me, and I love you and I can't—" He takes a breath. "You know when you eat a piece of candy, but it's not the normal kind, it's the sticky kind. It gets stuck to the roof of your mouth, and then your fingers when you're trying to dislodge it, and it's a pain, but it's so fucking good you keep going back for more. That's what it's like loving you, Jahlani. I'm stuck. It doesn't matter how far you go, nothing is changing for me."

She wipes her face with the back of her hand, shaking her head.

"But it changes everything for me."

His hand tightens around her jaw. "*Why?*"

She throws her head back, groaning before meeting his gaze. "Roman, picture in your head for just a second what that would look like. Flights aren't cheap, it's a thirty-five-hour drive, and a three-hour time difference. Most companies don't give PTO until you're at least a year in. Lucy can't go extended periods of time without you, and I wouldn't want her to."

He snorts, dropping his hands to his sides.

"You've got it all figured out, huh, Jahlani? Every *possible* reason as to why this won't work, you've figured out."

She narrows her eyes. "I'm being *rational*."

"Well then, rationalize us working," he yells, stepping back.

"I *can't*," she whispers. "I—"

"No, you *won't*," he says harshly. "And that's the difference between you and me. I can see us ten, twenty, *thirty* years down the line. Why can't you?"

She tilts her head back, before looking back at him. "Roman. I'm not the girl the guy chooses in the end. I'm the pit stop—the delayed layover to the final destination," she says quietly.

"That's bullshit, Jahlani," he says, through gritted teeth, pinching the bridge of his nose.

"Not bullshit," she whispers. "It's not."

The silence that surrounds them is deafening, and Jahlani takes a step forward when he pulls back, looking up.

"Okay, fine. Run away. It's your thing. It's what you do. You leave first now, right? So, you don't get left behind anymore."

Her lips part in shock. "What?"

He raises his fingers, letting them fall one by one as he speaks. "Your mom, your dad, your ex—they did that to you. They all left you. But I'm not them," he says, pointing to himself. "I'm not going anywhere. I'm stuck."

She wipes both cheeks with the front of her hand, sniffling. "You're right. I'm running away. I'm not ready for this. I'm not healed from them, and I'm not okay. I want to be okay, and I can't do that with you right now. You have someone else that needs you and one of these days, Roman"—her voice lowers—"you're going to wake up, and you'll have forgotten about me. I'll just be this … bump along the road when you meet the love of your life."

"That's you," he says in a thunderous voice, pointing to her. "You're the love of my life. You're the mother of my children. You're the wife. You're everything."

She nods, wiping harder as more tears spill over. "If you say so."

"I say so," he says, crowding her space. "I fucking say so."

And then he's gathering her in his arms, giving her a hot, erratic, desperate kiss. It's unlike any kiss they've shared. It's pleading, and interminable, and bruising and she can't *breathe* and it's everything.

It's perfect.

Need. Want. Mine.

But it can't be hers.

So, with all the strength that she can muster, she pushes against his chest, separating them. She can feel him shaking, or maybe it's her, but she steps back, untangling herself from him, unable to meet his eyes.

And maybe if the baby monitor he had set up on the island hadn't crackled to life, if Lucy's cries hadn't broken through, maybe he could have come after her.

But she's thankful that he doesn't.

$$x = \frac{-b + \sqrt{b^2 - 4ac}}{2a}$$

If this were a movie, this is the part where the guy and the girl go their separate ways. Perhaps, after the girl leaves his house, rather dramatically, and peels out of the driveway, almost hitting a lone jogger, she stays in bed the rest of the week eating ice cream, hanging with her girlfriends, crying about a boy. The scene cuts and the guy is moping around, but he's not all that hurt. In fact, his friends drag him out to a bar and convince him to lie under the next chick because there's *plenty of fish in the fucking sea* and all.

But Jahlani knows this isn't a movie. It's so much worse.

It's real life.

And if she's learned anything from her twenty-six years of life, it's that real life is punishing. It doesn't care if you're heartbroken. Even less when you're the cause of said heartbreak.

And so, she's not all that surprised when she receives an email two days later from the university, reminding her that she volunteered for commencement that weekend.

So, she scrubs her face with a ferocity she didn't think she was capable of, applies some lipliner before deciding to wipe it off.

When she checks in, she's ushered behind the stage, and is told she'll be handing name cards to the reader. At this, her stomach shakes.

Now, there's definitely no avoiding him.

"Jahlani."

Her head snaps up, and she meets Professor Jackson's somber stare.

"Professor Jackson? What are you doing here?"

He moves to stand next to her, placing his hands in his pockets. "I always work commencement. I didn't expect to see you here."

"I signed up a while ago."

He nods. "I see. What are your plans after graduation?"

Jahlani balks at how much he's talking and stammers out a response.

"Oh. Um, I'm ... moving to California."

His eyebrows pinch together. "California?"

She nods, her mouth drying. "Yeah. I didn't realize at the time—or maybe they changed the location after, but, yeah. I'm going. Thank you," she adds quickly, "for writing the recommendation letter."

"Huh."

Jahlani tilts her head, surprised by his nonchalance at her news. Most people would say "congratulations." But then again, he wasn't your average guy.

"What?" she asks, trying to gauge the expression on his face.

He shakes his head, scratching his temple with a single finger. "Nothing. I just thought—"

"What?" Her breaths quicken, and suddenly she's heart-poundingly *terrified* by whatever he's about to say.

He shakes his head. "I thought you were in a relationship with Mr. Hayes. Forgive me for my bluntness."

Her lips part and her tongue suddenly feels heavier than she remembers as she shakes her head.

"Why would you think that?"

He shakes his head, his lips turned upward in a grimace. "Forgive me, it's not any of my business. Congratulations on the job. I'm sure you'll do wonderful," he says, patting her shoulder twice, precise as ever.

"Thanks," she murmurs, sounding dazed because *he fucking knew* and her head hurts and she has *so many questions* but he's walking away from her.

"Professor Jackson," she calls out. He stops, turning to face her. "Thank you. I hope everything works out for you."

His eyes flash in understanding and he gives her a very minuscule smile, nodding his head before turning to leave.

As the hours trickle by, regret congeals. As she takes each name card, she becomes more disgusted with herself. She thinks about how she's torturing him, and herself. She thinks about how much this might ruin his day, and when she sees the top of his head, she nearly throws up. When he spots her, confusion flashes and then smooths into impassiveness.

And something raw and painful opens inside her.

"Congratulations," she says quickly, passing his card to the reader.

"Thanks," he murmurs, walking up the steps and onto the stage.

And just like that, it's over.

She stands until the final name is called, carved out, as she drops off the lanyard to walk outside to her car, fully prepared to go home and hide under her bed for the next three days, but a tall shadow leaning against it stops her.

"Roman," she says, startled.

A green gift bag sways in his hand, and his gown still hangs from his shoulders.

"Here." He sticks his arm out. "It's from everyone."

She shakes her head, refusing to move closer.

Why are you making this so hard?

His nostrils flare and his jaw clenches. "Take it, Jahlani. Danica will have my head if you don't."

She steps forward and takes the bag with shaky hands. "What's it for?" She asks, her voice quiet.

He drags a hand down his face and sighs. "You graduated this semester too, Jahlani."

She clutches the bag tighter, as her vision begins to swim. He turns to walk toward his car.

"Roman—"

He groans, stopping to face her. "Do you remember … when you asked me if this was just an itch that needed to be scratched?"

She nods, lowering her eyes. "I—sure. Yeah."

He exhales deeply, sliding his hands into his pockets. "I wanted to tell you that it wasn't an itch for me because I knew before you became my GTA. It was always a rash for me, Jahlani. Always."

She scoffs through a laugh that steadily dissolves into tears down her face. She presses her palms into her eyes and nods.

For me too.

"I hope you get everything you've ever wanted," he says softly.

"Don't say that," she says, wiping the back of her hand against her cheeks. "You're supposed to … pray for my demise. You're supposed to hate me."

He sigh is rough. "I could never hate you, Jahlani."

She opens her mouth to say something, but nothing comes out. With one last simmering look, he opens his car door and slides inside, not bothering to look back.

Want.
Need.
Not mine.

CHAPTER 36

Try Sleeping with a Broken Heart

Roman

Roman gets home after a late shift and tries to set his keys on the console but misses. They clatter to the floor, the sound echoing through the house. He stares at the metal for longer than necessary before stepping over it to enter the kitchen. The sound of a lone car passing greets him as he rifles through the kitchen medicine cabinet.

She left.

He knocks most of the bottles over, not *giving a shit* until he finds the ibuprofen. He swings the fridge open, grabs a water bottle, twists the cap off.

Jahlani left.

He tips the bottle for two tablets but the entire container scatters across the island and the floor. He blinks slowly, watching the island freckle white with pills.

It's over.

He reaches for two, turns for the water—misjudges—and backhands the bottle, sending it over the edge. He watches it tumble out like a waterfall before moving to the cabinet to grab a glass.

She left.

He flicks on the tap, fills a glass, shoves the pills in, and swallows. He doesn't mean to, but he drops the glass into the sink harder than he realizes, and it shatters.

Jahlani left.

He pushes his palms into his eyes until his vision spots before he stumbles into the bedroom, yanks off his socks—tears a hole—then slams a finger in the drawer hunting for sleep shorts.

"Fuck." He shakes his hand out and lowers onto the bed.

You're supposed to hate me.

He falls back against his pillow, throwing his non-throbbing arm across his face, breathing evenly. He'd laugh if he didn't feel so sick.

It's his fault. She warned him.

What if I'm the villain?

As he stares at the ceiling, trying to empty his mind, he wonders how long this will take, because this is his first time.

Trying to sleep with a broken heart.

And it fucking sucks.

"Okay, this is just getting pathetic."

Danica leans against the archway of his kitchen, arms folded across her chest.

"What?" He says, glancing her way when she drags out the stool across from him.

"*Really,* Ro? Look at you ... you look terrible," she says, looking around the house. "And the place is a mess."

He scratches under chin, before folding his arms over his chest. "Gee, thanks."

Her eyebrows raise to her hairline. "Seriously, we're worried about you."

He turns away from her, grabbing a Gatorade from the fridge. He finishes the whole bottle, shrugging his shoulders. "I'm fine. I've just been busy."

She continues to look at him.

He blinks at her. "Danica, I'm fine. Really."

She exhales, her eyes softening. "You're not fine. Tell me what happened."

He shrugs and she doesn't move from her spot on the chair, making it a point to drum her fingers on the table.

He lowers his eyes to the countertop, scratching the back of his head. "I'm not in the mood to talk, Dan. Can we do this another time?"

She shakes her head. "No, Ro. You won't talk to mom; you won't talk to Taylor or Vaughn—"

"What's there to talk about? She … left and I'm … here."

Danica's eyes soften. "Okay, there has to be more to the story than that."

He lets out a bitter chuckle. "How much time do you have?"

Danica and Roman sit on the couch together as they watch Lucy play on the floor in front of them. Alphabet blocks cover her playmat, as well as the toy Jahlani gave her two weeks ago. Roman sips from his glass as he waits for Danica to say something.

After a few moments of silence, Danica lets out a low "damn."

He blows out a breath, scratching behind his ear. "Yeah … so if I've been a mopey asshole the past few weeks, it's because I'm pretty sure I had my heart ripped out of my chest and … yeah. Everything just … hurts," he says, letting out a long exhale.

She nods, twisting her mouth. "Can I tell you something that you probably don't want to hear?"

He laughs. "Go ahead. Not like I can feel any worse."

Danica sucks in a sharp breath before turning to face him. "I think she was right—"

His eyes widen and he lets out a disgruntled noise. "Seriously?"

She holds up a finger. "*But* I still think there's a chance. I think you should go to her."

"What?"

"You should go to her."

He shakes his head. "I … don't think so."

"Why not?"

He clears his throat, standing up. "I don't know, let me think. She told me she doesn't want to be with me, we haven't spoken in *weeks*, and she lives on the other side of the country."

Danica twists around to follow him as he moves into the kitchen. "Roman, she cares about you."

He snorts, shaking his head. "She does not."

"She didn't want you to have to choose between her and Lucy, so she made the choice for you."

"That wasn't her place," he says, voice rising. "She didn't even talk to me about it, Danica. When you're in a relationship with someone … you communicate. You talk, you *share*, you compromise."

"Well, did you tell her that?"

"What?"

Danica stands from the couch moving to the kitchen. "Did you tell her that—about the communication part?"

"She's an adult. Pretty sure she knows how to communicate," he says, shaking his head.

"It's not the same, Ro. How me and you communicate is different. Communication in a romantic relationship is inherently different from just plain old communication. It's more nuanced. It requires ... *more*. Just, are you sure that she actually expressed how she felt? Is she even someone who's good at communicating romantically? Has she been taught that?"

Roman shakes his head because *fuck, she's making sense.*

"I don't think I could stand her saying no again."

"But hear me out ... what if she says *yes* this time?"

His chest tightens at the possibility. "I don't know, Danica."

Danica sighs, bracing her elbows against the kitchen island. "She might not have been ready back then," she says. "Timing matters. It's important. She might have been going through things that you will never understand. I know you said she had things going on with her parents, with her ex, with *life*. Just, please. Try one more time. She's worth it. She's different. You're different with her."

"I don't know, the past few weeks made me realize that I'm not in a good place."

She snorts. "When is anyone ever in a 'good place' when they meet The One? And so what? Does that mean you're supposed to put your life on pause?"

At this, he laughs. "The One?"

"Yeah, you know, boy meets girl, they fall in love, mom loves her, they live happily ever after. She's your girl from the story," she says, patting his back lightly before moving to kiss Lucy on the head. "Oh, here. Before I forget."

She drops a white envelope on the table. "It's the Thanksgiving film. Mom finally got it developed."

"Oh, nice."

She smirks. "Yeah, there are some ... interesting photos in there. Take a gander when you're feeling up to it."

Before he can ask her what she means, she's out the front door. Reaching forward, he lifts the flap, a slow warmth filling his chest as he thumbs through the pictures. After most of them, he starts to lose interest—until a particular head of hair catches his eye.

And suddenly his heart is leaping into his throat. Sliding the picture out, his eyes take in her dark braids, brown lips, and somber expression.

Typical Jahlani.

Except she isn't looking at the camera—she's looking at him. And maybe it's a *giant fucking leap*, but it's enough to seal one of the cracks in his chest.

CHAPTER 37

Step Into It

Jahlani

One Month Later

"Ms. Jones, you're needed in the conference room."

Jahlani sits up in her chair, looking over her monitor to stare at her assistant, Bonnie. She has eclectic tastes and is currently sporting two pigtails, a polka-dot top, and striped socks with peaches that reach her knees.

"It's just Jahlani, Bonnie," she says in the *politest* way she can muster. Bonnie continues to smile, holding the door to her office open. It's been a little over a month and she still can't quite figure her out.

Jahlani frowns, rising to grab her notepad. "Is something wrong with the Hudson report?"

Bonnie shrugs, adjusting her laptop, notepad, and pens. "I think it's a snag with another client's data." And then in a lower voice she adds, "Between you and me, Austin has been *slacking* since his divorce. It's not looking good for him."

Jahlani and Bonnie bypass his office, seeing his face pressed into the desk. Bonnie winces, shaking her head as her heels click across the floor. The glass walls of the conference room reflect the faint glow from the city's lights, though the tables inside are untouched, chairs neatly arranged around them as if waiting for the first sign of dawn. It's late, most having already left for the day.

Bonnie pushes open the third conference-room door, and Jahlani gauges the atmosphere. Two women sit across from her boss, Monique Chamberlin. The faint hum of the projector is the only sound she hears as she sinks into the chair beside Monique.

"Jahlani, thank you for joining us. This is Ember and Anna Mayfair."

Standing, Jahlani reaches out to give them both a *hopefully firm confident* handshake that doesn't display any signs of how she just might possibly expel her leftover burrito from two hours ago. Monique doesn't waste a second, sliding over a manila folder of data. They then spend the next thirty minutes reviewing the portfolio.

"What do you recommend, Jahlani?"

Every eye in the room lands on her and she freezes because *Monique Fucking Chamberlin* just asked for her input.

Jahlani lifts the paper, thumbing through the report. "There are a lot of gaps in the data. It makes it hard to get an accurate analysis from the survey. I would check the coding first and re-run the program—"

"What if we don't have time for that?"

"You could … skip that step, but then you run the risk of compromising the integrity of your data. The analysis might not be as valid."

"How long would it take you?"

Jahlani says, looking back at the report. "Two to three weeks."

"Which is it—two or three?" Monique asks.

Jahlani meets her stoic gaze. "Two?" And then, clearing her throat, she repeats with more confidence. "Two."

The Mayfair women look at each other before looking toward

Monique.

"She'll do it," Monique chimes in as she checks her watch, then offers a tight smile. "It's late. Jahlani's assistant, Bonnie Myer, will be in touch later this week to set up another meeting to finalize the project timeline."

All the women stand up, shaking hands. "Thank you for agreeing to meet with us, Monique and Jahlani. We're looking forward to collaborating with you."

Bonnie leaps up to walk them out, and Jahlani is left alone with Monique. She turns to her, sinking into her chair again.

"Did that just happen?" Jahlani asks, looking up at her as she reaches for her drink.

"It did."

"But … how?"

Monique leans back, studying her.

"I know you're new here, Jahlani, so I'll give you some advice: don't say "no" to career-altering projects, *especially* when you're fresh and you're being offered a client as big as the Mayfair's."

Jahlani's face flushes. "I'm sorry. I didn't want to overstep—"

She holds her hand up to silence her. "You weren't overstepping. I picked you because I know you can do it. Am I wrong, Jahlani?"

"No, of course not," Jahlani offers hurriedly, her palms sweaty. "I just—"

"Do you think you can do a better job than their original consultant?"

Jahlani licks her lips, trying to keep her eyes focused on the bridge of her nose. "It's a large project, and I figured someone who's been here longer would be the safer choice."

Monique shakes her head. "That's not what I asked. Do *you* think you can do a better job?"

Jahlani's mouth dries at her fierce gaze. "Yes."

Monique studies her, then offers a rare smile and stands. "You're good at what you do, Jahlani. Step into it. Embrace it. *Own it*. Don't let anybody in this building make you feel like you need to be smaller. That's not the kind of company I'm running here."

Jahlani nods, a flush spreading through her body, feeling as though she's being *scolded* by her favorite teacher.

Monique slides her purse onto her shoulder. "Go get some drinks, Jahlani. Celebrate with your friends, boyfriend, girlfriend— whoever. You're about to be very busy over the next few months," she says, squeezing her shoulder in a reassuring manner as she walks by.

"Monique?" Jahlani clears her throat. "I was wondering—"

Monique arches a brow, folding her arms.

Step into it.

"I want to be considered for the new branch—the one in Florida."

"Okay. Why?"

Jahlani rolls her shoulders back. "I'm highly qualified, and I was raised there. I know the people. I know the area. I have … people waiting for me. Family. Friends."

Monique nods her head. "I hear you, and I'll consider it, but you're too new for me to send out right now."

Jahlani swallows back the burn in her throat. "I understand."

Monique's eyes soften. "Let's see how the Mayfair project goes. It might speed things along."

Jahlani gives her a small smile, her heart swelling as she hears the soft sound of Monique's heels disappear down the hallway. Reaching into her bag, she slides out her phone as it vibrates, hope spiking in her chest because maybe–

"Hello?" She breathes, hopeful and flustered, pacing in the office.

A throat clears on the line. "Hey, baby. Are you free to talk?"

Jahlani pulls the phone from her ear, seeing her dad's contact, tears stinging her eyes.

She thought it would be *him*. But then again, why would he call?

"Sure," she says, her voice wavering as she works to fight through her disappointment. Settling into a chair, she drops the phone on the table, pressing the speaker button. She places her head in between her hands as she waits for him to speak.

He clears his throat again. "You sure? If you're busy, I can hang up."

"I'm not busy," she murmurs, sitting upright. "I'm just at work. I'm always ... at work."

He sighs, and she hears him shuffling on the other end. "Okay ... well, your mother called me a few weeks ago. She was pretty hysterical."

Jahlani sits upright, her skin tingling. "Oh. What did she ... tell you?"

"Everything."

Jahlani drops her head into her palm, sighing. "Dad—"

"I'm so sorry, baby."

Jahlani's hand falls to the table and she presses into it trying to ground herself.

"What?" She croaks out.

He sighs deeply. "Your mom ... she's been through a lot, and I'm not making excuses for her, but she's a ... complicated woman, and I should've done better. I just ... I made a choice to leave her, and I didn't think about how that would affect you. I thought about what you said to me that day, and you were right baby and ... are you still there, Jahlani?"

"I'm here, Dad," she says, whispering.

He clears his throat. "I know you're an adult now, so maybe you'll understand a little when I tell you why I left … or maybe you won't but … it got hard for me. She didn't support me in the way I needed her to and Celeste—your grandmother— she never liked me, and your mom just always went with what she said. It was like she wasn't her own person at certain times. So, it was difficult and I … I didn't tell you because … I gave up on her and I left you, and … I'm sorry."

Jahlani lets out a shaky exhale, wiping her face feeling *so fucking sick of crying*.

"Yeah."

He exhales again. "Okay, baby. Well, I don't want to keep you. But I wanted to let you know that I'm going to talk to your mother … try to get her on board with, you know … the therapy. I know you're in California, but I've seen that they do virtual sessions. Just … let me know if you need anything … anything at all."

Jahlani knows the thing she wants most, he can't give her, but she still nods letting out a strangled *'okay'*.

"Bye baby. I love you."

She hangs up, still not fully believing him, and not feeling ready to say it back, but knowing for the first time, she was taking a step in the right direction.

CHAPTER 38
Tell Her Again

Roman

January in Florida brings a strange duality to Roman's life. It's not that anything bad has happened. Mornings are pale as he heads to the bar; nights drop fast and cold, bundling him and Lucy on the couch.

It's not that there is nothing happening. There's a lingering sensation of something missing—of someone missing.

But there's nothing that he can do about it.

As Roman pulls into the hospital lot, the tires crunching over the rocks, he wonders how she's doing. If she's thinking of him the way he thinks of her. Turning off the ignition, Roman opens the car door and works to get Lucy out of her car seat.

"We're here, pretty girl," he says, unbuckling her and lifting her out. The wind blows her hair across her face, and she shoves sticky fingers into her curls, wrecking the parting he spent too long perfecting. "See?"

"We're here!" Lucy echoes, clapping softly.

Roman sets her on her feet before crouching down to zip up her jacket and pull her hat down over her ears. Making sure the door is locked, he grips her hand tightly and they walk across the parking lot.

As they make their way to the doors, Roman sees a familiar hue of brown waves.

"Audrey," he says, yelling as he picks up Lucy to walk toward her. She looks around, shielding her eyes from the sun before turning to him.

"Roman." Her smile brightens when her eyes drop to Lucy. He clears his throat, towering over her as he adjusts Lucy. "Say hi, baby."

Lucy drops her head into his neck, waving saliva-covered fingers at Audrey. Roman shakes his head, turning back to look over at Audrey.

"I'm not used to seeing you without your dinosaur and sailor scrubs. You going out somewhere?" he asks as she moves to the driver's side of her car, laughing.

"I ... actually have a date," she says, smiling up at him. He smiles, feeling genuinely elated for her.

"That's great. I'm glad to hear that."

Her cheeks redden as she looks at the ground before meeting his gaze. "Thanks. It's new but it's going really well. I'm ... happy," she says, and he believes her. It's hard not to when she looks like *that*. He shifts Lucy in his arms again, swaying her back and forth slightly.

"That's great to hear, Audrey. Really," he says, rubbing circles on Lucy's back.

She pushes her hair behind her ear. "What about you and Jahlani? How are you doing together?"

Together.

It must show on his face because all the energy she had been radiating earlier seems to evaporate. He clears his throat, looking toward the hospital

"She ... moved to California for work about a month ago."

Forty-four days ago, to be exact.

Audrey narrows her eyes, nodding slowly. "I see."

He shrugs, rubbing his neck with his free hand. "It didn't work out. The distance ... and just the timing of everything with Lucy."

Audrey closes her eyes, inhaling deeply before opening them. She crosses her arms over her chest, lifting her chin.

"So, if this were a different time and if I were the previous version of myself, I'd tell you that I'm sorry to hear that and that I hope you find your way back to each other. But, seeing as this is not, I'm going to be blunt as hell right now. Go get her back."

He laughs, shaking his head. "It's not that easy."

Her eyebrows raise. "Did you cheat on her?"

His head rears back. "Jesus, no."

"Did you lie to her? Manipulate her? Harm her in any kind of way?"

"No."

"Then go get her back," she says, raising her voice, looking as though she were on the verge of stomping her foot.

"Audrey," he says, shutting his eyes before opening them. "Don't you think I would if I could?"

"Roman," she says, exhaling slowly. "If there's one thing that I have learned from my mother's death, it's that life is too short not to tell somebody you love them while they still have air in their lungs. Skip the bullshit and tell them before it's too late."

"I *did*."

She steps closer, her eyes blazing. "Tell her again, and again, and *again*. Tell her until she's sick of you. Tell her until you're sick of your own voice. Tell her until she believes you. Because one day you might not be able to," she says, breathing heavily. "Now if you'll excuse me, I have a date to get to." She sends him one last pointed look before giving Lucy a sweet smile and sliding into her car.

As Roman takes the elevator up and sits in the waiting room, he replays her words.

Tell her again, and again, and again.
Tell her until she believes you.

Because, *fuck, he misses her.* It's been over a month and he's still stuck.

Dr. Newark runs through her routine check-up, turning to face Roman with a relaxed smile.

"The steroids are holding steady. Nothing in the urine; swelling is down. She looks good, kid. We'll keep monitoring, but I think in the coming months we can start to wean her off," Dr. Newark says, tapping his shoulder.

"Is she okay to travel?" he asks, sitting her up.

"Not yet. We'll make sure to keep monitoring her and as soon as she's clear for travel, I'll let you know. Where are you planning to go?"

She's your girl from the story.
Tell her until she believes you.
I'm not the girl the guy chooses in the end.

"California."

CHAPTER 39
Everything Means Nothing Without You

Jahlani

Jahlani spends her twenty-seventh birthday at the office. The glass walls of the conference room reflect the city's glow; the tables are untouched, chairs neatly arranged as if waiting for dawn.

Jahlani pushes the glass door open, taking in the still atmosphere. The faint hum of the projector is the only sound she hears as she sinks into the chair at the head of the oval table. For a moment, she pictures everything vividly—collaborating with her team, directing her projects, collecting her data with no one to stop her. She stands up, trailing a finger along the table before halting at the front of the room.

"You," she says, pointing to the empty chair, "I needed my report yesterday. Why hasn't it been done? And you"—she points her finger to another empty chair—"why do I have clients complaining to me about you not returning their calls after hours? Remember, without them, you have no job. Come on, people—did we leave our common sense at home today?"

She takes an exaggerated breath.

"You're right. I'm on edge. I apologize sincerely; nobody deserves to be spoken to that way. Everyone, lunch is on me. As a matter of fact, have the rest of the day off." She fakes a laugh. "No, thank you for being such hardworking, fastidious workers. Without you, there's no us."

She shakes her head at herself and waits for the familiar blanket of loneliness to settle in, before grabbing her bags and leaving.

When she enters the apartment building, she waves to Donny at the concierge desk, sidling up with a smile.

"Late night?" he asks, walking to the back to grab her packages.

She shrugs, dropping the powdered doughnuts on the counter for him. "I like what I do, Donny," she calls. "It's fun. I'm happy."

"Uh-huh. Whatever you say, girl. You remind me of my granddaughter. Always working," he says through heavy grunts. "You two would get along."

She leans over the counter, eyebrows drawn. "You alright in there?"

He rolls out a large box and drops it on the bellhop cart. Her eyes widen.

"That's for me?"

He holds up a finger, going back and returning with three more, and finally a bouquet of white tulips. When she gives him a questioning look, he shrugs, telling her to return the cart when she gets a chance.

After dragging the boxes inside, she decides she needs a shower. Face scrubbed and hair up, she grabs a knife to open the first box—then her phone rings.

"Hey, Mom." She breathes, dragging the knife through the tape.

"Happy birthday, baby."

Jahlani's chest tingles. "Thanks."

"I'm sorry I didn't get you anything. I didn't know what to buy you."

Jahlani's lips turn upward. "It's okay, Mom. This is ... good. This is nice."

They lapse into silence as Jahlani chews on her lip, contemplating what to say next. Despite their virtual therapy sessions, their phone calls are still tense. Unnatural.

"Do you ... have any plans?"

Jahlani looks around her apartment, lowering herself onto her loveseat, momentarily taken aback that her mom is *still* on the phone with her and that *she's* asked a question.

"I don't ... I just went to work, and now I'm in my apartment."

"Hmm. You should go out. Have some fun."

Jahlani nods, her brows bunching together. "Maybe," she murmurs. "I don't really like going out that much."

"That's true. I was like that when I was your age." Her mom continues, trying to recall how she spent her twenties, mentioning how she stumbled across a picture of the two of them from when Jahlani was little. She talks, and talks, and even though it's not perfect, and it's not fixed, she starts to no longer feel like she's on the back burner.

And when she hangs up, she feels better about them than she has in a long time.

Inhaling deeply, she moves to the kitchen to start prepping some cinnamon rolls. As the oven preheats, the boxes taunt her in the middle of her living room. Setting her wine glass down, she resumes opening the first box.

It's a stack of romance books. She thumbs through the pages, her eyebrows pinched together as she moves it to the left of her.

The second box is a pair of noise-canceling headphones.

The last one has her hands shaking. It's a limited edition Catan.

A knock at her door startles her, and her eyes immediately go to the clock on the stove. It's after ten.

Running shaky hands over her shirt, she checks her appearance in the circular mirror before opening the door.

"Roman," she says, her throat constricting as her body grows light.

"Jahlani."

His hair is in its familiar tousled state and even though it's been two months, it feels as though no time has slipped between them. She steps forward but stops herself when she sees he has something in his hand.

"I need to show you something, then ask you a very important question. Okay?"

She blinks, nodding in a daze. "Okay. Do you … maybe want to come in?"

Shaking his head, he hands her a small envelope. She tries to mask her disappointment at his refusal.

What did you think would happen?

"Open it," he says, his voice low. "Please."

With trembling fingers, she slides her finger under the flap, lifting out pictures. She looks down, blinking at him, then at the collection of photographs. She brings the first one closer to her face.

"They're pictures … from Thanksgiving," she says, slowly meeting his eyes for confirmation. He nods and she gently slides through them. Danica and Gwen. Gwen and Lucy. Gwen and Roman. Roman and Jahlani.

"What's that one?" he asks, his voice gravelly.

"It's a picture of you and me."

He nods. "That's right. Can you describe it to me?"

She clears her throat. "Your hand is on my waist and you're looking at the camera."

"And where are you looking, Jahlani?" he murmurs.

"I'm looking at you," she says, her pulse soaring.

God, please let this be what she thinks it is.

"And how would you describe that look, Jahlani?" he whispers, standing to his full height. She inhales slowly, looking over her features in the picture again.

"It's content."

"Hmm."

"Grateful."

"What else?"

"Caring."

He inhales deeply. "I think those are all fairly accurate, but I still think you're missing one. Can you tell me what it is?"

"Loving," she whispers, the photo slipping from her fingers. "It's a loving look."

"How do you know?" he asks, stepping closer until their chests brush.

"My eyes."

"If you say so, Jahlani."

"I say so, Roman," she says, reaching for the neck of his shirt. "If you'll still have me," she whispers. His hand snakes to her jaw and he tilts her head.

"I told you, I'm stuck."

As she closes the space between them, she thinks about how she lied to Donny not even forty minutes ago.

Because *this. This is happy.*

She pulls back, looking up at him. "I'm sorry about everything, about hurting you," she says, tugging him all the way in as he tries to deepen the kiss.

He closes the door with his foot before pulling her back to his chest. She folds her body into his as he unties her hair. He kisses her like they have all the time in the world, and they do, *she supposes*, her belly warming.

She pushes his shoulders back to look him in the eyes again. "Really, we should talk," she says, sliding from his hold to pace in front of him.

He blinks, leaning back against the door, watching her.

"God, why is this so hard?" she says, rubbing her forehead and shaking her hands out. Roman's eyebrows raise when she paces two feet before turning around again. "Shit, the oven." She rushes to the kitchen, turns it off, and finds him standing there.

He's here.

In California.

"Hi," he whispers, his eyes shining. He wraps an arm around her waist.

"Hi," she says, pushing her palms against his chest until they slide into his hair. He reaches down then, pressing his mouth to hers, and she loses her footing as his kiss becomes fast and searching.

Consuming.

She pulls back again, and he groans.

"Wait. Wait. I do have something to say."

"Tell me later," he says against her lips. "I need this now."

And she lets him press into her for a few minutes, his hands gliding over her cheeks to deepen the kiss, her leg raising to wrap around his waist, their breaths becoming one, but she pulls back again, forcing his eyes to her.

"Roman, I do–love you," she says, meeting his gaze. "But I won't be able to say it as much as you do … and express how I'm feeling as much as you do, but I do. And I know that's pretty shitty considering everything that's transpired, but if you're willing to … to work with me and give me a little more time … I can get better. I want to be better at this for you because I sit in this apartment, and it feels like,

like nothing. And my job is great, and I make more money than I could possibly spend now, but it's just … just a job, you know?" she says, exhaling slowly.

"And I know that this is what I asked for, this is what I said I wanted, what I thought I wanted, or, I don't know. The point is, it all feels so … meaningless. And I *know* that's shitty of me, believe me, I know. I wish I could take it back, and I've been beating myself up about this for weeks, about leaving you, but I thought it was a done deal, but you're here now, so I guess what I'm trying to say is, what I'm trying to *ask* is that you be patient with me, because I really do want this, okay?"

"Okay," he says. "Anything you want. But, Jahlani—this is it." He grabs her wrist. "If we're doing this, it's on my terms. No running away. Okay?"

She nods. "Okay."

His lips turn upward, before his eyes drop to her mouth. "Enough talking," he says, lifting her up. "It's your birthday."

"You remembered?" She breathes against his lips as he walks them into her room.

"Who do you think bought you all those gifts?" he says, depositing her on the bed, pressing a soft kiss to her mouth. "You know what else I remember?" he says, pulling off his shirt, then working his belt.

She leans on her elbows. "What?" She breathes. Lowering himself to her, he grabs her thighs, pulling her toward the edge.

"I'd rather show you."

$$x = \frac{-b + \sqrt{b^2 - 4ac}}{2a}$$

Low California light seeps past the curtains. The alarm sounds and she startles—briefly afraid she imagined last night with Roman, but she's pleasantly surprised to feel a warm, dormant Roman against her back. His arm drapes across her stomach and it feels so *good*.

She feels good, and warm, and *okay*.

Her arm snaps out to turn it off, but he's already moving.

"Sorry," she whispers, dropping back to the bed against his chest.

"S'okay. You have work?" he says, his voice low and sleep-filled.

She sighs, pressing further against him. "I usually go to the gym, but I don't want to."

He drags her closer, his fingers splaying against her abdomen as he presses a soft kiss to the back of her head.

"I don't want to go to work either," she says softly. "I just want to stay here in bed with you." He laughs into her hair, flexing his fingers against her, lowering them slightly. His touch is light as he skims back and forth in a gentle motion. His other hand moves to push the braids that escaped her wrap to the side to expose her neck. He shifts, brushing his mouth down the length of her throat.

"Go to work, baby. I'll be here," he murmurs, grazing the shell of her ear. She sighs, her stomach dipping as he drags his hand lower. He presses two soft kisses to her neck, then the shell of her ear again. "Pretend I'm not even here."

"That's impossible," she says as he slides his hand beyond the elastic of her shorts. "You're all I think about most days."

His teeth move to her earlobe and bite gently, before moving to track down her neck.

"Most days?"

She sighs heavily. "All the time, actually. Every day for the past few months, Roman." The motion of his hand on her stomach stops, and she turns in the bed to face him. "I'm so sorry about everything. The things I said to you," she whispers. "The way I left."

He shakes his head. "I shouldn't have pushed you. I understand why you did it."

"But—"

He presses a soft kiss to her lips. "Stop dwelling in the past. It's okay. We're okay."

"Roman," she murmurs when he pulls her back into his chest. "What are we going to do? How is this going to work?" she asks, looking up at him.

"I don't know. We'll figure it out together," he says, pressing a kiss to her nose. "We'll make it work, okay?"

She nods, but her mind still spins. It leaps. It tumbles.

It *spirals*.

But he's there, drawing her further into his chest as he rubs small circles against her back. "Relax, baby. Don't think so hard about it."

She pulls back, leaning on her elbow to stare down at him. "Roman, how long do I get to keep you?"

He laughs, reaching forward to pull her silk wrap from her head, pressing a steady stream of kisses down her chest. "Forever?"

She pulls back to look at him, sending him a pointed stare. "That's not what I mean."

"What do you mean?" he says, rubbing across her arms.

"When do you have to leave?" she asks, inhaling sharply. "I'm just trying to prepare myself."

He sighs, placing his forehead on her shoulder before rolling to his back. Jahlani taps his arm, watching as he scratches his eyebrow.

"Roman?"

He sighs, throwing his arm across his face. "The day after tomorrow."

So soon.

She tilts her head. "Like the movie?"

He cuts his eyes at her, and she falls back to the bed, laughing deeply. They lay next to each other, breathing, a light thrumming in her chest, head, fingers, toes.

Her lips twist as she continues to stare at the ceiling, listening to them both share the same space.

"Tell me what you're thinking," he says, now rolling on his side to face her.

"That's soon," she whispers immediately, no longer feeling the need to hide anything. "Sooner than I expected."

She turns to lie on her side, reaching out to trace his eyebrows, nose, jaw, lips, repeating the motion. Memorizing him.

"I know," he says, pressing a kiss to the tips of her fingers when she brushes over his mouth again. "I know."

She draws in a ragged breath. "What are we going to do?"

"We're going to come up with a plan to see each other as much as possible and we're not going to stress about it, okay? We're going to enjoy the time we have with each other right now," he says, drawing her to his side. "So, if you don't mind," he says, climbing over her, "there's something I've been meaning to do."

His weight lands on her and he's warm, and large, and perfect.

"So," she pants when his hand slides down to graze her over her shorts. Her hand flies to his roots when his tongue finds her neck and massages in sweeping circles. "Can I call out? Please—don't make me go."

He laughs into her side, pulling the skin of her neck with his teeth before sucking gently. "When have I ever made you do anything, huh? You're too stubborn," he murmurs, running his fingers over her faster.

"Roman," she sighs. He groans into her neck, pushing his hips against her, and then he's saying how much he missed her as he generously swipes, finding a rhythm that has her gasping and pulling his hair as she breaks.

When she can breathe again, he pushes her onto her stomach, working her shorts down over her thighs, and then his own, and then his weight is pressing down on her at a torturous pace, his hands tangling with her own to force them above her head.

"Despite what you think, Jahlani," he says, his hips driving impossibly slower, "I'll never get tired of this. I'll never get tired of you."

"*Roman.*"

"This is everything," he says, his hips moving harder. And it's not long before she's unraveling, her fists clenching as she ignites, her moans muffled into the pillow. "Shit. Jahlani," he groans, tensing above her. "*Shit.*" His forehead drops against her back as he breathes heavily.

He drops several open-mouthed kisses to her back before he moves to her side, pulling her close again.

Jahlani shuts her eyes, her body still trembling as she soaks in his presence next to her. And then, after almost drifting asleep again, she tells him she really *does* need to go to work and gets up, feeling lighter than she has in months.

EPILOGUE

It doesn't come easy for Jahlani. The distance. More often than she'd like, they go days without speaking, their schedules not aligning, him missing her phone calls, her being stuck in an important meeting. Every few weeks, when they finally get a hold of each other, she tries to end it. It's ridiculous, honestly. Most attempts are futile—he ignores the comment or changes the subject.

And every day, she loves him even more for it.

"No."

"No?"

"Roman."

"Jahlani."

She props the phone against her toaster and folds her arms.

"It's too complicated. Lucy is still in and out of the hospital, the time zones are ridiculous. We barely see each other," she says to his pixelated face.

He yawns, stretches, then nods. "We're doing this again?"

Jahlani scoffs, raising her hands, her mouth twisting.

"You'll find someone better than me. Someone who can meet you halfway—"

"Okay. So we're doing this again." Roman shakes his head, setting his phone down in front of him. She can see Lucy, the painting she bought for his bedroom hanging in the background. "I don't care if you meet me a quarter of the way. I'll be there. Also—you look beautiful."

Jahlani throws her head back in frustration, blinking at him through the phone. "What if you start to resent me—"

"I love you."

"What if I start to resent you—" She begins pacing in front of the camera, waving her hands.

"You're in love with me too."

"What if the distance is too much and you need it then and there?"

At this, he laughs. "You're the only one that I want it then and there with," he says, shaking his head. "Did you eat today, baby?"

She stops in front of the phone, her hands on her hips. "Roman, I don't want to argue with you about this."

He shrugs. "Fine."

"Fine," she says, and ends the call with enough force to topple the phone onto its side. The delicate drip of the tap gets to her, and she lasts all of three minutes before she redials his number.

"Fuck, I hated that. Let's never do that again."

He laughs. "Okay."

$$x = \frac{-b + \sqrt{b^2 - 4ac}}{2a}$$

Her flight lands early the next morning, and before she can even knock, his front door swings open. She isn't sure who grabs who first. All she knows is the lightness of being pulled into the arms of the person she can't breathe without.

"You're here," he says, pressing her against the door. His mouth lands on hers to push and pull. Twist and turn. His fingers cage her jaw, and his hand cradles the back of her head as he orchestrates their movements.

"Lucy," she says through a gasp when he slips his fingers over the front of her jeans, the pop of the button echoing down the hallway, the catch of the zipper making her head spin with what's about to happen.

"With Mom," he says, pulling back to tug his shirt over his head. "Until tomorrow."

Her hands splay against his chest, gliding up to his neck as she pulls him back down. His hands land on the door above her head as she opens her mouth to meet her tongue with his. She captures his top lip with her teeth, biting gently before pulling back to duck under his arms, earning a delicate groan from him.

"Great," she says, lifting her shirt as she walks backward. "No more talking. I waited two months for this."

$$x = \frac{-b + \sqrt{b^2 - 4ac}}{2a}$$

"Are you all plotting against me? What is this?" Roman asks, his voice carrying.

Jahlani shrugs, avoiding his eyes as she looks over at Danica, Teryn, and Taylor, all sitting around his dining room table.

"You all blocked my roads like assholes," he hisses, dropping his cards to the table, giving them a pointed look.

"Don't be mad, we're just teasing the birthday boy," calls Danica.

"Whatever," he says, pushing from the table.

Jahlani watches as he storms off, laughing behind her hand with Lucy in her lap.

"Uh-oh, I think we upset Daddy. Let me go check on him," she says, lifting Lucy off her lap and to the floor. Down the hall, she leans in his doorway, watching him mutter and curse.

"Don't be mad," she says, and his eyes flick to hers. "It was my idea. I know how competitive you get."

He doesn't say anything, and she sighs, glancing into the hallway before shutting the door and turning the lock. She's already halfway to him when he notices, and she looks up at him through dark eyelashes before slowly lowering to her knees.

"Jahlani—"

"Shh, I'm making it up to you," she says, unzipping his front. He grabs her wrist, shaking his head.

"But ... everyone's in the room right there," he says through harsh breaths when she shakes off his hand and works his jeans down his thighs.

"I'll be quick ... and you be quiet," she says, licking him slowly.

She watches his eyes drift shut, and it's not long before he gives in, his body shuddering, his breath coming out in bursts, her name a soft chant. When his eyes open, he helps her stand and kisses her hard before pulling back.

"Fuck," he says. "Please, just ma—"

Her eyes widen and she slaps her hand over his mouth shaking her head.

"Do not even think about asking me *that* after I just did *that*."

He grumbles, pushing her wrist away to kiss down her neck. "Okay, okay, but soon, yeah?"

Jahlani sighs softly. "Soon."

$$x = \frac{-b + \sqrt{b^2 - 4ac}}{2a}$$

Jahlani wakes to the sound of her phone ringing. She answers, blinking sleep from her eyes.

"Take a look at that," Roman says, his voice filling her quiet apartment. She gives the screen a bleary-eyed squint.

"What's this?" she asks through a yawn, her voice thick.

"You tell me," he says, unable to hold back his smile. She stretches her arms over her head before looking back at the screen more closely.

"Two plane tickets to … Los Angeles."

"For?" he presses, raising his eyebrows.

More squinting takes place. "Roman Hayes and Luc—*oh my God*. When did they clear her for travel?"

He chuckles, shaking his head. "This morning. Why are you crying?"

She covers her face with her hands, wiping her cheeks.

"These are happy tears."

$$x = \frac{-b + \sqrt{b^2 - 4ac}}{2a}$$

They lie parallel under his sheets. She watches his chest rise and fall evenly, tracing small, delicate patterns across the length of his arm.

"Roman," she whispers, sitting up to rest on her elbow, the covers falling from over them, exposing the mess they made a few hours ago. The room is dipped in darkness, the curtains drawn, shielding them from having to return to the outside world. The reality in which she only gets to wake up in his arms sparingly.

She hates it.

"Hmm."

His eyes remain closed, and she lowers back down so that her head rests on her arm.

"I don't want to leave you anymore," she says in a hushed tone. Her stomach dips at her confession, the weight of her words slicing through her.

His eyes fly open, and he lets out a soft laugh, drawing her to his chest. "Oh, well. Thank God," he says, his voice muffled by her hair. "Here I thought we were holding pretty steady. Guess I was mistaken."

Jahlani pulls back to look at him, shaking her head softly.

"That's not what I mean."

"What do you mean?" he murmurs against her cheek, dropping a swift kiss to it. She inhales sharply, her body molding into his warmth, like a flower bends to light.

"They're opening a new branch," she sighs, threading her fingers into his hair. "And they want to hire internally. It's been more than six months, and the salary is double what I make now, and I …" She loses her train of thought when his mouth travels to her neck next and spends a deliberate amount of time there with his teeth and tongue. "Ro," she breathes. "You're not listening to me."

She pulls at his roots, drawing his eyes to hers and he looks at her, his forehead bending as he frowns.

"I'm always listening to you."

Jahlani rolls her eyes and attempts to push him away, but he tightens his grip on her.

He nods and presses a kiss to her other cheek. "Go for it. It sounds incredible."

She nods, swallowing. "It is. Incredible."

He tangles his hand against the back of her neck, pulling it back to press an open-mouthed kiss to the column of her throat.

"When's the interview?" he asks.

Her nails press into his arm when his mouth sucks.

"It's … um," she says slowly, sliding her thigh over his, pressing closer. "It's February first."

Roman pulls back, staring down at her. "Jahlani—that was two weeks ago."

Her eyes blink open. "What was two weeks ago?"

He tuts, sliding his hand up her thigh. "Focus, love—new building. Potential promotion," he says, dropping soft kisses across her nose, forehead, and chin.

"Oh. Right. I got it. I got the job," she breathes. "I start next week."

He pulls back, staring down at her. "Shit, that's amazing." He grabs her face, pressing a firm kiss to her mouth. "You're incredible. Are you excited?"

She nods, rising to her elbows. "That's not the best part," she says, biting her lower lip.

"What is it?" he says, smoothing his hand over her stomach.

She inhales. "The new building. It's in Florida. Near you. Near Lucy."

His lips part and his eyes widen a fraction. "What?"

She laughs and pats his hand. "No more potential life-threatening earthquakes for you, my friend. From here on out, it's strictly hurricanes. What do you think?"

He runs a hand through his hair before falling back onto the pillow. For a while, he doesn't say anything. He stares at the ceiling, blinking, and for a second, Jahlani wonders if she's made a mistake.

"Stop it," he says, eyes fixed on the ceiling. Her eyes bounce to his.

"Stop what?"

"Stop assuming I'm thinking something bad."

Jahlani exhales, falling back onto the bed next to him. She shrugs, before turning to lie on her side again, facing him. "Well, you didn't say anything, so I just—"

"Assumed the worst, per usual." His eyes flick to hers. She shrugs again, and they fall into silence.

He sighs, rubbing his hands down his face. "I'm not thinking anything bad. I'm overwhelmed, Jahlani."

"Overwhelmed?" she says slowly. "In a good way?"

He turns to her, resting his hand on her hip. "In the best fucking way, Jahlani. I'm so in love with you, it scares me. I want to be sure we're on the same page, because I don't see myself with anyone but you. I want to marry you. I want more kids with you. I want a home with you. I want you, all the time, 24/7, and I'm scared that one day you'll wake up, and not want me."

Jahlani sits up, and he does the same. Reaching forward, she slides her palm into his, looking at him.

"There's nothing that I want more than to be with you and Lucy."

"Yeah?" He asks, his eyes bright.

"Yeah. I mean. Somebody wants us together, right?" she says, nudging her shoulder with his. "Otherwise, how do you explain us meeting twice that day in the grocery store?"

He laughs, throwing his head back before leaning toward her, his next words spoken against her lips. "I don't know. Some lady told me it's math and probability. That there's no such thing as fate."

"Well," she says, pressing a gentle kiss to his lips, "tell her she's wrong—and it's stupid to believe otherwise."

And then he's pushing her into the mattress, and she's laughing into his mouth. And they're holding each other with only thoughts of them living happily together.

Always.

ACKNOWLEDGMENTS

Wow. I never thought this day would come. The number of times I thought about giving up are immeasurable, but we did it.

I first want to thank my beautiful mother for being the complete opposite of the moms' you read in this story. Thank you for always uplifting me, for challenging me, for encouraging me, and for never doubting me. Without you, I wouldn't have written this novel.

To my dad: thank you for staying up late at night with us and reading those stories in the hallway. Because of you, my passion for reading and writing grew and persisted.

To my brothers: Justin, Kobe, and Shem, thank you for letting me live out my nerdy dreams. And no, none of the characters are about you (well maybe one).

To my family: Grandma, Auntie, Ashley, Mo, Michael, Mia, Moses, thank you for always being present and loving me. Please, read the content warnings before you pick this up.

To Elle: thanks for always asking for updates and checking in on me. I still have zero intentions of ever showing you this.

To my beautiful friends: Amrita, Anita, Alyson, Hazel, Geraldine, Rianna, and Janneese. Thank you for supporting me and all my indecisiveness with my life goals. One minute I want to be an actress, and interior designer, the next I'm a teacher writing romance novels on the side.

Amrita: my alpha reader, my romance guru, thank you for reading it in its baby stages. I hope you know that you had a major impact on the final product.

Anita: had you not bought me those blind book dates for my birthday, none of this would exist, so thank you for recharging a part of me that I thought was gone.

Alyson: my smut queen, thank you for all the real world experiences that you offered me. Thank you for staying up with me listening to my ramblings off all the worlds I intend to build.

Hazel: thank you for all your positivity and for just being you. Whenever I talk with you, you make my day a little bit brighter each time.

Janneese: thanks for answering my math and graduate school questions with your big, beautiful brain.

Rianna: I always love our little talks where I update you about me wanting to quit teaching and write all day and you encouraging it.

Geraldine: there are not enough words for me to explain how incredible you are. I am so grateful to you for designing the first character sheet for me, you really brought them to life, and that is something that is so rare and precious. I will forever be grateful for you.

To my cover designer: Alice, boy oh boy do I love you. We have never met, and you live halfway across the world, but I think fate drew me to your artwork. I am so thankful for the energy and effort you brought to bring my idea to life. It is one of the most beautiful covers I have ever seen, so thank you for that. I also thank you for putting up with all my last minute ideas and bringing them to life.

To my editor: Melissa, holy cow. I really don't know how you put up with me. The number of times I had to push the submissions back, and still sent you incomplete drafts, I would have dropped me as a client, immediately. In all seriousness, thank you for everything. From start to finish you were so helpful, and you definitely improved not only my manuscript, but me as a writer.

To Elena: thank you so much for checking over my work.

To Zaylee: thank you so much for beta reading and guiding me throughout this process. Without you, I still might have left some cringey lines in there.

To the reader community: thank you for taking a chance on me. And last, but not least, Logan: my love, my whole heart. Everything truly means nothing without you. Thank you for reading this, thank you for helping me with the math, thank you for pushing me to keep going when I wanted to give up. Thank you for doing my work so I could write. Thank you for doing the laundry, cooking, and cleaning. Thank you for being my witness and giving me purpose. Most importantly, thank you for loving me at my worst. I love you in this universe, and all the others.

ABOUT THE AUTHOR

Elizabeth-Jade Taylor is an avid reader of all things romance. Born in Florida, she spent her childhood in London before returning to the U.S. She's now settled in Houston with her high school sweetheart, who has since become her fiancé.

When she's not writing steamy, swoon-worthy romances you can find her napping, planning her wedding, or wrangling a bunch of middle schoolers together for a lesson.

Made in the USA
Coppell, TX
22 February 2026

72080627R00225